BOOKS BY MEARA PLATT

THE FARTHINGALE SERIES

My Fair Lily
The Duke I'm Going to Marry
Rules for Reforming a Rake
A Midsummer's Kiss
The Viscount's Rose

KINDLE WORLDS: REGENCY NOVELLAS

Nobody's Angel
Kiss an Angel

RULES FOR REFORMING A Rake

The Farthingale Series
Book 3

Cover Design by Greg Simanson
Edited by Laurel Busch

ISBN: 978-1-945767-05-0

A FREE NOVELLA

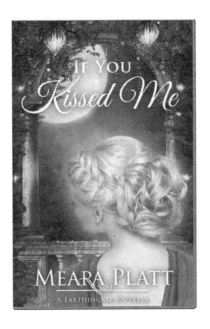

To Aaron, Ardaric, Cadence, and Reagan for always making us smile

CHAPTER 1

*To attract a rake, one must make an
elegant first impression.*

*London, England
Late February 1815*

"GABRIEL, DON'T WALK down that street!"

Gabriel Dayne turned in time to see his friend, Ian Markham, Duke of Edgeware, jump down from an emerald green phaeton and dodge several passing carriages as he raced toward him, waving his arms and calling for him to stop. Quickly scanning his surroundings, Gabriel reached for the pistol hidden in the breast pocket of his waistcoat and prepared to defend himself.

But from whom?

He saw nothing untoward on Chipping Way, one of Mayfair's prettiest streets. Indeed, the sun shone brightly, birds chirped merrily, and buds hinted of early spring blooms along the fashionable walk. Ladies and gentlemen strolled leisurely toward the park on this unusually warm day, and another elegant carriage led by a pair of matched grays with fanciful gold feathers on their heads clattered past.

Not a footpad or assassin could be seen.

"Put that weapon away," Ian said, reaching his side and pausing a moment to catch his breath. "I didn't mean to frighten you, just stop you from making one of the biggest mistakes of your life."

Gabriel frowned. "A simple 'good afternoon' would have caught my attention. How are you, Your Grace?"

"Me? I'm right as rain. But things have changed around here. I thought you should know." He withdrew a handkerchief from his breast pocket, removed his top hat, and proceeded to wipe his brow.

Gabriel gazed more closely at Ian's handkerchief... decidedly feminine... embroidered with pink hearts. He arched an eyebrow. "So it seems. You never mentioned that you'd acquired a wife."

Ian followed Gabriel's gaze. "The devil! Things haven't changed that much! I'm not married and hope never to be. No, this dainty piece of lace belongs to my new mistress. A shapely bit of fluff with cherry lips and hair to match."

"I see."

"Ah, but I don't think you do. I stopped by your townhouse shortly after your return from France to congratulate the wounded war hero, but you were in very bad shape—"

"Don't call me that," Gabriel warned, keeping his voice low, though they were quite alone for the moment. "As far as my family and London society are concerned, I'm the wastrel they believe I've become, shot by a jealous husband while hunting grouse in Scotland."

Ian gave another shake of his head. "I don't see the need to continue this pretense. The war's over. Why won't you and Prinny," he said, referring to the Prince Regent, "allow the truth to come out?"

"No," Gabriel said quietly. "It will come out in time, when Napoleon is no longer a threat."

"But he's in exile and under constant guard. What harm can he do now?"

"None, I hope. However, matters are still unsettled on the Continent. I may have to return." Though he was loath to do so. Having spent the last three years slipping from one hellish battlefield to another, and been close to death more times than he cared to remember, Gabriel was now eager to take advantage of this momentary lull to live life to the fullest.

Ian and he had saved each other from numerous scrapes with the enemy during the war and had become more than friends. One could say they were as close as brothers, though Ian did not care much for family. Indeed, Ian was an unrepentant rakehell with an excellent eye for the ladies, and just the person to guide him back into the carefree bachelor life. "Now tell me, does your delightful mistress have a friend?"

Ian laughed. "Veronique has several charming friends to suit your... er, needs. Come by White's tonight for a drink. We'll discuss your return to England and the joys of bachelorhood further."

"Look forward to it," Gabriel said with a nod. "Now, what is this nonsense about my making one of the biggest mistakes of my life?"

Ian tried to appear serious, but the corners of his mouth curled upward to form a grin. "The danger is real," he said, a glint of amusement in his eyes. "You must not take another step toward your grandmother's house."

Gabriel humored him by glancing around once more. For the life of him, there was nothing out of place on this street.

Ian took a deep breath. "Right, then. Your grandmother resides at Number 5 Chipping Way, and General Allworthy resides at Number 1 Chipping Way. He's no problem, of course, being the quiet, retiring sort. So is your grandmother the retiring sort, though I understand she was quite something in her younger day."

"Get to the point. I'm already late."

"Yes, well. The problem resides at Number 3 Chipping Way. The Farthingales moved in about three years ago, shortly after you went off to... well, you know. Ever since they took up residence here, this charming street has become a deathtrap for bachelors."

Gabriel frowned. "Your Grace—"

"Oh, I know it must sound absurd to you, but let me explain. The Farthingales have five beautiful daughters, and I don't mean just pretty. They're stunning and of marriageable age, which is a problem for us simple creatures."

"Simple creatures?"

"We bachelors, haven't you been listening? What chance do we have against a pair of vivid blue eyes? Soft, smiling lips? None, I tell you. Our brains shut off the moment our—"

"I understand your drift," Gabriel shot back, rolling his eyes. "But years of battle discipline have trained me well. I have an iron control over my body and therefore am in no danger from the Farthingale girls. They are mere females, after all."

Ian shook his head sadly and placed a hand on Gabriel's shoulder. "Julian Emory said similar words to me two years ago while on his way to visit your dear grandmother. He made it as far as the Farthingale gate, heard Rose Farthingale's kiln explode, and then heard her cries for help. She was trapped inside, along with her shattered pottery."

"A riveting story," Gabriel said dryly.

"Julian heroically dug her out of the rubble and lifted her into his arms, but as he carried her from the destruction, disaster struck. She opened her eyes and smiled at him. They were married before he knew what hit him. I doubt the besotted fool will ever recover."

"I'm not Julian."

"Curiously, your cousin, Graelem Dayne, said those exact words to me last year. We stood right here as I tried to stop him from visiting your grandmother. I failed, of course. He made it to the Farthingale gate, only to be trampled by Laurel Farthingale's beast of a horse. The beast broke Graelem's leg, but did your cousin care? No, because Laurel had jumped down from that four-legged devil, thrown her arms around Graelem, and cradled him in her lap while some medical relative of hers set his busted leg. Laurel and Graelem married a short time after that."

"Thank you for the warning." Gabriel started for his grandmother's house.

"Daisy," Ian called after him.

"What?"

"Daisy's next. She's the next eldest of the Farthingale girls. You know, first Rose, then Laurel, then—"

"Of course, Daisy Farthingale." Her name sounded as foolish as his friend's warning.

GABRIEL STRODE PAST General Allworthy's townhouse at

Number 1 Chipping Way, and then paused to look back at his companion because he had heard him mutter something about it being too painful to watch. Ian, along with his emerald green phaeton, was gone.

"Stuff and nonsense," Gabriel grumbled, dismissing his friend as an alarmist. Julian and Graelem had been ready to marry. It only took the right sort of girl to tame them. He, on the other hand, had every intention of remaining the unrepentant bachelor.

Indeed, marriage was the farthest thing from his mind. Bad women and good times were what he wanted.

He took a deep breath, squared his shoulders, and marched straight past Number 3... well, almost.

"You, sir! Please! Stop that baby!"

"Wha-at?" Gabriel turned in time to see a little boy toddle at full speed from the Farthingale drive onto Chipping Way. The infant was stark naked and headed directly toward a carriage that was traveling much too fast for this elegant neighborhood.

"There, sir! Please stop him!" a young woman cried, leaning precariously from one of the upper windows.

Gabriel tore after the little fellow, snatching him into his arms just as the little imp was about to fall under the hooves of the fast-moving team of horses. The boy squirmed in his arms, but Gabriel wouldn't let him go. "Let's get you back to your derelict governess, young man," he said, wrapping the unclad child in the folds of his cloak, for there was a chill to the air.

But the boy, having no enthusiasm for the idea, began to shriek. "No! No!"

Lord! Where was that governess?

Gabriel drew the inconsolable child against his chest, speaking to him quietly but sternly in an even tone until his shrieks subsided. As they did, Gabriel patted his small back and soothed his anguished sobs. "There, there," he said, quite at a loss. "No need to fuss."

His actions worked to some extent, for the boy did suddenly stop wailing. "Papa... Papa..." he repeated softly, resting his head against Gabriel's shirt as he emitted trembling gasps of air from his little lungs.

"I certainly hope not," Gabriel muttered, brushing the tightly coiled gold curls off the boy's moist brow. "Ah, there's a good lad. Feeling better now?"

The boy responded with a tiny nod.

Quite pleased with himself and the efficiency with which he'd restored order, Gabriel turned back to the Farthingale house as the young woman burst through the gate, followed by a small army of children in varying states of disarray. She paused but a moment to order her squealing troops "Back inside!" and to Gabriel's surprise, they promptly complied.

The young woman then turned toward him, her black hair half done up in a bun and the rest of it falling in a shambles about her slender shoulders. "Thank you! Thank you! You saved Harry's life! We're so grateful."

He frowned down at the seemingly appreciative girl. She was young and slight, barely reaching his shoulders. She took no notice of his displeasure, and instead smiled up at him, her eyes glistening as if holding back unshed tears.

Still smiling, she turned to the boy. "You gave me a terrible scare, you little muffin. I'm so glad you're unharmed."

Gabriel thought to chide her, but the girl chose that moment to smile at him again, and the words simply refused to flow from his mouth. Well, she did have an incredible smile. The sort that touched one's heart—if one had a heart—which he didn't, having lost it sometime during the war.

Her eyes were bluer than the sky.

His frown faded.

She shook her head and let out the softest sigh. "You're so wonderful with him. Do you have children of your own?"

"You ought to be more careful with your young charge," Gabriel said, clearing his throat and speaking to her with purposeful severity. The girl's attributes, no matter how heavenly, did not excuse her lapse in duty.

"Oh, Harry's not my charge... well, he is in a way. You see, he's my cousin. And the nannies have all quit our household, so I'm left all alone with the seven children until my family returns." She wiped a stray lock off her brow, then put her arms forward to show him her rolled up sleeves. "I was trying to bathe the littlest ones."

He noticed that her finely made gown was wet in several spots. "It seems they bathed you."

"What? Oh, yes. They did give me a thorough soaking." She laughed gently while shaking her head in obvious exasperation. "Harry was the last, but now I'll have to bathe him all over again."

"Don't let me delay you." He attempted to hand the squirming bundle back to her, but before he could manage it, Harry decided to leave him a remembrance.

What was the expression? No good deed ever goes unpunished? Gabriel watched in horror as an arc of liquid shot from the naked imp onto his shirt front, planting a disgustingly warm, yellow stain on the once immaculate white lawn fabric.

He didn't know whether to laugh or rage. He'd been undone. Brought to his knees by an infant and an incompetent guardian.

"Oh, dear," the girl said, closing her eyes and groaning. "I'm so sorry. So very, very sorry."

So was he. He ought to have listened to Ian, but not because the Farthingale women were dangerous. It seemed all Farthingales were dangerous. Young. Old. Male. Female.

The family and their servants were to be avoided at all costs.

"We'll pay for the damage, of course," she continued in obvious distress, her eyes remaining firmly closed, as if not seeing the damage would somehow make it go away. "We'll replace whatever needs... er, replacing. Please have your tailor send the bill to Miss Daisy Farthingale. I'll make certain it is paid at once."

Gabriel's heart stopped beating. Yes, it definitely stopped. And then it began to beat very fast.

"You're Daisy?" he mumbled, his tongue suddenly as numb as the rest of his body. Not that he cared who she was, or what Ian had warned. He wasn't afraid of any female, certainly not this incompetent slip of a girl.

She opened her eyes and graced him with a gentle, doe-eyed gaze. "I am."

Very well, Ian was right. She was a force to be reckoned with, but so would any woman be with glistening blue eyes, pink cheeks, and cream-silk skin.

"Sir, may I be so bold as to ask who you are?"

"I'm late, that's what I am." He plunked Harry in her arms and hastened to his grandmother's house.

CHAPTER 2

*A lady must be witty and clever, for a rake
is always enticed by good conversation.*

DAISY STOOD AT the front door of Lady Eloise Dayne's elegant townhouse, tightly gripping the shirt in her hand. The massive carved oak door swung open and Lady Dayne's gray-haired butler stepped forward. "Miss Daisy?"

She managed a small smile. "Good afternoon, Watling. How are you today?"

"Better than you, by the look of you," he said, gazing down at her in that perfectly expressionless manner only the finest butlers master.

"Indeed, I've had a terrible day." She let out a deflated sigh ending with a small, wincing groan.

His expression instantly mellowed. "Oh, dear. Oh, dear. Is there anything I can do to help, young miss?"

"Thank you, Watling, but I need to see Lady Dayne at once. Or rather, her visitor." She tucked a stray strand of her hair behind one ear, knowing she looked a fright even though her hair was now tied back in an unfashionably simple ribbon that felt as though it were already coming undone. Her new gown of pale blue velvet was still damp from her misguided attempt to bathe the children. Dark blue splotches dotted the delicate bodice and skirt.

His gray eyebrows shot up. "Ah, I wondered about his state. So you're the cause."

She shook her head sadly as he ushered her in. "I've left Pruitt in charge of the children, but can't expect him to keep them at bay for very long. Did Lady Dayne's visitor relate what happened? I brought him this shirt... it belongs to Uncle George, but he won't miss it. I thought it might do until his own is laundered. Is the gentleman very angry?"

An unexpected smile formed at the corners of Watling's mouth. "He didn't say. If he is, I'm certain he'll get over it."

"Yes, I suppose he will." She followed the kindly butler into the winter salon, a small and rather cozy room filled with ornate French-style furniture, flowers, and sunshine. There was usually a fire blazing in the hearth, but Daisy noted the lack of one today, for it was warm for late February, even for Eloise, who was elderly and easily took a chill.

"I'll advise her ladyship that you are here."

Daisy smiled in gratitude and didn't have long to wait before Eloise burst through the door, sailing toward her in a billowing mass of ecru satin. The lace ruffles at her throat and cuffs flapped in the breeze like raised sails on an English frigate as she wrapped Daisy in her arms. "You poor child! You've had quite a day!"

"And it isn't over yet," she said, trying not to sound utterly dejected.

"I know, poor thing. Now, sit down and tell me everything." Eloise, whose white hair and dark green eyes had retained every bit of their youthful vibrance, nudged her toward an oversized settee embroidered with pink roses.

"I will, but later. You're busy and I must get back to the children. I only stopped in to drop this off." She held up her uncle's shirt. "I thought your visitor might use it until his own is put back in shape. It's Savile Row and of the finest cloth, as his was before Harry destroyed it."

Eloise's eyes twinkled with obvious merriment. "Never mind about him. I gave him an old shirt of my late husband's that I dug out of storage. It'll do for now. More important," she said, urging Daisy onto the settee by patting the seat beside her, "tell me exactly what happened. Whatever possessed Harry to... er, unload... relieve himself?"

Daisy couldn't help but laugh as she settled beside Eloise. "I don't know. The incident was as hilarious as it was horrible. Oh, the look of shock upon your visitor's face when Harry let loose was priceless!"

Eloise let out a soft, but hearty, laugh. "I'm sorry I missed it."

"It was rather an interesting moment." Daisy giggled, then sobered. "Harry's going through a terrible time, and the nanny crisis at home hasn't helped. I warned Mother that one nanny couldn't possibly tend to so many children and that we had to hire reinforcements at once, but she's been so busy with our house guests that she keeps forgetting to send word to the agency. She won't let me do it," she continued with a sigh, "because you know what my family thinks of me ever since the incident last year. And now we have no nannies!"

"That's why you're looking after all the children?"

Daisy nodded. "And doing a rather poor job of it, but they're still alive and breathing, at least when I last checked. I suppose that's all that matters. Mother has taken our female relations shopping and won't be back for hours. Of course, I'm not complaining or trying to shirk responsibility, and I fully admit that I'm to blame for your visitor's... er, predicament. Is he very angry?"

The twinkle brightened in Eloise's eyes. "If he is, I'm certain he'll get over it."

"That's precisely what Watling said and in just that gleeful tone." She paused briefly to ponder the coincidence, then shrugged and proceeded with her story. "Miss Beardsley left us this morning."

Eloise shifted in her seat. "How is it possible? She just started last month."

"And was working out quite nicely until the Devonshire Farthingales decided to give their nanny one week's holiday. Miss Beardsley wasn't happy about that, but after some coaxing, she agreed to share the added responsibility with the other nannies. Then the Yorkshire Farthingales' nanny got sick and the Oxfordshire Farthingales' nanny eloped."

"Oh, dear. I'm getting dizzy just trying to keep track of all these visiting relations of yours."

"Imagine how little Harry must feel. Though he's a darling most of the time—"

"When he's not the very devil," Eloise said with a chuckle. "I do adore the boy."

"So do I." Daisy gave a sad shake of her head. "But he hasn't taken well to the upheaval in his life. He's been at a loss since his father's death and refuses to accept that he isn't coming back."

"And what is your Aunt Julia doing to help the boy?"

Unwilling to speak ill of Harry's mother, Daisy kept quiet.

Eloise pursed her lips and frowned. "Just as I thought, she isn't helping."

Daisy began to fidget with the shirt in her hand. She hadn't meant to cast blame on her aunt, though apparently Eloise had taken it that way. "Julia is grieving, too. But Harry's the bigger problem. He keeps running off to find his father. That's why Miss Beardsley left us this morning. She'd reached her breaking point, declaring we were all mad and she couldn't possibly stay on with us another moment. I can't blame her, really."

"I suppose not," Eloise agreed.

Daisy set the shirt on her lap and began to smooth it out, for she'd inadvertently crumpled the fine fabric while wringing her hands. "I want to help Harry through this difficult time, but how can I give him the attention he requires when there's no one left to look after the other children?"

Eloise cast Daisy a warm, motherly smile. "Dear girl, you can't take on the troubles of the world."

"Oh, there's no danger of that." She let out a small, mirthless laugh and rolled her eyes. "I can't even manage the Farthingale domestic problems. Mother's in a tizzy with the season about to head into full swing, and the house is already filled to the rafters with guests. I think she's forgotten that the children are not being looked after."

"How convenient for her," Eloise grumbled.

"She doesn't mean to overlook them. It's just that she's had her hands full helping all of us prepare for the upcoming balls and dinner parties." Daisy loved her mother, Sophie Farthingale; in truth she loved every member of her boisterous family. They had all loved and admired her in return, until that unfortunate incident last year. Now, just when she needed their support the most, they were certain she would run off and do something foolish.

In truth, their present lack of faith in her was humbling, something she hadn't considered would happen when she'd set out to help her sister. Well, no one knew what had really happened and she wasn't about to betray Laurel now that she was happily married to Eloise's grandson, Lord Graelem Dayne.

She would have loved to confide in Eloise and seek her guidance, but couldn't this time. The family relations were too close. In any event, it probably didn't matter. Her family would regain their trust in her soon enough and then these horrible few months would be forgotten. She certainly was doing all she could to return to their good graces. Indeed, taking care of the children was one of the ways she'd hoped to make it up to them.

Unfortunately, it wasn't working out too well for her.

"Are you ready for your first season, Daisy?" Eloise asked, distracting her from her thoughts. "You're to attend Lord Falmouth's ball in a few days."

"I am," she said with an ease she didn't feel. "Rose and Laurel used their connections to secure vouchers for Almack's. Rose and her husband took me there a fortnight ago, which in a way counts as my debut, though it shouldn't since my gown was borrowed from Rose."

"Borrowed," Eloise repeated with a slight frown.

Daisy dismissed her concern with a shrug. "It was a lovely tea rose silk confection. The gathering was a tame affair and not very well attended. The rooms were simple and the ratafia unpleasantly warm. However, we accomplished our purpose. Rose introduced me to Lady Barstow, one of the patronesses, who gave me permission to waltz."

The news seemed to please Eloise. "Well done. Now about your gowns, are they ready yet?"

"No, but they will be shortly," she assured, still unwilling to admit her own concerns. "I've completed the final fittings and Mother has arranged to have them delivered tomorrow, in plenty of time before the official start of the season."

Eloise clapped her hands. "Wonderful! I can't wait to see you in them. Madame de Bressard is a marvel."

"Indeed, she is. Some of her designs are quite beautiful, but the white satin I'm to wear to Lord Falmouth's has far too many bows and ribbons to be considered elegant." She paused a moment and wrinkled her nose. "Madame de Bressard wasn't keen on those frills either, but Mother insisted. No doubt she hoped they would make me appear more innocent."

Now she nibbled her lip, suddenly dreading her debut. Had rumor of The Incident begun to spread throughout Polite Society? Was that the reason for the curious glances she was receiving lately? Looking her best was the least of her worries, she supposed.

Eloise seemed to read her thoughts. "I'm sure you'll look quite charming and be well received by all. Do stop fretting, child."

"Am I that obvious?" Daisy rose from her seat with a sigh. "I do wish to make my family proud, restore their faith in me. I'll let you in on a little secret, Eloise."

"Ooh, I love secrets!" She leaned forward eagerly.

"Despite my fears, I will enjoy being thrown into the marriage mart. As madly paced as these next few months will be, it will be a pleasant improvement over the chaos presently reigning at home."

Eloise pursed her lips. "That's a logical observation, not a secret. Everyone knows your home is a madhouse."

"Speaking of which," Daisy said, backing toward the door while continuing to chatter, her gaze on Eloise and not on where she was going, "I shudder to think what the little devils are doing now. I really must go. And you must get back to your guest before he suspects foul play. I'll stop by as soon as Mother returns and—"

Eloise let out a gasp. "Daisy, look out!"

"*Oof!*" She bounced off something solid at the doorway and lost her balance, but was spared the indignity of a fall when a pair of large hands connected to muscled arms reached out and caught her. She found herself locked in the embrace of the gentleman who had earlier rescued Harry, her back pressed against his chest as he drew her against him to steady her. Did all gentlemen have rock-hard chests?

"We meet again, Miss Farthingale," he said in a soft, throaty rumble, slowly turning her to face him.

A crimson rush of heat shot straight into Daisy's face and fanned across her cheeks. Her heart began to thump erratically within her chest. *Oh, great balls of cheese!* Up close, the man was even handsomer than she remembered. "Yes, how nice to see you... er... er..."

He hadn't mentioned his name, and by the look of him, didn't seem inclined to tell her. Too bad she hadn't thought to press Eloise for the information, but it hadn't seemed important at the time. In any event, knowing his name would somehow make the horror of the encounter worse. He'd no longer be some stranger who had the misfortune to cross her path on the street.

She tried to stifle her embarrassment and turn away, but his eyes seemed to exert an invisible force that held her in place. There was something dark and dangerous in their tawny gleam. His lips twitched at the corners, as though he was holding back a laugh or a condescending remark. She knew what he really wanted to say was "you're a clumsy simple-brain and I'd like you to keep as far away from me as possible."

He continued to hold her, but made no attempt at politeness. A simple nod or smile would have sufficed, but he failed to offer either. Of course, why would he? She was the last woman on earth he cared to see, which was really too bad because he truly was one of the handsomest men she had ever encountered.

Indeed, quite the handsomest she had ever met, despite his scars. "You never told me your name."

He arched a wicked eyebrow. "I know."

Oh, he did look sinfully dangerous, too. In a way that made a girl's heart flutter as hers was fluttering now. Well, her heart was doing a little more than that, for it was practically in spasms and leaping out of her chest. *Drat!* Why did he have that effect on her? One would think the scar at his chin and the one above his eye would make him look cruel or scary, but they didn't. One would think that his size and solid muscles would be intimidating... well, they were, but in an exciting, melt-one's-resistance sort of way.

He looked wonderful in the ill-fitting shirt Eloise had loaned him.

She gazed at the shirt and the muscles rippling beneath it like perfect waves across the vast ocean. Chest hairs, as pure a gold as the hairs of his thick mane, peeked out between the straining buttons. She moved her gaze upward and groaned. Even his tawny-brown eyes were perfect, flecked with gold and slanted ever so sensually.

"Daisy, are you all right?" Eloise asked with some concern.

Why? Because she looked like a stunned trout with her mouth agape? Because she couldn't take her eyes off the man and his handsome features? It didn't seem fair that he should have a firm jaw, straight nose, inviting lips, and cheekbones as finely sculpted as his warrior's body.

She heard Eloise clear her throat and stifle something that sounded like a titter. "Daisy?"

Did the gentleman also believe she was two cards short of a full deck? Is that why he was now grinning at her and continuing to hold her despite his obvious reluctance?

She shook back to attention, or perhaps he was the one gently shaking her. "I'm fine. Just perfect, Eloise. I really must be going. Oh, sir. I'll leave this with you." She offered the gentleman the crumpled shirt still clutched in her hand, for she'd foolishly forgotten to hand it over to Eloise when she'd started for the door. "It might fit better than the one you presently have on, which seems rather tight... but not in a bad way... that is, you're big."

He released her and took it without comment.

Eloise sighed. "Honestly, Gabriel. I think you ought to thank the girl. By the way, Daisy, this is my grandson, Lord Gabriel Dayne, youngest son of the Earl of Trent."

Daisy inhaled sharply. "You're Gabriel?"

"I am," he said with a quirk of his eyebrow, which made him appear quite sinister.

"Oh." She refused to be disappointed in the knowledge. Of course, it meant that he had to be ruled out as a possible suitor. After all, the manner in which he'd earned the right to be called a lord, considering he was the younger son of an earl, had provided fodder for gossip for months on end.

Eloise had spoken about him and his elder brother, Alexander, quite often. While Alexander was a decorated war hero, Gabriel was an unredeemable wastrel and a dishonorable gentleman in every way, one to be avoided at all costs. However, Eloise loved him and firmly believed he was misunderstood.

Daisy wondered whether Alexander was as ruggedly handsome as his disrepute of a brother, something she would like to know since she was determined to marry Alexander. How else was she to be restored in her family's good graces? Alexander had an excellent reputation and pedigree and, because he was the eldest, would inherit the earldom and the Trent fortune that went along with it.

Yes, marrying Gabriel's brother was her brilliant plan and would be the perfect solution to her problems. She'd heard so much about his exploits over the past three years she felt as if she already knew him, as if they'd grown up together and been best friends.

Could love be far behind?

Of course, she'd have to meet him first.

Why wasn't he in town yet? And why did it have to be Gabriel Dayne who'd held her in his arms? Not that Gabriel *wanted* her in his arms. Nor did she wish to be in his arms.

He placed his hands on her shoulders again to steady her when she began to sway, mistaking her movements for a swoon, although there was absolutely no danger of that. She was merely uncertain whether to leave the room or stay and give him the set down he so richly deserved now that she knew he was the disreputable grandson. Swoon, indeed! The notion was ridiculous!

His big, confident hands tightened ever so slightly on her shoulders.

They were the sort of hands that knew their way around a woman's body. Were her cheeks still flaming?

"Sorry to disappoint," Gabriel said rather coldly, no doubt sensing her disapproval of him.

"You disappointed your grandmother. As for me... well, I don't know you, nor do I—" She stopped herself from saying more. Daisy disliked him for the pain he'd caused Eloise, and would continue to cause, if his behavior was any indication.

Now that she'd met Gabriel, she regretted having cried with Eloise upon learning he had been shot and lay lingering close to death for months—served him right for dallying with another man's wife. She regretted rejoicing with Eloise when learning he had pulled through. It had been a long recovery, for he'd truly been at death's door.

"Yes," he said with icy frankness, "she's among the many I've let down."

What had happened to change him? He'd been a wonderful boy, if Eloise was to be believed. She'd spoken often of Gabriel's youthful love of adventure, of his good nature and his valor. He'd even had a tender heart, particularly when it came to defenseless animals. Trent Hall, it seemed, became an infirmary for every stray cat, dog, bird, lamb, and frog whenever young Lord Gabriel was in residence.

"You have it in your power to make things right, my lord. You can be as good and kind as you once were." She mildly grieved for the loss of his precious, boyish innocence.

He didn't appear to be in the least moved by her words. "Is that so?"

She blushed, knowing she was being impertinent and meddlesome. Ah, yes. Meddling was a Farthingale trait. It's what got her into trouble in the first place and led to The Incident. "Of course. Don't you wish to be?"

"Do you want an honest answer?"

Something in his glib manner rankled her. She didn't wish to be rude, but she'd had a miserable day and this arrogant man was doing his best to make it worse. "No," she said with an exasperated roll of her eyes. "I wish to be lied to. Isn't it every girl's dream?"

She made no effort to hide her sarcasm, but now regretted that she might have overstepped the proper bounds. He was Eloise's grandson, after all. What was wrong with her today? She ought to have left well enough alone. A politely insincere "nice to meet you" would have sufficed. Or she might have made a passing comment about the slight family resemblance between him and his grandmother.

He'd just saved Harry. For that alone she ought to have been nice to him.

Instead of being angry, Gabriel let out a slow, devastatingly appealing grin. "I suppose I deserved that. As you may have heard," he said, glancing at Eloise, "I'm not known for my manners. My brother is though. I think I'll leave duty and honor to Alexander for now. However, thank you for worrying about me, Miss Farthingale. Few people do."

She shook her head in confusion. "Why would I worry about you?" In truth, she'd just insulted him.

"I don't know, but it appears you are." He glanced down.

Daisy followed his gaze, only to realize she had somehow put her hand on his arm. Worse, she was caressing him along the expanse of solid muscle. "I'm sorry. I don't know why I did that. It just seemed the natural thing to do. Yes, well... I'll pull away now."

But putting thought to action was not so easy when one was a simpleton and one's heart was madly thumping through one's ears. Why was her heart still thumping for this reprobate? His brother was the man she needed to marry. He'd said it himself, Alexander was the dutiful son. The worthy son. Finally, to her great humiliation, Gabriel took gentle hold of her hand and pried her fingers off his forearm one by one.

"Join me for supper tonight," Eloise called after her, but she was too busy dashing out of the house to answer.

"MISS DAISY, WILL you please untie me?"

Daisy glanced around the elegant Farthingale entry hall, searching for the body that went with the voice. She finally found it securely tied to the mahogany coatrack. "Pruitt! What have they done to you?"

She quickly untied their butler and helped him to shake the circulation back into his arms and legs. "Oh, this has gone from bad to worse! Where are the little heathens now?"

"I don't know, but I heard Cook scream a few moments ago. I hope they haven't tied her to the spit and roasted her like a stuffed pig."

Daisy hoped they hadn't either.

Yet Mrs. Mayhew was not the sort to surrender without a fight, and she had weapons at her disposal. A rolling pin, knives, mallets, meat forks. Yes, she could hold off a frontal assault for hours.

While Pruitt went through the house to check on the rest of the staff, Daisy hurried down the stairs to the kitchen, then came to an abrupt halt. The large room, usually bustling with activity, appeared deserted. All was quiet. Too quiet for this time of day.

The children had been here, she could tell, for the floors, walls, and worktables were covered in a white powder. A week's supply of flour gone, just like that. Could Mrs. Mayhew have been dispatched as quickly?

Daisy raised her skirts and was beginning to tiptoe across the debris left on the floor when she heard a giggle coming from the servants' dining alcove. She crept closer and peered around the corner. One, two, three, four, five, six, seven children plus Mrs. Mayhew and her two assistants, sitting around the table, as calm as you please.

All unharmed.

All present and accounted for.

She watched the children eagerly digging into freshly made apple tarts. "Thank you, Mrs. Mayhew," she said with a giddy sigh and stepped forward. "You're a marvel."

The stocky, middle-aged woman glanced up with a smile. "No trouble at all, Miss Daisy. The children were very helpful."

Daisy shook her head and laughed, pointing in the direction of the flour-covered floor. "I couldn't help but notice."

Mrs. Mayhew waved her hand as if to dismiss her concerns. "The scullery girls will clean that up, quick as a trice."

Daisy glanced around. "Oh, dear. About those girls, where are they now? Safe, I hope."

"They are," she assured with another wave of her hand. "I've sent them off to buy more flour and some other supplies."

Daisy breathed another sigh of relief. "I'll take over tending the children. I know you must have your hands full preparing the family supper."

"Soup's ready and bubbling on the hearth. The meat's in the oven, simmering in its own juices. Pies are cooling on the window ledge. All we have left to cook are the vegetables. Everything's in ship-shape order, thanks to the menus you prepared in advance for us."

"I'm glad it worked out."

"The meals are simple to make, yet present quite elegantly. Ye're doing a fine job of running the household, Miss Daisy."

"Um, I'm not really in charge, Mrs. Mayhew," she said with a modest shake of her head. "Mother is the lady of the house."

"She may be, but ye're the heart of this house, always looking out for everyone, getting things done and never taking credit. If ye ask me, ye've more than made amends for—"

Daisy knew she was going to mention The Incident and hastily changed the topic. "We'll discuss it later. Perhaps in a few months when our guests have all returned to their homes. However, I'd like to discuss something of greater importance. Are your nieces still visiting?"

"Indeed they are. As a matter of fact, they're enjoying London so much, they'd like to stay on permanently." Mrs. Mayhew pursed her lips and frowned lightly. "I'll have to find work for them, though I haven't had the time to attend to it."

"Perfect! Consider it done. Would they be willing to watch children? I mean, just until suitable nannies can be found."

The older woman glanced up in surprise. "They know how to tend children, that's for sure. They helped me raise my five boys after my husband died and did a fine job of it. But they don't come from genteel families. They're not the sort one would look for in a nanny. True, they speak softly and are well-mannered. I was hoping your mother might take them in as housemaids should the positions become available."

Daisy folded her arms across her chest as a plan formed in her mind. "I'm certain we'll have many openings before this month is through. In the meantime, your nieces would do me a great service by helping me with the children. I desperately need assistance and don't mind that they can't read the Greek classics or speak as finely as the Queen. We'll regain two of the Farthingale nannies by the end of the week, and I expect they'll want to keep your nieces on."

"Thank you, Miss Daisy. They'll be quite pleased."

"Have them report to me first thing tomorrow morning. And... ah, no sense burdening Mother with the little details. I'll instruct Mrs. Taft to add them to the list of household retainers."

Daisy allowed the children to finish their treats before marching them up to her room and instructing them to wash their hands. She turned the chore of washing into a game that even Harry enjoyed. Then she sat the youngest children on her bed, pulled up a chair, and began to tell them a story.

"Can we listen, too?" her twelve-year-old cousin, Lizbeth, the eldest of the children, asked.

"Of course." She waved her hand, motioning for the older ones to come closer, which they did with squeals and giggles. This small band of older cousins ranged in age from nine to twelve and were still considered too young to be allowed in the company of adults. They were at that awkward age, too young for more sophisticated conversation and too old to be forced to play with the younger children. She was pleased when they scooted closer, eager to listen to her read a story to the little ones.

"Tell us about the gentleman you met today," Lizbeth said, tossing back her blonde curls while taking a seat next to her.

Daisy felt the heat of a blush creep up her neck. Goodness, how much had the children seen? "Oh, I don't think—"

"Please, please, please!" Lizbeth persisted, an eager sparkle in her green eyes. "Harry met him, too." She was joined by the others in a chorus of begging.

Daisy let out a soft groan. "Very well."

Lizbeth cheered. "Harry liked him. We saw him hug the man."

She wondered what else her cousins had seen Harry do to the man. "Yes, well..."

"He seemed very nice. Is he a war hero?" Lizbeth cast her an impish grin.

"What's that?" four-year-old Charles asked with a sniffle, because it was a well-known fact that all little boys had runny noses. It mattered not if they were the offspring of a duke or a dustman. If they were little, their noses ran.

"Someone who's very brave," Lizbeth answered.

"The gentleman's name is Lord Gabriel Dayne and he's not a war hero, but his brother, Alexander, is one. I'm sure Alexander saved the lives of many young men and made lots of families very happy."

"Was Uncle Harrison with him?" Charles asked, referring to Harry's father, who had died in battle last year.

"Unfortunately, no." She glanced worriedly at Harry, but he seemed to be fine for the moment. "Alexander and Gabriel are grandsons of our neighbor."

"Grandmama Eloise?" Harry asked with a sniffle, his nose also perpetually running. Daisy withdrew the handkerchief tucked in her sleeve and efficiently cleaned his pudgy face.

"Yes," she answered with a nod. Eloise had been wonderfully generous with the boy, often allowing Daisy to bring him along on her afternoon visits. Harry had grown quite attached to their kindly neighbor. "Lord Gabriel has been sick for a very long time—"

"But he got better," Lizbeth said, punctuating her sentence with a squeal. "He looks very big and strong."

"Yes, Lizbeth." Daisy felt another jolt of heat rise in her cheeks as she recalled the firm hands that had gripped her shoulders and the powerful muscles bulging beneath his borrowed shirt.

"Who's very big and strong?" asked Daisy's youngest sister, Dillie, as she strode into the room without so much as a knock. She threw off her gloves and hat, then plunked down on the bed beside the little ones.

Daisy shook her head and laughed. "Hello, Dillie. Did you come back with Mother?"

"No, she took Aunt Julia and the rest of our female relations to visit Rose. Laurel joined them, but Lily and I decided we'd had enough of their jibber-jabber and asked to be dropped off at home." Dillie, always pert and animated, began to make clucking sounds and funny faces in imitation of their female relatives.

The children broke into giggles. Soon, they were all off the bed and following Dillie about the room like chicks marching after the mother hen. "Daisy, a thought just struck me. Why are all the children in your room? Where are the nannies?"

"Hadn't you noticed? They've all left us, though two should be back by the end of the week."

Dillie's eyes grew wide and her mouth gaped open. "Crumpets! Who's been watching the children all this time?"

Daisy waited for her to pass close on her turn about the room. "I have. Mrs. Mayhew and Pruitt have helped."

"Does Mother know? Wait, don't answer. Of course, she doesn't.

She doesn't even remember giving birth to you, me, or Lily. Her patience wore out after Rose and Laurel."

"You're not being fair," Daisy said, stifling a grin, for her sister's assessment was accurate. Their mother had simply been overwhelmed after giving birth to the first two daughters. It wasn't her fault really. "Managing a household as large as this one isn't easy, especially when it's constantly filled to the rafters with guests."

Dillie stopped in front of her, flapped her arms, and clucked. "Though you try to hide it, I know that you have been the one in charge of this household since Rose got married. Laurel was too busy grooming her horses to care, and Lily and I were too young. But more important, who is big and strong?"

"Lord Gabriel Dayne," Lizbeth interjected.

"He's a wart hero," Charlie added, his big, brown eyes widening as a mark of his earnestness.

"His brother, Alexander, is a *war* hero," Daisy corrected. "Lord Gabriel doesn't have warts, just a few scars."

"In very manly places, I imagine," Dillie said with a smirk.

"Dillie!"

"Is he handsome?" she asked, still smirking. "He must be. Your eyes have turned limpid."

Daisy held back a gasp. Oh, dear! Was she that obvious? "What you see is pity for poor Eloise. She's had to endure his outrageous conduct."

Dillie wasn't anywhere near finished with her interrogation. "Did you talk to him? When did you meet him?"

Dillie's twin, Lily, walked into the room just then. The pair were identical and even Daisy had trouble telling them apart at times. Lily was quieter, sometimes wore spectacles that hid her sparkling blue eyes, and always carried a book. Dillie's eyes, if one looked very closely, were a slightly softer shade of blue. Lily was studious and earnest while Dillie, also a clever girl, had a delightful tendency toward mischief. "Whom did you meet who's very handsome and doesn't have warts?" Lily asked.

Daisy sighed. "Come join us. You may as well hear about my most embarrassing moments."

CHAPTER 3

Although a rake might feign otherwise, as a gentleman of rank and breeding, he prefers the company of a serene and poised young lady.

"LET'S SEE NOW," Lady Eloise Dayne said, putting a finger to her chin and drifting off in thought. "Rose must be about twenty-three, and that would make Laurel about twenty-one. The twins, Lily and Daffodil—though everyone calls her Dillie—are just shy of seventeen. Now Daisy, that delightful girl, will turn nineteen next month. Did I mention their father acquired his wealth in the merchant trade? One would never guess it, for he has quite the manners and education of a gentleman. The girls are clever, too. Quite accomplished young ladies."

"Ah, just what I need, an accomplished young lady." Gabriel set down his teacup with a clatter. He glanced at the ornate wall clock hanging by the door of the winter salon, and noted it was almost five o'clock. He'd paid his duty call. Although he'd enjoyed most of the time spent with his grandmother, it was time to leave. "Grandmama, I fear I must be going."

"But Daisy—"

"Please, not another word about the girl. Did I in any way lead you to believe I gave a fig about her or her relatives?" *Bloody hell*, she couldn't seriously be considering him for Daisy, could she? If he were seeking to settle down—which he wasn't in the least—it would never be with an addled bit of fluff like her, even if she had practically stopped his heart with her beautiful smile.

"Well, no. But you and Daisy seemed to be getting along so well."

"Getting along well? Whatever gave you that impression? Her devil of a cousin emptied himself on me, and all she could do was flutter about me ineffectually, saying 'sorry, sorry, sorry' like a damned parrot with a one-word vocabulary. And later, when I joined you in this parlor, all she could do was gawk at me even as she chided me for my wicked ways."

Eloise let out a chuckle. "Well, you are a handsome man."

"Despite my scars."

"Most of them aren't that noticeable, and the two that are make you look divinely rugged. I imagine Daisy found them quite attractive."

Bloody hell again. Will my grandmother never give up?

"I'd be surprised if she noticed anything, for the girl seems to walk in a perpetual cloud. However, I will admit that even foggy-headed girls are consumed by one thing... marriage. I saw wedding bells mirrored in her blue eyes."

"Ah, you noticed the color of her eyes."

"No," he muttered and received a scowl of disbelief in return. Very well, so what if he had noticed? No man could overlook Daisy's magnificent eyes or her other splendid attributes. But it didn't mean he was interested or that she pleased him. The war years had trained him always to be vigilant and notice details, that's all. Her details happened to be spectacular, but it wasn't something one confided to one's meddlesome grandmother.

"You are being most difficult, Gabriel. Why won't you admit that you liked the girl?"

"Because I didn't. I found her quite unremarkable. She had nothing of interest to say. She lacked style. I think she forgot to brush her hair today. That dark mane of hers tumbled wildly about her shoulders."

Well, I do like that. Yes, indeed! Wild dark hair and big blue eyes, and a body—no! Daisy Farthingale was not the stuff of his fantasies.

"Her only lure is her wealth," he continued, "which isn't enough to tempt me. However, I'm certain she'll find some fop who'll fall in love with her dowry. With a little luck, he might even fall in love with her. After they marry, she and her family can slowly drive the wretch insane."

He expected a feisty response from Eloise, for he had truly gone on a spiteful rant. Instead she sat quietly, staring beyond him toward the door with a pained expression on her face. "Hello, Daisy," she said in a tight voice. "Don't believe a word of what Gabriel just said."

Gabriel felt as if an anchor had just been dropped on his stomach. He tried to stand but couldn't. Instead, he watched helplessly as Daisy remained at the door wringing her hands while trying to regain her composure. She looked beautiful and vulnerable.

She looked young and very hurt.

Where was Watling? Why hadn't he announced the girl's arrival? Or did the blasted chit just burst in whenever she pleased?

Eloise patted the seat beside her and motioned for Daisy to join her, but the poor girl couldn't seem to move either. "You look lovely, child. Your hair's done up quite elegantly."

Daisy patted her hair, which was now styled in a fashionable chignon, then slowly shook her head. "You're being kind as always, Eloise." Her chin began to quiver. *Hell in a handbasket*, was she going to cry? All his fault. "I only stopped by to inform you that I won't be able to ride with you to Lord Falmouth's ball." She let out a shaky breath and ran her tongue slowly across her full lower lip as she struggled to regain the composure that he'd callously shattered. "I know I promised, but I'm certain your grandson can manage that responsibility."

Her tongue darted out again, and all he could think of was the sweet sensation of her tongue and soft lips going down... Was there ever a man more depraved?

"I'd much rather have your company in my carriage. My grandson," his grandmother said, glaring at Gabriel, "won't be very entertaining. He's all bile and ill temper lately, and he's lost all sense of good manners."

Gabriel was about to admit that he had been in the wrong, but Daisy surprised him by coming to his defense. "Please don't berate him. He has every reason to think the worst of me, and as to his manners, I believe mine were worse."

"Nonsense, you're always delightful. You were a little distressed today, that's all. Nobody's perfect. We all have bad days. Still doesn't excuse his rudeness toward you," Eloise insisted, refusing to be mollified.

"Perhaps not, but let's not make more of it than necessary." Her beautiful lips were now stretched in a thin, tense line and her clasped hands were trembling. "I doubt I'll see him again and I do wish to explain about Lord Falmouth's ball. You see, I won't be attending."

Eloise let out a soft gasp. "Why ever not? You've been looking forward to it for ages."

"It seems Mother forgot to notify the dressmakers to proceed with the final alterations for my gowns. They won't be ready in time."

"Daisy, that's unpardonable!"

Gabriel rolled his head back and groaned. Obviously Daisy had endured a dreadful day, first chasing after her cousins—he did admit that looking after seven children was no easy task—and then learning that this much-anticipated event was not to be. A young woman's first season was a sacred rite of passage, not something to be trifled with or ignored by her family. Daisy looked crushed and he couldn't blame her.

Yet despite her miserable day, she'd found it in her heart to overlook his outrageous conduct—actually, to dismiss it as though he were irrelevant—well, he didn't like that. But he hadn't exactly swept her off her feet with his charm. He'd been cruel and callous, living up to the awful reputation he'd deliberately created over the years.

Damn.

He felt about as low as the scrapings on the soles of his boots.

Lower than those scrapings.

"She's had her hands full with the family," he listened to Daisy continue in support of her mother, and thought her too willing to forgive that obviously addled lady. "I don't mind, really. And the dresses will be ready in time for Lord Hornby's ball. I'll gladly ride with you then."

"Very well, it's settled," Eloise said with a slow nod of her head.

"I'll be off. I've left the twins in charge of the other youngsters and dare not stay away too long. Last time I was gone, the little savages took Pruitt prisoner. The poor man still has not recovered."

Gabriel found his legs and then his voice. "A moment," he called out, quickly striding to her side before she could turn away. "I believe I owe you an apology."

She lifted her chin and cast him a defiant scowl. "You're entitled to your opinion of me. I always prefer the plain truth to fancy lies."

"Then you shall have the truth," he said, his gaze riveted by her blazing blue eyes. A tactical mistake, he realized at once, for she did have the prettiest eyes. He cleared his throat. "My grandmother is right, Miss Farthingale. I did not mean any of the crass words you overheard. You were the unfortunate victim of my ill humor. I'd very much like to make amends."

"Not necessary."

"Quite necessary." The little widgeon was hurt and still angry with him. He folded his arms over his chest and stared down at her, hoping to intimidate her. Only a little, of course. He didn't wish to scare her—he merely wanted to impress upon her the importance of his apology. He owed her one and he was going to give it, whether or not she wished to receive it.

"I believe your description of me was accurate."

"Indeed, it was not. I insist on making amends. May I have the honor of a dance with you at Lord Hornby's ball?" *Gad!* Had he just asked this innocent for a dance? He'd only meant to mutter some contrite words and be on his way. He hadn't meant to prolong their association beyond this uncomfortable chat in his grandmother's parlor. She had to refuse him. He wanted her to refuse him.

He sighed, knowing he was trapped. She would accept him, for women always did. *Always.* When she did the inevitable, he'd endure with manly grace. How bad could one dance with this incompetent snip of a girl be?

She tipped her face upward to meet his gaze, her eyes an intense and fiery blue. "I don't think so. Please don't ask me again. *Ever.*"

"YOU'RE IN FOUL temper, Lord Dayne."

"Go away, Your Grace." Gabriel had just settled for the evening in a dark leather chair in the smoking room at White's, a stately room paneled in dark mahogany and filled with brightly polished tables, crinkled leather sofas, and comfortable wing chairs. He was still stewing over Daisy's refusal and in no humor for a pleasant chat with Ian.

Gabriel glowered at his friend in the hope he'd take the not so subtle hint to go away. Ian ignored both his comment and his dark scowl, instead taking a seat beside him. "Is there a reason for your ill humor?" he asked, casually lighting up a cigar. "Here, have a stiff drink. It'll help warm you up." Ian reached over and grabbed a whiskey off the tray of a passing servant. "By the way, you'll like Veronique's friend."

"Who?"

"My mistress's friend. Her name is Desiree, and she has red hair, sultry gray eyes, and a limber body that will render you speechless. It's all arranged. You're to meet her tonight. She'll warm you up if the whiskey doesn't."

"Can't wait," he said without a trace of enthusiasm.

Ian arched an eyebrow. "You don't have to meet her if you don't wish to. I know a dozen other men who would give their right arms to take her under their care."

"I just said I'd do it, didn't I?" He forced a smile. "And I'm looking forward to it."

"My, my. Seems the Farthingale girl has you quite turned upside-down. Well, it's to be expected now that she's grown into a beauty. Did your military training protect you from her onslaught?"

Gabriel shook his head and sighed. "What makes you think I met Daisy?"

Ian laughed. "You have the unmistakable look of panic in your eyes. You know, the look a deer gets when it realizes it's about to be shot. I warned you, didn't I? Now it's too late. Tell me everything."

Bloody hell. Had he spent years fighting Napoleon's army merely to protect a country of busybodies? "There's nothing to tell. The girl and I are not on speaking terms."

Ian set his cigar in a nearby ashtray and leaned forward, his gaze sharp and assessing. "But you were on speaking terms at one time."

Gabriel grumbled something indistinguishable.

"I heard you saved Daisy's cousin from a team of thundering horses. Also heard Daisy was most appreciative."

He grumbled again.

"Is that an affirmative? Never mind. What happened afterward? I know you remained at your grandmother's for quite a while."

He glared at Ian, annoyed by the interrogation. "Why don't you ask your spies? They seem to be quite thorough in their reporting."

"But it would be so much more interesting to hear the details from you. Ah, but you're not the sort to kiss and tell. Too bad. I'll have to watch the two of you at Falmouth's party and see how you behave toward each other."

"Daisy won't be attending," he said tightly, her look of disappointment still vivid in his mind. "Seems her gown won't be ready in time."

Ian's eyes widened as though he were caught by surprise, and then he shook his head and sighed. "Your cousin Graelem warned me this might happen. He and Laurel invited Daisy to stay with them in order to protect her from that chaotic family of hers, but she refused, claimed to be needed at home. Apparently, she keeps the household running. If you ask me, she seems to be doing a terrible job of it."

Gabriel clenched his teeth to curb his anger. He knew Ian was purposely goading him and refused to rise to the taunt. "She does an excellent job under the circumstances."

"I see." Ian took a sip of his own drink just delivered by a steward. "So, have you kissed her?"

"No, and I have no desire to. However, I will gladly kiss the sultry Desiree should she be willing."

Ian threw his head back and laughed. "You'll find her most accommodating."

CHAPTER 4

A rake's weapon of choice may be a blade
or dueling pistols, but a young lady's weapon is
her fashionable gown.

"DAISY, DO STOP fussing," Eloise gently chided as she and Daisy rode in Eloise's carriage one week later on their way to Lord Hornby's ball.

"I can't help it." Daisy wished she'd never been invited to the ball, though the night was perfect, another in a string of unusually warm evenings. The scent of lilac wafted in the air as they drove through the park, filling the compartment with a magical hint of early spring. "I feel like an enormous snowball in this hideous white satin and lace confection. I can't seem to get comfortable."

Eloise leaned forward and patted her hand. "You look perfect and I'm certain there'll be a dozen young men who'll declare that very thing to you before the night is through."

Daisy seriously doubted it. "Will your grandson be there?"

"Yes, Gabriel will—"

"No, not him." *Ugh!* "I mean Alexander." After all, he was the war hero and heir to the earldom. Gabriel, although handsome enough to send any woman into raptures, was an irritating bounder and she hoped never to see him again.

"Oh, I see. Unfortunately, Alexander is delayed at Trent Hall on important business. But Gabriel—"

"When will he return to London?"

"Alexander?" Eloise shrugged. "In about a month, I expect."

"That long?" How was she to meet her future husband if he refused to come to London? She hadn't considered the possibility when she'd first formed her plan. This was a major setback, she had to admit. What was she to do now? Wait for Alexander? But he could be delayed longer than a month, perhaps not make it to London at all this season.

Well, she could wait out the month, but she would have to form another plan on the chance that her first didn't work out. It was only prudent, after all. And how hard could it be to keep her eye out for other potential prospects? There were plenty of eligible bachelors around. Just not Gabriel Dayne.

Eloise let out a soft chuckle. "Gabriel will keep us company until then."

"What? Why him?" Daisy sank back in her seat and sighed. *Ugh, again! Never him!* "Must he? Forgive me, Eloise. I don't mean to be rude. I know you love your grandson and enjoy his company... that is, when he behaves himself. But he so rarely does. I wish I could help you to reform his rakehell ways, but he can't abide me. In truth, I don't like him very much either."

Eloise's eyes were suddenly agleam. "Hmm, help me to reform him? Now that's an intriguing thought, actually quite a wonderful idea. Thank you, Daisy. I'm so glad you offered."

At first, Daisy laughed. Then she realized Eloise was serious. Her heart shot into her throat and she grabbed the carriage door to steady herself. "No, that isn't what I meant at all."

Eloise was too busy grinning from ear to ear to pay attention to her protests. "We shall begin tonight. Why waste a moment?"

"Because it's a terrible idea," Daisy insisted, shaking her head in dismay. "I've never had any suitors. None. Not a one. How am I to deal with any man, much less a rake as dangerous as your grandson? I wouldn't know where to start. Or how to defend myself." *Or how to protect my heart.*

"Oh, dear. You're right." Eloise emitted a long, slightly disheartened sigh. "No, that won't do. You're much too innocent to understand the wicked workings of a rake's mind."

Daisy nodded in agreement. "I'm completely inept."

However, Eloise's eyes were still agleam. "But I have the perfect solution to our little dilemma. You—"

"There is no solution," she insisted, her frustration mounting.

"Nonsense, child. I know exactly what must be done to turn you into a worthy adversary for my grandson. I'm going to lend you a book."

"A... what?"

"Not just any book, but a brilliant exposition of warfare between the sexes. It's called *Rules for Reforming a Rake* and was written several decades ago by Lady Forsythia Haversham, one of the most respected strategists of her day. Never doubt that these rules still apply."

Daisy's eyes rounded in horror as Eloise continued. "My dear girl, you must look upon each ball, musicale, or soiree as a battle to be engaged, the enemy being the unrepentant bachelor." She leaned forward and patted Daisy's hand. "Said bachelor is ever on the alert, his ears pricked and body defensively poised to repel any attack on his freedom."

"Lady Forsythia explained all this in a book? Hasn't she gone through four husbands already?"

Eloise nodded. "All of them rakehells until she came along and tamed them."

"Killed them is more like it, for not one survived beyond their fifth year of marriage," Daisy muttered, trying to stem her rising panic. How long had Eloise been thinking of this? And how was she to dissuade her from pursuing this doomed and dangerous plan? "At the very least, Lady Forsythia herded each unsuspecting gentleman into an early grave." She swallowed hard and gave a sad shake of her head. "No, it's a terrible idea. I will never agree to reform your wastrel grandson. Put the notion out of your head at once."

Eloise laughed lightly and reached out again to pat her hands, which were now clasped and resting on her lap. "Gabriel isn't so bad once you get to know him. The two of you got off to a bad start, that's all. Think of it this way, your next encounter couldn't possibly be worse."

Daisy tried to muster enthusiasm for the knave, truly she did. But couldn't. She had problems of her own and didn't need to pile his atop them. She cast Eloise a polite but dismayed smile. "I doubt he and I shall ever meet again. We Farthingales have been your neighbors for over three years now and have never run into him before. I wouldn't have met him except for Harry's escapade. I'm certain he has every intention of avoiding me as well."

She hoped that was his intention, for she couldn't possibly be seen in his company. He was completely unsuitable for her, and he rattled her in ways she did not quite understand yet. Perhaps Lady Forsythia's book would explain why he made her feel so very uncomfortable. Not that she had any intention of reading it, but every time she thought of Gabriel, heat inexplicably shot into her cheeks. And her heart fluttered. Out of anger, no doubt. Even now, her entire body was growing hot at the mere mention of him.

Out of anger, she assured herself.

She would get over her ill feeling toward the bounder in a few days, for she was never one to hold grudges, even though he'd clearly been in the wrong. He'd also been arrogant and rude. He believed her to be a foggy-headed husband hunter with little polish and no sense of style.

What would he think of her when he learned of The Incident?

Why should she care? Indeed, she didn't. She let out a huff and straightened her spine, now quite put out. Who was he to cast judgment upon her when he was unfit to move about in civilized society?

The carriage came to a stop at the opposite end of the park. "Ah, here we are," Eloise said, drawing Daisy out of her thoughts.

Daisy lowered the window and stuck her face out. A light breeze tickled her nose. She noticed an imposing gray brick townhouse that appeared to be impeccably maintained. "This can't be Lord Hornby's residence. There isn't a soul on the street."

"Goodness, I meant to tell you, but it slipped my mind. Gabriel is to join us."

"Now? Here? This is his home?" She tried to keep the dismay out of her voice, but knew she'd failed. She had expected the man to reside in a den of iniquity. After all, he had a horrid reputation. But to reside in this magnificent abode?

"Yes, this is his London residence. Of course, his seat is in Derbyshire."

Daisy turned to her companion. "I'm curious about that, for you've never really explained how he acquired his seat. Certainly not through the Trent line, for he's the younger son. And there are so many rumors circulating about it that one doesn't know quite what to believe."

"Is it important? He's quite enterprising—acquired the Derbyshire estate and title all on his own."

"But how?" Probably by cheating at cards, Daisy mused. Or doing the Prince Regent some wicked favor to earn his gratitude. Hushed up a royal scandal, no doubt.

Eloise sat upright and quirked her head. "How odd! You know, I'm not certain how it came about. The news spread quietly one day that he'd been made Baron Summersby and given a charming estate to go along with the title. Gossip has it that he saved the life of an unnamed royal offspring, or perhaps it was some other royal relation. The point is, Gabriel must have rescued someone important, although the details were never disclosed."

"No doubt from a seedy establishment filled with cardsharps, cutthroats, and women of ill repute." Daisy closed her eyes and stifled a sigh of exasperation. "Is there a reason you asked him to join us tonight?"

Eloise's diamond earrings gleamed as brightly as her eyes. "I didn't. He asked to accompany me."

"He asked you? He ought to have been warned that I was to ride in your carriage. I'm sure he won't be pleased to find me here."

"Oh, he knew you were coming."

Daisy tried, but failed, to muffle her surprise. "He did? And he still agreed to ride with you... er, with us?" How odd, for the man detested her. Well, he didn't really. He felt quite indifferent toward her, which was in many ways worse, for hatred required some passion, while indifference was as exciting as sipping tepid soup. No flavor, no vibrance. Just watered-down bland.

"Good evening, Grandmama, Miss Farthingale."

"*Eep!*" Gabriel's whiskey-smooth rumble jolted her out of her thoughts. He'd moved so quietly that she hadn't noticed his approach. He now stood by the carriage, a smirk on his handsome face.

Eloise harrumphed. "Must you be so formal, Gabriel? This is my dear Daisy, and I insist you call her so."

"Very well," he said, filling the doorway with his presence as he climbed in and settled in the seat across from her. "Good evening, dear Daisy."

The bright streetlight illuminated his exquisite features.

Oh, she was doomed to an evening of torment! It wasn't fair that a man as wicked as Gabriel should look so good. The cut of his formal black coat accentuated his broad shoulders, powerful chest, and trim waist. The light shimmering into the carriage from the street seemed to form a halo about his magnificent gold hair.

"Good evening, Lord Dayne," she managed with a pronounced squeak to her voice. Be clever. Be clever. Now is your chance to show him you're not in the least affected by his presence.

"Please, call me Gabriel."

Unfortunately, he did affect her—she couldn't overlook the rapid beats of her heart or the butterflies fluttering in her stomach. She stared at his lips as they moved, unable to respond to his question. Wait, had he even asked a question? His lips were as tempting as hot scones slathered in butter. Made her want to sink her mouth on them and lick—*stop thinking of slathering Gabriel with anything!* Finally she managed an appallingly dim-witted reply. "What?"

He leaned close and began to speak to her as slowly as one would to a foreigner who did not understand the English language or to a person of limited understanding. "I... said... you... may... call... me... Gabriel."

Ah, this was going to be a very long evening.

"I... heard... you... the... first... time," she replied, leaning ever closer so that their noses almost touched as she imitated his manner of speech. "I... just... hadn't... expected... the... offer."

He chuckled lightly.

Their breaths mingled.

His was nice, as inviting as a soft May breeze.

Her skin grew hot and inexplicably began to tingle. *Not fair. Not fair!*

He chuckled again and eased his large frame so that his back rested against the polished leather squabs.

His long legs grazed hers as the carriage jerkily pulled away.

She let out a slight gasp— more of another *eep* really. *Definitely not fair!* She had better sense—or ought to have had better sense— than to respond to that knave's accidental touch. And why was she still thinking of his lips and wishing to lick them?

Eloise was now staring at her. "Did you say something, Daisy?"

How could she when she could hardly string two words together? "No."

"I thought you did," she insisted, casting Daisy an assessing smile. *Oh, dear.* Was Eloise really thinking of using her to civilize her grandson?

She had to disabuse her of the notion at once. "But I didn't say anything just now. Nor did I mean what I said earlier. You remember." She arched an eyebrow and subtly glanced in Gabriel's direction.

"Why not? I thought it was an excellent idea," Eloise persisted.

"I know. But it isn't."

"Ah, I see." Eloise's smile broadened as she also cast a subtle glance in Gabriel's direction. Fortunately, he didn't seem to notice. "I do see."

Daisy stifled a groan. "I don't think you do, Eloise."

"I'm sure I do."

"I don't think so." *Crumpets!* She recognized that look of determination. Eloise was going to match make. A terrible idea that would not end well for her or Gabriel.

"But I do."

Daisy heaved a sigh. "And I—"

"May I interrupt this scintillating conversation?" Gabriel asked dryly.

"Please do," Daisy said, certain this evening was headed for disaster. She couldn't possibly reform this rakehell, for she was an utter nitwit whenever in his presence. She didn't understand why, but his wretched smirk was making matters worse. How rude of him! Indeed, quite rude. She had forgiven his behavior at their first meeting, but had no intention of doing so now.

"Your grandmother and I were trying to hold an intelligent conversation... that is to say, we are usually capable of holding intelligent conversations... and often do... at least, your grandmother does... though we aren't having one just now, are we?"

Oh, dear. She was rambling and he was grinning.

A deliciously soft grin.

And now her entire body was doing the same odd, tingling dance it had done the first day they'd met.

"Yes," she continued, wishing he'd stop looking at her in that dangerous, heart-melting way. "That's why you sought to interrupt. Is there something clever you wish to say?"

"Clever?" He let out a throaty chuckle. "That puts me under quite a bit of pressure. I merely wished to thank my grandmother for allowing me to ride with her to Lord Hornby's ball. Thought I'd mention it before the evening wore on and I became distracted."

"Quite understandable... er, yes." Daisy began to fidget with her lace collar.

"Stop fussing," Eloise whispered. "Pay no attention to that oaf, even if he is my grandson. You're a delight and you look just fine."

"For a snowball," she whispered, feeling impossibly unsophisticated. Her gown needed more fabric at the bodice and less everywhere else. She felt miserable and uncomfortable, and Gabriel was still staring at her.

Finally he leaned forward, a mischievous grin on his lips. "Daisy—"

"Oh, dear! Please don't tell me what you really think of me tonight. Let me keep a shred of dignity!"

He drew back and regarded her with something resembling astonished sincerity. "Forgive me. I didn't mean to frighten you."

She shook her head. "You didn't."

"But you look scared."

"Not of you, but of the mistakes I'm sure to make tonight. You see, this is my first ball, and my first chance to make my family proud. I want everything to be perfect, but I'm so... so... and my gown is just... just..."

"Beautiful and so are you," he said with unexpected gentleness.

Her heart leapt into her throat.

He leaned forward and took her hands in his, imbuing her with his warmth. "Daisy, you do look lovely and that's the plain truth."

"Are you certain?" she finally eked out.

"Yes." He graced her with a long, lazy smile.

Daisy felt her cheeks flame. *Great balls of cheese!* The man was dangerous.

Is this how he'd seduced Lady What's-Her-Name? And why Lord What's-His-Name had shot him? *Be clever... be calm... do not acknowledge this rogue.* Oh, she desperately wanted to think of a smart retort to put him in his place. He had no right to be nice to her.

Certainly not this nice.

He flashed her another lazy smile.

The man was too, too handsome. And confident. And shameless.

His devastating smile was now causing her blood to bubble and her toes to curl in that pleasant way they curled beside a warming fire on a snowy day. Yes, they were definitely curling inside her slippers. Which meant she'd trip and fall flat on her face the moment she descended from the carriage, staining her dress—which really wouldn't be a bad thing—and probably scraping her elbows. That wouldn't be good.

Actually, none of it would be good.

She'd be a laughingstock, and Gabriel's brother would never take her as his wife. He'd seek out an Incomparable, a woman of elegance who spoke with intelligence and could bear him exquisite children. She, on the other hand, would be shipped off to the Farthingale country home in Coniston, left to dream of unrequited love while rambling among the fields of lavender and dense bracken, lamenting the only man she'd ever loved—Alexander, if she ever got to meet him—and how he might have loved her, if only she hadn't fallen flat on her face at her first ball.

"... which is why I hoped you would accept. Will you, Daisy?"

"What?" She slipped her hands out of his warm grasp. "I'm sorry, were you speaking to me?" *Lord, what did he just say?* "I... could you please repeat the question? Actually, I'd need to hear everything you said before the question."

He threw back his head and roared with laughter.

Eloise burst into laughter as well. "Oh, this is too, too funny!"

Daisy desperately gazed from one to the other. "What is? Please tell me."

"No," Gabriel said, still laughing. "You've unmanned me, left me mortally wounded and drowning in my own blood."

"I have? That sounds awful. I'm sorry for my inattentiveness, but I'm sure you'll find others at the ball more interested in what you have to say. No, no! I didn't mean it quite that way. I'm certain you're quite interesting when you're..."

"Not insufferable?"

"You're a fascinating speaker. Positively gripping. And I'm sure I would have been enthralled had I bothered to listen." *Oh, crumpets.* "Please tell me what you said."

"No, not even if my life depended upon it."

"I DIDN'T THINK it possible," Ian said, catching up to Gabriel in Lord Hornby's crowded gaming room later that evening. "You're afraid of the girl."

Gabriel stifled a sigh, knowing Ian would not relent in his quest to unearth the latest gossip about him and Daisy. "What girl, Your Grace?"

"Don't you dare *Your Grace* me. You're obviously trying to avoid the question, but you can't. I'm speaking of Miss Daisy Farthingale, of course. Could I be speaking of anyone else?"

Gabriel shrugged. "I don't know. By the way, thank you for Desiree. She was every bit as compliant as you indicated. We passed a most pleasant evening."

"Ah, very cleverly switching the topic of conversation. But it won't work. I know you spent the night alone at home and not with Desiree. I'm guessing Daisy had everything to do with that surprising decision and I'm now determined to learn everything I can about the girl."

"That's easily remedied. Why don't you ask her to dance?" Gabriel gazed through the double French doors into the Hornby ballroom, which was packed with revelers, the women in crisp satin and jewels, the men in white tie and black formal attire. Strains of a waltz drifted through the hallway toward them. "There she is by the door, chatting with her Aunt Julia and Lord Hornby's insipid son, Lumley. I'm certain she'd love to be rescued."

"Not by me. I readily admit to being too cowardly to approach any of the Farthingale girls. Can't risk being caught up in the whirlwind of marriage." Ian let out an exaggerated shudder. "No, very happy to observe from a distance. But you've actually exchanged bodily fluids with her cousin. Or rather, you were on the receiving end of his little gift."

"Damn it," he said, curling his hands into fists to stem his exasperation. "Three-year-old infants have accidents, and I grant you I'd be laughing heartily if it had happened to you."

"Gabriel, I don't mean to give you a hard time. It's just that you seem so calm about your impending... ah, how shall I tactfully put it?"

"Doom? No chance of it. I've exchanged nothing but pleasantries with the girl." That is, if one overlooked the heart-wrenching set down he'd subjected her to the first day they'd met. He still felt terrible about it.

"You're hiding from her."

"I am not. If anything, she's resisting me." Not that he blamed her.

Unaware of Gabriel's earlier rough treatment of the girl, Ian chuckled. "What have you asked her to do?"

"Dance. She has refused."

"That isn't possible. She's supposed to be chasing you and you're supposed to be fleeing. But she'll catch you anyway."

Gabriel uttered a silent prayer for this conversation to end. "Neither of us is chasing and neither of us is fleeing."

"I don't understand," Ian insisted with a shake of his head. "You're cursed. You walked down that street. You're a marked man. Your bachelor life is about to end, even though you put down a six-month deposit on a charming apartment on Curzon Street for the lovely Desiree."

Gabriel arched an eyebrow. "Kindly amuse yourself at someone else's expense. I do not like to be spied upon."

"I'm just trying to protect you. Now, you say the girl has refused to dance with you?"

"Yes," Gabriel said with a nod.

"And you asked her?"

He nodded again. "Yes."

"Nicely?"

"I asked her very nicely."

Ian shook his head again as though confused. "And she said no."

"Yes, she said no. The girl is not interested in me. I bore her to tears." Though she'd delighted him to no end on their ride to Lord Hornby's.

Ian cast him a painful look. "This isn't possible."

"Now you're the one looking like the deer about to be shot."

"This is no jest, Gabriel. If you're not the next victim of the Chipping Way curse, then who is?"

Gabriel grinned broadly. "Perhaps it's you. Perhaps you were meant to walk down that street, rescue Harry Farthingale, and fall in love with Daisy."

"Me?" Ian rubbed a hand across the back of his neck. "Is it possible? But I don't wish to fall in love with her. She's the silliest of the lot!"

Gabriel struggled to keep his hands at his sides and not circled around his friend's throat. "Don't you ever speak of her that way. She's clever and warm hearted. And we're just a pair of condescending fools who don't deserve her notice. If you ever—"

Ian smiled wickedly. "*Gad*, you're gullible. The girl is obviously delightful, but I wasn't sure you'd noticed." His wicked smile broadened. "It is you, after all. Thank goodness!"

CHAPTER 5

A rake enjoys a tempting morsel. A lady will permit his eye to wonder, but never his hand to wander.

IAN'S SILLY GAME had gone on long enough, Gabriel decided.

He had to put a stop to it before Ian—in a drunken slip—did or said something foolish, perhaps revealed to Daisy that he, Gabriel, had been shot while breaking up a spy ring loyal to Napoleon, not while bedding a married woman.

Yes, he had to put an end to Ian's game at once.

Daisy wasn't meant for him. Indeed, Eloise had assured him that the girl was mad for his brother even though they hadn't yet met. In effect, she'd fallen in love with Alex's reputation. Gabriel was glad of it. Indeed, he was. Alex was a good sort, proper husband material, and a viscount to boot.

He, on the other hand, wasn't suitable at all. He had a vile reputation, fully deserved, and he fully intended to do all in his power to uphold it. Now that he was home and his wounds were healed, he meant to spend his precious days making up for lost time in the company of loose women.

Love? Marriage?

Utter rubbish. Not for him.

He'd put an end to the nonsense by insisting Daisy dance with him, then calmly walk away once the set was through. That would put Ian and any fellow doubters in their place. All he had to do was find her in this crush.

Sweet, unspoiled Daisy.

Though he'd heard rumor of some incident in her past. *Bah!* He knew women, and she was still an innocent. He'd stake his life on it.

He spotted Eloise chatting with his cousin Graelem and approached them. "Have you seen Daisy?" he asked, not bothering with pleasantries.

The two exchanged smug glances.

"It's a simple question," he declared, growing impatient.

Graelem chuckled. "No, we haven't seen her."

"Well, not since she left the ballroom with Lord Hornby's son," Eloise added.

Gabriel regarded them incredulously. "And you let her go off with that... that... foolscap?"

Eloise shrugged. "You're hardly considered a prize and we would have let her go off with you."

No, you wouldn't.

"I overheard him say something about getting Daisy alone in the conservatory," Graelem teased. "You know, that steamy room filled with lush ferns and delicately scented flowers. Oh, and lots of dark hiding places. But don't worry, I'm certain the thought of kissing Daisy hasn't crossed his mind."

Had Graelem and Eloise, even Ian, always been this irritating and he simply hadn't noticed? Or had their characters changed for the worse during his absence from England? "The conservatory, you say?"

He marched through the crowded ballroom and strode past the gaming room and dining room, peering into each before proceeding down the long, dimly lit hallway. *Is Lord Hornby too cheap to provide adequate candlelight for his guests?* he thought testily.

He reached the door to the conservatory and was surprised to find it closed. He flung it open with his shoulder and immediately heard a giggle coming from behind an overgrown fern. Graelem truly had allowed Daisy to go off alone with that dull cabbage, Lumley! He couldn't believe it! Daisy was obviously inexperienced, unaware of the games played at such *ton* gatherings. "There'll be no more of that, young lady!"

He reached into the ferns and pulled out Dorothea Hobbs and the pimply-faced Tom Quigley. Dorothea squinted up at him, her lips curling in a too broad smile. "Lord Dayne, were you looking for me?"

"Er, pardon me. My mistake." He backed out of the conservatory.

Where was Daisy?

He began to open doors along the hallway. Billiard room. Study. Lady Hornby's parlor. Library.

He paused at the threshold of the library. "Daisy? What are you doing in here?"

She stood alone in the near dark, a lone, lit candle revealing her slight frame slumped against the fireplace mantel. "Please, leave me alone."

"Are you crying?" He was certain he'd heard a sniffle mingled with her words.

"You needn't concern yourself. You aren't responsible for these tears." She tensed as he stepped in and closed the door. "Just go away. I don't need your condescension to complete my perfect evening."

He started toward her. "I suppose I deserved that. Tell me what happened. What did Lord Hornby do to you?"

"Lumley?"

He nodded.

"Oh, him. Nothing really."

He came to her side, his heart slamming against his chest. *Nothing really?* What the hell did that mean? "Look at me, Daisy."

"No," she said and turned away.

He placed his hands on her slender shoulders and gently turned her once again to face him. She offered little resistance. "What did he do?" he asked in softest voice, straining to subdue his anger. Of course, it wasn't directed at her but at everyone who should have been protecting her and wasn't, particularly her parents, who seemed more concerned with accommodating their never-ending stream of guests than guarding their precious daughter. Leaving this beautiful girl untended in such surroundings was like dropping a lamb into a pack of hungry wolves.

"Truly, Lord Dayne. He did nothing at all."

"The name's Gabriel. If not Lumley Hornby, then—"

"No one bothered me."

Confused, he released her and ran a hand through his hair. "Then why are you crying?"

She hesitated a moment, obviously struggling to compose herself, and obviously about to lose the struggle. Her lips began to quiver. Her hands began to shake. Finally, she buried her face in her hands and burst into sobs. "I tried so hard... so hard to prove I was responsible. Now, I'll be forever branded the foggy-headed Farthingale, just as you accused."

Had he called her that?

"You were right about me and I was so wrong to resent you for it!"

He drew her close and wrapped his arms about her, surprised by the depth of her sorrow and alarmed by his sudden, overwhelming need to protect her. "Daisy, please tell me what happened."

"I lost the family heirloom pearls. I shouldn't have worn the necklace this evening because the clasp was broken, but Mother insisted it had been repaired. Rather than fight about it, I put on the necklace just as every Farthingale debutante has done for the last hundred years. I ought to have known better and should have said something, but didn't. Now it's lost and I've destroyed the proud family tradition!"

He held her in his embrace, knowing there was nothing he could say to cheer her spirits. Only finding the family heirloom would do. Perhaps this was his chance to make amends. He'd been too proud, too haughty to appreciate how badly he'd injured her feelings the other day. Retrieving the necklace would be the best sort of apology, better than his earlier offer of a dance. "When did you notice it was missing?"

She sniffled. "A short while ago. It fell off in the conservatory, I think. I tried to return to search for it, but didn't get very far. I wasn't alone in there."

He understood.

The Hornby conservatory wasn't the sort of place an innocent girl could handle without proper chaperone. He'd seen her attended earlier by her Aunt Julia, but apparently her aunt had found other distractions to occupy her time. He also suspected that Graelem and Eloise, despite their earlier teasing, must have believed she was still being chaperoned by her aunt or they would have taken up the slack immediately.

Daisy started to pull out of his arms, but he held her back, reluctant to let her go. She felt nice, he decided, surprised by how perfectly her slight body molded to his gruff contours. Her silky curls tickled his chin and her scent tickled his senses. She smelled of cinnamon and apples, as delicious as a Viennese dessert. "I'll help you search."

Her eyes widened in astonishment. "You will?"

He ran his thumb gently along her cheek to wipe away the trail of tears. "If you'll let me."

Leaning back to meet his gaze, she let out a long breath and cast him a dazzling smile. "Gladly. Thank you for the offer. I need all the help I can get."

"Good. Yes, then. It's settled." Reluctantly, he withdrew his hand from her cheek. There was something about her admission that roused his protective instincts. Ian would have called it a dangerous sign, but it wasn't. He'd survived to the age of twenty-seven by using his wits, by learning to defend himself against all enemies. This pretty slip of a girl wasn't much of an enemy and hardly a danger to his bachelorhood. "Now let's retrace your steps. Exactly where were you when you first noticed it was missing?"

"On my way back to the ballroom. But I'm certain I lost it in the conservatory. Yes, most certainly in the conservatory. You see," she said with a little hiccup followed by a harrumph. "Lumley Hornby lured me there in order to show me his... well... his..."

"His what?" he prompted, noting her hesitation.

"His *cucumber*!" she cried, her magnificent eyes rounding in horror. "Only it wasn't a cucumber at all!"

"Good Lord!" He'd always thought of young Hornby as a harmless twit, but obviously he wasn't. To expose himself to a respectable girl. No, not even Hornby could be that much of a muff. Hornby? He wasn't the sort. Was he? Gabriel shook his head, certain that he'd misunderstood her words.

"And then he wanted me to touch it!"

What?

"But I thought it more closely resembled a gherkin, so I refused. I mean, he led me to believe it would be enormous, the sort of thing one couldn't resist putting one's hands around and stroking."

Gabriel's jaw dropped open.

"Only it was this funny sort of twisted thing that hung limp on the end, like this." She curved her index finger and held it up to his view.

Did the girl realize what she was saying?

"I told Lord Lumley that if he thought to impress me by showing me that... that shriveled thing, he'd have to do a better job of it. Reminded me of a gherkin," she grumbled again. "Then I told him about your cousin, Graelem."

"What about Graelem?" Lord, what had his cousin done to involve himself in this imbroglio?

"Now there's a man with an enormous cucumber, but he doesn't go around bragging about it. Why are you looking at me so oddly? Surely you knew Graelem was an avid gardener. His beets and squash won first prize at last year's Midlands fair. Are you laughing, Gabriel?"

"No." Lord help him! The girl was actually speaking of vegetables. *Thank the Graces.* He'd been angry enough to grab that clunch, Hornby, and stuff his entrails up his skinny arse. He'd still have a private word with the man, for there was no mistaking the suggestive nature of his conversation.

"Yes, you are. It isn't funny. Gardening is serious business."

Oh, she'd bludgeon him if he revealed what he'd truly been thinking about Hornby's intentions. He dared not burst out laughing. *Ouch!* The restraint was killing him. "So you lost the necklace in the conservatory."

"I can't be certain, but I believe so. Do stop grinning. It's the last place I remember having it."

He took her arm and led her out of the library. "We'll start our search there, but let me go in first to clear the place out. It won't do to have you seen in there with me."

"Very kind of you to think of it. Why are you still grinning?"

"I didn't realize I was."

DAISY HAD THE distinct impression that Gabriel was staring at her derriere. Well, she ought to have known better than to reach over the oversized lungwort in order to better sift through the foliage and soil beds. She'd thrown herself off balance and was now tipped forward and fully exposed to his scrutiny. "Would you kindly help me up?"

Wordlessly he moved behind her, placed his hands on the sides of her waist, and drew her to a standing position. She stifled a groan as her back came to rest against his gloriously solid chest. The room was secluded, dimly lit, and lightly scented by the lilac in bloom.

His body felt warm against hers, the gentle touch of his hands at her waist, intimate. Now if only Gabriel would miraculously turn into Alexander. She closed her eyes and imagined Alexander turning her to face him, and lowering his heavenly mouth to hers... and seeking her lips for a long, lingering kiss.

She drew away with a start.

This was Gabriel!

Oh, she had to stop thinking about the delicious feel of his body against hers and concentrate instead on finding the necklace. After all, Gabriel would not indulge her very much longer. She'd heard him muttering under his breath, something about being punished for his wicked ways. No doubt he considered her a nuisance and had a hundred reasons to part company with her. Only extreme pity for her situation—or perhaps a sacred promise to Eloise to keep an eye on her so that she wouldn't make a complete ninny of herself—could be keeping him here.

Perhaps it was a little of both.

It certainly wasn't a desire to kiss her.

She certainly had no desire to kiss him, even if he did have the nicest lips. They gave a tell-tale twitch at the corners whenever he was about to smile.

"Wipe the dirt off your hands and put your gloves back on," he instructed, handing her back the elbow-length, white satin gloves that had been meticulously fashioned to match her gown.

"But we're not done searching."

"I'll continue to look through the plants and soil beds. Dirt won't show up against my black clothing, but there'll be the devil to pay if you stain your pretty gown."

"Do you really think this gown is pretty?" She slid the gloves up her arms but was unable to button the cuffs.

Gabriel sighed and turned her to face him. "Here, let me help you."

"Thank you," she murmured, allowing him to gently tug the gloves over her elbows and secure the buttons.

He tweaked her nose. "Keep them clean."

She nodded.

Did he think her pretty, too? He'd said so earlier in the carriage, but she had been distraught and he would have said anything to soothe her.

She studied him as he began to search. He was in very good shape for a debaucher of women and a general dissolute. Indeed, his body was remarkably well toned. So well, in fact, that he might have been mistaken for a Roman gladiator or other such symbol of masculine perfection.

She knew from the scent of his fresh breath as he'd leaned close a moment ago that he hadn't been drinking. Odd that he should be among the few sober men at the ball. Her host's son, Lumley Hornby, had imbibed too much—which explained why he'd tried to kiss her tonight. Tom Quigley had tried the same, calling her magnificent and chasing her around the conservatory when she'd realized her necklace was missing and returned alone to search for it the first time.

Then there had been the gentleman who'd pinched her by the punch bowl in the ballroom. Obviously, no gentleman.

Only Gabriel had acted with chivalry, which was quite ironic since he had the worst reputation of all. If he was so wicked, why hadn't he tried to steal a kiss from her?

Not that she wanted his kiss.

Still, it was quite insulting that he hadn't tried.

She shook her head and silently chided herself for the direction of her thoughts. Hadn't she learned the dangers of kissing a man? Even though she'd never actually been kissed, just allowed herself to take the blame.

And endured stiff punishment for it.

"I think it's safe to say that the Farthingale heirloom is not among the lungworts," Gabriel remarked, looking down among the plant beds. "Shall we search by the Cupid's dart? Perhaps you dropped the pearls there."

"No, I never went near them." He could use a good shot of Cupid's dart, right in the... no, he was being kind and helpful. It wasn't his fault that he had a terrible reputation. Well, it was. But even rakehells could be nice at times. Which explained why he hadn't tried to kiss her yet, assuming he wanted to at all.

Goodness! She had to stop thinking of Gabriel and kisses.

He ran a hand distractedly through the golden waves of his hair. "The orange trees?"

She squelched the urge to reach out and run her fingers through his glorious mane. Instead, she shook her head. "No."

"The eucacias?"

She gave another shake of her head. "No."

"The wild hoarhound?"

She sighed. "Quigley chased me by the orchids. Perhaps we'll find them there."

He quirked an eyebrow. "You mean young Hornby chased you."

"No, *he* tried to kiss me by the cucumbers—"

Gabriel's expression immediately darkened. "So, he did try something!"

She groaned, wishing she had not let that slip. "It was nothing, really. He left when I slapped him... well, perhaps it was more than a slap. I'd curled my fingers into a fist. You see, I accidently bloodied his nose and he was already in ill humor over the gherkin incident."

Now, both of his golden eyebrows were sternly arched. "You ought to have told me earlier."

She nodded. "I know. I'm sorry. But as I said, his amorous attempt failed and there was no harm done except to him. He was more irritated than hurt, though he let out an alarming howl when I struck him. He claimed to have very weak nasal cavities."

Gabriel smothered a cough, although she might have detected a chuckle mixed in as well. But his manner quickly turned serious.

"Tell me about Quigley."

"Must I?"

Gabriel took a step forward so that he was now standing quite close. "Yes, Daisy," he said, sounding quite protective. "You must."

Crumpets! She liked that man-seeking-to-defend-his-woman look about him. Clearly, he was not amused by Quigley and meant to do something about it. She wouldn't allow him, of course. Men brawling over her? Whatever was left of her reputation would be in tatters. "I'll tell you, but only if you promise not to do anything about him."

His scowl warned that he was about to leave right now and pound the truth out of Quigley. She placed a hand on his arm to hold him back, not that he'd made a move toward the door yet, but she was already distressed and could not afford to have him cause a scene. "Quigley was here when I returned and offered to help me, or so I thought, but what he really wanted to do was pull me down behind those eucacias and... is that all men have on their minds?"

"Some men," he replied, glancing at her hand, which was still on his forearm. She quickly removed it.

"Of course," she continued with a quick intake of breath, "I was forced to strike him over the head with a watering can that happened to be close at hand. He stumbled and let go of me, and that's how I made my escape."

"Very resourceful of you. I could have used you at... er, at my side."

When fending off that irate husband, she imagined. However, there was a look in his eyes, a dark, faraway expression that made her think just for a moment that he was noble and heroic and... no, he had spent his years carousing while his brother had gone to war.

Yet, there was something about him. Something commanding, and at the same time, comforting. He didn't look like a coward at all.

"One learns to hold one's own in a family as large and boisterous as mine," she said, shaking out of the thought. "I wasn't in any real danger from either gentleman."

She wanted to add that his cousin, Graelem, who was now married to her sister, Laurel, had taught her to shoot and to handle a knife as well as any man. He'd also taught her several tricks of defense, none of which she'd ever use on Gabriel if he decided to kiss her.

No! She meant *Alexander*. She'd never use those tricks on Alexander.

Gabriel furrowed his brow. "Your family ought to have been watching over you tonight."

"Yes, well. I'm certain they didn't mean to neglect me and I don't hold them responsible. They thought me capable of taking care of myself. Which I was. I dispatched one gentleman with a bloodied nose and the other with a lump on his head."

The furrow in Gabriel's brow deepened.

She let out a ragged sigh. "Oh, you have such an upright look about you, as though you intend to... please don't say anything to my parents."

"They must be made to understand the consequences of their inattention."

"There were no consequences. I defended my reputation quite capably. If you must know, I'm partly to blame. You see, I did something very foolish about a year ago and haven't quite lived it down."

"Daisy—"

"No, you'll have to ask Eloise about it, for I'll say no more." She turned away and sank onto a nearby bench. "Please, this evening has been a disaster and your exchanging words with those gentlemen or my family will only make matters worse."

He followed her, perching his foot on the bench and studying her quite thoroughly while he considered her request. He must have sensed her desolation and decided against adding to her worries, for he finally sighed and said, "Very well. I won't say a word."

"Thank you."

His frown returned. "Don't. I think you're wrong."

"Thank you, anyway. You've been the one bright spot in this dismal evening, chivalrous and valiant. My very own dragon-slaying hero. My very own Saint George."

He surprised her with a disarming smile that reached his eyes and made them gleam with the luminous warmth of the candles in the wall sconces. "I've been called many names before, most of them unmentionable, but never, ever have I been called a saint."

"Gabriel, I expected my first ball to be magical and the young men I'd meet to be charming. Instead, they were boors."

He let out a chuckle. "Ah, here you thought I was the only boor."

His gentle humor endeared him all the more to her. "You're not at all. In fact, I find you very charming and I'm enjoying your company immensely."

"I'm enjoying yours, too," he admitted softly.

She let out a bubble of laughter. "We seem to have made great strides since our first encounter."

"Indeed."

She gazed up at him and her eyes widened at the tender expression she saw on his face. Her heart, already beating wildly, now shot into her throat. "May I ask you a question?"

"If it's not too personal," he teased. "I have very delicate sensibilities."

"What were you and Eloise laughing about earlier in the carriage? I acted so silly, an utter dolt, but —"

He cupped a hand under her chin and gave it a playful tweak. "The jest was at my expense, not yours. I tried to charm you and you weren't even listening. I delivered a magnificent apology for my earlier behavior, short, sweet, sincere. Just the perfect balance of humility and contrition. Then I asked, no, begged you to accept my offer of a dance."

"You did?"

He grinned painfully. "And you never heard a word. It was a humbling moment for me. Well deserved, I may add. Daisy, I'm very sorry for what I said about you the other day. I didn't mean a single word."

She felt heat rise in her cheeks. "Truly?"

"Truly," he responded, taking her hands into his own.

A shiver of delight ran up her spine, which she quickly resolved to ignore. "I'm glad."

"Good. That's settled." He released her abruptly and resumed the search.

Daisy removed her gloves once more, and after promising to be careful not to dirty her gown and accessories, spent the next moments scouting through the last of the soil beds with him, lifting every pot and searching in, under, and around every leaf. They found a lady's mirror and an earring under a bench, a man's glove and a shoe buckle among the ferns, but no sign of the necklace.

"Does your offer still stand?" she finally asked miserably. "I mean, about the dance. I'd very much like one. It'll be the only pleasant memory salvaged from this disastrous evening."

"Perhaps later. First, let's find your heirloom."

Daisy's cheeks suffused with heat. She sputtered an apology about not meaning to force him to do anything he did not wish to do, and that he needn't dance with her ever, or feel compelled out of politeness or by order of Eloise to endure her company.

"Daisy, I do wish to dance with you. I just assumed our top priority was to find the lost necklace."

"It is. It's just that you've been so patient and—"

"You hate to impose further on my time?"

"Yes, exactly."

"I'll let you know when you become an imposition. Come here, you have a smudge on your nose." He drew out his handkerchief and stepped toward the small fish pond to moisten one edge of the fashionable cloth. "I'll be damned," he muttered, staring into the water. "I thought you said you looked in here."

"I did." She came to his side and followed his gaze. "It's clear enough to see straight through to the bottom."

"But you didn't stick your hand in it."

"No, why should I? My vision is perfect and there's nothing swimming in the pond but two goldfish."

He sighed and pulled his cuff up as far as it would go. "Your knowledge of science is limited. Not your fault at all, but rather the idiocy of society in restricting the formal education of women."

She turned to him in surprise. "That's quite forward thinking of you."

"You sound shocked. Did you believe me to be as stodgy as the fossils who run the Royal Society?"

"Indeed, no. But neither did I expect you to hold such radical views about women and their rights to an education," she said with a nod of approval. "What does losing my necklace have to do with science?"

"Do you see how the light plays on the water?"

She returned her gaze to the small pond and studied the movement. "Yes, it's quite beautiful. But what are you doing?"

"Hopefully retrieving your heirloom." He dunked his hand into the shallow water, feeling about the bottom, and finally pulling out—a miracle!

"You've found it!" she gasped, watching the strand of pearls shimmer like starlight between his fingers.

He laughed, obviously feeling quite proud of himself. "Crisis averted."

She gazed at him in amazement. "How did you know?"

"I stayed awake during physics class at Cambridge," he said with a wry grin. "Though I never expected to put the theory of refraction of light to such good use. The bottom of the pool is deeper than it looks, you see." As though to make his point, he held up his jacket sleeve to show that even his drawn-up cuff had gotten wet. Fortunately, not too badly.

"I don't know what to say. 'Thank you' doesn't seem enough," she whispered in relief. She felt giddy, elated, and in danger of actually starting to like Gabriel.

"Put them in your pocket," he suggested after wiping droplets of water off each shiny bead with his handkerchief.

"I haven't one. This gown wasn't designed with much fabric to spare," she said with a wince, feeling the heat of a blush creep up her neck and onto her cheeks. Her gown had been purposely fashioned to cling in the most obvious places.

"Ah, um... I see the problem." He studied her attire, his gaze slowly drinking in every curve of her body as though he could see through the fabric. He coughed as he stuffed the necklace into his breast pocket and patted it. "I'll hold it for the moment."

She wondered how she might feel cozily tucked against Gabriel's chest. However, she quickly shook out of the bumble-headed thought. "My sister, Lily, tried to teach me about physics. She's brilliant and an excellent tutor, but we'd hardly begun before the family caught on and put a quick end to my studies."

"Not seemly for a debutante to be spouting equations while

waltzing with a dashing duke, I suppose."

"Lest the dashing duke find her a crushing bore." She grinned before continuing. "So I'll have to wait until the season is over before learning more about Sir Isaac Newton and his writings. Have you read his *Opticks* or the *Principia Mathematica*?"

He arched an eyebrow. "You know about those works?"

"Surprised?"

He shook his head and smiled. "I should be, but somehow I'm not. Daisy, you are a rare young lady."

"In a good way or bad?" she asked with a sudden pang of doubt.

He seemed surprised by her confusion. "Good, of course. I meant it as a compliment." He sighed. "If I help you, will you do something for me?"

"Help me? With what?"

"Well, do you wish to learn more about Newton or not?"

"Yes... no... it depends."

"On what?"

"On what I must do for you in return." He'd found her pearls and saved her from disaster, but she wasn't so foolish as to sacrifice her virtue for a lesson in physics. She didn't need to read Lady Forsythia's book on reforming a rake to know that. "What is it you wish from me?"

His brilliant smile simply melted her bones. "I wish to dance with you."

CHAPTER 6

*A lady repays a debt to a rake with no
more than a polite thank-you.*

THE GIRL GREW prettier with every breath, Gabriel decided,
offering Daisy his arm and escorting her onto the dance floor. Once
in place among the other dancers, he took her gloved hand in his,
and resting his other hand at the small of her back, brought her as
close as he dared. "You're trembling."

"With relief," she said with the softest quiver to her voice. "I'm
amazed. I don't know what to say. You saved my evening. You
saved *me*."

"Very heroic of me, I must say."

"It was. Thank you... Saint Gabriel." She smiled up at him.

Once again, he made the mistake of gazing into her vivid blue
eyes and quickly found himself enthralled by their magnificent
depths. He was still gazing as the music started. And as the first
dancers bumped into him.

"Gabriel? The music."

And as her soft, incredibly tempting body yielded to him.

He was going to kiss her tonight, damn the consequences.

One harmless kiss.

Sweet.

Short.

"Did you forget the steps?" she asked, reaching up on tiptoes to
whisper in his ear. "Shall I lead? We can sit this one out if you don't

feel like—"

He stopped her as she was about to pull out of his arms, and moving with the music, began to twirl her about the floor. She swayed gracefully in her white satin, following his steps with ease. Surprisingly, she was an excellent dancer.

"I'm not incompetent in all things," she murmured, seeming to read his thoughts. In truth, he didn't think her incompetent at all, just young and inexperienced, and at times distracted by her boisterous clan and the burdens they unwittingly placed upon her slender shoulders.

"I'm sure you are a very accomplished young lady."

She pointed her pert nose into the air and cringed. "Oh, dear."

"I intended it as a compliment."

"I know, but it's such a hideous expression. My father often describes his Aunt Hortensia that way. She's an utter ogre."

He shook his head and laughed. It felt nice, he admitted, to hold Daisy in his arms. "You're not an ogre at all."

She let out a deliciously breathy sigh. "I'm not all that accomplished either."

"Is that so? You don't seem the sort to butcher Beethoven sonatas or sew crooked hems."

"Oh, but I do so constantly," she said with a twinkle in her eyes.

"Those aren't important talents. Kindness and generosity such as you've shown my grandmother throughout the years of my absence are the virtues that count." He knew it had been a harrowing time for his entire family. They must have felt helpless, no doubt blamed themselves as they watched him earn the reputation as the family disappointment.

The dance ended and he knew better than to try to continue the conversation by seeking Daisy's hand for another. No, he'd already caused enough damage to her reputation by choosing to partner her in this one. Then there was the time spent in the library and the conservatory, innocently of course, but vicious rumors often started with much less.

Apparently, she'd already felt the sting of gossip a year or so earlier and suffered for it. He'd ask Graelem about that *incident* later.

His situation was different. He'd endured the lies told about him—indeed, encouraged those lies in order to maintain his disreputable appearance. Easier to slip in and out of France without being noticed. Easier to infiltrate the lower orders, make contact with Napoleon's agents and make them believe he would betray his country for a few shillings.

He escorted Daisy to his grandmother's side and settled her in one of the red velvet tufted chairs beside the lovable old harridan. "Don't let her out of your sight, Eloise."

His shrewd-eyed grandmother glanced from him to Daisy then back to him. "I'll watch her like a hawk," she assured, casting him a wry smile.

He turned to Daisy, intending to issue a stern warning... Well, he'd meant to speak sternly, but his tone might have softened in response to her delightfully earnest gaze. "You're not to leave my grandmother's side for the rest of the evening."

He expected mild protest since the night was young, she was beautiful, and her admirers were many. Young Albert Dawson, lean and sharp-nosed, was already circling Daisy like a buzzard awaiting his meal. "And do not talk to him."

Daisy looked around, confused. "Who?"

He turned and stared pointedly at Dawson, who had the good judgment to quietly slink away. "Never mind, he's gone now."

"Oh, him. He didn't look very pleasant. Indeed, none of these young men look at all appealing. I'll do exactly as you say. I'd much rather spend my time with Eloise." She smiled up at him, doe-eyed and utterly delicious. Having found her heirloom necklace, he could do no wrong, at least for tonight.

Gabriel smothered a grin, feeling quite the cock-a-hoop, for the girl had a way of making him feel quite capable and important. "Good."

She took a little breath and wiggled in her seat. "Yes, I'll tie myself to this chair and never leave it. I won't give you another moment's worry."

Oh, he liked that little wiggle.

And the thought of Daisy tied to a chair... perhaps naked and tied to a chair... perhaps naked and aroused and tied to his...

Thwap!

Hellfire! His grandmother had caught him squarely across the back of his head with her reticule as he'd innocently bent over Daisy's hand to bid her farewell. Well, perhaps not so innocently, he knew, struggling to subdue his body's response. Of course, getting walloped by one's interfering grandmother went a long way toward cooling off all lust. Lord, what had she stuffed in her reticule? A cannonball?

"Leave us, Gabriel," the beloved harridan intoned. "Go tend to your business."

MUCH LATER THAT evening, Daisy snuggled in a corner of Eloise's carriage and gazed out the window into the darkness that was about to lift with the coming dawn. There was an enchanting stillness to the London night, something warm and cozy about the gentle rocking of the well-oiled carriage springs and the nicely padded leather seats, something appealing about the light musk scent of Gabriel's cologne and his comforting presence.

Eloise had always been her friend.

She now considered Gabriel a friend.

Tonight, he'd been more than that, he'd been her hero. Her very own *wart* hero, as her young cousin, Charles, would say.

She allowed her thoughts to stray as they rode in silence.

"What are you thinking about?" Gabriel asked in a whisper.

She must have had an odd expression on her face because Gabriel hadn't taken his eyes off her the entire ride. He'd remained seated directly across from her, studying her since they'd left the Hornby townhouse. Well, she thought he had been studying her, but couldn't be certain because there was hardly any light in the carriage and his eyelids were half closed. Perhaps she'd imagined it and he had briefly drifted to sleep.

Eloise had fallen soundly asleep the moment they'd started the journey home. Even now, her soft snores mingled with the rhythmic groaning of the carriage wheels.

"Oh, I was thinking of many things," Daisy whispered back, hoping not to wake his grandmother, who was bundled in a thick fox fur and almost hidden from view. "Mostly of this beautiful night and how I survived my first ball, thanks to you."

He shook his head. "Any friend would have helped out."

"But only you did. I hope I may return the favor someday."

He arched an eyebrow as he shifted slightly toward her. "A good deed is its own reward."

She let out a merry, but hushed, laugh. "You sound like a minister at a Sunday sermon."

He gave a mock shudder. "Who me? No, I'm an unrepentant sinner."

She was a sinner, too. The thoughts now whirling in her head while gazing at him were undeniably wicked. She'd have to speak to her married sisters about these new sensations. Or read Lady Forsythia's book. Even though she had no intention of reforming Gabriel, what harm could there be in learning the workings of a rakehell's mind?

Certainly no harm in better understanding her body's response to Gabriel. Unmarried females weren't supposed to think or feel or even know about what went on in the marriage bed. But Daisy had overheard enough of her sisters' conversations to understand that the quickening of her heart, the warm tingling of her body, the yearning in her breast, were symptoms of desire. Did she desire Gabriel—*crumpets, she couldn't*—or was she mistaking these sensations for gratitude?

Would she respond as eagerly to Alexander?

In truth, she liked the naughty way Gabriel made her feel. There was a quiet promise in his soft glances, as though they were a prelude to something wonderful.

But what?

She'd have to ask Rose and Laurel.

"Are you cold, Daisy?" His voice was a husky rumble of concern.

"A little," she said, though she wasn't in the least. But how else could she explain away her shiver of excitement?

"Here, take my coat." He removed it and then drew her forward to wrap it about her shoulders. His taut muscles shifted beneath the white expanse of his shirt. His vest, shot through with silken threads of silver, gleamed as brightly as the moon on a crisp winter's night.

He drew the coat tightly about her, his hands gentle against her skin. There was something wonderful about being enveloped in his scent. "Better?"

She tilted her head toward his. "Much."

His hand lingered at her neck.

She held her breath. *Please. Please!*

No! She was mad to want him to kiss her! And hadn't she already gotten into trouble once, even though she hadn't really done anything wrong?

And what of Alexander? Would he ever forgive her for kissing his wastrel brother? Goodness, she'd never even met Alexander. What if she never met him?

It seemed a terrible shame to waste this opportunity.

Gabriel was a man of experience. Surely, he'd know just what she needed. And what harm could he do with Eloise snoring right beside them?

Ever so gently, he began to trace the outline of her jaw with his finger.

"I've never stayed up all night before," she whispered tremulously.

"Perhaps it shall be a night of firsts for you," he murmured, his thumb now caressing her cheek. "Your first ball."

She nodded.

"Your first waltz at a ball." He drew her closer.

She blinked her eyes. "My first ball gown."

"And a lovely one it is." He drew her closer still. "You were the prettiest girl at Lord Hornby's tonight."

"Very kind of you to say." She suppressed a sigh as their breaths mingled. "Thank you."

"Don't mention it. Daisy—"

She let out a small gasp. "The answer is yes."

He eased back, seeming confused. "To what?"

"The question you were about to ask. Yes, you may kiss me."

His lips twitched upward at the corners. "I wasn't about to ask the question."

She groaned, certain she was the silliest debutante ever to exist. It was bad enough she'd given him permission to kiss her, but to assume he'd wanted to... and now it was humiliatingly obvious that he didn't. She ought to have kept her mouth shut until she'd read Lady Forsythia's book. She'd probably botched a dozen rules on the short ride home. "I'm so sorry. I thought... ridiculously foolish of me..."

He held her as she tried to pull away. "Shut your eyes."

"Why?" she sputtered.

"Because I *am* going to kiss you. I just hadn't planned on asking permission. Rakehells never do." His mouth slanted across hers before she had the chance to protest, gently at first, his lips pressing against her own in a whisper-soft caress that sent a wave of heat through Daisy's body. The kiss was lovely, politely restrained, and more pleasant than she'd expected, but instead of bringing the kiss to a natural end, Gabriel suddenly let out a quiet growl and began to increase the pressure of his lips against her mouth.

In the next moment, she was on Gabriel's lap, deliciously wrapped in his strong arms, her body tingling madly as he circled one hand about her waist and allowed the other to linger at her neck, his thumb caressing a wildly sensitive spot behind her ear.

She let out a gasp. "*Gabriel.*"

"Hush, Daisy. Don't speak, just feel," he said with aching gentleness and slid his tongue along the soft, throbbing flesh of her lips to tease them open. He eased his tongue into her mouth and she welcomed the invasion.

Great balls of cheese and hot, buttered crumpets! She closed her eyes tightly and did as told, taking in every exquisite sensation. No doubt she'd just broken every rule in Lady Forsythia's book, but she didn't care. Her surrender yielded a rich bounty in return, for with each barrier Gabriel conquered, with every probing surge and teasing feint against her lips, he gave a part of himself to her.

Oh, she knew that she was an incompetent innocent and held little seductive power over him. Nonetheless, she enjoyed the moment, allowing herself to grow reckless and wanton, for she was eager to match him touch for touch, and savor him taste for taste.

Her body was hot and trembling with desire, but so was his. At least, she hoped so.

"*Daisy,*" he said in a ragged whisper and kissed her again, his kiss igniting a fiery torment deep within her soul. Fireworks exploded in her heart and a flaming heat spread throughout her limbs.

Oh, they were going to hell!

She couldn't wait to get there.

CHAPTER 7

Never kiss a rake!

DAISY SLOWLY MADE her way down the stairs of the Farthingale townhouse at noon the following day, still nursing a throbbing headache. Moments earlier, Lily had diagnosed her condition as imbibing too much at Lord Hornby's ball. Nonsense! She'd sipped only two glasses of champagne the entire evening, or was it three?

And what did her younger sister know? She was a little bluestocking who always walked around with a book in her hand, but she knew nothing about real life. Dillie was the twin who understood people and their unpredictable feelings.

Ugh! I feel wretched. Perhaps she had imbibed four glasses of champagne, she decided as her throbbing eyeballs began to pound in rhythm to her head.

Or five. Couldn't have been more than six.

She sighed.

Perhaps seven, for she must have been more than a little drunk last night to allow Gabriel to kiss her. If one could call the locked-lips, sucking, and plundering dance that went on with their mouths and tongues something as tame as a kiss. It wasn't.

Not that she blamed him for that all-devouring, shockingly delightful occurrence. Indeed, no. Not this time. This kiss—her first and only kiss, to be precise—was all her fault. Her first kiss *ever*, and she'd practically thrown herself atop him, jumping onto his lap... or had he drawn her onto it? She couldn't recall.

A little of both, she finally decided with dismay. They'd each been clutching and groping and breathlessly needing to draw one another closer. *Oh, good grief!* Had she really been that wanton?

Making her way into the dining room, Daisy smiled at her mother, who was busily chatting with Aunt Julia by the tulipwood buffet. Neither her mother nor her aunt appeared to notice her entrance, for they failed to return the greeting.

Since the pair were obviously lost in the midst of an important conversation, Daisy decided not to interrupt them. In any event, she was still quite muzzy headed and could offer nothing of significance to the discussion.

She settled into a chair at the dining table and motioned for one of the serving maids to bring her a cup of tea. As she sat quietly, Julia's chiding words reached her ears. "You're right, Sophie. Her performance last night was disgraceful. I don't know how else to describe it."

"Quite the scandalbroth," her mother agreed.

"Who was disgraceful?" Daisy asked.

"Goodness!" Julia dropped the silver lid to a tray of eggs and sausages.

Daisy winced as the lid made a resounding clang.

"When did you come in? I didn't hear you," Julia accused, turning to face her. As always, Julia was immaculately groomed, her hair styled in the latest fashion and not a golden curl out of place.

Daisy's mother frowned. "If you must know, we were speaking of you."

"Me?" Daisy gripped the edge of the dining table.

Had they seen her kissing Gabriel last night? No, they couldn't possibly have been watching Eloise's carriage or seen what was going on inside. That kiss—or rather that long string of kisses that blended into one because neither she nor Gabriel had bothered to come up for air—would have given her mother quite something to rage about.

Even now, the thought of the glorious encounter brought a heated blush to her cheeks. Her entire body warmed to the memory. She would endure whatever punishment her family had in store. Gabriel's kiss was worth it. His touch, the taste of his lips, the magical union of their hearts was a dream come true for her.

Oh, goodness! I must still be drunk!

Her mother pinned her with a stern glance. "What do you have to say for yourself?"

That she'd confused Gabriel for his brother.

That it should have been Alexander's kiss last night, and would have been had the clunch bothered to come down to London. But he was still at Trent Hall, so she'd wound up in Gabriel's muscled arms, pressed against his manly body, and breathing in his divinely subtle, musk scent.

That had she been sober—alas, she wasn't—and not giddy from too much champagne... no, that wouldn't work.

That it had been a harmless kiss.

That Gabriel would never kiss and tell.

Crumpets! What if he were the sort to kiss and tell? He was a rakehell, after all. She'd be ruined. Disgraced. She'd have to run away and live out the rest of her life under an assumed identity. Perhaps disguise herself as a boy and sign on to a pirate ship.

Her mother gently rapped on the table to regain her attention. "Daisy! Are you listening to me?"

And last night she'd kissed him back with undeniable ardor, pouring her heart and soul into that kiss. She hadn't meant to, but he'd told her to close her eyes and simply feel. She had. *Hot, buttered crumpets!* She'd felt every muscle and sinew of his big, powerful body.

"Daisy!" Her mother was still rapping her knuckles on the breakfast table. "Honestly, child!"

Daisy grabbed the cup of tea just set in front of her and took a gulp. Too hot! She gagged and dribbled most of it onto her napkin.

Julia groaned.

Her mother sighed. "Oh, for pity's sake. What am I to do with you?"

Daisy muttered a lame apology. "I'm a little off my stride this morning. I'm so sorry, Mother. I'm trying very hard to be on my best behavior."

"You didn't try hard enough last night," Julia declared, mimicking her mother's frown. "You punched Lord Hornby's son in the nose."

Daisy set down her napkin and smothered a sigh of relief. They were angry because she'd walloped Lumley? "Oh, that. He tried to kiss me and I didn't want him to. I set him in his place with a very gentle slap."

Her mother pursed her lips. "You should not have been alone with him in the conservatory. Do you see that you are to blame for provoking the situation?"

"Me?" She shot out of her seat. "Perhaps, had I gone in there alone with him, but Julia was with us at the time."

Julia gasped. "Are you blaming me?"

"Well, you did traipse off with friends and leave me trapped with that muggins—"

"Because I don't recall being appointed your chaperone."

"Indeed, you were not," her mother agreed, patting Julia's hand in sympathy.

Daisy wondered who, if anyone, had been charged with her care? A little detail neither her aunt nor her mother deemed significant.

"Because I have myself and young Harry to think about, so how can I think of you as well?" Julia withdrew a handkerchief from her sleeve and waved it about dramatically. "Life is not easy when one is a widow with a small child."

"I'm glad you mentioned Harry," Daisy said, ashamed that she'd provoked the confrontation with her aunt. Even though Harrison Farthingale had been dead for over a year, poor Julia was still mourning him. But she was still Harry's mother and he desperately needed her attention. "I'm terribly concerned about him."

"Don't bring up that nonsense about the boy missing his father," Julia said with a flash of pain in her eyes that cut straight to Daisy's heart. "He's a baby. He hardly knew Harrison and can't possibly understand that his father is gone."

"But he does," Daisy said, trying to remain calm despite her mounting frustration. Why wouldn't her family listen to her?

"He's my son and I say he's fine! However, I am not. I've suffered a terrible loss and have you ever shown concern for me? Have you ever wondered who will take care of me now that my husband is dead?"

Daisy once more gripped the table's edge, finding it safer than wrapping her hands around Julia's throat. No, that was cruel. All the elders were still reeling over the loss of Harrison Farthingale, most of all Julia. However, Julia also had her faults. She was a beautiful woman who thought of herself first, last, and always. Unfortunately, her little boy suffered for it. "You know that you have a home here for as long as you wish. Papa has told you so, many times."

"Be that as it may, I'm a grown woman and not a charity case. I need to be in my own home, taking care of my own husband. Giving him children."

Daisy struggled to remain calm. "You already have a child."

Julia frowned. "And I'm young, healthy, and able to have more."

In truth, she had been a good wife to Harrison Farthingale, he being the sort of person suited to her temperament. Daisy's uncle had enjoyed doting on his wife as much as Julia enjoyed being doted upon. Now, she had no man to pamper her. To Julia, that was a serious problem requiring immediate remedy. Having mourned husband number one for the requisite respectable length of time—and she truly had mourned him, Daisy had to admit—she was ready to move on to securing husband number two. "I wasn't about to waste my time with you and Lumley Hornby when Lord Malinor was so... so eager to gain my attention."

"Lord Malinor?" And thank you so much for thinking me a waste of time.

"He's quite important in the Ministry of Finance."

Lots of shillings jingling in his pockets, Daisy imagined. "You might have warned me. I wouldn't have followed that muggins out of the ballroom."

"Stop calling poor Lumley that," her mother chided. "He's a very accomplished young man. And stop blaming Julia for your mistakes. I suppose you'll also blame her for your jaunt with Lord Gabriel Dayne."

Daisy pursed her lips.

"Oh, yes. I know you spent a shocking amount of time in his company. Don't try to deny it."

"I wouldn't call our time together shocking," Daisy said with an exasperated shake of her head. Except, of course, during the carriage ride.

Oh, worth a lifetime of punishment for that ride!

And that kiss.

Was it possible for a man to kiss a woman like that and not be in love with her? Or did Gabriel kiss all his women, outside of his family, of course, that way? Had she misinterpreted the significance of the moment? Had there even been "a moment" between them? All questions to jot down and ask her older sisters as soon as the opportunity presented itself.

She studied her mother's expression, then Julia's. No, she couldn't ask them. She'd sooner read Lady Forsythia's ridiculous book. Reforming a rakehell, indeed!

"I expected better of you, Daisy. I worked so hard to mold you into a proper young lady. Is this how you repay me? By traipsing about with that inconsiderate dissolute?"

She wasn't sorry. No, not one bit.

"Don't give me that impertinent look. You and Lord Dayne were seen dancing together! Your very first dance at a ball! Oh, why did it have to be with him?"

"Because he was the first man to ask me? What is so shocking about that?"

Her mother sank back in her chair. "Julia, please tell me where I went wrong with this child. What did I do to turn her out so badly?"

"I'm not the village idiot, Mother. Nor am I some wanton female... er..." Well, she had been a tad out of control when responding to Gabriel's kiss, but that didn't count. Did it? "I won't deny that I made some mistakes last night. Minor errors, and no irreparable harm was done. As for Lord Dayne, he graciously helped me with a problem."

"You should have come to me with your problems."

"Yes, of course, and I will in future. However, since I couldn't find either you or Father in the crush at Lord Hornby's, I had no choice but to rely on a friend."

Her mother clasped a hand to her heart in a gesture Daisy considered both cheap and theatrical. She and Julia must have practiced their histrionics together. "You are never to consider that man a friend! He is never to be trusted!"

"Very well, I'll be politely cool to him from now on. However, I would like it noted that he was a gentleman at the ball."

"Don't make light of his behavior," her mother warned, shaking her head so sternly that her fashionable chignon threatened to come undone. "He is no gentleman. Never has been and never will be. His poor parents. They must be suffering greatly."

Daisy frowned. She'd heard the gossip about Gabriel many times before, but meeting him in person... well, he just didn't seem to be the coward, the dissolute everyone said he was.

"Now he's taken up with that lightskirt. That... that Cyprian!"

"What are you talking about?" Daisy asked with a shake of her head.

"His new mistress," Julia intoned, her green eyes aglow as she related the gossip. "It was quite the *on dit*, all anyone spoke of last night. Weren't you paying any attention to the whispers?"

No, she'd been too busy searching for her necklace.

"Daisy, dear," her mother said more gently. "There's something I must tell you about Lord Dayne. He's a scoundrel of the lowest order. Julia, didn't I tell you that a man with scars as prominent as his just had to be depraved?"

Julia's golden curls bobbed prettily as she nodded. "Indeed, you did."

"He wasted no time in resuming his life of debauchery, setting up that woman on... well, it's time you learned that such places exist... Curzon Street."

Daisy's heart sank into her stomach, though she couldn't imagine why she should care. "His mistress?"

"I hear she's beautiful in an indecent way," her mother continued with a blush. "Why else would he set her up so finely?"

"Are you certain?" She'd actually believed Gabriel had enjoyed their kiss. Well, she was a foolish, naive girl.

Her mother shook her head impatiently. "Many men keep mistresses, even happily married men indulge. I'm not surprised that Lord Dayne did so, but he showed a shocking lack of respect by taking up with her so openly, and a foreign girl at that, when perfectly suitable English girls are available."

Daisy choked back a mirthless laugh. "I see."

"I doubt you do, Daisy. You're too young to understand the sordid depths to which some men descend."

Oh, but she did understand. She'd kissed Gabriel with utter abandon, with womanly passion and longing, and may have allowed more had the journey lasted longer. Gabriel didn't love her—she knew that—nor did she love him. But he had wanted to make love to her in a very real sense that extended beyond the proper bounds of courtship. An important distinction. Love led to marriage. Making love led to scandal and ruination.

"Tell her all of it," Julia urged. "She's better off knowing the worst."

"There's more?"

"Lord Dayne has informed his parents that he will never marry. Having made his fortune in who knows what sordid ventures, he is determined to enjoy life to the fullest, *sans* wife. Such behavior cannot be tolerated in any man of noble bloodlines. But what is his family to do? He's independently wealthy and doesn't care if his father cuts him off without a shilling."

"Surely, he'll change his mind in time." Daisy wasn't certain why she should rise to his defense, but this gossip about Gabriel felt wrong. "Marriage is not a prison to all men. Indeed, his own cousin is very happily married to Laurel."

Odd, he and Graelem seemed very close. She wasn't imagining it. Graelem did like and admire Gabriel despite his horrid reputation. Why?

"Lord Dayne has renewed his friendship with that reprobate Ian Markham, Duke of Edgeware, and everyone knows his views on marriage."

Julia shook her head and *tsked*. "A shocking waste of wealth, respectability, and good title, if you ask me."

What had happened to Gabriel? What had led him to shed his boyhood dreams and pursue a life of depravity?

"Ask Eloise, if you don't believe me," Julia insisted. "She's distraught over the whole affair."

Daisy managed a nod, though her entire body felt numb. "Poor Eloise. She never mentioned a word about his mistress. Of course, she must be deeply ashamed of his behavior."

"I suppose she wouldn't have mentioned it to you, dear," her mother said, her manner once more gentle and her gaze pitying. "You're an innocent. And it's not as if you needed the warning. He isn't likely to take serious notice of you."

"I suppose not." Although Eloise had other plans, but that had been earlier in the evening, before the gossip about him and his new mistress had spread throughout the ballroom. Surely Eloise had thrown up her hands in disgust and given up on making a match between her and Gabriel by now.

"You're lovely, darling," her mother continued, her pity intensifying. "But you're not the worldly sort. No, not his sort at all. Though I do wonder why he asked you to dance."

"Eloise must have begged him for the favor," she responded, the numbness now firmly lodged in her heart.

"I suspected as much. He danced two waltzes with Lady Olivia Westhaven. Now, she's more his type. A merry widow, that one. Just twenty-two and already outlived two husbands."

"They did make a striking couple," Julia mused. "And if he were ever to change his mind about marriage, she's just the sort he'd want as his wife. She wouldn't care if he carried on with every woman in London. That would leave her free to take on her own lovers."

"Excuse me, Mother. Julia. I think I'm going to be ill."

DAISY SPENT THE next hour alone in her bedroom, pretending her pillow was Gabriel Dayne's head and ripping it apart. She resolved to write herself little notes that read "Warning—do not ever use the word 'yes' when in the presence of Lord Gabriel Dayne."

"Oh, this can't be good," Dillie remarked, stepping in and quickly closing the door behind her. "Mother will have a fit when she sees what you've done to this room."

Daisy followed her sister's gaze to the little white feathers littering the floor and her peach satin bedcovers. Several more feathers had floated onto the fruitwood bureau and a few were caught in the lace curtains. She glanced into the mirror and brushed off the ones trapped in her hair. "Why is life so complicated?" she cried, collapsing onto her bed.

"Ugh! You're becoming as theatrical as Julia."

"Oh, Dillie! I've had a terrible day and it couldn't possibly get worse."

"Would you care to wager on it? Mother sent me up here to retrieve the necklace. You know, the one you almost lost last night."

Daisy poked her head toward the door to make certain it was closed. "Hush! Only you and Lily know about that."

"And so will Mother when you don't come up with it. She wants Julia to wear it tonight to Lord Malinor's dinner party."

"Why wouldn't I... oh, duck feathers!" She slapped a hand to her forehead. "Lord Dayne still has it. Dillie, what am I to do?"

Her sister shrugged. "I don't know, but you have less than four hours to track him down and get it back."

Daisy rose from the bed and scampered to the bureau. "There's plenty of time to set matters right. I'll have Pruitt send someone around to his townhouse. Just give me a moment to write a note."

"Pruitt doesn't have a man to spare."

She paused in the middle of pulling open the drawer where she kept her writing materials. "Surely, someone must be available."

Dillie shook her head sadly. "No one on the staff is free. I've already asked, discreetly, of course. Mother has everyone running about madly preparing for the arrival of more relatives."

"Just what we need, more Farthingales." Daisy let out a sigh and began to nibble her lower lip as she considered her alternatives. "We can't ask any of the adults. They wouldn't understand about my losing the necklace in the first place. And the children are too young. That leaves me, but I can't go alone. It wouldn't look right, and what if someone saw me?"

Dillie wiggled her eyebrows. "It would cause quite the sensation."

"Oh, Dillie. Too bad you can't go to him."

"Me? Visit that rakehell?" She laughed. "Not unless he promises to kiss me as thoroughly as he kissed you."

"Dillie!" Honestly, her sister wasn't helping matters at all.

"Sorry, couldn't resist teasing you. Don't worry, he isn't my type. Not that I have any notion of the type of man I could love. One thing is certain, rakehells aren't for me. I want the solid, decent sort who'll love me as much as he loves himself. Hopefully, more so."

Daisy grimaced. "So do I. Unfortunately, I haven't come across any such creatures yet. The men I met last night were all boors. Except Lord Dayne, and he turned out to be the worst of the lot. Shows you what I know."

Dillie cast her a sympathetic smile. "I can't go alone, much as I would like to put paid to the problem. I'm far too young and innocent to be trusted on my own."

"We could go together. You, me, and Lily. There's safety in numbers. We might get away with it."

"How will we get there? The family carriages are all in use."

"Drat! Perhaps Eloise—"

"She isn't at home," her sister said with a shake of her head, quickly dispatching that idea. "I saw her leave about half an hour ago."

"That's right. She mentioned something last night about visiting family. We'll have to take a hired hack and hope we don't get caught. Oh, if only we had a male chaperone."

Dillie snapped her fingers as another idea suddenly came to mind, decidedly wicked if the gleam in her eyes was any indication. "I know where we can find two males and they're just perfect. Harry and Charles will act as our chaperones."

Daisy couldn't help but laugh. "They're just boys, in fact little more than babies."

"They'll have to do and they'll make the perfect cover. If asked, we'll say we're taking them to play in the park."

"But we'll really be taking them to Lord Dayne's townhouse. I never realized my sister had such a devious mind." She enveloped Dillie in an enormous and heartfelt hug. "Dillie, I'm quite proud of you."

CHAPTER 8

*A lady must never visit a rake unless
gentlemen of her family are present to defend
her honor.*

GABRIEL HAD NEVER seen his butler look so perplexed. "Is there a problem, Hobson?"

"You have company, my lord. A delegation has arrived on urgent business."

Gabriel set down the disturbing letter he'd just received from General Wolcott and pushed away from his desk. "I'm not home to visitors today. I thought my instructions were quite clear."

"Indeed, they were. But the matter seemed extremely important."

He rose from his chair, his brow knitted with concern. "A delegation you say? From General Wolcott?"

"No, my lord," Hobson said with an almost imperceptible grin.

"Then from the Duke of Wellington himself?"

"Hardly."

Hobson never grinned. Ever. Now Gabriel's curiosity was piqued. "Must I guess or will you enlighten me?"

"Miss Daisy Farthingale is here with two male members of her family among others. They wish to speak to you on an urgent matter, of a delicate nature. The gentlemen were quite adamant."

"Hellfire," he grumbled under his breath, his collar suddenly feeling uncomfortably tight. Daisy must have told them about the kiss—that unbelievable, incredible kiss that should never have happened, but of course did happen—and they were here to settle the score. "Are they carrying weapons?"

"I don't believe so, my lord. Though one gentleman is carrying a sack of marbles."

He paused with one hand on the doorknob and turned a quizzical eye toward his butler. "What sort of man carries a—? Good Lord! How old are these gentlemen?"

Now Hobson's lips were twisted in a full grin.

Gabriel moaned. "Don't tell me you've left the little Farthingales alone! They'll cut a swath of destruction through this house the like of which you've never seen!"

He raced out of his study and into the visitor's parlor. The place was sure to be in ruins. His home, his cherished sanctuary, was under siege by that miniature Mongol horde!

Well, perhaps not.

He stopped abruptly at the doorway and surveyed the scene. Daisy sat calmly on the claw-foot sofa, holding Harry on her lap while reading aloud from the day's newspaper. Another young boy, who appeared no older than four or five years of age, sat beside her intently listening to her every word, and two girls who looked so much alike it would be impossible to tell them apart occupied the chairs across from Daisy.

He couldn't blame the boys for being enthralled with Daisy. She had an angel's voice, sweet and melodic. And an angel's body hidden beneath her simple gown of soft gray velvet. And an angel's mouth. Lord, what a beautiful mouth!

No wonder he'd kissed her last night. And kissed her again. And again.

"Good afternoon, Miss Farthingale. To what do I owe the honor?"

He expected a smile, perhaps a delicate blush in response, but was surprised to find her tense and frowning. She rose abruptly, sweeping Harry into her arms as she lifted to her feet. "We're sorry to have disturbed you, my lord. We won't keep you long."

My lord? The sudden formality surprised him, especially since she'd been delightfully *informal* last night. "Not at all. I welcome the distraction. The document I happened to be reviewing was particularly dry." He turned to Hobson. "That reminds me. Bring refreshments for my guests. You must be thirsty after your ride."

"Oh, that won't be necessary," Daisy said, seeming eager to depart. "It wasn't all that long a ride. In any event, we can't stay."

"Surely you can spare a moment."

The boys nodded.

"Good. That settles it." Though he hadn't expected Daisy's visit, he was glad that she had come. Somehow, being around her allowed him to forget the uglier side of life, the ugly reality of war and broken truces. He needed to put General Wolcott's letter out of his mind for this short while. Nothing he could do about it at the moment.

He turned to the two girls who had settled opposite Daisy. They were seated in a pair of mahogany chairs gifted to him by the Prince Regent in honor of his war service, though rumor was spread that he'd won them in a game of cards. Obviously, the girls were her younger sisters, Lily and Daffodil. Though he'd never met them, they were the right age and bore a striking resemblance to Daisy, similar dark hair and deep, blue eyes.

They'd require a few more years to blossom into Daisy's impressive beauty, he decided, regarding them with the same curiosity as they regarded him.

"You must be Daffodil," he said to the twin with the mischievous twinkle in her eye. "A pleasure to meet you."

She let out a little gasp. "How did you know? Even our mother mixes us up. Please call me Dillie. All my friends do."

"Very well, Dillie." He chuckled and turned to her mirror image. "And you must be Lily. I hear you're quite the avid reader. Please feel free to peruse the books in my library. Borrow any you wish."

Her eyes, not quite as vivid a blue as Daisy's, lit up. "Thank you. May I see them now?"

Daisy let out a soft gasp from behind him. "Lily!"

"Oh, Daisy. Please let me go. Lord Dayne did offer."

"Indeed, I did. The library is just across the hall. First door on the left." Lily was off before he'd finished his sentence. He felt a persistent tug at his jacket and glanced down.

"I'm Charles," said the little boy who had earlier been seated beside Daisy. He held Gabriel's pocket in a death grip.

"A pleasure to meet you, Charles. My name is Gabriel." He knelt down, pried the boy's hand off the pocket, and gave him a gentle, but fervent, handshake.

"I like marbles." Charles rattled the bag he had clutched in his other hand. "Daisy got me the best one. It has seven colors."

He turned to Daisy and grinned. "Yes, she is a wonder."

She blushed and stared at her toes, obviously made uncomfortable by his direct gaze, but he was in no hurry to look away. She was the prettiest thing ever to adorn this room. Indeed, ever to adorn his townhouse, and he was not about to let the moment pass without drinking in his fill.

"Daisy always gets us the best things. She got Lizbeth a doll and Lizbeth said it was her favorite."

Gabriel caught Daisy glancing at him and cast her a gentle smile. "As I said, she's utterly perfect."

Charles nodded earnestly. "Want to play with me?"

He continued to watch Daisy, surprised by how pretty she looked in the simple gown. Her hair was done up quite simply, as well. She looked as delicate as a porcelain doll, but not at all happy. "I'd love to, Charles."

"We mustn't impose on your time," Daisy insisted, the blush now spreading to the tips of her ears. "You're a very busy man, and we only stopped by to retrieve the necklace. I meant to ask you for it last night while we rode home in your grandmother's carriage, but..." Her cheeks flamed crimson. "I became distracted."

"Ah, yes. It was rather an interesting carriage ride." *Hell in a handbasket!* They'd practically blown the roof off the carriage with the explosive force of that kiss. "I'll have Hobson bring down the necklace at once. In the meantime, join us in a game of marbles." He settled Charles beside him on the Aubusson carpet, motioned for Dillie to join them, and was pleased when she eagerly did so.

Even young Harry cooperated by trying to squirm out of Daisy's arms until she had no choice but to set him down. She knelt beside him, holding the infant loosely by his chubby waist. Now, Daisy had no choice but to join in the game.

"Haven't played in years," Gabriel said, perusing the youthful faces and their wide, innocent eyes. "I used to be quite good, you know."

"I'll bet you're still good at a lot of things," Dillie remarked not so innocently.

He coughed and glanced at Daisy, who returned his glance with a pained one of her own, revealing she had told the twins about their kiss. Obviously she hadn't told her parents, or else her father would have been at his doorstep with something significantly more threatening than a sack of marbles.

"Set them on the carpet, Charles," he said, finally turning his attention to the boy. But his thoughts remained on Daisy. She had looked terribly serious and he was curious to learn why, for the answer was not immediately apparent.

Though Gabriel had proposed the game in order to prevent Daisy from retrieving the necklace and rushing off, he understood that it meant entertaining the rest of her family. However, he quickly decided they were quite tolerable. In fact, as the hour wore on, he found them a pleasant surprise. Their laughter and genuine sense of delight reminded him of his own boyhood, of idyllic summers and utter contentment.

He hadn't felt this lighthearted in a long time, he suddenly realized. In fact, he'd forgotten how enjoyable life could be, how precious and sweet. Until last night and Daisy's kiss.

"Is something wrong, Lord Dayne? You're suddenly frowning."

"No, Dillie. Just thinking of the business I'm neglecting."

Daisy shot to her feet. "Then we mustn't take up more of your valuable time."

He let out an exaggerated sigh which the boys thought very funny, took her hand, and urged her down beside him. "Nonsense. We haven't finished the game."

"But—"

"Are you trying to beg off because you're losing? Coward."

Surprised by his light goading, she laughed. Finally, she shook her head and reluctantly settled back on the carpet. "I'm an abominable marbles player, just ask Charles. He manages to beat me every time. He, on the other hand, plays brilliantly."

The boys and Dillie were all sprawled on their stomachs, busily studying the positions of their marbles and how to best knock each other out of the game. He noted the gentle manner in which Daisy handled the boys, her genuine friendship with Dillie, and he decided he heartily approved.

She was easy to be with, to talk to, and to tease.

"It is clear to me," Gabriel said, taking aim at the largest of Daisy's marbles, "that you lack the instincts of a killer. It is an admirable trait in a young lady, but quite the liability on the playing field. You had the opportunity to knock me into oblivion earlier but passed it up. Now, you shall pay for the mistake."

She took his teasing with humor and grace, and only pretended to mind when he shot her marble to the opposite side of the room, causing her to lose the game. Then an amazing thing happened. Her sister gave her a little hug and said, "You'll win next time. I just know it."

Charles kissed her cheek. "You tried your best. I'm proud of you."

Harry, who had never left her side, crawled onto her lap and used her breasts as handholds while reaching up to kiss her on the cheek. Clever, clever boy. "*Wuff* you, Daisy." Which Gabriel understood to mean *love you, Daisy.*

"Your turn," Charles said, staring at him in expectation.

"We always console the loser," Dillie explained with a wicked grin. "It's a family rule. Good sportsmanship and all that."

"Excellent rule." Though he couldn't use Harry's handholds trick, much as he would have liked to. Instead, he lifted the boy off Daisy's lap, then helped her to her feet, taking her pale hands into his large, calloused ones. She began to protest, but her resistance seemed weak. Still holding her lovely hands in his, he slowly, tenderly leaned forward to touch his lips to her cheek. The afternoon, which had seemed quite unpromising at the start, now held great—

"Gabriel! What are you doing in front of these children?"

At least, it had been promising until his grandmother, sounding quite liverish and wearing a ridiculously large purple feather in her hair to match the purple silk of her gown, intruded. He might have found the ornament stylish, indeed quite fashionable, if she hadn't just put him in foul humor. "Hello, Grandmama. Your timing is impeccable. What brings you here?"

He felt another jolt of disappointment as Daisy skittered out of his grasp, her fingers sliding from his with haste. Though he couldn't be certain, she did seem as disappointed to let go as he was in letting her go.

"More to the point, what are the young Farthingales doing here?"

"Playing marbles," Charles replied with youthful innocence. "Daisy lost, so we had to be good sports about it."

Gabriel stifled a chuckle. "So you see, I had no choice. I was ordered to console her."

Eloise eyed him shrewdly. "If memory serves me correctly, you're better at giving orders than obeying them. In fact, you're positively dreadful at obeying them."

"Yes, but not in this instance. I couldn't disappoint the children. What are you doing here? I don't recall inviting you."

"I was at Dayne Hall, which is where you should have been an hour ago."

"Hellfire," he mumbled softly so the children wouldn't hear, but their eyes popped wide and their ears perked so he knew that despite his best intentions, they had heard. He'd forgotten all about the command performance for his parents.

"I volunteered to search for their derelict son. That means you, unless your father has taken steps to disown you, in which case you'll soon be referred to as the—"

"You mean he hasn't yet?" He sighed, already regretting the end of the surprisingly pleasurable afternoon. "Never mind. I'll be along shortly."

"I'll wait," Eloise intoned before he had the chance to suggest she run along ahead.

"We were just leaving," Daisy assured, her cheeks once again an intense shade of crimson. Then she let out an adorably breathy groan that made Gabriel wish the rest of his guests would conveniently disappear so he could coax more breathy groans from her perfect lips. "I'll fetch Lily."

Eloise tossed him a withering look. "Lily's here too?"

"Yes," Dillie answered before anyone had the chance. "I'll collect her. She's in the library, no doubt looking for books on her latest passion—baboons."

Dillie grabbed the boys and hurried out, leaving Gabriel alone with Daisy and his frowning grandmother. "Well, this is cozy," Gabriel murmured as the three stared at each other in awkward silence.

The dark red blush in Daisy's cheeks spread across her face and neck. "Eloise, please don't tell Mother you found me here. She wouldn't understand, not after the warning about *him*. And I'll be lectured again about consorting with *him*. And I didn't even want to come here. I only meant to retrieve the Farthingale heirloom necklace that he'd tucked into his pocket for safekeeping last night after I'd lost it. But one thing led to another. As you know, your grandson can be very persuasive and I, unfortunately, seem to be very easily persuaded by him."

Gabriel regarded her thoughtfully. "You were warned about me?"

"Yes, about your wicked ways," she said in anguish. "I tried to keep my distance, but you made us all feel so welcome, and I... we enjoyed your company so much, especially the boys did. So did my sisters."

"I enjoyed this afternoon, too. It was a rare moment of fun for me. The first since my recovery."

She raised her beautiful, round eyes to him, betraying disbelief. Of course, he realized in that moment, she must have heard all about the disreputable business he'd set in motion over the past few days. Her mother must have warned her about his distaste for marriage, and *damn*, about his newly acquired mistress. Had the news crushed Daisy, this lovely innocent who believed in all things good? Was it possible she believed there was still some good in him?

No, to allow her to think so was dangerous.

He'd spent too many years developing his repugnant reputation, for the good of England, of course. He wasn't about to allow the girl to undermine all his hard work. Despite appearances, the war against Napoleon wasn't over. Though exiled on Elba, the little Corsican had just escaped. All hell was about to break loose.

Gabriel knew that the Prince Regent would turn to him first for help. He'd operated behind enemy lines for years and knew the terrain better than anyone else. He'd quietly be ordered back to

France within a matter of days, before everyone learned of Napoleon's escape, and before Parliament voted one way or the other on a renewed war effort. That vote could take weeks. Every hour lost when dealing with the French menace on the Continent was dangerous. The little general had to be stopped before he caused more trouble.

Gabriel knew he'd be receiving his orders soon. He alone couldn't stop Napoleon's progress, but he could track him and relay sensitive military information back to the Duke of Wellington.

He glanced at Daisy, wishing he could reveal just how much her unexpected visit had meant to him, how profoundly her good humor, her laughter and affection toward the children, had moved him. She would make too much of it, perhaps hold out hope for something more between them.

Of course, it wasn't possible. Now, more than ever, he had to maintain his wastrel reputation. He couldn't change his wicked ways. Marriage was out of the question, for he would not leave behind a grieving widow or fatherless child. Not if he could help it.

Not while Napoleon remained a threat.

He spared Daisy another glance, hoping to catch her eye, but she was once again looking everywhere but at him. He'd taken advantage of her last night and wasn't feeling very proud of himself right now. She'd been so willing and irresistible, and he'd indulged at the expense of caution.

There was also the thorny matter of hearts. While hers was fragile, his had long since turned to stone. Yet this afternoon, for a few precious hours, he had felt its joyous beat, felt alive for the first time in years.

"I'll see what's taking the children so long," Eloise said, making her way to the door. "In the meantime, Gabriel, I expect you to do what's right. You owe Daisy an apology."

"For the little consolation kiss on the cheek he was about to give me when you walked in?" Daisy asked.

"No, for the scorching kiss you thought I didn't see last night," she said, firing her cannonballs before blithely walking away.

Daisy, looking quite pained, stood with her mouth agape.

"Seems we were caught," Gabriel said, lifting a finger to her chin and gently nudging her mouth closed.

"You don't owe me an apology. I enjoyed last night. That kiss should not have happened, of course. But it was harmless enough, wasn't it? I mean, it didn't signify anything, certainly not to you."

Though it had to her, Gabriel suddenly realized with concern. Lord, what had he been thinking?

"However," she continued, "others may make more out of the incident. I suggest we never mention it or think of it again."

"Ah, pretend it never happened?"

Daisy nodded emphatically. "Yes."

"Very well. Consider it forgotten." He knew it was for the best. She was a good girl, not the sort to be trifled with, and he was duty bound to be bad.

CHAPTER 9

*Propriety and modesty, not the rake's
desires, will determine how much bosom a lady
will display.*

GABRIEL HAD LONG ago realized that the Dayne family produced good fighters and terrible diplomats, which explained why he and his father constantly argued. If forced to do one thing, the Dayne male instinctively rebelled and did the opposite. All men in his family were that bullheaded by nature, except Alexander, who was kind and perfect, and Gabriel loved him because Alexander, though easy-going and pleasant, was no toady. He stood up for himself and had always, *always*, looked after his younger brother Gabriel.

They'd shared the strongest of brotherly bonds, a bond Gabriel had been forced to break in order to maintain his cover as a boozing, brawling disrepute.

However, he'd promised his mother to be on best behavior today and not ruin her quiet tea party. He regretted the concession the moment he entered her fashionable salon and found it crowded with eligible young ladies and their parents. "How are you, Mother?"

He dutifully leaned forward to buss her offered cheek. His heart tugged as he noticed the threads of gray among her blonde curls and small worry lines at the corners of her green eyes. However, she returned his smile with a warm one of her own and her eyes brightened a little as he fell out of character for a moment and hugged her. "Dear boy, I despaired of seeing you here today," she whispered rather shakily in his ear.

He drew back and gave a little shrug. "I promised I'd put in an appearance."

Her smile faltered. "So you did, but you've broken so many promises lately... I wasn't sure. Never mind. You're here now and that's all that matters. Your father will be pleased to see you."

Gabriel doubted it, for he'd done a thorough job of disappointing him as well. "Who are all these people? I thought this was to be a quiet family gathering. You and Father promised not to goad me further on the matter of marriage. Yet, you seem to have invited every eligible young lady in London. Bloody hell, even the Fribble sisters." Those females could talk the hind leg off a donkey and he was not about to be that donkey.

"Gabriel! Mind your language." She shook her head and sighed. "It was your father's idea to invite them all. Go bother him."

He didn't have far to search, for his father had seen him entering and was fast making his way through the crowd toward him. "About time you showed up," he said, his face set in a glower. "You had your mother worried."

"Good afternoon, Father. I see you've been busy concocting your matchmaking schemes, no doubt in consultation with Grandmama," he said, referring to Eloise. "Quite an assortment of sweet temptations you've gathered here, but it won't work. I'm not in the least interested." He glanced at Lord Fribble's two daughters to emphasize his point. The Fribble estate bordered Trent Hall, and the families had been friends for years. Gabriel had known the girls since they were irritating children and had always done his best to avoid them.

Hortense cast him a gap-toothed smile when she caught him looking in her direction. Gwendolyn just giggled. He stifled a groan as they approached, the pair still giggling in a high-pitched titter that assaulted his eardrums. "Afternoon, Miss Fribble. Miss Gwendolyn."

Lord, save me.

"We've just had a lovely chat with your cousin, Lord Graelem," Gwendolyn mentioned, batting her eyelashes at him through dull, watery eyes. "A delightfully long chat."

"Have you?" Better his poor cousin than himself.

"Indeed." She tittered again. He tried his best not to wince. "We persuaded him to reveal the secret to his marmalade."

"His is always so thick and robust," Hortense added.

"A potent swallow," Gwendolyn agreed.

Gabriel cleared his throat. "I hear he's growing a magnificent cucumber as well, but no one is allowed to touch it but his wife."

His father's glower deepened. "Gabriel! The *ladies* were speaking of marmalade. Ladies, you were saying that he revealed his secret."

Hortense shook her head in dismay. "Yes, but it is all so confusing, first selecting just the right oranges and there was mention of orange rind. I can't keep it all in my head. He promised to write down the recipe for us."

"Then I'm certain he will," Gabriel intoned, "for he's a man of his word."

"Unlike you," his father muttered for his ears alone.

"Where's my cousin now?" Gabriel's gaze scanned across the elegant room filled with ornate silver, antique porcelain, and overly dressed young ladies. Daisy, in her simplicity, would outshine these stuffed partridges. "Ah, there he is. Forgive me, ladies. Duty calls, but I'll return shortly."

"You had better," his father grumbled.

But he wouldn't. To do so would only heighten hostilities and he wasn't about to humiliate his mother in front of her friends. Though he had to remain in character as the black-sheep son, merely feigning animosity toward his father would adequately serve the purpose. There was no need to cause more of a scene by pretending to be drunk and insulting their friends.

He crossed the room to join Graelem by the window, determined to remain in moderate seclusion for the remainder of the afternoon. In any event, he needed to speak to him about General Wolcott's letter. Though they couldn't discuss the contents at length for fear of being overheard, they could arrange a suitable time and place to meet with the select few men who would be assigned to this impending mission.

Graelem shot him a grin as he approached. "I thought you weren't going to show, you devil. Your mother trapped me into joining her and the ghastly Fribble sisters. Gad! Never met more boring creatures in my life."

Gabriel followed his gaze and gave a mock shudder. "Almost got trapped myself. They give new meaning to the word 'empty-headed.' But enough about them. I have more important concerns right now. Can you meet me and Ian at the club tonight?"

His cousin took a step back to stare at him, then burst into laughter. "No! Keep me out of your *concerns*. Is that what you and Ian call your nightly adventures in debauchery? Laurel will have my hide if I'm caught with you two reprobates in tawdry evening amusements."

Gabriel tamped down his irritation. Obviously, his cousin had mistaken the reason for his request. The purpose was business, not pleasure. Still, his cousin's desire to stay close to home surprised him. Few married men were that attached to their wives. "It didn't take Laurel very long to put you on a short leash."

Graelem arched an eyebrow. "You can stop the pretense. No one's paying attention to us now. We're quite alone in this corner."

"What pretense?"

"Of the dissolute bachelor. That short leash comment. Wait, you're serious?" He scowled at Gabriel with the full force of his dark eyes. "What's wrong with you? Did you purposely come here to insult me?"

"Of course not." Gabriel let out a sigh. "Sorry, I'm not at my best just now. I know you're happy in your marriage."

"And that irks you?"

Gabriel held up his hands as though in surrender, for his cousin still appeared put out. "Your capitulation is none of my business."

"Capitulation?" His cousin eased his scowl and slowly shook his head. "Is that what you see when you look at me? A man with the headache of an independent wife."

"Laurel is headstrong, you must admit." Why were they even having this conversation when matters of far more importance needed to be discussed?

"And I wouldn't have her any other way. She has fire, spirit, and intelligence." He glanced at the Fribble sisters. "No woman with boiled potatoes for brains will do for me."

"Nor for me, but Laurel comes with a very large and boisterous family."

"Ah, you refer to the Farthingale horde." Graelem shook his head and laughed. "Yes, those relatives can infest one's home like pests in the woodwork, but they're not so bad once you're used to them."

"And you are?" Gabriel asked, surprised by his cousin's new-found domesticity. Things certainly had changed while he'd been away. Friends and family had moved on with their lives, little realizing Napoleon was still a threat. His spy organization remained active, not only on the Continent but in England, and Gabriel had been working to destroy it. He'd been shot for his efforts. In truth, he'd been shot several times in the past three years—mostly minor injuries, but the last time had been serious.

He was still alive because of Ian's efforts and would be eternally grateful to him for it. Ian had rescued him from the French abbey where he'd been hiding, slowly bleeding to death from his injuries. Half the French army had been scouring the countryside for him at the time, for he'd gotten hold of sensitive French military maps. Fortunately, those soldiers hadn't quite known whom they were looking for.

If not for that, and Ian's timely rescue, he would never have seen his family again.

He'd missed so much in all that time away, including Graelem's wedding.

"Yes, in fact I'm quite used to the Farthingales. I particularly like Laurel's sisters," Graelem said, reclaiming his attention.

Gabriel nodded. "I've met Daisy and the twins."

His cousin laughed. "Yes, you seemed quite attentive to Daisy during Lord Hornby's ball. And Grandmama told me just how attentive you were in the carriage."

Gabriel shifted uncomfortably. "Must the entire world know that I kissed the girl? I assure you, it won't happen again."

His cousin arched an eyebrow. "Why not? She's charming."

"It was a mistake." Had his entire family been enlisted in Eloise's matchmaking schemes? Even Graelem? "I'm not interested in her."

"Are you certain? Because I'm sure I tripped over your tongue a time or two at Lord Hornby's ball. It seemed to roll out of your mouth onto the ground every time you caught sight of Daisy."

Gabriel crossed his arms over his chest and glowered at his cousin. "Thank you. You're ever so helpful. Any other inane comments?"

"Seriously, Gabriel. Don't you wish to settle down now that the war is over?"

Gabriel relented, accepting a cup of tea and slice of cake offered by a passing servant. "That's just the problem," he said in a whisper when they were once more alone in their corner of the parlor. "It isn't over. In fact, we may be in greater danger than ever from Napoleon. That's why Ian and I need to speak to you as soon as possible. I'll soon be ordered to return to France."

Graelem noticeably tensed. "Damn. What has happened?"

"Can't tell you here," he said, glancing around and noting the curious stares he was now receiving in return.

"Oh, hell. Your father's approaching. He doesn't look at all happy." He gave Gabriel a slap on the back, as though to bolster his courage. Not that Gabriel needed it, for he was used to his father's ire. This was the worst part of the necessary pretense, sending his father into fits of apoplexy. Shaming the honorable Dayne name.

His father stopped in front of him so that they were standing almost nose to nose. Of course, he was slightly taller and broader in the shoulders than his father. Still, the man was an imposing presence. "How dare you abandon the Fribble sisters."

Gabriel shrugged, forcing all warmth from his voice and trying very hard to keep his heart from aching. But the anguish in his father's eyes, in the eyes of the man he loved most dearly, cut like a knife straight through him. "I didn't see the point in returning since I have no intention of marrying either of them, or any of your sweet young guests, for that matter."

His father shook his head slowly, sadly. "What's happened to you? I used to be as proud of you as I was of Alexander."

"By the way, how is the dashing war hero?" Lord, he'd missed Alex's bright smile and the good times they'd shared as boys. But to reveal the truth, to give his family hope of his redemption was impossible. The deception had to be perfect or Napoleon's spies would know he was a fraud.

He'd spent years acting the immoral dissolute to earn their trust, handing over bits of information about English troop movements that were purposely given under Wellington's orders and with approval of the Prince Regent. If not for that hard-won trust, he would never have been able to travel to France and gain access to Napoleon's inner circle. "I haven't seen my brother in years."

"You will soon. He's returning to London with his betrothed to formally announce their engagement."

Gabriel shook his head. "His what?"

"Surely, you remember Lord Broadhurst's daughter, Jillian."

"Ah, his childhood sweetheart. Good old Alex. He always was the steady sort. Loyal, trustworthy, a perfect candidate for marriage." He was happy for Alex, but truly saddened that he'd missed those years with him as well. He was now a stranger to his family and they were strangers to him.

"I don't understand you," his father said, letting out a ragged sigh, "or your desire to shed all obligation and do whatever you bloody well please. I've kept silent and allowed you to lead your life of debauchery, believing you'd soon tire of it and that would be the end of the family crisis."

Gabriel arched an eyebrow as though bored. "But I haven't."

"I'll let you in on a little secret—remaining free to do as one pleases isn't really pleasing at all. It's a hollow existence, but you'll see that as soon as you meet the right girl. There will come a time for you to marry and assume your respectable place in society."

He let out a mock shudder. "I certainly hope not."

"Bah! I don't know why I bother with you." His father spoke not so much out of anger, but out of pain. *Hell.* Gabriel much preferred the anger.

"Wait, Father!" He placed a hand on the older man's arm to stop him as he was about to turn away. "Tell Alex that I'm happy for him. Send him my best wishes."

"Tell him yourself. He'll be here by the end of the month." He turned abruptly and left.

"And you'll be back in France by then," Graelem muttered, "scouting behind enemy lines. Lord, this is a mess."

More than his cousin realized. Gabriel watched his usually proud father retreat toward his mother, his shoulders slumped in disappointment. He ached to tell him the truth, but couldn't.

Forcing himself out of his own anguish, he turned the conversation to more pleasant topics. "I didn't mean to insult you or Laurel earlier. Please accept my apologies."

Graelem nodded. "No harm done. You have a lot resting on your shoulders."

"So will you quite soon." He grinned at his cousin, forcing himself to forget about Napoleon for the moment. "How is she faring? When is the baby due?"

Graelem's expression suddenly softened. "Any day now. Laurel's perfect and I'm an utter wreck. I suppose that's because I'm about to become a father. Strange things happen to a man when he realizes he has created new life. He looks at the whole world differently, gains new respect for the woman he's chosen as his partner in life."

Gabriel's thoughts unwillingly drifted to Daisy, but he tried to shake them off. A partner in life? Living with Daisy would be chaos. Oh, and those relatives. So many of them. And what if he and Daisy were to have children? The little heathens would run rampant over his tranquility, and she... well, creating those little heathens would be quite pleasant, especially with her. She'd shown exquisite innocence and passion in their first kiss.

In truth, bedding Daisy would be something quite spectacular.

"I need a drink," Gabriel said, suddenly finding the room quite warm. "Something stronger than this wretched tea."

"Let's raid your father's library. I spotted an excellent brandy in there earlier."

"Perfect."

"I'm obligated to attend Lord Malinor's dinner party tonight," Graelem said upon entering the library and shutting the door behind them for privacy, "but I can stop by the club afterward. Laurel won't mind since she's the one constantly pushing me out of the house to attend these affairs without her."

"Damn, I forgot all about Malinor's party. I'll be there, too."

"We can talk then," Graelem suggested.

Gabriel shook his head. "Perhaps, briefly. Too dangerous to discuss plans in any detail. Besides, we'll need Ian and the others."

"What can you tell me now?" Graelem crossed to the decanters standing on a small table beside the bookshelves.

Gabriel sighed. "The Corsican Wolf is loose and on the prowl, eager to stir up trouble on the Continent. Apparently, he escaped Elba a few days ago with a handful of men. He'll soon have a rag-tag force of a few hundred loyal soldiers."

Graelem paused as he was about to pour their drinks and shrugged. "We can stop a few hundred men."

"Indeed, but can we stop a hundred thousand? That's how many will take up arms at Napoleon's behest unless we stop him now. The French will flock to his side, they still adore him. He'll pick up more support every day."

Graelem shook his head as he handed Gabriel his brandy. "But a hundred thousand men?"

Gabriel nodded. "He'll have a formidable army by the time he reaches Paris. Once Paris is conquered—"

"*If* it's conquered," Graelem interjected.

"It will be, and then Napoleon will look outward to start new offensives beyond his borders. We have to stop him before he regains his full strength."

Graelem poured his own brandy and returned to Gabriel's side. "Do you really think Napoleon can pull it off? Defeat his own French king? I don't see how."

"I've seen him, Graelem." He absently swirled his glass so that the amber liquid spun against the crystal, gleaming as it caught the firelight. "I know the nature of the beast, witnessed the power he has over the French masses. Wolcott is right to be concerned, particularly if this early report he's received is accurate."

He drained his glass and began to pace, though neither the drink nor his pacing relieved the knot of dread now twisting in his stomach. "Wolcott never believed the peace negotiated with Napoleon would hold and he was right. Wellington was of the same opinion. Prinny's concerned. He fears Parliament will demand more proof before embarking upon another French campaign."

Graelem stepped in front of him and put a hand on his shoulder. "That's why you'll be ordered back to France, to give Prinny time to sway Parliament and provide the proof of Napoleon's designs. I have a better idea. Let me go in your place."

"Are you mad? You have a wife and child to think about. I have no one." The memory of Harry Farthingale, that sad little boy desperately missing his father, flashed vividly before his eyes. He silently vowed never to allow the same fate to befall Graelem's child.

"But I can fight," Graelem insisted.

"Which you may do at length with your wife, but not with the French. However, I'll need your help to organize my supplies, quietly secure my passage across the Channel."

"Damn it, Gabriel—"

"No, I'll listen to no more argument. Besides, I hear Grandmama calling us." He placed a hand to his ear and leaned toward the closed door. "Yes, she'd like us to join her and the delightful Fribble sisters."

"Bloody hell, not them," his cousin said with a laughing groan, but he clamped a hand on Gabriel's shoulder to stop him as he was about to walk out. "This discussion isn't over."

"Yes, it is. I'll see you at Lord Malinor's tonight."

DAISY WAS DETERMINED to make her family proud, but first she had to find a quiet spot in Lord Malinor's bustling townhouse in order to fix her gown. Julia, in her eagerness to descend from the carriage and reach that wealthy widower's side before some other predatory female snatched him up, had stepped on the hem of Daisy's newest gown and soiled it.

Drat! Daisy stared glumly at the exquisite blue satin as it shimmered divinely by candlelight. Could it be salvaged?

"It isn't fair," she grumbled, recalling the first rule in Lady Forsythia's book: *To attract a rake, one must make an elegant first impression.* Her first meeting with Gabriel hadn't gone well at all. Neither had their second. Not that she intended to pursue the scoundrel. She didn't. Certainly not now that she'd read the first few pages of Lady Forsythia's book and realized how dauntingly perfect one had to be in order to conquer a rake's heart.

Eloise had instructed her butler to deliver the book to her shortly before they were all to leave for Lord Malinor's party. It came bound in pink ribbons, no less. Poor Eloise. She wanted Gabriel to marry, but wasn't it painfully obvious that she and Gabriel were not suited?

The twins had taken the book from under her pillow, pleading for something to entertain themselves while left behind at home with the little ones. She hoped they would have fun reading it. No doubt they were giggling over its contents right now.

Daisy's mother came up beside her. "Darling, what's wrong?"

"Nothing." Daisy quickly hid the damage to her gown.

"Then stand straight and don't crush the delicate fabric. Why are you holding the train so awkwardly? You have it in a death grip. You can't walk about like that all night."

"I thought this was to be a simple dinner party."

Her mother gave her shoulder a soothing pat. "It is, dear. I doubt there will be more than a hundred guests in attendance."

"Oh, dear." That meant two hundred prying eyes and one hundred heads shaking in disapproval.

"Come along and meet our host. He's eager to know all of Julia's family. Can you imagine? What a coup for the dear girl!" She paused a moment and eyed her with a sudden, speculative interest. "Lord Malinor's son, Auguste, is unattached. He's a handsome fellow. A good, solid sort. I'll make certain you're introduced to him before the night is over. Your father and I ought to have thought of him sooner. You and he will make an excellent match."

As her mother turned away to greet friends, Daisy hurried off in the opposite direction. She rushed past a jovial crowd gathered in the ornately decorated red and gold salon. Those guests amiably chatting and sipping champagne, ignoring the gentle strains of a harp plucked by a rather large woman hidden behind an abundant green fern.

They ignored her as well as she tried to edge her way to the stairs leading up to the ladies' retiring room, blocking those stairs and making it impossible for anyone to pass. She gave up and glanced down a long hallway that appeared deserted, deciding to sneak into one of the many empty rooms along the hall.

She paused by a closed door and knocked softly. "Is anyone in here?"

No response.

Good. She opened the door and found herself in Lord Malinor's library. The warming fire in the hearth cast a golden glow across the soft leather chairs, mahogany desk, and finely oiled bookshelves. Stepping in, she crossed to one of the red leather chairs angled beside the hearth. And now to fix the problem.

She raised her hem, and was about to brush off the dirty footprint, when a large hand suddenly gripped her shoulder. She let out a yelp and turned to her assailant, gloved fists raised. "Honestly, Gabriel!" She uncurled her fists and set one hand over her heart. "You scared the wits out of me. What are you doing in here?"

"Seeking solitude," he grumbled, his gaze fixed on her ankle, which was exposed to his scrutiny along with the rest of her leg since she'd raised the gown above her knees.

She quickly smoothed the fabric back into place and shot to her feet. "I was here first and I'm trying to be good, so you'll have to leave immediately."

"What I've seen of you is very good," he said with an arch of his eyebrow and a rakish gleam in his eyes.

She tipped her chin up and turned away, determined to ignore him. "I suppose you think yourself very witty, but my predicament is serious. I've been warned to be on best behavior tonight. That means keeping away from rogues such as you."

He tucked a finger under her chin and turned her to face him so that her gaze was back on him. "It seems you've failed."

"Did you purposely follow me in here?" Oh, she'd be in for it if her family found them together, especially after the scathing lecture she'd received on the carriage ride over here.

"You look adorable when you scowl." He cast her a deliciously tender grin that heated her insides more efficiently than any fire ever could. "Your eyes blaze an intense blue and your lips—never mind." He shook his head as though to clear his thoughts. "What I mean to say is that actually, I was here first. I didn't follow you anywhere. You followed me."

She eyed him skeptically. "Why didn't you speak up when I knocked?"

He tweaked her chin and then released her, folding his arms across his chest. "I was hoping you'd go away."

"That's not a very nice thing to say. Well... oh, it doesn't matter. I'll go as soon as I fix my hem."

"Need help?" he asked, bending on one knee beside her.

She gripped his jacket by the shoulders... my, they were massive shoulders... and urged him up. "No, you may not help me," she declared, suddenly feeling quite small beside him. "I'm quite capable of handling this mishap on my own, and I'll be in so much trouble if you're seen in here with me. It'll cause quite the scandal. I'll be ruined and you'll be forced to marry me. Neither of us wants that. So please go away, just for a little while."

"I suppose I should. That's rather a large footprint on your dress."

"I know." She emitted a ragged sigh. "Please go."

He shook his head and *tsked*. "It won't come off with gentle wiping."

"Any more helpful comments?"

"But you might try gathering the train and holding it like this, and..." Suddenly, he drew her away from the chair, pulled her toward him, and wrapped his hands about her hips.

The momentary feel of his hard body against hers, of his arms gently cradling her and the whispered scent of musk against his skin, tantalized her senses and left her so weak-kneed she was barely able to stand.

Would Alexander Dayne's touch be as divine?

Oh, it simply didn't matter. Alexander wouldn't have her now that she'd kissed his brother with utter abandon. Perhaps had it been a chaste, you-remind-me-of-my-maiden-aunt sort of kiss, it would have been all right. But the kiss they'd shared was one of those you'll-be-damned-in-hell-for-eternity kisses that could never be taken back. Or forgotten. *Blessed angels*! She'd really liked that kiss.

And once again, Gabriel's touch was muddling her senses. Why else did she desperately wish to kiss him again? "Stop it, you scoundrel. What are you doing?"

She tried to push away, not from horror, but from shame at her own sense of delight. His hands felt wonderful against her body while he deftly worked to hide the stain by rearranging the drape of her gown.

"Stand still, Daisy. And don't fidget or you'll tear the fabric. There, much better. However, you still need something more. Something daring to distract the eye. Ah, yes. This must go."

He pointed to the lace at her bosom.

She gasped. "You insufferable cabbage head! Are you suggesting I remove my *fichu*?"

He shook his head and laughed. "You'll expose just enough *there* to draw everyone's eye away from your hem and toward the endowments with which the Good Lord has blessed you. And make no mistake, you are amply blessed."

"I hate you," she whispered, wishing he would stop looking at her as though she were a ripe cherry that he'd like to pick. Only he wasn't looking at her in a leering, boorish sort of way, but in an oh-hell-I-think-I'm-losing-my-heart-to-you, endearing manner that turned her legs to pudding. Of course, it couldn't be so. Rakehells were good at pretending.

"No, you don't, Daisy," he said, his voice taking on a sudden seriousness. "You simply hate my wicked ways. Sometimes I hate them too."

Her eyes widened in surprise. "You do?"

He shrugged. "But not enough to change them."

"My family thinks I'm wicked too. Oh, I don't know why I just said that. I suppose I simply want you to understand why I'm so desperate to have you leave."

He leaned closer and whispered against her ear. "But I like wicked girls."

She balled her hands into fists and was about to do damage to his manly chin when his tone suddenly mellowed. "Ah, but you're not really wicked, are you? Everyone just thinks you are because of The Incident. Eloise told me about it, how you were caught in the stable with Lord Kirwood's lack-wit son, Devlin."

She gazed at him in defiance. "So what if I was?"

"I am hardly one to pass judgment," he assured. "However, I don't believe a word of that fable, about the pair of you being caught while trying to elope. It simply doesn't ring true."

"It doesn't?" She took a deep breath. "Why not?"

"Because I'm your first. The only man ever to kiss you," he said with such tenderness that she wanted to throw her arms around his neck and cry on his shoulder. "It's obvious, so don't bother to deny it. You've never been in love, never been swept off your feet, and certainly not by Devlin Kirwood."

The accuracy of his statement and the tinge of arrogance with which he delivered it unsettled her a little. "You're wrong, I have been in love. Um, with your brother, Alexander. I think he's wonderful."

Gabriel's eyes darkened, and his lips twisted into a small grin, indulgent and at the same time mirthless. "Yes, well, everyone loves Alex. He is wonderful, as you say. But the Kirwood incident may pose a problem for you. Alex, being perfect in every way, expects the same in his wife."

She tipped her chin upward again, not quite understanding why she felt the need to defy him. He was the first person to see through Devlin's lies and believe her. "He'll forgive me when I explain it to him."

"Explain what? That you went to the stable hoping to prevent something romantic from happening between you and Kirwood? Staying home, safe in your bed, would have sent Kirwood a more effective message."

Daisy bit her lip. No, she wasn't going to reveal the truth about that night! She and Laurel had sworn each other to secrecy. It wasn't her fault that Devlin Kirwood—that clunch—had tripped and fallen against her at an inopportune time, or that her father had come upon them at just that moment, or that Devlin had lied through his teeth about his plan to elope with *her*, thus giving rise to the false story known from then on as The Incident.

Gabriel's voice gentled as he spoke. "I'm not sure why you were in the stable that night, but I do know that you've unfairly suffered the consequences. It explains why those two fools, Lumley Hornby and Tom Quigley, attempted to kiss you the other night."

"I don't care about those oafs." She gazed into Gabriel's tawny eyes, curious as to what he might be thinking, but she could discern nothing. "What hurts most," she admitted, letting out a long, ragged breath, "is the disappointment I see every day in my parents' eyes. They've lost all faith in me, won't ever trust me again, and I've been feeling quite miserable about it for a long time."

"I know," he said softly.

She gazed up at him and sighed. "You do?"

He nodded. "They'll realize their mistake soon enough. I suppose it isn't much consolation now. However, I know you didn't do anything wrong. Just remember that whenever you're feeling particularly low. I know who you really are, Daisy. Any parent would be proud to call you their daughter."

Her heart welled with joy. Gabriel understood! Why him, of all people?

"Oh, there you go being nice to me again." She gazed at him in confusion, wishing she understood him half as well as he seemed to understand her. "Even after I uttered that silly remark about being in love with your brother. Truth is, I've never even met him."

Gabriel chuckled lightly. "Perhaps you will one day. He's a good man, a loyal brother."

"Is he as nice as you? Not that it matters any more," she said, slumping her shoulders in surrender. "I had this foolish plan to make my family proud of me by marrying the perfect gentleman. You see, I want so desperately to regain their trust, but something goes wrong every time I try. That kiss we shared, for example. Not that I regret it," she hastened to add. "I'm glad you were the first to kiss me, Gabriel. You did a commendable job of it."

He arched an eyebrow and grinned. "Did I?"

She nodded. "It was a wonderful first kiss. I suppose I shouldn't have said that either, what with your ghastly reputation. And I'm certain Lady Forsythia's book advises never to make such an admission to a rake, but I feel safe with you and relieved... no, elated that you recognize The Incident for the nonsense it is. How can you know me better than my own family does?"

"What book?"

She sighed. "Lady Forsythia Haversham's *Rules for Reforming a Rake*. Your grandmother loaned it to me. She's of the misguided opinion that I can change your wicked ways. It's silly, of course." She glanced down at her hem. "I can't even take care of myself."

She expected a flippant response from Gabriel, but he suddenly looked as though his best friend had died. "You're just as you ought to be, Daisy Farthingale, and never let anyone tell you otherwise. You have more to offer than you realize."

"Beyond my ample endowments?" She glanced at her breasts while making the poor attempt at levity.

He followed her gaze, but his smile was more appealing than it was lascivious. Then he stepped back to study her from top to toe, as though he needed to absorb her entire being, needed to remember her the way she looked tonight, the way she smiled and how she moved. "Yes, quite more than we pitiful males deserve."

Moving quickly and with unwavering purpose, he lightly touched his fingers to her cheek. "I've handled this very poorly... indeed, treated you very poorly from the start though you've been wonderful to those dearest to my heart, helped them make it through some very difficult years."

She understood he referred to Eloise.

"Daisy," he said, his voice whisper soft, "I'm eternally in your debt for that."

No wonder women found him irresistible. Even Julia had thought him splendid until Lord Malinor and his shillings had distracted her. Of course, Gabriel's determination never to marry had further dulled Julia's enthusiasm.

If only she were as sensible about men as her aunt.

Her breath quickened and her cheeks began to heat under the force of his stare. She wished she understood more about men, because Gabriel seemed to be looking at her with an intensity beyond mere lust or base desire.

He let out a soft, animal growl.

Of course, rakes earned their reputations by seduction and pretense. They were masters at feigning interest. What she needed to know, and would have to rely on her older sisters for an answer about, was whether men could fake love. "Well, I had better return to Lord Malinor's party before I'm missed. Thank you for fixing my gown. It is fixed, isn't it? What do you think? Am I presentable?"

He responded by sweeping her into his arms and covering her mouth with a hot, most exquisitely uninhibited kiss that set off a fiery tempest in her body, a raging wildfire that scorched a path straight to her heart.

Oh, bad boys were very, very good.

CHAPTER 10

*If a rake confesses his ungovernable
desires, a lady must immediately retreat and
take no further notice of him.*

GABRIEL HAD MEANT only to gently trail his tongue along Daisy's lower lip and taste lightly of her nectar before dipping into her honey-sweet mouth, but instead he found himself breathless and hungry, plunging his heart and soul into kissing Daisy. He experienced a pleasure so hot and unexpected, so purely sinful and at the same time so divine, that it was beyond anything he'd ever felt before.

No woman had ever affected him like this.

Damn. His blood and body were on fire, all from a simple kiss. Daisy's kiss.

"Don't pull away, Gabriel," she pleaded, her breasts gently heaving against his chest as she struggled to regain her composure. Or was it his own heart pounding through his chest? She was an innocent, easily bruised, and he was a brute, hot and lusting, needing to touch her *everywhere* and aching to possess her heart.

To what end? A momentary pleasure, and then he'd be gone to scout out the French military positions. He had no illusions about his mission. Chances were, he'd be dead before the end of the month. He eased his hold on the girl. "I must, Daisy."

One of them had to show some sense. Not for his sake, but for hers. It amazed him, and in truth confused him, that he held this seductive power over the young beauty, yet couldn't bring himself to take advantage. Oh, perhaps he'd taken a little advantage, but nothing compared to what he wanted to do, needed to do in his current state of arousal. His lust and her innocently passionate nature were a dangerous combination. "I've made a mess of you," he said, his fingers trembling as he smoothed her gown and then attempted to right himself. "Not at all what I intended."

She smiled at him, her eyes aglow with hope and confusion. "I think I must be wicked. I should be appalled, horrified, but I'm not a bit sorry we shared another kiss."

He let out a long, weary sigh and ran his hand along her silky curls. "Daisy Farthingale, you complicate my life."

He didn't want her... no, that wasn't quite right. He wanted her, but not in any respectable way, for he didn't dare to think beyond tomorrow. He wanted her body without the responsibility of courtship. He wouldn't act upon it, though. He had yet to sink that low, to destroy her future because he couldn't keep his hands off her.

Her smile deepened the dimples in her cheeks. "I'm glad that I'm a complication for you," she said, her dewy-eyed gaze never wavering.

"Don't be. I'll only end up hurting you."

She pulled away slightly and turned to gaze at the flames leaping in the fireplace. "Is that what you think?"

"I know it for a fact, Daisy. That's what I do. I seduce women and then break their hearts." They had no possible future together. How could they when England was once more about to be thrown into war and he was likely to be in the vanguard?

Even if he wanted to make her promises—which he didn't—but even if he did, he couldn't. There were no guarantees he'd return safely.

No, that wasn't quite right. There wasn't a chance in hell that he'd return in anything other than a wooden box.

DAISY KNEW SHE was as much to blame for ignoring her own resolve to keep her distance from Gabriel. She'd allowed him to kiss her, saying *yes, take me* with her heart and her eyes, practically begging him. Goodness, she'd been quite swept away by this rogue.

Yet she also understood that Gabriel was not completely immune to her charms. She had affected him to some small degree and was glad of it. "Why did you kiss me so desperately just now?" she asked, returning her gaze to his.

He let out a bitter laugh. "Did I?"

"The way you held me, as though you were sinking into a boggy moor and needed me to pull you safely back to solid ground. There's a darkness about you tonight, perhaps it's always been there. Is that dark torment what compels you to follow your dissolute path?" She reached up and gently touched a finger to the red puckered scar at his chin, only to feel him tremble as she lingered there. "How did you get this one?"

"Jealous husband."

She trailed her finger along his neck and down his chest, resting her hand gently against his heart. To her disappointment, it was beating in a slow, steady rhythm. Hers was pounding wildly and with as much discipline as that of a rabbit just escaped from a farmer's shotgun. "What about the one above your eye?"

"Jealous mistress."

She regarded him thoughtfully. "I wonder what the rules say about a rake and his scars."

"That damned book," he muttered. "It probably warns never to stroke your fingers delicately along them, or to look at a rake's scars as though you want to kiss them and make them better. It probably says that you ought to run as fast as you can from a rake before lust gets the better of him and he does something really stupid."

"Such as kiss me? You've already done that." She sighed. "Your visible scars have healed, but they're mere physical wounds and easily repaired. It's your other wounds, the hidden rips and tears to your heart, that are causing you pain. They lie concealed from view, raw and festering beneath your polished surface."

"You don't know what you're talking about," he said, his voice gruff and suddenly filled with disdain.

"Oh, but I do." She'd just felt his heart skip a beat, and every sinew in his body had tensed. That response was tantamount to a volcanic eruption from a man determined to suppress his feelings. She didn't understand why he needed to distance himself from his family, to disdain commitment and marriage for the sake of pursuing a life of empty pleasures.

"How did you get this scar?" she asked again, touching the one that ran along the corner of his eye. "The truth this time."

"Brawling in a seedy alehouse." He took her firmly by the shoulders. She saw that he was struggling to restrain his temper, to keep from shaking her as though she were a dusty mop. Finally, he gave in to exasperation and released her. "Daisy, what's your game?"

"I don't have one. You're the one who's good at playing games. Why do you pretend to be a sot and a coward? Don't bother to deny it. I know it's all a pretense."

"You're wrong." His tawny gaze seemed to bore straight through her.

"Not in this. My father has an expression, rather simple on the surface, but really quite profound. He says that people don't change."

"Which should warn you that I'm an unredeemable cad."

She tipped her head up to meet his gaze. "Quite the opposite. It tells me that you're a wonderful man because you were a wonderful boy, and don't bother to deny it. I visited Eloise every day while you were lying on your deathbed. She always told me stories about you, about how you always cared for the sick and wounded animals on the Trent estate. How you brought joy to your family. As a child, you were known for your kind heart. People don't change," she repeated.

He folded his arms across his chest and cast her an angry frown. "You're mistaken. That little boy died long ago."

"Gabriel," she said in a whisper, "that is an utter and complete lie."

GABRIEL LET OUT a soft string of curses. "Right, that ought to be a warning to you. Telling lies is something rakes do all the time, particularly to women in order to get them into bed."

She shook her head as though confused. "You don't appear all that eager to get me into your bed. In truth, you keep pushing me away. Not that it matters, for we aren't a suitable match. However, there is something going on that troubles you deeply. You seemed preoccupied earlier today when playing marbles with Harry and Charles."

She paused, as though debating whether or not to confide in him. She nibbled her lip and then decided to continue, a sign that she trusted him. He ought to have been pleased, but her faith in him only put him in greater torment. He didn't want to be thinking of her while he was in France. He didn't want to think of the life they might have shared together if only Napoleon hadn't escaped.

"Afterward, when I and the children returned home," she said, "I overheard my father and Uncle George speaking of a rumor. I think it was about Napoleon. My uncle is a brilliant physician and many of his patients are of the Upper Crust. I couldn't hear most of what he said, only that nothing's been confirmed yet." She paused again and raised her beautiful eyes to stare at him. "Are we to be at war again?"

He tried to shrug it off. "I pay little attention to such matters."

Her lips curled in a mirthless smile. "You'll be joining Wellington's forces, won't you?"

He put his hands on her shoulders. "No. I'll be running as fast as I can in the opposite direction."

"You needn't lie to me. I'll keep your secret." She held up a hand to interrupt his protest. "We're kindred spirits, you and I. You understand my shame and frustration because you're experiencing these same feelings. My situation is inadvertent, caught in the wrong place with a petty, mean-spirited gentleman I disliked. But you purposely want your family to think the worst of you. Why?"

"You're wrong." The damn girl was slight and slender, her head barely reaching his shoulders, yet she'd managed to shake him with such force his heart had shot into his throat. Perhaps that's why it took him a moment to regain his voice. "Daisy, war is not a game. It isn't something soldiers gossip about over tea, or at *ton* dinner parties. Bad things happen on a battlefield, men die. Horribly and unfairly."

"You speak as though you've been there. I knew it." She reached out once more to place her hand over his heart.

"I haven't. I don't know a damn thing about Napoleon, nor do I wish to." He nudged her hand away, cursing at his slip. He had to destroy all trace of good feeling or respect Daisy might ever have felt for him. "I decided long ago never to be one of those pitiful men who risk all for king and country. The only *war* games I play are games of seduction. The only *battles* I fight are battles of the sexes. Stop looking at me with starlight in your eyes. Unlike yours, my sordid reputation is well-deserved."

Daisy tilted her delicate chin upward and frowned at him. "Thank you for the warning, though it isn't necessary. I know what you are, Gabriel."

"Good, then I suggest you leave now. I'm suddenly feeling quite wicked and fully intend to steal more than a few kisses. You don't want to be the scandalous topic of next month's dinner conversation, do you? I doubt your family will recover from a second disappointment."

She gazed at him in confusion and suddenly scampered away to put a little distance between them. "You wouldn't—"

"Your first mistake." He took a step toward her.

She took a hop back. "I don't care what others say about you. You're a gentleman—"

"Your second mistake." He took another step closer.

Her eyes rounded in surprise. "I don't believe you."

He crossed his arms over his chest. "Your third mistake."

"Why are you suddenly so angry with me?"

He frowned. "Get out of here, Daisy."

She cast him a wounded look. "Gladly." She hurried out of Lord Malinor's library, shutting the door behind her with a quick slam.

Once alone, Gabriel pounded his fist into the padded leather back of a nearby chair. Daisy was a torment to him, believing him wonderful and special and all those nice things everyone else had long ago stopped believing him to be.

He was glad they'd shared those kisses, for they were as special as Daisy. But giving in to temptation came at a steep cost. He couldn't confirm his involvement in Napoleon's war. He didn't want

118 | MEARA PLATT

her believing he was a man of honor, didn't want her falling in love with him.

Nor did he wish to fall in love with her.

All he had to do was avoid her until he left for France... if only his heart would let him.

"What did you do to startle your little dove?" Ian asked, ducking into the library just as Gabriel's fist struck the seat back again with a soft thud.

"She thinks I'm a damn hero. I had to convince her otherwise."

Ian quirked his head. "No wonder she ran past me as though demons were chasing her delightful tail."

"Shut up, Your Grace."

Ian dropped into the chair Gabriel had just been pounding. "Desiree tells me you've visited her only the once since setting up your cozy love nest."

"That is also none of your business."

"And even that visit consisted only of talk."

"That is definitely none of your business. Where's my cousin? He's supposed to join us."

"By now, I expect Graelem's busy keeping the wolves away from his delectable sister-in-law. Daisy does look exceptionally fetching tonight. Malinor, that old buzzard, can't seem to take his eyes off the girl. Auguste, the younger Malinor, has noticed her as well."

"Enough, Ian. Forget about her. She isn't important."

Ian sighed. "No, I suppose she isn't. We'll conquer a city's worth of virgins after we conquer the French army. How does that sound to you?"

"Jolly good sport."

"Now you're sounding utterly morose. Gabriel, I have to know your mind is on the mission and not on the Farthingale chit."

Gabriel settled in the chair across from his friend. "Consider her forgotten."

Ian shook his head and let out a mirthless laugh. "Right. Forgotten. Any more news from Wolcott?"

"Yes, none of it good."

When Graelem quietly slipped into the library moments later, Gabriel relayed the latest instructions. "Napoleon is making faster progress than anyone thought possible. I have to sail to France without delay. Graelem, that gives you about two days to gather the supplies I'll need and arrange my passage across the Channel."

His cousin scowled. "It's too bloody dangerous for you to undertake this mission alone. We could go together. I don't see why you're always taking on the dirty jobs."

"You're needed here. So is Ian, especially now that Napoleon's spies have infiltrated the highest echelons of English society. You need to be attending the London balls and parties, keeping your eye on anyone who seems to be acting suspiciously." Gabriel eased forward in his chair and motioned for the pair to come closer. "Napoleon's spies must believe that Prinny's chosen John Randall and Edward Gaffney for this secret assignment. While they watch John and Edward," he said, glancing at Graelem, "Ian and I will contrive some ruse to explain my sudden absence. Wolcott's preparing those fake orders concerning John and Edward as we speak. I'm to hand over this supposedly secret information to those spies at Lord Hastings' ball tomorrow night. If they believe I'm on Napoleon's side, they'll stop watching me closely."

"I have a hunting lodge not far from the Scottish border," Ian said. "A few dropped hints and everyone will believe we two bachelors—desperate to escape feminine shackles—intend to ride off shortly on a hunting excursion."

Graelem ran a hand across the back of his neck. "It might work if news of that hunting trip spreads before Napoleon's escape is made public."

"I'll take care of the problem this evening," Ian said. "All I need to do is mention our plans to Lady Phoebe Withnall and she'll spread the word throughout the elegant salons of London within a matter of minutes."

Graelem grunted. "Incorrigible gossips serve a useful purpose, I suppose."

Ian nodded and then turned to Gabriel. "The day before your scheduled sailing, you and I will ride off together on the north road toward Scotland. Once we're certain no one is following us, we'll break away at the first opportunity and ride eastward toward the sea."

"Eastward to your doom," Graelem muttered, frowning at Gabriel. "There must be a better way to slow Napoleon's progress than to send you back into that deathtrap. What can you do on your own against Napoleon's army?"

"I don't know, but Wellington needs time and that's what I intend to give him. My job will be done once the English army is properly supplied and transported to the Continent."

Ian appeared equally displeased. "I'll join you as soon as Prinny permits me. He'll grant me that permission as soon as the House of Lords votes to approve a new campaign against Napoleon. I'll speak to Prinny tomorrow, just to be certain I'll have his permission before you set sail."

"Count me in," Graelem added.

Gabriel scowled at him. "I don't need you. At least Ian speaks French, and Edward and John know all about munitions. They'll go about London supposedly gathering their supplies and weapons, doing what they must to put the French off my scent for as long as possible. Even if you were useful to have along," he said, pausing briefly to emphasize his next words, "I'll not turn Laurel into a grieving widow. Nor will I allow your child to grow up without his father."

This was the pact they had made at the start of the war—no attachments, no wives or sweethearts left behind to grieve, no children to shed tears over the loss of a father. Now that Graelem had married and Laurel was with child, sending him off on this dangerous mission was out of the question.

"Right, that's settled." Ian slapped his hands against his thighs. "If I do say so myself, I like this idea of a hunt. It also gives us the excuse to be seen with John and Edward should the need arise. Everyone knows they're avid sportsmen. In fact, we can meet them tonight at White's, share a few drinks, let word spread of our bachelor outing, then return to my townhouse for more detailed planning."

Gabriel nodded. He'd also have to put his affairs in order before he left. "Graelem, I—"

"I know," his cousin said with a grumble, rubbing his hand roughly across the nape of his neck. "You can count on me to manage your estates while you're away. Write a note to your parents. I'll hold on to it and turn it over to them if the need arises. It had better not. I'll expect you to get your sorry arse safely back home as soon as possible."

Gabriel nodded. "I'll do my best." He rose to signal the end of the conversation. "Well, time to return to my wastrel ways."

Graelem rose with him and gave him a hearty pat on the back. "Be careful. One slip and the wretched mission fails."

Just as he'd slipped with Daisy? How much did the girl really know? Probably nothing. Still, he had to be careful around her. He'd spent much of the war years being thought of as a coward, a drunk, and a cheat by friends and family. He needed Daisy to believe it as well.

He closed his eyes, hoping to expunge her from his mind.

He couldn't.

Gabriel took another moment to compose himself before slipping back to the party. When he did, Lord Malinor instantly cornered him, shoving a glass of champagne into his hand. "Been looking all over for you, Dayne. Where the devil did you run off to?"

"Talking to my cousin in your library," he replied, stepping back to avoid his host's breath, which reeked of stale spirits. With his red, bulbous nose, the man reminded Gabriel of a modern-day Bacchus, or what he imagined Bacchus might have looked like when debauched and in his cups. "Hope you don't mind. He's about to become a father, you know."

Lord Malinor burst into a chuckle, and then winked at him. "I hear your cousin's wife has been giving him the devil of a time. Did he want advice on how to handle her? Beautiful gels, those Farthingales, but high spirited. They require a delicate touch."

Gabriel assumed a bored manner, though the little hairs at the back of his neck were standing on end. What did Malinor want with the Farthingale girls? "Don't all women?"

"But Lady Laurel's got a temper. Don't know that any man can handle her. Now, the young one over there's a tempting morsel, an attractive bit of goods. My son's taken a fancy to her." He pointed to Daisy. "Gad, what a body on the gel!"

Gabriel's fingers tightened around the glass he held in his hand.

"Yes, she has an interesting look about her, but she's a little slip of a thing. Easily overlooked in the crowd."

"Oh, one would have to be as dead as mutton to overlook that vision," Lord Malinor said, licking his lips as he stared at her. She stood a short distance away, beside her mother and surrounded by several admirers, including Malinor's son, Auguste. "What I wouldn't give to have that young flesh tingle beneath my fingers."

Gabriel excused himself before he gave in to the urge to lift the worthless man by his lapels and shake him till his wig fell off and yellow teeth popped out. "Pardon me, Lord Malinor. I believe my grandmother is summoning me."

Lord Malinor held him back as he started to move away. "About the gel, any interest in her?"

"I'm not in the habit of discussing such matters."

"Don't bite my head off, Dayne. It's not as if you intend to marry her. You've made no secret of your loathing for the institution, but she's a beauty and if you don't want her there are others who will. Just making sure you haven't changed your mind, but I see by your scowl that you haven't. Leaves the field clear for the other poor sods. Lucky for them you're not interested. They'd be hard pressed to compete."

Lord Malinor left him to join his son and the circle of men now formed around Daisy. Auguste Malinor, more formally known as Viscount de Veres, had inherited his mother's good looks and his father's scheming nature—a bad combination, to Gabriel's way of thinking. When the elder Lord Malinor passed on, Auguste would inherit the vast Brayfell holdings and assume the title his father now held, Earl of Brayfell.

He watched Daisy chat and smile and thoroughly charm Auguste and the throng of popinjays dancing attendance around her. She'll be married before the year is out, he realized, suddenly feeling a tremendous sense of loss. Perhaps she'd marry before he returned from France.

He stared at her, marveling at the stark contrast between them. She was carefree and unburdened, eager to rush headlong into the future. He had no future, or none that he dared to think about.

CHAPTER 11

*A lady must never insert herself in the
business or political affairs of a rake.*

"WAIT FOR ME, Lily. I'm coming with you," Daisy called the
following afternoon, rushing downstairs to catch up with her sister
as she prepared to walk out the door. The day was overcast,
uncommonly cold, and Lily was already bundled in a fetching forest
green pelisse to match the green of her merino wool gown. "Just give
me a moment to find my gloves."

Lily sighed. "Very well, but hurry up. I don't wish to be late."

Daisy hastily donned the dark blue wrap that matched her gown,
grabbed her reticule and the gloves she'd forgotten she'd tucked
inside the reticule, and then turned to her sister only to meet her
skeptical glance.

Lily stood by the doorway, her arms folded over her chest, and
she was tapping her foot with marked impatience. "You do realize
I'm on my way to a lecture at the Royal Society."

Daisy nodded. "I understand Lord Allenby is to speak on Sir
Isaac Newton's *Philosophiae naturalis principia mathematica*. I find the
topic fascinating and can't wait to learn all about it."

Lily tossed her head back and laughed. "What rot! You wouldn't
even read Lady Forsythia's silly book, but Dillie and I finished it last
night while you were at the Malinor ball. It's actually quite
fascinating. The rakehell's character very much resembles that of a
dominant male baboon."

Daisy rolled her eyes and laughed. "You're jesting."

"Not at all. It will make for interesting research. However, Newton is far more interesting to me at the moment. Apparently, to you as well. Why the sudden fascination in principles of mathematics?"

"I've had a lifelong passion for the subject," she said with a merry gleam in her eye, "but never the time to pursue it."

"Hmm, to pursue it or Lord Gabriel Dayne? Shall I feign surprise when we run into him at the lecture hall?"

Daisy's gleam faded. "I doubt we'll see him, Lily. Even if rakehells were about town at this time of day, I doubt they'd spend much time at the Royal Society. However, he spoke so highly of Lord Allenby and the topic of his lecture that it piqued my curiosity."

"When did he have the chance to speak to you? Last night?"

Daisy blushed as she tried to avoid Lily's assessing gaze. "Yes, several times. He helped me fix my gown after Aunt Julia accidentally stepped on it. After that, he tried his best to avoid me, but I heard him and Graelem talking about the lecture, so I asked them about it. That was shortly before Gabriel joined Lord Malinor at the card tables."

Lily rolled her eyes. "And not a half hour later drunkenly accused Malinor's son, Auguste, of cheating?"

Daisy's eyes widened in surprise. "Where did you hear that?"

"From Aunt Julia. I can pry all sorts of information out of her at will, so don't try to deny it happened."

"Wouldn't think of it," Daisy said with a resigned sigh. "I don't understand him, Lily. Perhaps you can help. It's as though there are two sides to him, one intelligent and charming, and the other slovenly and deceitful. I know the terrible effect too much drink can have on a man, but I just can't believe he was that deeply in his cups. There must be a logical explanation for his behavior."

"And you're determined to discover it." Lily took her hand and squeezed it gently. "I like him, too. So does Dillie. And since we're such clever young ladies, we can't all be fooled by our instincts. If he were truly bad, we'd sense it."

"Precisely. So what do you think is the cause of his bad behavior?" Although Lily was younger by almost two years, Daisy often turned to her with difficult problems. Lily was the smartest person in England, as far as she and her sisters were concerned, and they greatly admired the nimble workings of her brain, although most of the family and certainly everyone outside the family seemed put off by her.

Lily shrugged. "I'd have to spend a little more time in his company to figure it out. I'll do it for your sake, and who knows? I might also gather insight from his behavior that I can apply to my baboon research."

"Ugh! Lily, kindly stop thinking about your baboons."

She shrugged again. "I can't. They fascinate me, just as Gabriel fascinates you. Will you allow him to kiss you again?"

"Hush," Daisy said with a laughing groan. "Don't remind me of my mistakes. I don't know why I allowed those kisses to happen."

Lily pursed her lips in thought. "You told me that he made you feel safe."

"Ridiculous, isn't it? Especially since those kisses signified nothing to him." But they'd affected her and she couldn't get them or Gabriel out of her thoughts.

Lily nodded. "If we think of him not as a man but a dominant—"

"Honestly, Lily!"

"Well, it's true. You know even less about men than I do, Daisy. At least I've read Sir William Maitland's early findings on male baboons, and when aroused, they'll kiss anything female that moves. *Anything*. The little I know about rakehells indicates they aren't so very different."

Daisy simply shook her head and laughed. "I love you, Lily. But you've become quite the cynic."

Lily shot her a grin that reached into her big, blue eyes. "I prefer to think of myself as quite sophisticated."

Daisy laughed again. "Mother and Father will be so proud. Come on, we don't want to be late."

They entered the Royal Society's oak-paneled lecture hall and found seats just as Lord Allenby struck the gavel to summon the meeting to order. The *thuck* made by the gavel as it struck wood carried over the din and resounded through the hall.

Daisy glanced around, noting the place was packed mostly with older gentlemen.

"Fossils," Lily muttered under her breath.

She noticed several young bucks who were far too smartly dressed in silks for the scholarly assemblage, and a smattering of matrons in ghastly bombazine gowns and hats as oversized as their bosoms. Several matrons sported egret feathers atop their hats, and one had an entire bird perched atop her head.

Daisy unfastened the bow to her simple bonnet—a most unfashionable bonnet judging by the disapproving glances cast by these older ladies—set it on her lap, and glanced around once more. She and Lily were the youngest females by about thirty years.

"We'll never spot your Gabriel in this crush," Lily said with a sigh.

"Shh! And he isn't my Gabriel."

"Perhaps not yet," she muttered, "but I have every faith he will be. I see his friend, the Duke of Edgeware, over there."

"Where?" She craned her head to see.

Lily pointed toward the front rows. "There, in the second row."

Daisy frowned. "I wonder what he's doing here."

"Probably took a wrong turn on the way to his favorite den of iniquity."

"At this time of day?" She laughed softly. "I suppose even he must have interests outside of drinking and debauchery. The man is reputed to be very clever."

"By whom?" Lily asked, as though the source were relevant.

"Oh, I don't know, but I've heard general talk among the *ton*."

Lily gave a little snort. "Anyone who can buckle his own shoe is thought of as clever among that vaunted assemblage. And if that buckle happens to be made of pure gold, why, the man will be thought of as brilliant."

"Indeed, you're quite cynical for a youngster," Daisy said with a shake of her head. "And don't you dare claim to be sophisticated."

"I'll leave that title to you. No, I'm just observant."

So am I, Daisy thought, nudging Lily's shoulder. "Look, someone of interest has just entered the hall."

She'd recognize that thick mane of gold hair and muscular shoulders under a jacket of dark blue superfine anywhere. Gabriel.

Her heart skipped a beat... no, many beats.

"Oh, yes. I see him."

Daisy's frown deepened. "But who is that ugly little man with him?"

Lily got up on tiptoes to peer over the row of tall hats. "Where? I don't see anyone."

Daisy scanned the crowd around Gabriel but could no longer spot the odd-looking man. "I'm sure he was just there." She lowered her voice to a whisper, suddenly gripped by an inexplicable sense of uneasiness. "Yes, there he is. He's handing something to Gabriel."

"A lecture schedule? They're handing them out at the door."

"Oh, Lily. Must you always be so logical? The hairs at the nape of my neck are standing on end. I think something untoward is going on. Let's move closer."

Before she'd managed so much as a step, Gabriel turned suddenly and pierced her with his rapier-sharp gaze.

"Oh, no! He's seen us!" she said in an urgent whisper, clutching Lily's hand. "More important, have we just seen something we weren't supposed to?"

Lily frowned. "I haven't seen anything. What are you talking about?"

"I'm not certain myself." Daisy began to nibble her lower lip. She'd never seen a colder, more deadly look in anyone's eyes. Or had she been mistaken?

Lily appeared irritatingly calm. "Do you think he'll come over to greet us?"

"Haven't you been listening to me? I think something nefarious just took place. Or is about to take place. What if Gabriel suspects I know?" If Gabriel did come over, would his greeting include a knife blade between her ribs?

No, she was being utterly ridiculous. They were practically family, for his own cousin was married to Laurel. One didn't kill family, did one?

Unless he was utterly deranged. She'd read about that Yorkshire strangler who'd murdered his wife and assorted relatives, and then calmly disposed of their bodies on a desolate moor. The newspaper account was quite chilling and sensational.

She let out the breath she'd been holding, realizing that she was behaving as theatrically as Julia again. Gabriel wasn't deranged, but he was up to something. She followed his movements as he left his unsavory companion and settled beside the Duke of Edgeware. Daisy watched intently as he and the duke exchanged a few words, and was caught unaware when the duke suddenly turned back and glanced at her.

Did that mean he was involved in Gabriel's shady business? Was there any shady business going on?

Gabriel frowned and said something in return to the duke.

Daisy gripped Lily's hand again. "I think we had better leave."

"Oh, no." She squirmed out of Daisy's grasp. "I've waited six months for this lecture. I don't care what scheme you think Gabriel is plotting."

"But—"

A lady with an enormous hat suddenly took a seat at the end of the row, effectively blocking her escape. "Oh, perfect. We're well and truly stuck here."

"Daisy, you're fluttering like a bird trapped in a cage. This isn't like you at all. I'm certain there's a logical explanation for what you think you saw. Just ask Gabriel when the lecture is over. Let's shift down two spots. At least we'll be able to see Lord Allenby's podium."

"Don't you girls know it isn't polite to stare at a gentleman's podium?" said a teasing voice from behind them. Gabriel. *Cheeseballs!* "Certainly not one as large as Lord Allenby's. Good afternoon, Daisy. Lily. I didn't expect to find you girls here."

"We often come for the lectures," Daisy replied, hoping she sounded quite casual. In truth, her heart was hopping like a mad rabbit. He stood so close she easily breathed in his divine musk scent. The fragrance, as light as a whisper, wreaked havoc on her senses. She didn't know what to think. "I hadn't noticed you were here."

Gabriel arched an eyebrow, now looking quite sinister. "Hadn't you?"

Oh, he was a clever character, pretending to ask a casual question when he really wanted to know exactly how much she'd seen. He settled his hand on the back of her chair and leaned close enough to raise disapproving eyebrows from a pair of matrons to their right. But in true rakehell form, he flashed them a smile that drew blushes and girlish giggles from the ladies.

"Well, perhaps I caught a glimpse of you out of the corner of my eye. But you know how it is amid a crush, one can hardly see beyond one's own nose." She ended with an inane titter that probably roused his suspicions.

He hopped over the empty chair beside her and settled into it. "I noticed you, too. I'm glad you're here."

He sounded warm and sincere, not chillingly sinister. "You are?"

"Very much so," he said, casting her a devastatingly soft smile that reached his tawny eyes. "By the way, you look charming."

"Thank you." She muffled her surprise and tried not to look quite so confused. There were so many questions racing in her mind, so many pieces of the Gabriel puzzle that would not fit together. And now he was seated beside her, looking alert and sober. How could he be so well put together after the spectacle he'd made of himself at Lord Malinor's party?

She cast him several furtive glances. Shouldn't he look muzzy headed and disheveled? Shouldn't he still reek of spirits? How long did the stench of whiskey, or brandy, or whatever gentlemen drank, remain in one's system?

She cast him another furtive glance. His eyes were clear and gorgeous.

Lord Allenby banged the gavel one last time, signaling the commencement of the lecture. The last of the members took their seats and all chatter quickly subsided. The room turned silent except for the embarrassingly loud thump, thump, thumping of her heart — not out of fear, but out of... drat, why did she feel so wonderful whenever Gabriel was close by?

And why did he always look so wonderful?

And wouldn't her senses warn her if he were up to something sinister?

He withdrew a lecture schedule from his breast pocket and casually perused it as Lord Allenby began to speak. Daisy stifled a groan, realizing she'd been an utter dolt. There had been no nefarious exchange, just an odd little man handing a program to Gabriel.

"Welcome, ladies and gentlemen, to the world of Sir Isaac Newton, one of the greatest minds ever to have graced this earth. Today we shall discuss his masterwork the *Principia*..."

"Ah, I promised to help you through Newton's works, didn't I?" Gabriel whispered, leaning close once again and causing her insides to melt in a puddle of delight. That little rabbit previously thumping in her heart was now splashing around joyfully in that puddle.

She ought to be ashamed of herself! He'd melted her resistance without the slightest effort and she had capitulated like a wax candle held over a flame.

Lily leaned across her and cast Gabriel a grin. "You did promise to teach her all about Newton in exchange for one dance," she whispered. "Daisy told me all about it. She's thrilled—"

"Honestly, Lily. *Hush*." Until today, she would have been pleased that he'd remembered the offer made at Lord Hornby's ball. Most men pretended to be forward thinking, but were really unrepentant fossils when it came to educating women. She had expected the same of Gabriel, but he was nothing like those brash young men who preened and strutted and lacked substance. She wasn't sure what he was yet, just that he wasn't like those young men. He was better... the best, or so she had felt in her heart. But could she trust her heart? "Generous of you to offer, but I don't expect you to—"

"To keep my word? In truth, I rarely do."

She turned to gaze at him, hoping to find something beyond his bored expression. "Then why keep it now? Last night you couldn't wait to get away from me."

"Because Newton is special."

"Oh." She wasn't special, Newton was.

"The talk may be a little dry for someone unfamiliar with his publications," he continued in a whisper as though she hadn't seen him with that unsavory man, or that he hadn't seen her seeing him, "but listen carefully and absorb whatever you can. I'll take you and Lily to the bookseller's after this lecture. We'll select suitable reading material for you."

Her eyes widened in surprise. "I don't think we should."

"Thank you," Lily interjected. "We'd like that very much."

"Then it's settled," Gabriel said before she could raise another protest.

Daisy didn't know how she'd ever make it through the lecture with Gabriel seated so close and throwing her senses into a jumble, but Lord Allenby's presentation proved to be most entertaining. After a while, she stopped fretting and sat enthralled through the two-hour program.

She even sighed in disappointment when he called for a brief recess before answering questions. The gentlemen and ladies in the audience slowly came to their feet and began to mill about the room. Several gentlemen left the room to grab a breath of air and perhaps a smoke.

Though Gabriel rose, he remained by her side and cast her another of his devastating smiles. Really! How was she to think straight when he insisted on leaving her breathless?

"Well, Daisy? What do you think of Sir Isaac now?"

"I'm impressed," she admitted. "One discovery would have assured him a place among the greatest men in history, but to have given us so much... his writings on gravitation, his theories on optics, and his development of calculus are astounding."

"Some credit Leibniz with that advancement in mathematics," Lily interjected because she somehow knew everything about everything, which worried their mother to no end, but simply made Daisy proud. Though just sixteen, the girl could hold her own against any man in this room.

"No loyal Englishman would ever acknowledge that foreigner's work," Gabriel replied with a chuckle. "Besides, there's no doubt that Newton derived it independently."

Daisy stifled her frustration and joined in with a smile of her own.

And now Gabriel was smiling back at her in that devastatingly gorgeous way. And his eyes were warm and the most beautiful shade of dark amber.

When Gabriel was good, he was very, very good. But was he good or very, very bad?

"I understand he was a shy man," Daisy said, unable to fend off the urge to ramble, "often needing to be coaxed into publishing his work. I marvel at his humility when compared with the breadth of his knowledge."

"Makes one feel quite insignificant," Gabriel said.

She nodded in agreement. "Indeed, it does."

"I'm personally fascinated by his theories of motion and gravitation," Lily said.

Gabriel glanced at Daisy and grinned. "Ah, yes. The mysterious force that attracts one planetary body to another."

That attracts one heart to another, Daisy thought, finding it easier to comprehend the mysteries of the universe by seeking their parallel on a human level. And the way he had leaned close to her, as though attracted to her planetary body... was it possible he yearned for more, possibly for her heart?

"It's quite romantic, really," Daisy said with a sigh. "Two heavenly bodies traveling in the night, each on its own path until suddenly their paths cross. They're irresistibly drawn to each other, and try as they might, they can't pull away. Though still two bodies, they now move as one, bound to each other for eternity."

"Or until one can escape the other's orbit," Gabriel pointed out.

Daisy rose and frowned at him. Was he warning her to escape his orbit? "Why should one feel the need to escape?"

"One simply does," he said with an annoying quirk of his eyebrow.

"Honestly, Lord Dayne. Moving alone through eternity is a most unappealing proposition."

He arched his eyebrow again. "Is it?"

Really, she found him most vexing. "Yes. Certain bodies are meant to be together."

"You mean like the moon and the earth?"

Like you and me, you dolt! Goodness! Where did that come from? "Earth and moon, yes, that is one example."

He ran a hand roughly through his hair as though unsettled. Good! She wanted him to think about more than an unencumbered life filled with tawdry entertainments. He needed to think about his future... about his happiness... about his future happiness with her. *Oh, crumpety crumpets.* She was doing it again, thinking of him as marriage material when she ought to be thinking of running as far away from him as possible.

"And what if those bodies are not meant to be together?" he asked.

Now Daisy wanted to throttle him for his stubbornness. "If they were truly meant to be apart, their paths would not keep crossing, would they?"

"Um," Lily said, "would you mind explaining what you two are talking about?"

GABRIEL STARED AT Daisy. The little widgeon was right, damn her, even if she had taken the greatest laws of science and pared them to their simplest human terms. Love, much as gravity, attracted one body to another. The male to the female.

Was he attracted to her? Certainly, for he'd ignored his own instincts and the little remaining sense he possessed to settle beside her during the lecture. But love and attraction were quite different matters.

Men such as he did not fall in love.

And after the scene he'd caused at Lord Malinor's last night, Daisy ought to have known better than to fall in love with him.

The adorable scowl on her face revealed that she did know better. She liked him, that much was obvious. But she didn't want to like him, and that was also obvious. She certainly didn't trust him.

So what harm could there be in spending one more day in her company?

Besides, Ian had ordered him to find out exactly what she saw pass between him and General Wolcott's aide, whose disguise had been excellent. Anyone glancing at him would have thought he was the lowest form of life, never suspecting the cur who had passed on vitally important information was an army major. And that small packet of information was now burning a hole in his breast pocket.

He needed to slip away to read it carefully. Part contained the bit of false information he was to hand over to the French agents tonight. The other part held further instructions for him.

Offering to fetch Daisy and Lily refreshments, he left their side. While briefly out of sight behind a large marble column, he withdrew the letters from his pocket and perused them. Then, with his smile fading, he tucked them back into his breast pocket.

As expected, General Wolcott had included a separate letter meant for his and Ian's eyes alone. He'd practically been ordered to keep Daisy and Lily by his side all day. Well, not precisely, but he had to make preparations for his mission while pretending to be a man of leisure and what better way to avert suspicion than to keep the girls by his side?

Ian had already suggested it.

The letter merely reinforced Ian's opinion.

He'd already offered to take the girls to Gresham's bookshop, where he was to pick up forged identity papers. He hoped anyone watching them would think he and the girls were innocently buying books.

Then, he needed to get to Blakney's Confectionery, the pie shop across the street from the bookshop. He'd invite them once they'd finished at the bookshop. He glanced around, sensing Napoleon's spies were all over this lecture hall, already curious about the timing of his hunting trip. He'd noticed several men hovering close by as he'd settled in the seat beside Daisy.

Of course, the girl was beautiful and those men might simply have been trying to gain her notice. Most of them probably were, but among them could have been a French spy sent to watch his movements and report back.

He frowned.

There was another complication. Spending more time in Daisy's company was dangerous to her reputation—one that was already mildly tarnished. She couldn't pass the entire afternoon with him and not have tongues wagging.

"Do it," Ian whispered, coming up beside him. "There are no morals when it comes to winning a war. I know what you're thinking, that being seen too often in the company of a rakehell such as you isn't wise for her, but it helps us. Her little tarnish is what makes her so perfect as your cover. It makes your interest in her believable."

"I don't have to like it."

"Make sure you pick up your travel papers today. Gresham has them ready." He shook his head and sighed. "I know you're worried about Daisy. Graelem and I will fix any damage your attentions toward her have caused."

"You had better," he grumbled.

Ian, never one for coddling his ill humor, indulged him this time. "I will. I promise."

Gabriel nodded. "I'll also do what I can before I leave." A few drunken curses muttered at Lord Hastings' ball tomorrow night about the priggish virgin who had rebuffed his advances would go a long way toward repairing any damage.

He returned to the girls with a glass of ratafia in each hand.

Daisy took hers with a hesitant smile.

Did she suspect something?

The gavel pounded again, signaling commencement of Lord Allenby's question and answer period. "I'll take you to Gresham's Antiquarian Books as soon as the lecture is over," Gabriel said.

"And afterward to Blakney's Confectionery for some strawberry tarts?" Lily added as they resumed their seats.

Bless you!

Gabriel laughed, but he doubted the laughter reached his eyes. "Yes, you impertinent little bluestocking."

The lecture ended promptly at three o'clock. Gabriel introduced the girls to Lord Allenby, then excused himself to bid farewell to Ian and make further arrangements to meet him tonight.

"She's pretty enough to set any man's heart on fire," Ian said, nodding toward Daisy, who was gently laughing at some remark of Lord Allenby's.

Gabriel watched the man puff up with pride as Daisy graced him with a dimple-cheeked smile.

"Not even Allenby is immune to her charm, and he's one of the few happily married men I know. Take this friendly bit of advice—"

Gabriel tensed. "I've heard it before."

"Don't lose your heart to Daisy Farthingale."

He nodded. "Furthest thing from my mind."

"Spend your last days in mindless pleasure with Desiree. She's undemanding, willing to please. Trained to please. That's why you set her up in your love nest, isn't it?"

"I'll visit her tonight," he said, more to convince himself to do it than to assure Ian he would.

"And every night until we leave for our hunt?" he asked, grabbing Gabriel's arm when he tried to turn away.

Gabriel shrugged him off. "What's it to you, anyway? We'll be gone in another day or two."

"It's enough time for you to get up to your eyeballs in trouble with Daisy. You're in danger, my friend. I don't wish to see you break a sacred vow."

"No broken hearts, no grieving widows," Gabriel muttered, repeating the pledge he and his bachelor companions had reaffirmed last night. "I know what I'm doing. Leave me alone, Ian. Tend to your own affairs."

"I'm trying to, but part of my business is to keep you alert and attentive to your mission. Do whatever you wish when you return. Damn it, just don't falter now."

"Right," he said quietly, "when I return." Ian, of all people, had to know that sheep headed for slaughter never returned.

<hr/>

GABRIEL ESCORTED THE girls to Gresham's, a musty bookshop run by an even mustier elderly gentleman of the same name who lived alone above the shop. Every corner of the establishment, including his living quarters, was lined with shelves, each shelf crammed with books of higher learning of every size and shape.

Everyone knew Gresham's establishment was a gentleman's realm existing for the fulfillment of scholarly pursuits. Indeed, Gabriel had never seen a woman in the place in all the years he'd been coming here. Well, Daisy wasn't just any woman.

Gresham would quickly find that out.

"No shilling shockers here," Daisy commented as they entered.

"Indeed," Lily said, her eyes wide and brimming with excitement. "Walking through the shop is like walking through a maze. I've never seen so many books in my life."

Gabriel helped the girls to step over several lofty tomes that were too big to fit on the shelves. Gresham had stacked them wherever space could be found on the floor. The old bookseller liked his clutter and often declared that he found more comfort between the sheets of a book than the sheets of his bed.

That may have been true until today, Gabriel mused with a chuckle.

After a mere half hour with Daisy, the old man appeared ready to toss aside his life's work, polish his dancing slippers, and join the ranks of her admirers.

Yes, Daisy was something quite special, for she was sincerely kind and caring, and genuinely unaware of her allure.

"These two annotations of Newton's work are suitable for a beginner," Gabriel said, placing the reading material in Daisy's gloved hands.

"Thank you," she managed before Gresham reclaimed her attention.

Indeed, after slipping him the forged identity documents, Gresham had followed Daisy about like a lovesick schoolboy, so enthralled by her it seemed as though he'd never seen a young woman before.

"I'll take the annotations, Gresham." Though reluctant to deny the old man the pleasure of Daisy's company, Gabriel knew it was time to end the visit. They had another stop to make.

"They are first editions, my lord."

Which meant the old scoundrel intended to charge him double what they were worth. Apparently, his work for the Crown did not diminish his desire to make a healthy profit. "Very well."

Daisy flashed the bookseller an adorable smile.

"They are for Miss Farthingale?" He wiped his hands, gnarled by age, across his dusty apron.

"Yes," Gabriel said and was graced with an equally adorable smile from Daisy. He drank in her loveliness, treasuring the simple moment. Eventually, she'd grow to detest him when rumors of his drinking and whoring while at the Duke of Edgeware's hunting lodge reached her ears. None of it would be true, of course. But the lies would persist long enough to keep Napoleon's agents off his scent.

"Then you may have them as a gift," Gresham said.

Until today, the man had been as tightfisted a merchant as ever existed, but one smile from Daisy and he was merrily giving his stock away. "Nonsense, put the books on my account and wrap them as quickly as you can."

Daisy pursed her lips. "On your account? I think I ought to pay for them."

"Gresham, I'll string you up by your short hairs if you take so much as a ha'penny from either Miss Farthingale. Is that understood?"

"Yes, my lord." The old man cast him a curious glance, no doubt wondering why either of them was offering to pay for something he'd just offered as a gift.

In truth, Gabriel wasn't certain why Gresham's gesture had irked him, for Daisy wasn't his wife nor was he courting her. She was free to have admirers, even crotchety old men such as the bookseller.

And now Lily was studying him as though he were one of those male baboons she had been going on about earlier. Perhaps there was a slight resemblance, he reluctantly admitted. He suddenly felt quite possessive, and didn't want another man giving Daisy presents.

He ignored Lily's grin and purchased two books on African swamp baboons for the little bluestocking, deciding it was necessary to divert the gossips just a little. Not that there would be much to whisper about, for handing Daisy a gift of Newton's works would hardly be considered in the same light as a gift of jewelry or perfume.

"It's getting late," Lily hinted not so subtly.

"Yes, on to Blakney's." He escorted the girls across the street to the large shop painted strawberry red and smelling of freshly baked pies. The crowd was sparse, and the few ladies and gentlemen present were unfamiliar to him or the girls.

The jovial proprietor, obviously a man who enjoyed sampling his wares, welcomed them in with enthusiasm and cheerfully led them to a decorative wrought iron table surrounded by red and white striped cushioned chairs.

Once they were seated, he scurried into the kitchen and returned rolling out a large cart filled with hot pies.

"Oh, I think I'm in heaven," Daisy said, closing her eyes and inhaling the delightful aroma of apple, cherry, apricot, mince, quince, meringue, and a dozen more scents. "I would have studied harder had I realized learning was this much fun. Of course, if I finished every session with a visit to a pie shop, I would be the size of a horse by now."

And still beautiful, Gabriel imagined. He watched, fascinated by the changing expressions on her face as she perused the enticing display. "They all look so tempting. I don't know which to choose."

He knew what tempted him and it had nothing to do with pies.

"I'll have an apple tart, if I may," Lily said to the proprietor.

"Um, I'll take the meringue," Daisy said.

"And you, my lord? What's your pleasure?"

I'll have Daisy, thank you. No fork necessary, I'll use my tongue.

"May we have a pitcher of lemonade?" Lily added.

Gabriel nodded. "Of course. An excellent idea. I'm feeling a little parched myself."

And sensing prying eyes upon him.

He was now certain they'd been followed ever since leaving the Newton lecture. He hoped neither Daisy nor Lily had noticed. He also hoped no one had noticed Gresham slipping him the forged documents or Blakney slipping the little note under his plate that revealed the time, date, name, and location of the ship upon which he was to sail to France.

He suspected that French agents had been following him for several days now, and it had taken tremendous effort on his part to pretend to be unaware. He'd spent years building up his tawdry reputation, selling them information about England's battle plans — with full knowledge of the Crown, of course — and was about to give them more tonight. He'd been feeding these French agents useless bits of information without problem for years.

The information was always accurate, but given a day too late. Sometimes even an hour too late. Sometimes given timely, but since the English knew the information was in the hands of the French, the generals were able to plan around it.

He eased back in his chair and turned his attention to Daisy, doing his best to convince the French spies that this outing had nothing to do with preparing for his mission and all to do with a rakehell's lust for a beautiful girl.

Daisy closed her eyes and ran her tongue ever so slowly along the dollop of meringue on her fork. Images of Daisy running her tongue ever so slowly along his... no, too exquisitely painful to dare hope!

Had he worried about convincing those spies?

It was all he could do to keep his eyes from bulging out of their sockets... or hiding the hard bulge elsewhere on his body.

CHAPTER 12

A lady must never allow a rake to lead her
down a garden path.

DAISY ENTERED LORD Hastings' residence escorted by the Mongol horde also known as her family. They presently surrounded her and pushed her along on their slow migration up the receiving line, paying more attention to her than usual during their progress. Her mother was going on and on about Auguste Malinor and Daisy was now concerned that everyone would make too much of his attentions toward her. She wasn't about to smile and pretend to be in raptures over a man who didn't make her tingle.

Too bad, for she sincerely wished to adore Auguste.

Unfortunately, Gabriel was the one who made her tingle. All over. Every body part. She glanced around. Had he arrived yet? Careful planning was required to slip away from her family and find him, a few choice words... well, very small lies... to her parents and particularly to her Uncle George. Very little escaped his notice, so she'd have to move quickly the moment he was distracted.

"You seem pensive this evening," Uncle George said, boring into her with his keen gaze. He was a big bear of a man and more clever than anyone she'd ever met, other than Lily. She adored him, usually. Right now, he was an obstacle, for he sensed she was up to something.

"I'm overwhelmed by the magnificence of the Hastings home." She pretended to study her surroundings. The ballroom itself was painted in a cheerful shade of apricot yellow with crisp white trim. Above the trim was a beautifully painted ceiling depicting angels frolicking in an Italian style villa. Four massive crystal chandeliers lined the ceiling, each chandelier ablaze with floral-scented candles. The shimmering light played tricks on the eyes so that the angels appeared to dance among the crystals. "Don't you find it lovely?"

He arched an eyebrow. "Hmm."

She turned to inspect the crush of splendidly dressed lords and ladies filling the large room, her gaze trained on the taller gentlemen in the crowd, hoping one of them was Gabriel. Despite her initial reluctance, she'd had fun with him at the Royal Society lecture, and afterward at the bookshop and confectionery.

"Are you looking for someone in particular?" her uncle asked, not at all fooled by her casual glances.

"Yes, I've lost Mother. She's walked on ahead. I think I had better find her." Again, a very small lie.

Harmless, really.

Still eyeing her warily, her uncle cleared his throat. "I see her standing beside the marble column. I'll take you to her."

She forced a smile. "How kind of you. Don't trouble yourself. I—"

"No trouble at all." He tossed back an equally forced smile.

"Oh."

George took her by the elbow and guided her through the festive throng, his grip light, but still managing to convey his determination to remain close to her all evening. How was she to be rid of him?

Lord Malinor, dressed in extravagant peacock blue silk, approached as though in answer to her prayer. "I need you for a moment, Farthingale."

George frowned—actually, he uttered something not very polite under his breath—but Lord Malinor appeared too busy drinking in her appearance to notice. "Miss Daisy," he said with an eager smile, exposing his yellowing teeth, "you look charming, simply delightful. Indeed, you're the loveliest young lady here tonight. The stars pale—"

She let out an uncomfortable laugh, for the man was obviously in his cups and staring at her too avidly for her liking. "Confess, my lord. How many young ladies have you flattered with precisely those words this evening?"

"I assure you, you are the one and only." He took her hand and tossed her a courtly bow which he managed with only one small stagger.

"And I second my father's opinion,"Auguste Malinor said, his dark eyes alight with merriment as he approached her. "I hope your dance card is not yet filled."

She smiled politely. "It isn't, my lord."

"Good, then I shall put myself down for two," he said, staring at her meaningfully. He claimed the fourth and seventh dances, which was surprising for her dance card was empty and she'd expected him to claim the first.

Still, she was flattered. His request for two dances amounted to a declaration of interest, of possible courtship, and she ought to have been pleased.

She was pleased.

Auguste was tall and handsome, rich and powerful, and possessed of a venerable title and unmistakable air of refinement. He appeared quite the dashing gentleman, the black of his coat a shade darker than the black of his long hair. His eyes were the color of rich, dark earth. A deep, vibrant brown. Indeed, he was handsome and she ought to have been delighted by his attention, but there was a subtle arrogance in his demeanor that... no, she was merely out of sorts this evening. "I'm honored, my lord."

He took her hand and graced her with a courtly bow, and though she caught the scent of spirits on his breath, he was in full control of his body. Unlike his father, he had not a trace of a drunken stagger. "The honor is mine."

Lord Malinor slapped his son on the back. "Well done, lad! He takes after me in some small way, you know. Has the same fine eye for the ladies. For the prettiest ladies," he remarked, once again staring at Daisy. "Fortunately for him, he takes after his mother — may she rest in peace — when it comes to looks. He's a handsome lad and the ladies can't resist him."

Auguste shook his head and cast Daisy a sheepish grin. "Father, pray stop or you'll frighten Miss Farthingale away."

144 | MEARA PLATT

"Nonsense, she isn't easily frightened. Are you, m'dear?" Once again, his gaze bore into her a little too avidly for her liking, but she put it down to his attempt to concentrate.

Daisy ignored him and smiled back at Auguste. "No, my lord."

"Good, that's what I like. A girl with spirit. Come along, son. And you too, George. It pains me to have to leave your side, m'dear. Important business to discuss, affairs of state and all that. Forgive us for abandoning you."

Daisy tried hard to appear disappointed, especially since her uncle was still frowning at her. "Of course."

Lord Malinor hiccupped. "Ah, you are a delight."

"I'll return shortly," her uncle warned, leading her to the marble column where her mother stood chatting with friends—and bless her distracted soul—too intent on the latest *ton* gossip to pay her any notice. "You are not to leave her side."

Daisy waited until her uncle was out of sight—after all, she hadn't promised—then edged toward one of the massive floral displays lining the walls at measured intervals. The pale lilac flowers sewn on her gown of ivory silk blended well among the flowers and her hiding spot provided the perfect vantage point to watch for Gabriel.

"Viscount Sanford's father is in terrible health," Lady Warrick said to her shy daughter as they passed by the floral display, ignorant of Daisy's presence. Lady Warrick pointed to a young man with curly, orange-red hair. Daisy had never seen anyone with hair so bright a shade of orange.

"I'm so sorry," her shy daughter said. "The poor viscount must be distraught."

"Melissa! Don't be silly, child! He'll soon be an earl and needs to take a wife. Come, let's move closer. Now's our chance. He's talking to that old goat, Lord Barrington."

Poor Melissa Warrick! Her mother was as subtle as a battering ram and certain to humiliate her in front of that carrot-haired viscount.Daisy shuddered, knowing her fate would have been little better had she remained by her own mother's side. Except her mother would have been droning on about the "feeling" in her bones that an offer of marriage would come tonight—her mother always had these "feelings" about her daughters and marriage proposals, and she was always wrong.

Thank goodness!

Besides, who would offer for her tonight?

The only eligible young man with whom she'd spent any time was Auguste Malinor, and she couldn't imagine him tossing all caution to the wind and proposing. They'd hardly exchanged two sentences.

Also, there was something about him that struck her as calculating. Or was he merely trained to be careful? Coming from one of the most important families in England, he had much to consider, for the future of the Malinor family rested upon his finding a proper wife to sire his heir.

Then there was Gabriel, but he was no gentleman, although he had been very nice to her at the Newton lecture. She sighed. When he was nice, her body responded to his presence in a most embarrassing way.

Still, he didn't love her.

Nor did she love him.

When I fall in love, it will be wholly and completely. I want all of my husband, not bits and pieces of him. Not riddles and puzzles.

Speaking of riddles and puzzles, Daisy saw Gabriel making his way across the ballroom. He seemed to be heading toward the terrace.

Where was he going?

She was about to slip from her hiding spot and follow him, but Auguste chose that moment to emerge from the room where the important meeting was being held. He appeared to be searching for her. *Drat!* Had he seen her? She had to come up with an explanation for lurking behind the overgrown floral display.

He appeared to be looking straight toward her, although she wasn't sure how he could have noticed her crouched behind the display. Which was why she was momentarily startled when he said, "Ah, there you are, my passion blossom."

He wasn't speaking to her but to another young woman whose back was to her. She couldn't make out who it was, for all the debutantes wore similarly demure, white silk gowns, and their inane titters all sounded the same. "Meet me in the garden," he coaxed the breathless young thing, "by the fountain. Don't be long. I'm so hot for you, my little minx." He then proceeded to tell his *passion blossom-minx* just what he intended to do to her.

Daisy resolved then and there to break a chair over Auguste's head if he ever dared call *her* by that hideous endearment. The wretch had just engaged her for two dances, stared at her in a meaningful way that spoke of the seriousness of his intentions, and in the next moment made an assignation with another young lady.

Daisy felt wretched as she watched the pair move away from each other and melt back into the crowd.

Did all men behave this way? She'd only skimmed through the rest of Lady Forsythia's book in the few hours before the ball. She silently resolved to read it carefully and thoroughly tomorrow. Indeed, wouldn't leave the house until she'd memorized every word. No rake would ever get the better of her. *Not ever.*

Having made her resolution, she stepped out from her hiding spot and walked into the ballroom in time to see Gabriel slip outside through the large doors that led onto the Hastings terrace. Him, too? She glanced around, trying to determine which debutante he meant to lead to ruin in the garden. No young lady followed him out.

Perhaps the foolish girl was already waiting for him.

Daisy shook her head and let out a soft, mirthless laugh. Perhaps this was just the jolt she needed to dismiss Gabriel from her thoughts, to prevent him from ever capturing her heart. She hurried after him, stepping outdoors into the night only to find herself quite alone, a chill wind biting her flesh.

She was immediately struck by the folly of her intentions and considered turning back. She would have, had she not heard Auguste's rumbling laugh and a high-pitched trill coming from a row of bushes beside the nearby fountain. Who was the girl with Auguste? In truth, she didn't care.

Gabriel was another matter. He was the first and only man ever to kiss her. She was in danger of losing her heart to him. "You can't let it happen," she whispered to herself as she rubbed her hands along the sleeves of her gown. The delicate silk offered little protection against the cold.

Where was Gabriel?

Fiery torches drew her eye along the terrace to the dimly lit garden walk. The large garden appeared dark and abandoned, in stark contrast to the vibrant ballroom with chandeliers aglitter and bejeweled dancers waltzing.

More noises emerged from the bushes beside the fountain where Auguste and Passion Blossom-Minx were hiding. She heard his deep grunts and her urgent moans, and then her cries for him to go deeper. Harder. To squeeze her... she gasped and fled deeper into the garden, for she'd never heard a young woman use such coarse language.

Now into the garden, she strained for a glimpse of Gabriel amid the shadows, but the full moon and vibrant stars were obscured by wisps of clouds and offered meager light. Then those clouds passed and she saw him, a dark, masculine shape against the suddenly bright night, making his way along the stepping stone path into the outermost recesses of the Hastings garden.

She followed him beyond the row of golden torches.

Beyond the reach of silver moonlight.

She followed despite her sense of unease. There was something forbidding about this winter garden, perhaps the manner in which the lifeless branches jutted out like jagged silhouettes, sharp and menacing against the moonlight.

She shivered as another icy gust of wind bit her flesh, a warning to return to the ballroom and the safety of a crowd. Instead, her legs propelled her forward, past another young couple—she hadn't noticed them before—doing their best to keep each other warm. She heard groans and giggles, and then she heard silence.

Did everyone engage in this sort of sport?

Was she the only fool who didn't?

She quickly dismissed the thought, for there was another man leaning against a distant tree. This man was shorter and more rotund than Gabriel. Was he meeting Gabriel? Not a lover's tryst but something far more sinister?

In the next instant, he was gone.

Had she imagined him?

No, someone had been standing beside that tree.

She heard another man behind her, ambling along the stone steps in no particular hurry or direction. His steps were heavy, as though he wore boots and not dancing slippers—which meant he had not come to the Hastings ball to dance.

She stopped to gaze at her own delicate slippers, the silk already wet from treading on damp grass and trudging through small puddles of mud. They were ruined and her mother would demand explanations.

"Gabriel," she called out softly, losing sight of him.

Her heart skipped a beat for the garden was suddenly eerily quiet.

Too quiet.

Which meant the gentleman behind her had stopped walking when she had.

On purpose? Or mere coincidence?

She tried to still the now rampant beating of her heart to better hear the stranger's footsteps as he crept behind her. She started walking along the path again and stopped. Twice.

He did the same.

"Bother," she muttered, her decision to follow Gabriel now seeming immensely foolish. What was she to do? Returning to the ballroom was impossible, for she'd have to walk past the man who was standing between her and the safety of the ballroom.

Her senses warned it wasn't a good idea.

Indeed, they were now screaming for her to run.

Run!

She whirled around, intending to make a desperate dash for the terrace, but someone suddenly covered her mouth with his large hand—yes, definitely a strong, male hand—and yanked her behind a row of sculpted boxwood. "Bloody hell," he said in an angry whisper. "What are you doing out here?"

Gabriel!

He'd moved with such stealth she hadn't heard so much as a crunch of leaves.

"Don't scream," he warned, his voice still a whisper as he slowly removed his hand from her mouth and circled his arms protectively around her body.

She shuddered with relief and melted into his embrace, feeling quite safe in his arms. "There's a man following me."

Gabriel tensed. "Did you get a look at him?"

"No." She hesitated a moment, her heart still pounding wildly. "What shall we do?"

"Just follow my lead. This ought to dissuade him." He made a show of lifting her up against him and slowly twirling her in his arms, no doubt to scout the nearby hedges to see where the man was hiding. "My love, I've ached to hold you since we were last together. It seems forever ago," he said with surprising ardor, his warm lips suddenly descending on hers, easing her fears and... *sigh*... providing comfort in a consuming kiss she hoped would never end.

She circled her arms around his neck, eager to respond. She knew this was merely a pretense, but he was awfully good at it, and since she'd gotten herself into this scrape, she had no choice but to be grateful and play along.

Indeed, she was eager to—

She froze as Gabriel pressed something hard against her thigh, something her sisters had explained about, that men sometimes... except it wasn't *that*.

Gabriel had a very big, very sharp knife pressed against her body.

"ARE YOU ATTICS-to-let?" Gabriel growled softly, his mind quickly working through several plans to get Daisy safely out of the garden now that she'd charged in where she didn't belong. Fortunately, he and Napoleon's spy had completed their exchange of information, so there was no reason for his contact to linger now that he had the English military "secrets."

But in following Gabriel, Daisy might have unwittingly drawn more attention to herself. Who was this other man following Daisy? Gabriel feared it was another of Napoleon's agents, for they often operated in pairs. If so, he couldn't allow the man to believe she was in any way involved in this intrigue. He dared not think what these blackguards might do to her if they believed she was in the service of the Crown.

The only plan that sprang to mind was to pretend he and Daisy were lovers meeting in secret.

Could Daisy pull it off?

He nibbled her ear—*Lord, she smelled good*—to stall for time while he thought the plan through or came up with a better one. Simply walking her back was out of the question, for he'd seen the glint of a weapon in the man's hands when he'd lifted Daisy in his arms and slowly twirled her.

She moaned softly. "Gabriel, I saw you—"

He stopped her with another deep kiss before she blurted something that would get them both killed. Anything to keep her from talking!

She shouldn't have followed him out here. He'd worked years to develop his dissolute reputation, to gain the trust of enemy agents, and she was about to destroy all that hard work in one evening.

"I—"

He thrust his tongue against her rose-petal lips, purposely invading her mouth. "Daisy," he whispered upon ending the kiss, "you must do exactly as I say." He slid his own knife clear of her body to defend her if the need arose. "I'm afraid you've muddled things and I need to get you out of here alive."

She leaned her head against his shoulder and nodded. Her breaths were short and ragged, a sign of her fear. "I'm so sorry." She swallowed hard, seeming to understand the foolishness of following him into the garden. Too late, unfortunately. "Can you put that knife away?"

"No, sweetheart. I can't. But I won't hurt you. You know that, don't you?"

Once more, she nodded against his chest. "I'm frightened, Gabriel."

So was he. They were trapped in a dangerous game of cat and mouse, he and Daisy being the mice, while Napoleon's spies decided whether he was as reputed—a wastrel lord who seduced innocent maidens and was not above selling secrets to the French—or an English agent feeding them false information, in which case they would be attacked before he drew his next breath.

"Listen carefully and do exactly as I say. Don't speak, just nod if you understand."

Which she did, probably because she couldn't string two words together. She was scared and the wild beat of her heart against his chest confirmed it. He felt the light heave of her breasts with each ragged breath she took.

"We're lovers," he continued softly, struggling to concentrate on the immediate danger and not be distracted by his rampant desire for the girl. "It's our only chance."

"Meeting in secret, like Romeo and Juliet," she whispered back.

He touched his forehead to hers and groaned softly. "The point is not to die in each other's arms."

"Ah, poor choice on my part. I think you had better kiss me again. Oh, and I give you permission to do whatever you must to get us out of here alive."

"I intend to." He kissed her hotly at the base of her throat, hoping Daisy would respond with innocence and passion. He knew she was not immune to his touch, but fear of death was a powerful force and Daisy was unpredictable.

Her skin felt soft against his lips. He dusted kisses along her throat and up toward her lightly parted lips. He felt her body shiver against his own as he continued to whisper instructions on how to respond. She was too innocent and wouldn't know how to fake passion. "Give me a breathless moan and tell me not to stop."

"Oh! Oooh. Gabriel, don't stop."

His own breath momentarily caught in his throat. *Hell in a handbasket*, she sounded achingly good. "Who taught you that?"

"No one," she whispered. "I overheard a young woman a few moments ago and imitated her cries."

He stifled a laugh, relieved and at the same time furious with her for wandering into danger. Yet he also felt a sudden possessive pride in knowing he was the only one ever to touch her. "Good. Do it again."

"It'll be easier if you help out." She took his hand and placed it on her breast. *Lord help him!* The knife almost slipped from his fingers, the force of his body's response almost dropping him to his knees. All at once, fireworks exploded within his body, every organ erupting with its own display. Was the girl attics-to-let? She might have warned him of her intention.

No, Daisy wasn't at fault. He was the dolt. What was wrong with him anyway? He knew his way around a woman's body. The mere feel of her breast against his open palm should not have sent him into spasms of ecstasy.

But Daisy wasn't just any woman. She was... his ruin? His downfall? Whatever she was, she happened to be methodically demolishing his best-laid plans. To his amazement, the little widgeon had no idea she held this power. He meant to pull away, but her breast felt so good against his hand, the lush mound fitting so perfectly in the cup of his palm, as though she were meant for him and no one else.

He suddenly felt like a boar marking his territory.

He wanted Daisy, didn't want anyone else to have her. It mattered little that he had no right to ache for her body or yearn for her heart. His only duty was to keep her safe from Napoleon's agent.

Would the man never leave?

Growing impatient, and now concerned that the ruse wasn't working, he shifted slightly and felt her nipple harden beneath his thumb. He glanced heavenward. *Lord, you aren't helping!* In truth, the Good Lord seemed intent on torturing him.

He tore his gaze from Daisy and trained it on the man still standing in the shadows. The weapon was still drawn and glinting in his hand. "You're not doing enough to convince him," Daisy whispered, tossing him a frown. "He won't believe we're lovers if you hold back."

He wasn't about to slip the gown off Daisy's shoulders and bare her glorious breasts, not while that vermin looked on.

He let out a soft growl, his hand still frozen on her breast. And growled again, knowing he would never take Daisy this way, no matter how desperately he yearned to tease and suckle her hard, pink nipples and taste... the man suddenly moved.

Gabriel tensed, his gaze following a dark shape outlined in the moonlight.

He heard a soft rustle and quickly drew Daisy behind him so that her body was sheltered between him and the tree under which they now stood.

His tightened the grip on his knife, ready to kill the man if he got too close to Daisy. *Hell.* He reached back to make certain she was all right. Her breaths were short and erratic, and he knew her heart had to be pounding in that same, erratic beat.

"Thank the Graces," Gabriel muttered, for the man was now at the garden wall and attempting to scale it. The agent he'd met earlier to hand over the false information had left in the same manner. That both had chosen to leave by that route was too much of a coincidence. If the second man had been a mere guest, he would have simply walked back to the party.

"He's gone," he said as the man went over the wall. He drew her into his arms and caressed her as she trembled against his chest. "You're safe now, Daisy."

"Who was he?" He heard the lingering fear in her voice and wished he could soothe her, but he wasn't at liberty to give her any answers.

"I don't know." In truth, he didn't know the man's identity, only that he was working for Napoleon. Yet it felt like a lie. His existence, his dissolute reputation, everything about him... all lies. He tucked his knife into the sheath hidden within his boot, all the while keeping hold of Daisy. For some reason, he couldn't let her go.

She burrowed closer. "What happens now, Gabriel?"

He ran his hands up and down her arms to warm her, for she was shivering. Her skin felt cool and silky. He bent his head and kissed her lightly on the lips. She tasted as sweet as sugared apples. "You'll be missed by now. I had better return you to the party."

She gazed up at him, unshed tears glistening in her eyes. "What if I don't want you to let me go?"

He let out a short, harsh laugh. "I'm not keen on it either. In truth, I'd like to hold on to you forever, but it isn't possible." He gently wiped a tear that had fallen onto her cheek. "Daisy, I don't wish to hurt you. Let me do the right thing and take you back."

She nodded. "I think I broke every rule in Lady Forsythia's book tonight. I don't know what's wrong with me. I can't seem to do anything right."

"There isn't a blessed thing wrong with you." He studied her face by moonlight, noticed the tension in her mouth and the tears still shimmering in her eyes. He bent his head to kiss her one last time. "You're perfect."

He kissed her again, knowing he needed to break off and return her to her family. Instead, his hand was somehow back on her breast, his thumb skimming across its straining tip. She gasped and arched into him, running her hands up his chest and circling them about his neck. "Gabriel, don't stop."

"This is madness," he murmured, sliding his hand along her back and down the delicate silk of her gown to cup her buttocks and draw her even closer so that their bodies were in full contact, the evidence of his lust hard and throbbing against her hip. Would she leap back in shock? Would she cry?

She smiled up at him. "Thank you for not calling me your passion blossom minx."

"What?" He had trouble understanding her thought, although he was having trouble with everything just now. His body. His heart. His brain that had obviously stopped functioning. He'd never experienced anything like this hot need to possess Daisy, to cover her creamy breasts with his mouth and swirl his tongue over her sweet, pink nipples. The girl had turned him upside down, had destroyed every vestige of his good sense and annihilated the last of his resistance.

He released a tortured shudder as her gloriously taut nipples brushed against his chest. He tried to be gentle, tried to be a gentleman—*oh, hell*. He wasn't a gentleman, didn't want to be. He couldn't be just now, for the need to stroke and touch, to rouse Daisy's unawakened desires, was overwhelming. This would be his last chance, his last memory of Daisy and he was going to take full advantage.

He eased the gown off her shoulders and exposed her breasts to his view. "Daisy," he said, sucking in a breath, "you look like an angel in the moonlight." He bent his head and delicately took one rosy tip in his mouth, flicking his tongue across it and feeling every throb and shudder as she closed her eyes and wound her fingers in his hair, holding him against her breast as he licked and tasted the sweetness of her skin.

"Oh, Gabriel!" Her eyes were closed and body arched toward him. Her head tipped back and she let out an achingly soft moan. *"Oooh, Gabriel!"*

"Stop me, Daisy. This truly is madness." *Sweet, glorious madness.* He wanted to make love to her all night long, yearned to feel her hot, naked body move with exquisite passion beneath his own.

His heart beat faster as he forced himself to draw away. The fantasy would have to wait until he'd carried out his mission. For now, the feel of her soft skin beneath his fingers, the taste of her rose-tipped breasts, would have to be enough.

He could make Daisy no promises, no matter how fiercely he wanted her. All of her. For himself.

She was reckless and passionate... so incredibly passionate. But it was time to end the dream and return her safely to her family. He slid his fingers to hook the bodice of her gown and draw it back over her breasts. "Sweetheart, I can't do this to you, much as I'd like to help you break every damn rule in Lady Forsythia's book." *Sweet mother of mercy!* His hand trembled against her smooth flesh.

She was about to push him over the edge... way over, into molten, scorching—

"Daisy!" a male voice rang out from the opposite end of the garden. "I know you're out here! Answer me or I'll have bloodhounds and every Farthingale in existence raking these grounds in search of you!"

Gabriel released a gush of air, his relief profound. He heard the rustle of bushes as George Farthingale approached.

"You had better go," Daisy said in a whisper.

He let out a soft growl. "And leave you to face your family alone? Not going to happen."

She glanced at him with concern. "But this isn't your fault. It's mine. There could be consequences."

"I'm sure there will be." He made certain Daisy's breasts were secure within the confines of her gown and the stray wisps of her silky hair were properly tucked behind her ears. "And you're not going to face them alone."

CHAPTER 13

A rake will never cherish a lady who
challenges him in gentlemen's pursuits.

THE FOLLOWING MORNING, Daisy was surprised to find Gabriel waiting for her beside the mews where Laurel housed her horses. She had agreed to take her sister's beast of a horse, Brutus, through his early paces and had not expected to find Gabriel here. She'd left him talking to her uncle after they'd returned to Lord Hastings' party. Obviously, nothing had been said to her parents or she would never have heard the end of it last night.

It was a little after sunrise and far too early for any respectable member of the *ton* to be up and about. The point of riding was to be seen by one's peers, not by common dustmen or grooms. The fashionable riders would be out later, once the sun was up and had burned away the morning dampness. At this early hour, there was a chill to the air and a lingering fog that partly obscured the stable and surrounding streets.

Gabriel stood with his shoulder propped against the door, looking not at all tired from last night's intrigue and every bit the imposing lord in his polished Hessians, buff breeches, and finely tailored chestnut jacket.

In short, he looked divine.

And here she stood, dark circles under her eyes from lack of sleep, dressed in well-worn boy's clothes consisting of baggy breeches, a stained black jacket, and a cap large enough to hide the fat braid she'd tucked in it.

Gabriel frowned at her. "After last night, you ought to know better than to go anywhere alone."

"Laurel asked me to take Brutus for his morning exercise." Why else would she dress like a rag-tag boy and be up at this unholy hour? "One of our footmen escorted me here. More important, what were you really doing in the Hastings garden last night?"

His frown deepened. "None of your concern."

She may have acted foolishly, inadvertently placing them in danger, but last night's incident was clearly one of his own making and he owed her an explanation for that unsettling business. "Nor is my helping out Laurel any of *your* concern. Why are you here? Where's Graelem?"

"My cousin is busy this morning. He asked me to look after you."

Which only added to her confusion. Obviously, Graelem trusted him. So did her heart, for it was fluttering again as it always did whenever he appeared. "Is that so? As you looked out for me last night? Who was the man following me?"

"I don't know. Probably an admirer who noticed you walk into the garden and sought to take advantage."

She shook her head and sighed. "If you thought that's all he was, you wouldn't have drawn your knife, or placed your body protectively between mine and his, or made a grand show of pretending we were in love."

"Daisy—"

"Why is it so hard for you to tell me the truth?"

She expected a dismissive retort; instead he remained silent and there was an undercurrent of sadness in his expression. She was mad as an English hatter to expect more from him, to want more from him. Yet, there was a moment last night when she thought... No, rakehells didn't believe in love or commitment. "I kissed you with all my heart, Gabriel. Those kisses were as real as the knife you held against my body. Do you always carry it with you?"

He nodded. "Most gentlemen do, for protection."

"To defend themselves when in unsavory places? Such as Lord Hastings' garden? You met someone there."

He placed his hands on her arms and shook her lightly. "Damn it,

Daisy. Stop asking questions. Stop trying to reform me. It won't work, no matter what it says in Lady Forsythia's damn book." His hands were still on her arms, gently restraining her. "Didn't you learn anything from last night?"

She responded with a scowl, although she felt more hurt than angry. She wanted so badly to walk away and never think of him again, but she couldn't.

He released her and raked a hand through his hair, the gesture nudging one golden curl over his forehead. He had large, strong hands, exquisitely gentle last night when stroking her body to calm her fear.

The memory brought flames to her cheeks.

"I did learn something... about myself." She expected him to shoot back a careless response, but he simply remained silent, jaw clenched, his brooding amber gaze warning not to provoke him.

She simply wanted the truth.

Dropping her hands to her sides, she sighed. "My heart skips beats whenever you look at me. I wish it didn't. I want to look into the mirror and be proud of myself. I want my family to be proud of me. Auguste Malinor is courting me and yet all I can think of is you. No wonder my family doesn't trust my judgment. How can they when *I* no longer trust my judgment?"

The anger seemed to drain from him, escaping in a feral groan. "Daisy—"

"But that doesn't mean I like you or respect you, especially if you're conducting shady business. I thought you might be meeting another woman. In truth, I hoped you were. I needed something to shake me to my senses and remind me how dissolute and untrustworthy you are. Instead, I—" She was about to mention Auguste and his tryst, but decided against it since it was none of Gabriel's business. In any event, Auguste had not made formal his intentions, so she had no claim on him or right to feel betrayed.

She was being ridiculous, of course. Faithfulness was something one hoped for in a marriage, perhaps during a courtship. She and Auguste had shared two dances and he'd barely spoken to her during all that time. Hardly a courtship.

She dismissed her thoughts of Auguste and returned her

attention to Gabriel. "Are you smuggling French goods into England? Or are you involved in something more sinister? Perhaps providing ministry secrets to the French. Are you capable of betraying Eloise, your parents, and your own country? That's what I keep asking myself... but what would you gain by it? A fee to be squandered at the gaming tables?"

She studied his face and found it devoid of all expression. Though disappointed, she pressed on. "That's why I followed you into the garden, to find out the truth."

"And what would you have done if I were spying for the French? Stopped me from continuing down that foolish path?"

"Something like that." She blinked her eyes and took a deep breath. "Are you?"

He shrugged. "You've found me out."

"I haven't at all," she said, swallowing her frustration. She wanted to pummel him. "Despite what I just said, I don't believe you're a French spy, or a gambler, or a reprobate. I believe you're a wonderful man caught up in something dangerous and I can't figure out what it is."

"Don't you dare try," he growled with a depth of feeling he'd never shown before. He did have a heart after all and it held some small affection for her. She had been starting to wonder about that, because until last night, he'd done a good job of making her think he didn't care. "Just trust that I'm trying to keep you safe. Stop asking questions."

She curled her hands into fists in frustration. "Not until you provide some answers."

"You're the stubbornest, most meddlesome little Farthingale." He shook her again gently, as though to emphasize his point. "I can't and won't explain myself to you. Nor will I protect you the next time you stick your nose in something dangerous."

"Now that is a lie," she said with a wistful laugh, placing her hand over his heart. She felt its steady beat beneath her palm. "Do you know what I truly think?"

He muttered something under his breath; she wasn't certain what he'd said, but it didn't sound pleasant or like a "yes."

She decided to tell him anyway. "I think you'd fight to the death to defend me, no matter when or where. You were prepared to do so last night."

"Had I known you'd be so irritating, I might not have."

"Don't try to deny it or make a jest of it. I know the sort of man you are."

"You don't."

"I think you're a hero," she said softly, deciding to trust her instincts, "even more heroic than your brother because he receives praise and accolades while you go quietly about your difficult business, suffering in secret heartbreak."

"Bloody hell," he said with ragged breath, his eyes now dark with pain. "Don't say another word, Daisy. I'm a bastard, plain and simple."

Her eyes suddenly welled with tears—Lord, why should she cry over this impossible man? She struggled to hold them back and finally gave up, allowing her feelings to show, for she was tired of deception. More important, she sensed Gabriel was tired of the burden he was carrying... the agonizing burden he insisted on bearing alone.

She reached out and began to trace the long, jagged scar above his eye, her finger moving slowly over the rough pink flesh in order to absorb every agonizing detail of his injury. "And if you are that silent hero, the one who tackles the dirtiest missions, endures the worst hardships without complaint or expectation of reward... then... then... I think I could fall desperately in love with you."

"Hell."

"Let me amend that. I think I may already be desperately in love with you." She hadn't conceived of loving him until the words spilled out of her mouth. And now that they had, she didn't know how to take them back or if she wanted to take them back.

"Bloody hell."

"Please say something else," she whispered, humiliated because he looked nothing like a man in the throes of rapture. There was so much pain etched on his face she couldn't bear it.

He looked wretched, as though he'd just been handed a death sentence.

She'd just admitted that she loved him, had just thrown away her chance to make her family proud. Her parents would never allow her to marry Gabriel. They'd be appalled. He was too much of a scoundrel. Not that he'd ever consider offering for her anyway.

What was she to do now? Having admitted that she was in love with Gabriel, how could she encourage Auguste Malinor's courtship? She wasn't the sort to hide her feelings. Auguste wasn't stupid, he'd know her heart belonged to another. And would Auguste continue to stray if ever they were to marry? She sensed that he would. Fortunately, it would never come to that. He'd never offer for her. "Oh, what's the use? I don't even know why I care about you."

She pushed past him and made for Brutus' stall.

He held her back, spinning her to face him and tracing her jaw with his finger. "Daisy—"

She inhaled sharply.

"Don't lose your heart to me," he said with an aching groan. "I'm a bastard, not a hero. I'll never be *your* hero."

DAISY GAZED AT him with her sad, beautiful eyes. "I know you're not. I was mad to hope even for an instant that you were. Forget everything I just said."

"But will you?"

"Yes," she said, sounding quite unconvinced. "Please let me go. I have to saddle Brutus."

"I've already saddled him for you," Gabriel said, struggling to maintain his composure, to contain the ache in his heart that was as raw as an open wound. He really needed to kiss Daisy, desperately and deeply. He needed to lift her into his arms, carry her onto the freshly cut hay and bury himself inside her soft body.

Daisy needed to be protected from him because that damn vow— no broken hearts, no grieving widows—would be broken if she didn't stop just being Daisy. No matter how foolish she'd been to enter that garden alone, she'd done it for him.

She cared for him.

She believed in him.

Here she stood, practically dressed in rags and sniffling like a street urchin, and all he could think of was how beautiful she looked and how badly he wanted her.

"Laurel's beast allowed you near him?" she asked, interrupting the thoughts he was desperate to hide from her. "How did you manage it?"

Gabriel moved away from her and strode to the temperamental stallion, approaching him carefully because Brutus enjoyed going after strangers and pounding them with his massive hooves if they dared come too close. The beast had almost killed Graelem, but that unfortunate encounter had led to his cousin meeting Laurel, so Graelem considered himself coming out ahead. A beautiful wife that he loved deeply in exchange for a broken leg.

A badly broken leg that had acted up today. For that reason, Graelem had summoned him and asked for the favor of accompanying Daisy on her morning ride. Or had Graelem purposely schemed to throw him and Daisy together as much as possible before he left for France?

Hell.

Brutus was another problem. Handling the beast had been a challenge, but one he had mastered. He and Brutus were arrogant males and understood each other.

Handling Daisy was quite another matter—one didn't handle her so much as simply watch over her and try to hold her back whenever those compassionate instincts got the better of her. But love her?

That was out of the question.

He couldn't risk his mission, not even for her. "I'll tell you how I managed Brutus while we ride to the park. It's getting late and he's restless."

Daisy tucked her long, black braid securely under her cap and then glanced at the open stable door and the rays of sunlight beginning to poke through the morning mist. "My family doesn't know I'm helping Laurel while her groom is ill."

"After last night's incident," he said, maintaining a casual tone despite the unbearable tension between them, "I'm surprised they haven't placed armed guards outside your door."

"They would have, had Uncle George mentioned that he'd found us together in the Hastings garden. I don't know why he didn't. Unless he trusts you." She sighed. "I doubt he trusts me. Nor should he. I stuffed pillows under my covers so anyone peering into my room will believe I'm asleep in my bed. I should be safe for a few more hours."

He nodded. "I'm eager to see you put Brutus through his paces. I hear he's as fast as the wind and as sturdy as an English oak."

Her eyes brightened with obvious pride. "There's no finer horse in England."

"Graelem claims he's faster than my Goliath."

She smiled for the first time this morning. "Care to find out?"

"Are you challenging me and Goliath?" He'd also heard she was an excellent rider. Indeed, she had many talents, yet remained modest despite her accomplishments.

He had wanted to refuse Graelem's request to escort Daisy this morning, he really ought to have, but he was like a bee drawn to a flower. No matter how hard he tried or how often Ian warned him of the danger, he couldn't keep away.

Daisy intrigued him.

He wouldn't allow himself to feel anything more.

She gazed at him, her beautiful eyes gleaming. "Well, what do you say? Goliath may be fast, but Brutus and I will have you eating our dust."

He shook his head and laughed. "How can I resist the challenge?"

Happiness was a creature of the moment, requiring no promises and leaving no broken hearts. Happiness was safe, if kept contained. "Twice around Hyde Park and we finish back here," he said.

"Agreed."

She led Brutus out of the stable, patting his nose and cooing endearments while Brutus gently nuzzled her cheek in return. Gabriel couldn't help but be amazed. The beast—and that stallion truly had the heart of a demonic beast—was as docile as a lamb under Daisy's touch. Still, he was a large animal and Daisy looked so small beside him.

"Let me help you up," he said.

Her big, blue eyes rounded in alarm. "Don't! He'll bite if you get too close."

"My, but you're a fidgety little thing this morning. The only one likely to do any biting is you. Brutus won't harm me. We've reached an understanding."

"What do you mean?"

He cast the beast a conspiratorial wink. "He's promised not to make a meal of me. Isn't that right, Brutus?"

"And what have you promised in return?"

Never to break your heart.

His hands slid along her waist as he hoisted her onto the saddle, lingering for an exquisite moment before he cupped his hand about her foot to guide it into the stirrup. "That," he said with a catch to his voice, "is a secret."

Which was not a very clever thing for him to say, he realized as her grin faded. He was full of secrets and she deserved better.

She bent down to whisper in her stallion's ear. "You'll tell me, won't you?"

Brutus angrily shook his head and let loose with an impertinent whinny.

She let out a surprised laugh. "Goodness! Do all males stand together?"

"We must." Otherwise, they'd be defenseless against headstrong young women with eyes the brilliant blue of a mountain lake and a smile as enchanting as a meadow flower. He muttered something about fetching Goliath and turned away to do precisely that.

"He's magnificent," Daisy said, eyeing the deep-chested bay he led out of the stable a moment later.

"Goliath, meet Daisy. She's a slip of a girl, but don't be fooled. She's a force to be reckoned with."

GABRIEL HAD A fine eye for horses and a masterful way with them, Daisy realized. She'd never seen Brutus warm to anyone so quickly. Of course, she'd warmed to Gabriel almost as quickly, but she was a female and couldn't help herself.

Gabriel, with his brooding eyes and ruggedly handsome face—the few scars only adding to the irresistible force of his attraction—had a devastating impact on women.

"Tell me more about this understanding between you and Brutus," she said as they ambled toward Hyde Park. She had taken months to develop a rapport with the stallion, but Gabriel had gained his respect immediately... which had to mean Gabriel was valiant and not at all the villain he would have everyone believe.

Animals had excellent instincts.

"It's very simple really. We faced each other and established the bounds of our territory."

She tipped her head in confusion. "How do you establish bounds when you don't speak the same language?"

"Oh, but we do, just not the King's English. He snorts at me. I growl back. We take the measure of each other."

She rolled her eyes. "I would hardly call growling at each other the basis for a lasting truce."

He leaned closer and arched an eyebrow so that he looked appealingly wicked. "That's because members of your sex do not understand the language of men."

"The language of possession, pride, and conquest? Nonsense, anyone can growl."

"You can't," he said, his expression so tender it made her heart ache.

"Of course I can." She let out a low, strangled sound.

He shook his head and sighed. "Feeble."

She tried again.

He winced. "Stop, you're hurting my ears."

"I am not," she said with a soft laugh.

"Indeed, you are. That noise you're making more resembles a squirrel begging for a nut."

She frowned. "It sounded fine to me."

He drew even closer and leaned forward in his saddle, his seductive gaze doing thoroughly inappropriate things to her body.

"Try this." He released a low rumble that traveled from the depths of his stomach to the back of his throat before finally escaping in a sensually feral growl that caused her blood to heat and body to quiver.

The noise was more than the mere expression of male dominance. It was a mating call and she was responding to it like a mare in heat.

Great balls of cheese!

The man was dangerous. No wonder she'd fallen in love with him... and admitted it to him... and couldn't take it back even if she wished.

"THE FOG'S LIFTING," Gabriel said, the short canter from Graelem's stable to the park leaving him in torment, but when was he not in torment when close to Daisy?

He forced his attention to the sandy trail known as Rotten Row. Several grooms and trainers were already on the trail, exercising their master's mounts. All appeared as it should, business as usual and no strangers who didn't belong. More important, Napoleon's spies were no longer following him since Daisy had thoroughly confused them last night.

Which also meant they weren't following *her*.

That's all he cared about, keeping her safe.

"Keep that cap low on your head and don't make eye contact with anyone," he reminded, although she wasn't likely to be recognized. The fashionable set was never out this early, but one couldn't be too careful.

"You needn't worry. Those men will be looking at our horses and not at us."

"Not if they catch a glimpse of your face." Daisy's incredible blue eyes and sooty lashes would give away her disguise.

She let out a little harrumph; however, her indignation passed quickly as she put Brutus through his paces. When she turned to him again, she had an adorable grin on her face. "Brutus needs to warm up before our race."

"Very well. Let's see what he can do."

She spurred Brutus to a gallop, leaving Gabriel once more in amazement as horse and rider covered the track with incredible speed. Daisy was one of the most adept riders he'd ever seen, confident and utterly fearless, she and her mount seeming to move as one.

"Well, Goliath? Are we going to let a little girl beat us?" The stallion needed no urging to take off at a gallop, but there was too much distance to make up and Gabriel knew he'd manage little more than keeping Daisy in his sight.

He finally caught up with her by the Serpentine. She had dismounted and was casually standing by the water's edge, her arms folded and impertinent chin upraised while Brutus stood beside her, lapping water.

Gabriel dismounted and released Goliath to join his equine companion.

"Took you long enough to catch up," Daisy teased.

He tucked a finger under her chin and smiled. "Those shall be my precise words to you after I win the race."

She laughed merrily. "Typical male, all preen and bluster! Are you ready?"

"Yes. We've already drawn unwanted attention," he said, nodding in the direction of the grooms and trainers who were looking their way and beginning to edge closer. Those men couldn't help but be drawn to superb horseflesh, nor could they resist a good race.

"Brutus loves an attentive crowd, makes his winning all the more rewarding."

He arched an eyebrow. "And what about concealing your identity?"

She nibbled her lower lip. "You're right. We had better go."

"As I mentioned earlier, we'll take two laps around the park and finish at Graelem's stable. No one will follow us through the London streets. First one to reach the stable is the winner. Agreed?"

She cast him another adorable smile. "Agreed."

Daisy and her Brutus edged out Gabriel and his Goliath by a nose, though Gabriel knew he could have won had he not held Goliath back that littlest bit at the end. Nevertheless, Daisy ran a brilliant race and he wouldn't take the hard-earned victory from her.

She reached the stable a few strides ahead of him and, leaping out of her saddle with grace and agility, let out a triumphant cheer.

168 | MEARA PLATT

"Victory is mine!"

He threw his head back and laughed. "That's not very sportsmanlike."

"Indeed, not at all!" she agreed without a trace of remorse.

He stifled a groan as she tugged the cap off her head, unbound her braid, and slowly, sensually shook out her long, black locks. Her beautiful mane cascaded over her shoulders, flowing down her back in dark, rippling waves.

Did she have any idea how lovely she looked?

"Winner gets to pick her prize," she said, tossing him the dare.

He dismounted and strode toward her. "What's it to be?"

She trained her still sparkling blue eyes on him. "The truth about last night."

"No," he said gently. "Speaking about it will place you, me, and countless others in greater danger. Do you understand? You are never to discuss this incident with anyone. Not your parents, not your sisters. No one."

He expected an argument, but she merely shook her head slowly. "Will you ever tell me the truth?"

"I don't know. That's as honest as I can be."

She sighed and shook her head again. "Very well, I'll pick another prize."

He nodded. "Go ahead."

"A kiss from the loser."

She was determined to torture him.

He should have said no again.

"Well?" She arched a dainty eyebrow and folded her arms over her delightfully ample breasts. Glorious breasts. Damn glorious. The memory of his lips against her soft mounds and their hard, pink tips was about to send him over the edge.

He should have insisted they unsaddle the horses and return the saddles to Laurel's grooms to be properly oiled and polished.

He should have said absolutely no.

And retrieved pails and brushes to feed and curry Brutus and Goliath.

He had watched Daisy ride Brutus, her legs straddling his sweat-sheened body, urging him faster and faster to the finish, her own lithe body moving in perfect rhythm to the beast's strides—and had imagined her, naked and hot, riding atop him with equal rhythmic fervor.

A kiss?

He ached to bury himself inside her body and claim possession of her soul, ached to carry her to majestic heights, her senses soaring in one, incredible burst of passion. "Very well, but my way."

She gazed at him in confusion. "Your way? Are there different ways of kissing?"

He swept her into his arms, molding her body to his so that her utterly and incredibly perfect breasts were pressed against his hard chest and her long, slender legs rested against his thighs. He lowered his hungry lips to her honey-sweet mouth, needing the hot, urgent memory to sustain him through the bitter French nights.

He cupped one lush mound—so soft and perfect—teasing its rosy bud with his thumb, gently stroking and caressing through the coarse fabric of her shirt until she moaned and shuddered in a wave crest of desire.

He slid his hand inside her shirt, his palm rough against her smooth, pink flesh and pebble-hard nipples. He yearned to free her from her cumbersome clothes, yearned to taste her sweet, hot flesh and inhale the intoxicating scent of her passion.

"Merciful heavens, Miss Daisy!" The shocked cry came from behind him, instantly and painfully dragging him back to his senses, for he was hot and hard and on the verge of losing control.

A pail clattered to the ground, also behind him.

"Amos!" Daisy cried out, pushing out of Gabriel's arms.

"Who's Amos?" Gabriel followed her gaze to a young man the size of an ox. His face was as red as a beet, but it was a kind face despite his brawn.

"He's one of our footmen," she explained in a short, breathless gasp and crossed her hands over the front of her shirt to hide its disarray. "He brought me here."

"And waited to escort you back?"

"Yes," she said, a blush now staining her cheeks. The gleam of passion remained in her eyes, revealing that his touch had affected her. Her lips were pink and lightly swollen from his kiss. "I'm not so foolish as to walk through the streets of London on my own."

Yet she'd had no qualms about traipsing through a dark garden on her own, or sneaking out of bed to ride a beast capable of crushing her with barely a flick of its hooves. Nor had she discouraged him from swallowing her up in his kiss.

He'd gone far beyond a mere kiss. Her shirt was open down the front and so was his, so desperate was he to touch and taste her sweet, silken skin.

Foolish?

They were both—he and Daisy—mad as hatters and bound for Bedlam.

"I'll be right along, Amos," she said, scrambling to put order to her clothing. "Please wait outside."

Gabriel helped with her buttons and ties, stifling yet more groans each time he grazed her warm skin and ran his fingers through her silky mane to tuck it back under her cap. She cast him a dewy-eyed gaze that made him want to kiss her again. "You held Goliath back during the race, didn't you?"

"Yes," he said after a moment's hesitation. He didn't wish to disappoint the girl, but neither did he wish to lie to her—he'd already lied about too many things.

He needn't have worried about hurt feelings, he realized in the next moment as she cast him an impish grin.

"I did the same with Brutus. No matter what you think, I really did beat you."

CHAPTER 14

*A lady must never accept the assistance of
a rake, for his motives are always suspect.*

GABRIEL DECIDED TO pay a call on his grandmother later that morning, his purpose to discuss Daisy and undo the muddle he'd made of matters by his inability to keep his hands off the girl. The little innocent had efficiently demolished his iron discipline and he was sinking as fast as an English frigate with a gaping hole in its keel.

He had to repair the damage before he left London, for he wasn't going to leave Daisy with hope in her gorgeous blue eyes. She needed to move on, settle down with someone who would offer her a safe, secure marriage.

He also needed his grandmother to get Lady Forsythia's damn book out of Daisy's hands. The girl, by her own admission, hadn't followed a single rule about how to reform a rake, and her constant misadventures were wreaking havoc on his composure.

Surely, nowhere in Lady Forsythia's book did it say to take the rake's hand and place it on your breast. Nowhere could it possibly have said to tell the rake you love him and then trust him to do the right thing.

"Gabriel, how lovely to see you," Eloise said, motioning him into her chamber. She was still abed, in her robe and nightgown, finishing the last of her breakfast. Her silver hair was tucked under her cap except for a fat curl falling on each cheek.

"I've come too early." His heart tugged at the sight of her, for the smile she had for him was broad and filled with affection.

"Nonsense," she said with a laugh, "I've slept too late."

She instructed her maid to remove the breakfast tray and leave them to discuss matters in private. "That's better," she said once they were alone. "I'm glad you're here, but is there a reason for your visit?"

He drew up a chair beside her bed. "I'll be leaving town soon and wanted to pay a call upon my favorite girl before I did."

"I heard about that hunt you and Edgeware are planning." She tried to sound casual, but he heard the undercurrent of reproach in her voice. "How long will you be gone?"

He shrugged. "I don't know, depends upon the weather."

Eloise shook her head and sighed. "Two of the *ton's* most eligible bachelors gone for an indeterminate period of time just as the season starts, that ought to send the marriage-minded mamas into a frenzy. I hope you don't stay away too long."

He reached out to squeeze her hand. "I'll try not to."

She gave his hand a light squeeze in return and pursed her lips. Gabriel knew that her mind was busily working up another plan to match make, so he wasn't surprised when she said, "Will you be attending Lady Baldridge's musicale this evening?"

"Yes." But he'd leave soon afterward, for he had the identification documents and supplies he needed. His passage to France was also in order. There was nothing to keep him in London any longer.

"Have you spoken to Daisy about your trip?"

"No," he said with an exasperated sigh, releasing his grandmother's hand. He ought to be avoiding the girl, not aching to spend every moment with her before he left town.

"She's a lovely girl, you really ought to get to know her better."

He arched an eyebrow. Had his grandmother always been this meddlesome, or had she acquired that trait from spending too much time with the Farthingales? "Perhaps when I return from the hunting trip." He noted the hopeful glint in her eye and hastened to quell it. "I can't promise anything, Eloise. Anyway, you were never any good at matchmaking. Don't start now."

The fat curls of silver framing her face bobbed as she quirked her head. "You're being utterly ridiculous."

"For wishing to avoid marriage?" He shifted uncomfortably in his chair. If only she realized how little encouragement he needed to pursue Daisy! He should never have kissed her that first time in the carriage. Hell, he should never have done a lot of things with her.

"Not just marriage, but marriage to Daisy," Eloise said with a frown. "No other girl can compare. She's the best."

"I like her," he said quietly. "Truly, I do. I don't wish to hurt her. That's why I want you to encourage her to move on. She needs to find a more suitable gentleman to marry. One who'll make her happy as I never can."

The fight seemed to drain out of his grandmother. "Oh, Gabriel," she said softly, "I wasn't born yesterday. There are sparks enough between the two of you to light the entire town on fire." She paused and pursed her lips once more. "Love is a rare and precious gift. Don't squander it. Indeed, I would urge you to act fast. Auguste Malinor has been quite attentive to her lately."

Not that sneaky worm. "I hadn't noticed."

"I've been watching them together. There's no fiery heat between them, not like you and Daisy."

He leaned closer. "I'm a rakehell, Grandmama. Sparking fires in women is what I do best. And since we're on the topic of fires and sparks, what were you thinking in lending Lady Forsythia's book to Daisy? The girl is a menace with those rules. She hasn't properly followed a single one."

His grandmother chuckled. "That's what makes her so delightful."

Hell, yes. But it isn't something one could ever admit to one's own grandmother.

"Daisy insists there is something noble in you," she said, her merriment suddenly fading. "What does she understand that we don't? When she looks at you, she doesn't see the debauched creature who offends everyone. She sees a man worthy of her love."

"No doubt that silly idea was put into her head by Lady Forsythia's book. Get it out of her hands before she causes irreparable harm to herself."

"Is that the reason for your visit?" She frowned at him. "To berate me for lending her the book?"

"No, sweetheart. I just wanted to see you before I left." He slapped his hands against his thighs and rose. "And now that I have, I believe it's time for me to go."

Her curls bobbed and a little *harrumph* escaped her lips. "So soon? You've just arrived."

"I love you, Eloise," he said, wanting their last moments to be tender, especially if this was to be their last meeting. He'd be off on his secret mission by tomorrow at the latest and wouldn't return until Napoleon was defeated. Death, if it came on this mission, would be swift and he was prepared for it.

However, lying to his family, agonizing over their hurt and disappointment, was an enduring scar that cut deep into his heart.

She reached out and gave him a fierce hug. "I love you, too. I'll never stop loving you, Gabriel."

"I know, sweetheart." He appreciated her words more than she would ever know. He'd tried to see his father before coming here and been curtly turned away. His father was still angry over his slight to the Fribble sisters.

Gabriel could have pushed his way in and confronted him, but there was nothing to be gained by it. He'd hurt his father too badly, broken too many promises to fix the situation in a matter of minutes.

He gave his grandmother a final, lingering embrace. *Stay strong for me, Eloise! Look after Daisy for me.*

She gazed at him as he drew away, and suddenly appeared quite distressed. She placed a hand over her heart. "Dearest, you must be very careful on this hunt. I held you just now and had a vision of you swathed in black. Veils of black. Gabriel, I saw death all about you."

Damn it. He wasn't the superstitious sort and his grandmother was never known to have the "gift" of foresight. "You mustn't let it upset you. We're going off on a hunt, so we're bound to kill a few game birds."

She cast him a pensive frown. "No, these were men I saw around you."

He bent down and kissed her on the forehead. "I've dealt with jealous husbands before and survived. You must have eaten a bad kipper for breakfast."

"I had eggs." Her frown deepened.

He shook his head and drew away. "Watch out for those runny eggs. Farewell, Eloise."

THE SKY HAD turned from cloudless blue to ominous gray, Gabriel realized as he strode down the steps of his grandmother's townhouse a short while later. A groom rushed forward, leading Goliath. He thanked the lad and mounted.

"Wind's picking up, old boy," he said, patting the stallion's neck and glancing up at the approaching wall of gray clouds. "But I don't think it will rain. Sun will come out again within the hour, I'll wager." He'd just turned onto Chipping Way when he heard shouts coming from next door. *Hell in a handbasket.* The Farthingale residence.

He looked up when a young, female voice cried out, "Up there!"

He glanced among the leafless branches of the towering oak which stood in the Farthingale's front garden and saw little Harry making his way up to the very top. "Harry!"

Eloise had just sensed death.

It wasn't going to be that little boy's death.

He drew up Goliath, leaped the stone fence, and rushed toward the tree. The twins and several children and their nannies were gathered under it, most of the children crying.

"Daisy's climbed up after him," Lily said as he reached her side.

He flung off his jacket and tossed it to the ground.

It damn well wasn't going to be Daisy's death either.

He saw that she was already halfway up the tree, her gown hiked up to her knees and her shoes off, leaving her only in her stocking feet. He swung onto the first branch and continued upward, quickly reaching Daisy, who was now having difficulty making her way up the smaller branches because her stockings were catching on the tree bark. "I'll get him. Climb down, Daisy. It isn't safe up here."

She smiled in surprise. "What are you doing here? I mean on Chipping Way, not in this tree."

"Visiting Eloise. I was riding home when I heard the children's shouts." He put his arm around her waist, preparing to ease past her. A damp wind rustled through the branches and carried the apple-sweet scent of Daisy on its steady gusts. "Let me get Harry."

"No, these smaller branches will break under your weight." She refused to let him pass, so they momentarily remained pressed against each other, each stubbornly determined to take the lead and wait for the other to give in. "Let me do it," she insisted.

He would have been happy to spend the rest of the afternoon in this position, Daisy's soft body molding to his hard muscle, but Harry was in danger and this was no time for argument. Daisy was right. Those slender branches would crack under his weight. What if they couldn't hold her weight either? "I'll stay close as I can to catch you if you lose your footing."

"But—"

"I'm not about to let you or Harry fall. We'll work together. Let me hold you while you try to reach the boy."

"Work together?" She cast him another of her soft, Daisy smiles. "I like the idea. In truth, I'm glad you're here. I'm never scared when you're beside me."

He didn't know what to say, so he kissed her on the nose. "Start climbing."

"I suppose I shouldn't have admitted that to you. Lady Forsythia's rules specifically forbid a young lady from revealing her feelings to the rake in question." She stepped up to a higher branch so that her breasts were aligned with his mouth. He had only to tip his head forward and— "I suppose I shouldn't have admitted that I love you, either. I've decided not to take it back. I'm not sorry that I love you, Gabriel."

She climbed higher still so that the junction of her thighs was now aligned with his mouth. He refused to consider the possibilities. Then she accidentally knocked him in the teeth with her knee, a punishment he heartily deserved because he *was* thinking of all he would do if he ever got her naked with his head between her thighs.

Lord, he couldn't help himself.

He wasn't a eunuch, nor was he dead as mutton.

"Gabriel, I'm sorry! Did I hurt you? I'm not quite as steady as I hoped to be. I'm worried about Harry. What if he falls?"

"He won't," Gabriel said with an authority he did not feel. Harry was so young, hardly more than a baby. How could his little hands clasp those branches?

Daisy continued to chatter.

Gabriel realized it was her way of relieving her own fears. She began to rattle on about Lady Forsythia's book again. "So if a young lady is not permitted to express her true feelings, then how is the rake to know that she likes him? You see, Lady Forsythia's rules really make no sense."

He muttered something in agreement and placed his hands on Daisy's waist to lift her higher still. She stopped talking when she reached those perilously thin branches, now busy concentrating on saving the boy.

"Harry," she called out, her voice deceptively calm as she edged closer, "wait right there. Don't move."

The boy began to cry. "Too far!"

"I know. Take my hand, little muffin. Hold on to me." Her voice trembled and Gabriel knew that she was struggling to hold back tears. He also knew that she'd never allow herself to cry until the danger had passed, until Harry was safely on the ground.

"No!" the boy wailed and scooted higher. "Too far! Too far!"

Gabriel hoisted Daisy onto his shoulders, providing a sturdier foothold than those offered by the delicate branches. Indeed, those thin upper branches were barely capable of holding Harry's weight.

He hoped the boy wouldn't make a sudden move.

Daisy tried once more to coax the boy down. "Hold still and look at me, Harry. I'm almost there."

"Want to go higher!"

"It isn't safe, muffin. Don't move. Just look at me. Shall I sing you a song?" She reached out, but he was ever so slightly out of her grasp. "What song would you like to hear?"

"No... want Papa!"

"Your Papa had a favorite song. Take my hand and I'll sing it for you," she said, glancing downward and suddenly losing her footing. She let out a soft cry as she slipped off Gabriel's shoulders.

"Daisy!" He caught her as she was about to tumble out of the

178 | MEARA PLATT

tree, and with his own heart now pounding wildly, he drew her close and swallowed her in his arms. He felt the savage beat of her own heart as she clung to him. "Don't ever do that again."

She let out a short, tremulous laugh. "I'll try not to." She took several calming breaths. "I almost had him. Lift me up. I'll get him this time."

He glanced at Harry, saw that the boy was afraid and desperately clinging to the thin branches. "There's no time to lose," he said with a nod. "Be careful, Daisy."

Her hands were cold and shaking as they clasped his. "I will. I promise."

She balanced her weight on his shoulders when he lifted her above him, and grabbed one of the sturdier branches. Once her hold was secure, she reached out to Harry and cried out in elation when she managed to catch his hand. "I have him!"

But as she circled her arm around the boy to draw him closer, the boy began to struggle and squirm. "No! No! Want Papa!"

"Gabriel! He's slipping! I can't hold him!"

"Harry, stop that at once!" he commanded in a booming tone of authority that he hoped would work as well on children as it did on disciplined soldiers. To his surprise—and immense relief—Harry did as ordered.

However, unlike trained soldiers, the boy was undisciplined and his obedience would only last a moment. Fortunately, Daisy moved quickly to secure Harry in her grasp. "You're brilliant," she said in a whisper, handing the boy safely into his outstretched arms.

He tucked the boy in one arm and helped her onto the sturdy branch upon which he stood. "Tell me that again once we're safely on the ground."

She cast him the sweetest smile and kissed him on the cheek. "Sorry, my lips slipped."

He returned her kiss with a thorough one of his own, pressing his lips against her slightly open mouth and not ending it until Harry began to slap his nose. Only then did he ease back with a grin. "Sorry, mine too."

Daisy's face was a delightful shade of crimson.

He heard the twins giggling and cheering down below and heard a chorus of gasps from the nannies, who were no doubt shocked by his behavior. He expected they were relieved as well. After all, those nannies were charged with the care of the children. "Can you make it down on your own, Daisy?"

She nodded, smiling at him again.

He struggled to ignore the ache she roused in his heart. How many of Lady Forsythia's rules had she broken in the last five minutes? Never climb a tree. Never risk your life to save a child stuck in a tree. Never kiss a rakehell in a tree.

Never kiss a rakehell under any circumstances.

He held her back a moment to kiss her again. *The hell with rules.* "Not sorry for this kiss. My lips didn't slip. I meant to do it. You were the brilliant one."

She rested her head against his chest and laughed. "We'd better get off this tree before we give our audience more of a show than anyone bargained for."

Gabriel climbed down first, the boy now clinging tightly to his neck. Once on the ground, Harry continued to cling to his shoulders and began to sob against his shirt. "I want my Papa. Papa! Up there! Up there!" He tearfully pointed toward heaven.

Gabriel hugged the boy, hoping to soothe him, but it was to no avail. "Harry, you can't reach him by climbing a tree. It's too dangerous. Your papa would never want you to get hurt, but he knows how important it is for you to see him. Do you wish to see him?"

The boy's eyes rounded in astonishment... and hope. For that reason, Gabriel had to be very careful about what he said next. "There's a place, one place that's very special to your papa. It isn't far from here. I'll take you there if your mama will give me permission."

The boy nodded.

"And when you're in this special place, you'll find him looking back at you. And if you want to hear him, all you have to do is close your eyes and listen very carefully. Do you think you can do that?"

The boy nodded again.

"Because if you close your eyes and listen, you'll be able to hear your papa right here." He pointed to the boy's heart and tapped it gently.

Harry shut his eyes tight, then pounded on Gabriel's heart before opening his tear-filled eyes and smiling.

"There's a good lad."

The small crowd around him had turned silent as he spoke to Harry, but when the boy smiled at Gabriel and began to giggle, Dillie stepped forward and offered to take him from Gabriel's arms. Harry wouldn't let go. "No! Very thpecial! Want to go!"

"Go where?" Lily asked.

"Thpecial," Harry said.

Dillie stepped back with a sigh. "He's stuck to you like a barnacle to the keel of a frigate. No one's prying him out of your arms."

He glanced up to see how Daisy was doing and saw that she was still struggling with her gown entangled in the branches. Fortunately, she had made her way onto the lower branches so she was in no real danger even if she slipped. "You girls will have to help your sister down."

They laughed.

"She doesn't need our help," Dillie said.

He frowned and was about to insist when Daisy swung down from the tree, landing as gracefully as a gentle swan gliding onto a crystal lake.

She knelt to put on her slippers, then rose and smoothed out her gown.

"Well done," he was about to say, but was drowned out by a string of hysterical female shrieks.

"Daisy! This is all your fault!" Julia cried, leading an assortment of female relatives in a cavalry charge out of the house. The Farthingale men followed close behind.

Gabriel recognized Julia, and Daisy's uncle George, and her parents, but he hadn't been introduced to the other Farthingales and had no idea whom most of them were. No matter, they had no right to be scowling at Daisy.

Julia spoke up first, her angry gaze trained on Daisy. "I warned you about putting dangerous ideas into Harry's head."

"Foolish ideas," another elderly women muttered and others agreed.

"He's just a child and could have died falling out of that tree," Julia declared with a theatrical wave of her scented handkerchief.

Gabriel's heart tightened. *Damn them all.* Daisy was the only one who understood Harry's anguish, the only one who'd tried to fix the problem. She deserved their praise and commendations, not a public scolding.

He moved protectively to her side.

She gazed at him, startled. "My family won't hurt me."

Perhaps not physically, but their words could be as wounding. He saw the pain reflected in her beautiful eyes whenever she looked at her parents and met with their disappointed gazes.

"Gabriel's right," Lily said as she and the children gathered to her side. "It's time we all took a stand on Harry's behalf. He's been neglected far too long."

"Yes, far too long," Dillie said, curling her hands into fists.

Daisy sighed. "Honestly, you'd think we were about to battle Huns."

"Sometimes this family can be worse than Huns," Lily muttered.

Julia reached for her son to tug him out of Gabriel's arms, but the boy refused to be drawn out. "No! Want Papa! Papa!"

"He isn't your papa," Julia insisted, reaching for him again.

"No! Take me to Papa! Papa!" He pointed to his heart.

Julia began to cry.

"This is your fault, Daisy. *He* wouldn't be here if it weren't for you," Daisy's mother said, holding back her own sniffles as she comforted Julia, but not before she shot Gabriel a glower.

Gabriel was used to such glares. Indeed, he'd endured far worse and would endure far more dangerous encounters within the next few months.

"Be thankful Lord Dayne was here," Daisy said, turning to point at the towering oak.

"Harry only climbed the tree because you told him Harrison was up in heaven," Julia hotly retorted.

"And you told him nothing," Lily answered in Daisy's defense. "The boy was terrified, confused, and crying out for answers. We all ignored him, except Daisy. You should be thanking her."

"Thanking her? When her inattention allowed him to climb up

there in the first place," one of the family members, a man the others referred to as Rupert, accused.

Gabriel struggled to contain his anger.

"It isn't Daisy's fault," young Charles said. "Harry was napping with Aunt Julia."

Julia took a step back. "What if he was? I had the door closed. I... I must have fallen asleep, but someone had to have let him out."

"Indeed," Daisy's mother said. "He couldn't have turned the knob all by himself. He isn't tall enough."

"I know how he did it!" Charles bounded into the house and ran back out moments later with an object in his hand. "He used this!"

Julia gasped. "What are you doing with my footstool?"

Daisy's father let out a weary sigh. "Now we know how he got out of Julia's room, but how did he make his way out of the house?"

Dillie stepped forward. "I might not have properly closed the front door. Lily and I, with the nannies, of course, took the other children out to play. We were running in and out of the house and..."

"The point is not to cast blame, but to attend to Harry's problem," Daisy said as Dillie's voice trailed. "Lord Dayne has a solution. I think you ought to listen to his idea."

"Thpecial place," Harry said, as though understanding the nature of the conversation and adding his opinion. "Want to go now."

Julia frowned. "What does that rakehell know about children? His talent is in breaking up families."

Daisy stepped forward with her fists clenched. "Julia! That's uncalled for."

"Indeed," Daisy's father said. "I think this... er, special place has merit. Would you care to tell us your idea, Lord Dayne?"

Daisy's mother appeared horrified. "John! You can't take his side! Hasn't Julia suffered enough?"

"This isn't about her suffering, Sophie," he said, his manner gentle as he spoke to his wife. "It's about Harry's. I think we've ignored the boy long enough. Go on, Lord Dayne. We're listening."

DAISY HAD NEVER visited Uncle Harrison's regimental headquarters before, though her father and Uncle George had often spoken of the place with pride. Gabriel also seemed familiar with the headquarters, which surprised her at first, but upon reflection she decided nothing about Gabriel surprised her.

"Will you look at this place," Lily said, enthralled as they entered the massive stone building near St. James's Palace.

Daisy, little Harry, and the twins had accompanied Gabriel and their Uncle George.

Julia refused to join them for fear of reviving too many painful memories.

To Daisy, entering the barracks was like entering a fortified castle complete with heavy iron gates and sentries standing on alert. Soldiers drilled in the courtyard, the metal of their sabers and belt buckles gleaming in the sun.

Daisy wrapped her cloak about Harry's little shoulders, for there was a slight chill to the air despite the sunshine. She hurried inside, keeping the boy securely in her arms. He appeared to be content but curious.

While Gabriel and her uncle spoke briefly with the commander, she and her sisters stood in the entry hall, passing time by peering out the windows and watching the soldiers as they continued their drill. Harry also looked on, fascinated by the display of military precision.

"I think we ought to purchase Harry his own set of tin soldiers," Dillie said in a whisper.

Daisy and Lily nodded in hearty agreement. "Ah, here come Gabriel and Uncle George."

Gabriel introduced them to Colonel Croft, the regimental commander, a gruff but jovial man. "I insist on giving you a personal tour. Especially you," he said, saluting young Harry.

The boy responded by tugging on his moustache.

After an exchange of pleasantries the commander escorted them on an extended tour, guiding them through the gate house, the mews, the dining hall, the chapel, several meeting rooms, the dungeon—fortunately, it was not occupied—and finally into a stately hall with dark oak paneling and dozens of paintings lining the walls. "I believe this is the room you had in mind, sir," the commander said to Gabriel.

Gabriel nodded.

Harry had taken it all in, as though understanding every word issuing from Colonel Croft's lips. Even now, as they walked through the portrait hall, his eyes were wide as saucers, taking in every detail, the large windows, the brightly polished dark wood, the decorative swords and shields hanging between portraits of the regiment's commanding officers.

"And now that we're here, you must excuse me for a moment," Colonel Croft said. "I'll return shortly."

While her sisters and her uncle lingered over the swords and shields, Daisy accompanied Gabriel to the far end of the hall, pausing before a portrait of her uncle, Harrison Farthingale.

"Painted shortly before the regiment shipped off to Spain one last time," Gabriel murmured, taking little Harry from her arms. Their hands touched as they made the exchange, and Gabriel, to her surprise, gave her hand a little squeeze.

It wasn't a flirtatious squeeze, just an acknowledgment of something special between them, almost a thank you for helping him unite father and son, though he'd managed that on his own. She had tried for months without success to make her family listen and had never thought to bring Harry to his father's regimental headquarters. Yet this place more than anywhere else captured Harrison's essence, his sense of honor and duty which extended beyond family, to king and country.

"That's your papa," Gabriel said to Harry, holding him in his arms with a casual ease that evoked a sigh from Daisy. There was something quite exquisite in the way he held the child, quite caring and fatherly.

The loss of Harrison Farthingale had struck their family hard. They'd all mourned him, but watching Gabriel, the kindness and patience with which he dealt with little Harry, somehow eased that pain and simply conquered her heart. She turned away to wipe a stray tear from her eye before it fell upon her cheek. If one tear fell, she knew others would follow in a pitiful, gushing stream. She refused to have Gabriel think of her as a blubbering ninny.

"Take a long look at him," Gabriel said to Harry, but he spared her a concerned glance. "Do you see how he's smiling at you?"

As Harry nodded, Colonel Croft returned with a box in hand. "Here it is, Lord Dayne. The medal and ribbons you requested."

Daisy stared at Gabriel in confusion. "Medal and ribbons?"

He nodded and opened the box with one hand, dug out an ornate gold cross hanging on a red ribbon, and handed it to her. "A replica of the Cross of St. George, the regiment's highest award for valor. It was awarded to Harrison on one of the early Peninsular campaigns."

She stared at her uncle's portrait, then turned back to the medal. Julia had the original safely under lock and key at their townhouse, for the medal had jewels encrusted on it, several diamonds among rows of smaller sapphires. A drawing of it was pinned to her uncle's chest in the portrait.

"Harry's too young to be entrusted with the real one," Gabriel said as she continued to stare at the portrait. "Your aunt will keep it safe until he comes of age."

In the meantime, the lad would have the replica to wear. She ought to have thought of it herself. Indeed, why hadn't her father or Uncle George considered it? She glanced down the hall to where her uncle stood with her sisters and caught him looking back. His remorseful gaze spoke volumes. In truth, she expected that Julia, her parents, and the rest of the Farthingale elders were feeling quite ashamed for their dismissal of little Harry and his loss.

Gabriel tweaked the boy's chin. "See, Harry. Just like your father's."

The boy looked at his medal, then up at his father's portrait and the one displayed on his chest. His face lit up with the brightest smile. "Just yike Papa's."

Daisy chuckled. "Yes, just like your papa's."

She turned to Gabriel, now hopelessly in love with him, and wishing he felt the same about her. Of course, that would take a miracle, especially since she'd botched every one of Lady Forsythia's rules.

"I don't know what to say, or how to thank you," she said, a little breathless and quite in awe. He'd known exactly what to do, had thought of everything short of returning Uncle Harrison to them.

Not even Gabriel could accomplish that feat. But as he stood beside her, she felt his warmth, his reassuring presence, and almost believed him capable of performing miracles.

"You would have done the same," he mumbled and walked back to the twins and George with Harry safely tucked in his arms.

She stared at his retreating back, her mouth open in surprise, for he seemed decidedly embarrassed by the compliment. She felt another tug at her heart. Indeed, she was in danger of falling ridiculously and deeply in love with him. *More* in love with him than she already was.

"Didn't know Lord Dayne had it in him," Colonel Croft said, standing beside her and watching Gabriel, "what with his wretched reputation. I suppose there's good in everyone. Sometimes you have to look very hard."

No, Daisy thought in despair. His valor was there for all to see, but those looking were simply too blind to notice.

Gabriel was a hero.

An English hero, not a blackguard or a scoundrel. Not a smuggler, or gambler, and certainly not spying for the French.

Problem was, he refused to be her hero.

CHAPTER 15

*In a dire situation, a lady must defer to the
authority of a gentleman, even if the
gentleman is a rake.*

"DAISY, WHAT'S TAKING you so long?"

"I'll be right down, Mother," she said, hastening to dress for the afternoon jaunt she'd agreed to take with Julia. More precisely, she had been invited by Julia to ride in Hyde Park in order to be "seen" by all the right people. Unlike her gloriously free and unfettered morning jaunts on Brutus, this afternoon's excursion was crafted with the strategy of a Wellington battle plan, the objective to show her off to greatest advantage.

Having been exonerated of wrongdoing with respect to the Harry incident, and thanked by her parents upon returning from the regimental headquarters, she was quite pleased with the way everything was turning out. Even the sun continued to shine brightly and the air had warmed, making for an unusually lovely day.

Julia had apologized to her and extended the invitation to ride, a generous peace offering, so they were off to the park, happily reconciled and in search of husbands. Not that she had any interest in finding a husband. She'd found the man for her, chosen by his charming but interfering grandmother, who had given her a book on how to reform his wicked ways.

She let out a dejected sigh, knowing she was incapable of

reforming anyone, least of all Gabriel. Quite the opposite, she was likely to end up as another of his conquests. She *hoped* for it, wanted to be thoroughly scandalized and ruined by him. He wouldn't do it, of course. He was too sensible.

She was the lovesick fool.

"Take the carriage," Uncle Rupert advised as she passed him on the stairs. Even now, the elders were interjecting their opinions on whether she and Julia ought to be riding.

"A stroll along the Ladies' Mile is just the thing," Aunt Eunice vociferously insisted.

Daisy had no say, no one believing it relevant that *she* was the one going to the park and might perhaps have a preference, or wish to express it. But no, such decisions were made by committee, every adult member of the Farthingale clan convinced that his or her opinion was of vital importance and had to be expressed no matter how unwanted or inane. To question the family's decisions was unheard of and a waste of breath, Daisy had long ago learned.

She'd obediently donned her new riding habit of dark blue velvet and polished boots of finest black leather, cutting a fine figure (if she did say so herself) as she pranced down the stairs, because she wasn't going to stroll or take the carriage, no matter what the elders decided. She enjoyed riding and that's what she was going to do.

Her mother cast her a warm, doting smile. "Don't you look pretty, dear."

"I've ordered Amos to saddle Bessie for you," her father said, casting her a stern glance because he would not allow any Farthingale female, certainly not one of his dainty daughters, to tear through the park like a hellion on horseback. The way he studied her, Daisy was certain he suspected that she had crept out of the house this morning to ride Brutus and was now punishing her for it.

She let out a groan. "No, Papa. Not her!" Bessie was a lovely old mare, barely capable of walking, much less breaking into a gallop. Little Harry could toddle faster than the docile mare could trot.

"You'll ride Bessie. I'll hear no more about it!" And whenever her father used that expression and in just that tone there was no changing his opinion.

Crumpets, as the twins would say!

Daisy smothered her annoyance and walked toward the mews where Julia awaited her, now friends again. Daisy had readily forgiven her for her harsh accusations, relieved to move on now that Harry seemed to be feeling better. Julia appeared contrite and eager to move on as well.

Daisy came upon her fussing with the skirt of her emerald green riding habit, busily draping it across the rump of her roan filly to create the unstudied effect of a lavish, green wave. The filly, a frisky animal by the name of Windy, refused to cooperate, each time knocking the expensive fabric off her rump with a flick of her tail.

"Oh, bother! I shall die an old maid," Julia muttered, overlooking the fact that she had been married and produced an adorable child.

The remark required no response, so Daisy wisely chose to keep her mouth shut and not comment. Instead, she concentrated on the horses. Windy pranced and skittered in front of the stable, a sharp contrast to good old Bessie, whose joints creaked as she hesitantly crawled out of her stall, coaxed into the sunshine by Amos.

"You be careful with her, Miss Daisy. She's a frail little thing."

"I will." She cast him an assuring smile, knowing he had a soft spot for the old mare. Although Amos was as big and strong as an oak tree, he would weep like a baby if any harm befell the gentle horse.

She supposed it was for the best that she'd been given Bessie. After all, she'd had a busy day, first riding Brutus, then saving Harry and visiting the regimental quarters, and now going for a ride with Julia. Tonight they were expected to attend Lady Baldridge's musicale. Indeed, it was to be a long day, but if she found herself yawning, she'd settle in a dark, quiet corner as soon as the recital started and nap through it.

"I wonder whom we'll meet," Julia remarked with a surprisingly girlish squeal as they made their way to the park with Amos and another of the household retainers following at a discreet distance.

Daisy wished she could be as excited and filled with innocent hope, but her heart had spoken and she wasn't ready to dismiss the man it had chosen. It mattered little that the man in question was doing his best to avoid commitment.

"Well? What do you think?" Julia asked after they'd exchanged greetings with several riders as they entered the park.

Daisy turned to Julia. "Of what?"

"Those gentlemen we just passed."

Daisy could not help but roll her eyes. "Lord Wilsey is arrogant and without good cause. Lord Armbrewster is a sot and Lord Henley has bad teeth."

Julia surprised her by agreeing.

"He looks promising," Julia said a moment later, discreetly pointing to an elegantly dressed gentleman riding toward them. "He's six thousand a year."

"Hello, Lord Six-Thousand-a-Year," she jokingly muttered before he was close enough to hear her, referring to him as Julia had, by wealth and not by name. "Oh, there goes Lord Flat-Broke."

Julia cast her a light frown. "Honestly, Daisy. Marriage is a serious business. You would do well to encourage the suitable young men who've shown interest in you. Auguste Malinor, for one. We've all noticed how attentive he's been to you lately."

A hot blush crept into Daisy's cheeks. "I know, but there's something about him that puts me off." She wondered whether to confide in Julia that he seemed to have a roving eye and she sensed he would not be faithful in their marriage, assuming he ever would consider marriage to her, which she doubted. Curiously, she thought Gabriel would be faithful, for everyone knew that reformed rakes made the best husbands, or so it said in Lady Forsythia's book.

"I was fortunate the first time," Julia admitted. "Harrison was a good man and I loved him dearly, but marriage is a mercenary business. Women don't have the ability to make their own fortunes, so they must marry well. Why don't you like Auguste? He seems quite charming."

"He's a little intimidating, I suppose." So was Gabriel, but not in the same way. What was it about Gabriel that set her heart aflutter? And why couldn't Auguste evoke even a blush from her? He was handsome and clever, and he hadn't really done anything wrong. True, he had gone into the garden with another woman, but he was still free to do so. The true test would come once he declared for her. She silently berated herself. His sort did not propose marriage to daughters of merchants, not even wealthy merchants.

"You needn't be in love with Auguste to marry him," Julia said, interrupting her thoughts. "The Malinors are among England's most prominent families. Auguste is a viscount in his own right and will inherit the vast earldom upon his father's death."

Daisy's thoughts drifted once more as Julia droned on about convenient marital arrangements and discreet understandings, none of which held any appeal for her. She was going to marry for love and would settle for nothing less.

"... though you're not nearly as clever as Lily," Julia remarked, regaining her attention. "You'd find a way to coax a marriage proposal out of young Lord Malinor if you really tried."

She shook her head and laughed. "Julia, I'm not an idiot."

"Of course you're not. I never said any such thing." She drew up her mount and paused to study Daisy, finally giving a nod of approval. "You have a natural beauty and a genuine sincerity that men find quite attractive. Thank goodness you're nothing like that bluestocking sister of yours. Few men will want Lily, for the brain on that girl is intimidating. She'll probably die an old maid surrounded by her books. But, as I said, you are nothing like your sister and have great possibilities."

"Oh, that makes me so feel much better." She laughed again, amazed by her aunt's ability to insult her and Lily in the same breath. Lily was too brilliant to attract a man and she, Daisy, was too empty headed. She understood that Julia did not mean to insult her. She loved the woman, but often found her exasperating, as she was now.

"And if you don't wish to pursue young Malinor, then consider Lord Six-Thousand-a-Year. He'll make you far happier than Lord Dayne ever could. You must keep away from that scoundrel. He's no good. He'll only hurt you, Daisy. You deserve far better."

"How can you say that after all he's done for Harry?"

Julia pursed her lips and raised her chin daintily in the air. "He humiliated me in front of my own son, in front of my entire family."

Obviously, that remained a sore spot for her aunt. "He didn't, but even if he had—which he didn't—can't you see the wonderful change in Harry?"

Her chin tipped higher. "No, I can't. Harry's always been

wonderful and that hasn't changed."

Daisy let out a resigned sigh. No amount of logic or reasoning would alter Julia's resentment toward Gabriel.

Their horses hadn't gone more than a few steps further before Julia suddenly reined in her mount and let out a soft cry of delight. "There's Auguste Malinor and he's riding toward us. Here's your chance, my girl. I wonder if his father is here, too." She craned her neck to get a better view, then let out a *huff*. "Oh, drat. I don't see him."

Daisy couldn't imagine the elder Lord Malinor fitting his rotund frame upon a horse. His jowls would bounce about like soft pudding. However, Auguste cut a trim, striking figure in his black riding jacket and buff breaches. He sat astride an enormous gray gelding, exuding confidence and authority.

"Good afternoon, Lord Malinor." Julia sat a little straighter in her saddle as she greeted him.

"Good afternoon, Mrs. Farthingale." He nodded to Julia, then allowed his gaze to drift to Daisy, one eyebrow tilting up in mockery as he noticed her poor little mare. He smiled, revealing a row of perfect white teeth. "Miss Farthingale. What a pleasant surprise. Then again, I shouldn't be surprised to see you here since you're known to be an excellent rider. But your riding tends to take place in the early morning I understand."

A tingle of unease crawled up Daisy's neck. "I help my sister out with her horses on occasion, if that's what you mean."

His smile seemed frozen on his face and she felt its coldness. "Very thoughtful of you to lend her a hand."

"She appreciates the assistance," Daisy replied, wondering at his comments. He had no right to berate her for taking Brutus through his paces this morning. And how did he learn of it anyway?

"I have no doubt. Family loyalty is an honorable trait."

"We're a large, but very close family," Julia interjected. "We're all loyal to each other, even those who *marry* in."

She'd stressed the word "marry."

"And what of your sister, Miss Farthingale? Does her loyalty lie with her family or Lord Graelem's family?"

"I should think both."

Once again, he arched a dark eyebrow. "Both?"

Daisy did not care for his manner. "My lord, are you suggesting there is a reason for her to choose sides? If so, which side must she choose? Pray enlighten us, for you seem to have a point to your comments."

"Forgive me," he said, his gaze now lowering to her hands, which were now curled into fists on Bessie's reins. "I don't mean to suggest there is a conflict, although it is common knowledge that not every male in the Dayne family has turned out quite as well as hoped."

"You mustn't believe all the gossip you hear." She silently counted to ten to restrain her temper, which was about to erupt with volcanic force. This conversation was beginning to feel like an interrogation and she wished to put an end to it before she damaged his delicate nasal cavities with her fist.

"It is fact, not gossip, Miss Farthingale. Gabriel Dayne is a dangerous man."

Bloodying one young lord's nose might be overlooked, but bloodying two young lords was certain to have her banned from society. No one wanted an ill-bred, slightly tarnished hellion in their midst. Not that she cared, but her family had gone to great expense on her behalf and she did not wish to disappoint them more than she already had.

"Aren't all men dangerous?" Julia chimed in with a merry laugh, obviously trying to lighten the conversation. "And is that not why well-bred young ladies are under constant watch by their chaperones? The Daynes are an honorable family, as are the Farthingales. What Daisy means to say is that there isn't likely to be a conflict. Of course, she understands that a wife's duty is to her husband. Isn't that right, Daisy?"

She was spared the need to respond—neither Julia nor Auguste would have liked her response anyway—by the timely appearance of Lord Lumley Hornby, he of the delicate nose. Daisy winced, for his nose was still red and more than a little swollen. Perhaps she had struck him harder than she'd realized.

Wishing to make amends, she tossed him an overly cheerful smile. "Lord Hornby, how nice to see you." Of course, the incident had been his fault. He shouldn't have tried to kiss her beside his gherkins... nor should Gabriel have kissed her, for that matter, but she'd been the one eager to kiss *him*, not the other way around, so it wasn't at all the same thing. Was it?

"*Harumph, grumph,*" was all Lumley said, followed by a frosty stare. Obviously, he was still angry over their last encounter. Would he ever forgive her?

He was far more polite when greeting Auguste, and practically tripping over his tongue in raptures the moment his gaze fell on Julia. One would think he was a man dying of thirst and she was his cool drink of lemonade. He continued to lavish compliments on Julia until Daisy wanted to put her finger in her mouth and make gagging sounds.

Point made, you muggins. You like her, hate me.

Julia did not look *that* exquisite in her dark green riding habit. And her gold hair, though pretty, did *not* match the brilliance of the sun.

Never one to resist flattery, Julia fell into animated conversation with the young lord. Or as Julia might call him, Lord Five-Thousand-a-Year.

Daisy stifled a chuckle. Having been rebuffed by her, was Lumley now considering Julia as a prospective wife? And—*gasp*—was Julia seriously considering him as husband material?

Her aunt and Lumley rode ahead, forcing her to lag behind with Auguste.

She and Auguste also made an odd-looking couple, she decided, he on his muscled gray and she on the creaking Bessie, but she was determined to make the best of it, so she tried to turn the conversation to something light and inconsequential. "Nothing like a clear blue sky to cheer up the day."

"Makes for excellent traveling weather. I hear some of your friends are planning a trip."

"My friends?" Goodness, had he taken lessons in the art of conversation from the Spanish Inquisitor himself, Torquemada?

"Lord Dayne, for one."

She reined in Bessie and cast him a scowl. "Lord Dayne, again. I wouldn't know about his plans. Indeed, I hardly know him."

Which was the truth. She knew very little about Gabriel, though not from lack of trying.

"Ah, then I'm mistaken. I thought you and he were on quite friendly terms, Miss Farthingale."

"I'm quite good friends with his grandmother," she corrected. "And as you know, his cousin is married to my sister. For that reason alone, we meet on occasion."

"Then you won't mind if I repeat my warning. He is a dangerous man."

"I should think it beneath you to engage in malicious gossip."

"The whispers about him are true." Auguste suddenly grabbed her elbow and drew her closer. "Just a few hours ago," he said, his voice cold and menacing, "Lord Dayne had a row with Wellington and," he glanced about before leaning forward to speak in her ear, "insulted the Prince Regent. No one knows quite what it was about, but I have it on good authority that they fought quite bitterly."

Daisy frowned. "Whose authority? Your father's?"

"I'm not at liberty to reveal my sources, but it is someone in a position to know. Anyone who associates with that scoundrel now will be tainted by his reputation."

Something she could ill afford if she was ever to get back in her family's good graces. Obviously, Auguste was trying to protect her, though she cared little for the manner in which he sought to accomplish it. "I'll keep it in mind. Truly, I will," she said with more sincerity than she felt. "Thank you, my lord."

His lips curled in a smile. It wasn't a soft smile, for there really wasn't anything soft about Auguste. He was all hard, calculating angles.

As they continued together, Daisy attempted to learn more about him, to give him a chance to dispel her unfavorable impression of him, but with each passing phaeton and carriage, his condescension, not only toward Gabriel, but toward almost every member of respectable society encountered during their ride, became quite evident.

The man was insufferable.

Daisy took the opportunity to rejoin Julia and Lumley when Auguste was momentarily trapped in conversation with the dowager Duchess Langwell, a long-time friend of the Malinor family and a woman too powerfully connected for him to ignore.

However, the conversation between her aunt and he-of-the-swollen-nasal-cavities was equally uninspired. In truth, it was painfully awkward. While Lumley's attention was openly fixed on Julia, she was droning on about the elder Lord Malinor.

"Yes, I'm sure simply *everyone* will be out this afternoon," Lumley agreed, "even *him*."

It was no secret that the elder Malinor had been exceptionally attentive to her aunt these past few days. While Daisy wasn't keen on him as a prospect for Julia, she wasn't about to discourage her aunt, either. The man was wealthy and influential, able to offer Julia a very good life and many advantages for young Harry.

Indeed, Lord Malinor might prove a good mentor for Harry. But Lumley, despite being a bit of a dolt, had a kinder disposition and would offer her his heart.

Lord Malinor finally did make his appearance, a spectacular one at that, driving a magnificent yellow phaeton that had all in the park gawking as he passed. He drew up the reins to stop beside them, eliciting a squeal of delight from Julia. Lumley's expression turned unmistakably glum. Daisy almost felt sorry for the young lord, for he was on the whole a decent fellow, just dull and predictable, certainly no competition for the prominent elder Malinor.

Once again, Daisy's attention lagged as they exchanged pleasantries. She strained in her saddle to peer beyond Lord Malinor's carriage as a rider in the distance caught her notice. Was that Gabriel astride Goliath? Yes, it was, and he was talking to a young woman seated in a sleek carriage. Daisy eased back, hoping for a better view of the woman.

Her heart sank into her stomach.

Gabriel's companion was the merry widow, Lady Olivia Westhaven, and the two of them engrossed in conversation, though one could hardly call Lady Olivia's leaning out of her carriage and jiggling her large breasts in front of Gabriel a civilized form of conversation.

Daisy refused to acknowledge the sudden lump in her throat.

"My dear," Lord Malinor said, startling her out of her thoughts, "would you care to join me for a ride?" He loosened his grasp on the reins of his pair of matched grays and reached down to offer her a hand. "You can tell me all about my son. I hope he has been treating you well."

"He is a perfect gentleman," she said smoothly, although he wasn't really. Auguste was still insufferable, but at the moment she was quite put out with Gabriel. The cur was openly ogling Lady Westhaven's still-bouncing breasts.

Would those things never stop jiggling?

"Miss Farthingale?" Lord Malinor held out his hand to help her onto his splendid conveyance.

Having no desire to hurt Julia's feelings, she politely declined.

"Don't be shy, my dear. The view's wonderful from up here. One can see everything going on in the park. The phaeton's new, just delivered today. Paint's hardly dry on the door." He pointed to the family crest, two maces across the bloody head of a boar. Unfortunately, there was a startling resemblance between Lord Malinor and that boar. "Here, take my hand, my girl. I'll help you to climb up."

Daisy smothered her annoyance at his persistence. Not even the possibility of stealing a better glance at Gabriel and his merry widow could tempt her to accept. To make matters worse, Julia appeared distraught. She had wanted to be invited first, and despite all, Daisy loved Julia and would never do anything to hurt her feelings.

She spared another glance at Julia, saw that her lips were quivering and there was pain evident in her glistening eyes. Daisy wished Julia was pitching daggers at her instead, for anger was so much easier to dismiss than anguish. Why had Lord Malinor invited her first, anyway? Did he have a particular motive? "Very well, you've convinced us, my lord. Julia, won't that be fun? You go first and I'll go next. I'll wait right here while you take your turn. How kind of you, Lord Malinor." She tugged old Bessie's reins and the horse responded by backing away two steps, just out of reach of his pudgy, outstretched hand.

"Indeed," he said with a smile that didn't quite reach his eyes.

Julia, now beaming, dropped her mount's reins into Lumley's hands without a moment of hesitation and hopped up beside the elder Malinor.

Daisy sighed. She had appeased Julia, but crushed Lumley. She almost felt sorry for him, recognizing his look of unrequited adoration. She'd felt much the same about Gabriel.

Whatever Lord Malinor's intention, he recovered well and smiled at Julia. "You're looking well, Mrs. Farthingale. We'll take a quick turn, if you don't mind, for I have very little time to spare. Caught up in pressing business these days."

"I don't have a head for business. Thank goodness this country has competent men such as you to guide us." Julia batted her eyelashes, looking every bit the helpless widow. Daisy stifled a laugh. Her aunt could count up a row of columns faster than any man alive, and Lord Malinor, also known as Lord Forty-Thousand-a-Year, had lots of shillings to count.

"I would consider it an honor to guide you in your personal affairs," Lord Malinor responded warmly, "should the need ever arise. You have only to ask, my dear."

"As would I," Lumley interjected. "You... er, can ask me too."

Poor Lumley, he was an earnest dolt. What chance did he have against Lord Malinor, England's finance minister?

"Will you be attending Lady Baldridge's musicale this evening?" Lord Malinor asked Daisy, on the surface appearing to include her once more in the conversation, but she couldn't get over the feeling he had an ulterior purpose.

"Indeed, my lord. I hear her daughter, Elspeth, is an accomplished harpist and will regale us with ancient Celtic tunes."

"Surely she's not as accomplished as you. I'm told you have a lovely singing voice. I hope you'll grace us with a song or two."

"My talent is adequate, at best," she said with a chuckle. He'd confused her with her sister, Dillie, who had the voice of an angel.

"Ah, you're beautiful and modest. No wonder my son—" He broke off sharply and gazed in the distance. "Devil take it, what's he doing here?"

Daisy followed his gaze and saw Gabriel riding toward them. Having obviously accomplished his business with Lady Westhaven, he had murder in his eye. *Oh, dear.* He was glowering at the Malinors. She'd never seen him look so cold and determined before.

"This doesn't bode well," she muttered under her breath.

"Changed your mind yet, Dayne?" Lord Malinor asked curtly.

"No."

"Then we have nothing more to say to each other." Lord Malinor tightened the reins in his hands, preparing to move his matched grays along. "My apologies, Mrs. Farthingale. We'll have that ride another time. I must leave you now, but look forward to seeing you and Daisy this evening. Come away, Auguste. The air has suddenly turned unpleasantly foul."

Hiding her obvious disappointment, Julia accepted Lord Lumley's assistance in dismounting, though Lumley was bordering on euphoric now that she'd returned her attention to him.

"Changed your mind about what?" Daisy asked Gabriel as he reached her side, but Gabriel wasn't paying attention to her. "You were quite rude to the Malinors and you're being rude to me now. Gabriel, did you hear me?" She was about to repeat the question when he suddenly wrapped his arm about her waist and drew her onto his lap. "What are you —"

The protest caught in her throat as a shot rang out.

Daisy felt something whiz past her ear and heard Gabriel's soft grunt.

Julia screamed.

Another shot rang out, but she couldn't tell where it came from for Gabriel's body was over hers, and as she grabbed his arm, something warm and liquid dripped onto her fingers. "You've been hit!"

Gabriel whirled Goliath so that his body remained between her and the direction of those shots. "Hornby, take the ladies home. Now!"

"Gabriel, wait!" But he'd plunked her back on Bessie, determining the danger had passed, and he was off, leaving her to Lord Hornby and the two Farthingale footmen, who were now shielding her like a solid brick wall.

How badly was he hurt? Where was he going? He seemed to be riding toward Lord Malinor's phaeton, which had taken off the moment those shots were fired, but she couldn't be certain because Amos, the big ox, was in front of her, herding her out of the park.

At the Park Lane gate, staring straight at her as bold as you please, was Gabriel's ugly little man, the very man she'd spotted passing Gabriel a note at the Newton lecture and whom she thought she'd seen hiding in the Hastings garden. What was he doing in the park?

Had he fired those shots?

CHAPTER 16

A lady must never get her hands dirty.

"I PROMISED TO take you home," Lumley insisted when Daisy stopped in front of Laurel's townhouse. "Lord Dayne will have my guts for garters if I disobey."

"And I promised Laurel I'd visit her today," she retorted, her heart pounding through her ears. Gabriel's blood coated her fingers and some had dripped onto her riding habit. Not that she cared a whit. He was hurt and there was nothing she could do about it, but Graelem could help. He had to know what was going on. "Amos will remain with me. I'll be safe with him."

"Do as you please," Julia said, her gaze darting up and down the street, as though fearing the assailants were still after them, "but my nerves are frayed and I wish to go now."

"I'm certain the danger has passed. Those shots could not have been intended for us," Daisy assured her. "Who'd want to harm us?"

"I'm sure I don't know." Julia continued to gaze up and down the street.

Daisy turned to Lumley. "I'll be fine here. You had better take my aunt home."

He gave a sober nod. "Very well, but we'll wait until you're safely inside."

She handed Bessie's reins to Amos and then hurried into the house in search of Laurel, now feeling some remorse for almost breaking Lumley's nose. He seemed genuinely concerned for her and Julia.

Daisy found her sister curled in an oversized chair in the parlor, quietly reading beside the fireplace. "Laurel! Do you know why Lord Malinor is in a rage about Gabriel? And have you heard the latest rumors?"

Laurel glanced up, startled. She was about to reproach her for bursting into the room, then noticed the red stains on her palms and riding habit, and gasped. "Daisy! What's happened?"

"I'm sorry. I didn't mean to frighten you." She glanced at Laurel's swollen belly.

"My baby's fine." Laurel slammed her book shut, tossed it onto a nearby table, and awkwardly attempted to rise. "But you're not, you have blood on your hands!"

"It isn't mine." Daisy motioned her sister to remain in her chair. Laurel, who was the size of a small whale and quite ungainly in her condition, sank back without protest. Daisy took full advantage. "Where's Graelem? I need to speak to him."

"He isn't home. But I'm right here and you had better tell me everything. Now."

Daisy nodded and crossed to the bell pull to tug on it. "First let me ring for tea and a damp cloth to wipe my hands."

"And freshly made scones. You can eat while we talk. It will help to calm you down. You're as jumpy as a toad."

"You would be too if someone had taken a shot at you."

"What?" Laurel once again struggled to rise and Daisy once again motioned her back in her chair.

"Those fiends weren't trying to harm me." She quickly related all that had happened, starting with little Harry's climbing the tree, then their visit to the regimental headquarters, and finally her ride in the park with Julia and the shooting. As she finished, she pursed her lips and frowned. "In truth, I'm not quite certain who the fiends were aiming for. It could have been Lord Malinor. He's the most obvious target considering his rank and position in government."

Laurel nodded.

"But they shot Gabriel, grazed his arm as far as I can tell. He can't have been too badly wounded because he took off after Lord Malinor's phaeton... well, perhaps he took off after him. I can't be sure about that either. Amos, the big ox, blocked my view." She let out a resigned sigh. "That's why I need to know more about the ill feelings between Gabriel and Lord Malinor."

Laurel held her response as Billings, her elderly butler, scuttled in. She asked for refreshments and the damp cloth, then waited for him to bustle out before returning her attention to Daisy. She pursed her lips and frowned. "I wish I had answers to give you, but I haven't heard anything about bad blood between them." She glanced at Daisy's hands. "Sorry. I shouldn't have mentioned that word. Where is Billings with that cloth?"

It didn't take long for the efficient butler to return. Daisy quickly wiped her hands clean while Laurel poured a cup of tea for each of them. "Go on," Laurel urged when they were once more alone. "Tell me everything else that happened."

"There isn't much more to tell." Daisy's hands were cold and trembling, so she wrapped them around the teacup to warm them. "We were all in the park. Gabriel joined us. Someone took a shot—several, I think—possibly aimed at Lord Malinor, but Gabriel was hit."

Suddenly, there was a commotion at the door and on cue, as though she were in a sensational stage play, Gabriel strode in. His gaze instantly went to hers. "Damn it, Daisy. What are you doing here?"

"I might ask the same of you." But she rose and hurried to him, for he was clutching his arm and blood was running down his fingers. "Sit over here." She pointed to a footstool beside the fireplace. She then hurried out and ordered Billings to fetch a basin of water, more clean cloths, and a bottle of whiskey. "Not Lord Graelem's finest. Any will do. It isn't for drinking purposes. And send a footman off to fetch Uncle George. He'll need his medical bag. Send another to find Lord Graelem."

Daisy hurried back to Gabriel's side, surprised but pleased that he'd followed her instructions and settled onto the stool. She thought it odd that Laurel had remained in her chair, doing nothing more than eyeing her and Gabriel curiously. Laurel was as meddlesome as any Farthingale in existence. So why was she sitting there silently, doing nothing to assist Gabriel?

She turned her attention back to him. He wore a prideful, stubborn glower on his face that warned he would not obey any more of her commands.

Stubborn dolt! She was going to fix him up whether he wanted it or not, and he was sadly mistaken if he believed that she gave a fig about his strong, silent, I've-been-shot-but-will-bear-it-with-manly-grace look. She knelt beside him, for the footstool was low and she could better treat his wounded arm in this position. "Can you remove your jacket? Here, let me help you."

"I don't need your help," he said, pain punctuating every word. "It's just a flesh wound."

"All the more reason to stop acting like a little boy in knee pants and do as I say." She reached for his good arm first and helped him to shrug out of the sleeve. Then she eased the jacket off his injured arm. There was a hole in the fabric, just below his shoulder where the bullet had struck. The blood around the hole was still wet, not dry and caked, which meant his wound was deeper than he had let on and still oozing.

The shock of dark red against the stark white of his Savile Row shirt sent a shiver up her spine. "Now for your shirt," she said, swallowing hard.

He glanced between her and Laurel, his gaze coming to rest on her. "No."

Since he wasn't the modest sort, she realized that he was thinking of her modesty, which was ridiculous since he'd already seen her breasts and explored them... well, now was not the time to think about that wondrous experience. By the sudden, hot smolder in his eyes, she knew his mind had wandered along the same path. Heat rushed into her cheeks. "Don't be ridiculous. You're still bleeding."

"I don't care. What does Lady Forsythia's rule book say about sipping tea in your cousin's salon with a shirtless man? I'm sure it is written in big, bold letters, DON'T."

"First of all, I'm not sipping tea. Second, this is my *sister's* salon. Third, you aren't shirtless yet, but you will be in another moment, and I'm sure the rule book would say to do whatever one must to save an injured man, even if said man is an arrogant and infuriating rakehell. *Especially* if that rakehell just saved one's little cousin," she added, letting out a soft breath.

"Well said, Daisy." Laurel smirked as she turned to Gabriel. "You may as well give up. She's clearly won this battle. And before you tell me to mind my own business, which I can tell by your expression, you are about to say, keep in mind that if she doesn't tend to your wound, I will. However, I won't be anywhere near as gentle as Daisy. I'll take a hot poker to your shoulder and simply burn that wound shut. And if you dare say another word about your delicate sensibilities—of which you have none—or of my sister's delicate sensibilities—apparently, when it comes to you, she has none either—I will take that hot poker and stick it somewhere up your body that will really hurt."

Laurel then smiled sweetly and popped a scone into her mouth.

Daisy struggled to suppress her laughter, but that struggle ended with her emitting a string of very unladylike snorts. Gabriel shook his head and grumbled, but ultimately cast her an endearing grin. "Very well, I surrender. You may have your wicked way with me, Daisy Farthingale." He paused a moment and then his grin broadened. "I beg you, be gentle."

She managed a hesitant smile back, understanding that he was teasing her. "I'll do my best."

In truth, she was shamefully eager to put her hands on him, to cleanse his wound, first and foremost. But she also wanted to feel his warm skin against her fingers, to touch him and make him feel as exquisite as she'd felt with his hands and mouth on her breasts the other night.

"We'll compromise," Gabriel said, clearing his throat and seeming to wince as she began to unbutton his shirt. "Leave it. Just tear off the sleeve."

She nodded, relieved that he'd made the suggestion, for her heart was already in palpitations and she was in grave danger of swooning. She'd drop to the floor like a stone the moment he removed his shirt. "Brilliant. Excellent idea. I should have thought of it." Of course, she had and immediately dismissed it because a bare-chested Gabriel was a fantasy she'd hoped would come true... oh, dear. Her heart was palpitating again.

She shot to her feet as Billings walked in with the supplies she'd requested. "Ah, good man." She took the bottle of whiskey and clean cloths from him, then motioned for him to set the basin and pitcher of water on a small table beside the fireplace.

She spared a glance at Gabriel. Blood still slowly dripped from his wound, fortunately landing on the polished stone surrounding the hearth and not on Laurel's expensive Aubusson carpet. "Perhaps we ought to have done this in the kitchen," Daisy mumbled.

"And scandalize my cook and scullery maids?" Laurel shook her head and laughed. "No, much safer here where I can properly chaperone the two of you. I have my eye on that poker and will not hesitate to use it on Gabriel if he steps out of line."

What about me? Daisy was in peril of ravaging Gabriel. She returned to his side, kneeling too close to him and reveling in the glorious heat radiating off his body and the subtle scent of musk and sweat along his throat. *Great balls of cheese!* She really wanted to do thoroughly inappropriate things to his body.

She placed her hand on his arm to tear away the sleeve and groaned softly as her knuckles grazed hard muscle. Truly, she was in serious danger of mauling the poor man. What was it about him that set her body off like fireworks?

Everything.

Silently berating herself, she tore off his sleeve, tossed it into the fire, and quickly rose to dunk a cloth into the basin. Laurel was on her feet and had already poured water into the basin. "Thank you," she said.

She turned back to Gabriel and forced herself to ignore all but his wound. In truth, it wasn't as bad as it had first appeared. The bleeding had now slowed, and she saw that the bullet had only grazed the fleshy part of his skin and torn through. She wrapped her hand around his arm just below the wound to hold it still while she cleansed it. In truth, Gabriel had no fleshy parts, for he was all hard, solid muscle.

She took a long breath, for her heart was furiously beating again. And wasn't it awfully warm in here? She and Gabriel were close to the fire, which was the logical reason for her discomfort. However, the parts of her that were fiery hot and smoldering could not possibly feel heat from those flames. "This will sting quite a bit,

Gabriel."

She poured whiskey onto a fresh cloth and applied it to his now clean wound. He covered her hands with one of his as they began to shake. "You're doing a fine job, Daisy."

She let out a soft, quivering breath as his deep, gentle rumble washed over her. "I think you'll need stitches. Where's Uncle George? Why isn't he here yet?" She wrapped one of the cloths around his wound now that it had been properly cleaned. In no time, a dark red stain spread across the white cloth. "You're still bleeding." She hastily unwrapped the cloth, tucked a thicker square of cloth beneath it, and bound the first cloth tightly about his arm once more. "How are you feeling? A little lightheaded?"

He cast her a tender gaze. "Only a little. You needn't fret. I'll survive."

"I hope so." She pursed her lips and cast him a scowl that quickly faded to a look of worry. "What happened in the park? Who shot at you? Or did they mean to hit Lord Malinor?"

"I don't know, Daisy. Graelem will report the incident to the Prince Regent and he'll order a royal investigation."

She nodded. "It isn't every day an attempt is made on the life of one of his ministers... or one of his rakehell friends. But why must you wait for Graelem to report it? I'll ring for Billings to fetch you some notepaper, quill, and—"

"Prinny and I are on the outs at the moment," Gabriel interjected. "That's why I came in search of Graelem. I need him to pay a call on Prinny."

Daisy shook her head, recalling her earlier conversation with Auguste Malinor. He'd indicated that very thing, but it still rang false to her. "You're on the outs with him? When did this happen?"

He shrugged. "This afternoon."

Her eyes narrowed, for she was angry and hurt that he sought to dismiss her so casually with yet another of his lies. "How is it possible? You were with me at sunrise, with your grandmother in the late morning, with me again at the regimental headquarters in the early afternoon, and not an hour later with me again in the park."

Laurel quirked an eyebrow. "You're spending quite a good deal of time with my sister."

"Unintentional, I assure you." He ran a hand roughly through his hair and scowled. "I don't have to account to you for my precise movements."

"I never said you did, but I'd much rather you tell me to mind my own business than spout lies to me."

He shrugged again. "Very well, none of your business." He turned to Laurel. "None of yours either. I mean it, Laurel. If the pair of you dare open your mouths about this affair, you'll put me and Graelem in danger."

Daisy rushed to Laurel's side when her sister paled. "Laurel, sit down," she said gently, now truly angry with Gabriel for frightening her sister while she was in her delicate condition. However, even she was surprised by her sister's sudden weakness, for Laurel was all fire and spit, and nothing ever frightened her. She supposed it was Laurel's love for Graelem that had suddenly turned her blood cold, the mere thought of losing the man she loved clearly rattling her.

Daisy turned to Gabriel, her hands curled into fists. "We'll keep your horrid secrets. Even though I don't trust you" —*but I love you*— "I do trust Graelem. He would never betray his country, so whatever intrigue the two of you are involved in must be on behalf of the Crown. But you're wrong to keep the truth from us. How can we protect you unless we know what's going on?"

He frowned at her. "You can't. Don't even try. Who else must get shot to make you understand?"

She let out a little *huff*, but made no further comment. She was worried about Laurel, who appeared even more shaken than before. "You're ashen. Why don't you go upstairs and rest?"

"No, you can't stay alone with Gabriel."

"Nonsense. Uncle George will be along soon, and even if he is a little delayed, there's no harm done. I'm spitting angry and not kindly disposed to *him* right now." She turned to Gabriel, intending to scowl at him, but forgot all about her anger the moment she noticed a small, dark red stain across the cloth she'd just used to bind his wound. The blood was still oozing and threatening to soak through two squares of cloth. "You're still bleeding."

Laurel set her hand across her belly and moaned.

Daisy tamped down her alarm, not sure whom to tend to first. She decided on her sister. Gabriel had been shot and his wound might be more serious than she'd realized, but Laurel was in danger of giving birth to her first child in the middle of her salon. "Here, Laurel. Sit down. I'll send a footman to summon the midwife."

Laurel laughed gently. "No, not yet. The babe is quiet. I'm the one feeling a bit queasy."

Daisy rang for Laurel's maid, and after a bit of a fuss, Laurel was helped upstairs. That left Daisy alone with Gabriel. Her eyes rounded in alarm as he slowly rose to his full, imposing height and started toward her. It took him only a step or two to reach her. "What are you doing? I promised Laurel I'd behave."

"And I promised no such thing." He wrapped his uninjured arm about her waist and drew her much too close.

Though her mind urged her to draw back, her body had quite other intentions. Unbidden, her hands came to rest against his broad chest because she needed to touch him and feel the strength of his body against her open palms. "Where is Lady Forsythia's book when I need it?"

He let out a soft laugh, but it quickly died. "I don't want you going anywhere alone for the next few weeks." His tone was gentle, no longer arrogant or angry, and the look he cast her was tender but somber.

She brushed back a lock of her hair that had fallen over her brow and absently tucked it behind her ear. "Why? I wasn't in danger in the park. Surely, the assailant was aiming at you or Lord Malinor."

"Perhaps, but I'd like you to be careful until we find out more. The fact remains, had I not thrown my body over yours, that shot would have killed you."

DAISY WAS FRUSTRATED, but not surprised, when she and her family arrived late to the Baldridge musicale. Her mind was still reeling over what Gabriel had said, but surely the assailant had simply missed his mark. She couldn't have been the intended target, could she? The possibility had brought her polite and sheltered world crashing down about her ears.

She hoped to learn more from Lord Malinor, but by the time she caught sight of him, he was already standing at the opposite end of the entry hall surrounded by his friends. She despaired of catching him alone before the recital began. "Drat."

Her mother, who was standing beside her and no doubt scanning the crowd for Auguste Malinor, turned to her. "Did you say something, Daisy?"

"No, Mother." After returning home, she had gone straight to her room and not said a word to any of the elders about the incident in the park. Perhaps she ought to have mentioned something to her parents, but neither of them were home at the time. No doubt they had gotten an earful from Julia, although she suspected that Julia had gone on at length about Lord Malinor's new phaeton and ended with an account of the shooting that was so sensational her parents had probably dismissed it as another of her theatrical embellishments.

Uncle George knew the details for he'd stitched up Gabriel, but he'd refused to discuss it with her afterward. What had they said to each other? She had been ordered out of her sister's salon while her uncle had tended to Gabriel, so she had no hint of what the pair had discussed. Of course, she'd tried to listen in from the next room, but they spoke too softly to be overheard.

How inconsiderate!

"Daisy?" Her mother studied her with concern. "Perhaps you ought to have stayed home this evening."

She smiled and assured her mother that she was in the pink of health.

"Well, you let me or your father know if you wish to go home. Imagine, shots ringing out in the park! I'm so glad no one was injured."

Her smile faltered. Had her uncle said nothing about Gabriel's injury? Had Julia been too hysterical to notice? Surely, Lord Lumley had been aware, but he might have been asked to keep quiet about it.

"Ah, here comes Lord Malinor. No doubt he wishes to make sure that you and Julia have recovered from all the excitement. Wait here while I find her." She gave Daisy a quick inspection and frowned. "You're not quite yourself yet. I can see that, child."

"I will be once the music starts. Nothing like harp music to get one's toes tapping."

Her mother laughed lightly. "Or put one straight to sleep." She squeezed her hand. "That's my girl. I love you, Daisy."

"Love you, too."

"Well, now to find Julia. I'll return in a moment." Her mother soon disappeared into the crowd.

As soon as Lord Malinor saw that she was alone, he swooped down on her like a hawk seeking its prey. However, hawks did not dress in garish leggings of scarlet silk. "My dear! How are you?" He leaned close and lowered his voice. "Quite a shock you must have received this afternoon."

"I will admit I'm still a bit rattled. More important, are you all right?" She was genuinely concerned, for his eyes were red and watery, and the wine on his breath already smelled stale. He must have started drinking early, no doubt to calm his own frayed nerves.

"Yes, yes, I'm quite well." He seemed to wave off the incident in the park. "The bounder wasn't shooting at me. Obviously aiming for Lord Dayne. Another jealous husband to be sure. Terribly disappointed in the man."

"Everyone seems to be." However, she didn't believe the assailant had been a jealous husband. Going after Gabriel while he stood amid a crowd didn't make any sense. She'd felt the shots whiz past her ear, too close for comfort. All she remembered after that was Gabriel swallowing her up against his big body, his arms as hard as granite as he shielded her against his chest.

And what about the ugly little man she'd seen in the park? She'd noticed him earlier in the week, had seen him handing a letter to Gabriel at the Royal Society lecture she'd attended with Lily. Were Gabriel and the ugly little man part of a greater scheme? Some intrigue on behalf of the Crown? None of it made sense to her. Why would that little man shoot one of his own colleagues?

Lord Malinor reached for a glass of champagne from the tray of a passing servant, drank it down quickly, then grabbed another two and handed one to her. "You look fetching, my dear. Quite fetching."

She took the offered glass but had no desire to drink its contents. Her stomach was roiling and she wasn't certain she could hold anything down. "Thank you. How did Lord Dayne disappoint you?"

"What?"

"Lord Dayne. Disappointing you." Were all men incapable of answering the simplest questions?

"Not just me. He's let down the entire country," he said with theatrical flair, as though giving a speech in Parliament.

"How so?" She cast him a demure smile, hoping he was drunk enough to let something slip.

His chest puffed out, reminding her of a rooster. An overly perfumed rooster. She continued to smile and batted her lashes, perhaps overdoing it a bit for she wasn't used to flirting with men. Whatever she was doing seemed to have the desired effect. "You keep away from Lord Dayne, my girl," he warned, now scowling although not at her. "He's a bad one."

"How is he bad?" She added a delicate hand to her throat to heighten the impression of helplessness. "Please tell me. I can't protect myself if I don't know."

He hesitated a moment, then moved close so that his hot breath ruffled the curls beside her ear. "No harm in telling you now, I suppose. Word of his row with Prinny and Wellington has already spread throughout Parliament. It'll be all anyone talks of tonight."

Her fingers tightened around the glass of champagne still in her hand as she fought off her disappointment. She'd hoped to learn secrets, but what she was about to be told was a rehearsed lie. Gabriel had not had a falling out with the Prince Regent, but everyone was meant to think he had. To what purpose?

Lord Malinor glanced around, then leaned close again. "Lord Dayne refused to cancel his hunting trip."

Obviously, this trip was important in some way, but why should anyone care if Gabriel left London for a few weeks of hunting? And why should Wellington in particular care? "How is that significant?"

Lord Malinor tensed, as though fearing he'd said too much. "Sorry, m'dear. I'm not at liberty to say more."

Daisy struggled to hold back her frustration. She gazed across the entry hall and saw her mother and Julia slowly making their way toward her. She was running out of time to pry the information out of Lord Malinor. "Surely, you can tell me something. After all, if members of Parliament know about it, how much of a secret can it be? And those shots came awfully close to striking me. Don't I deserve some explanation for that alone?"

She whipped out her lace handkerchief and held it to her trembling mouth. "I'm quite overset. Really, my lord, this is too cruel of you."

"Now, now," he said, uncertain how to deal with a young woman on the verge of hysterics since his wife had dutifully given him sons and not any daughters before passing away. If not for that, he would have seen through her little performance at once. "No cause for alarm, my dear. We've had a minor disturbance in France. Nothing to worry about. Wellington asked Lord Dayne to delay his hunting trip and travel with him on the Continent. It's his duty as an Englishman, but he behaves as though he's Trent's eldest son and heir when he clearly is not. The man is shameless."

"Why is he so important?"

Lord Malinor shook his head and let out a forced laugh. "I wouldn't call that bounder important so much as convenient. Dayne speaks fluent French and knows the terrain. Travels as a young man... that sort of thing. He was involved with a French countess for a time. Point is, Wellington needs him there. Being a scoundrel doesn't excuse him from all duty to the Crown. The man's a damn coward."

She shook her head. A minor disturbance in France? Had something happened to Napoleon? And why should Gabriel be involved even if he did speak French? Most gentlemen learned languages in school. Many had traveled to France and throughout Europe. "Why should Wellington want him when he's considered so unreliable? What's really so important about Lord Dayne?"

Lord Malinor paled. "Nothing. He isn't important. The point is, when you receive a royal request, you obey it."

"I see." But she didn't really. The royal request would not have been made unless something important had happened or was about to happen, obviously in France since Gabriel had an excellent knowledge of that country, according to Lord Malinor. What could be so vital not only to the Prince Regent, but to his most trusted military advisor, the Duke of Wellington? Not to mention the top ministers in England?

She tried to put the bits and pieces together and could come up with only one conclusion. "Has Napoleon escaped?"

Lord Malinor's eyes rounded in alarm and he ran a fat, clammy hand across his collar. "Where did you hear that?"

"You just told me. Why else would—"

"Gel, keep your thoughts to yourself!" He suddenly seemed quite angry, so she hastened to reassure him that she'd speak no more of the matter since she was here to find herself a husband and not to interfere in excruciatingly boring matters of state.

She fluttered her handkerchief and then drew it to her trembling lips. Lord Malinor was immediately contrite. "Forgive me, dear gel. I didn't mean to overset you. In truth, the cat is certainly out of the bag by now. The news will be all over the London papers by tomorrow. Not much of a secret that Napoleon has escaped. Er... but do keep it to yourself for now."

She nodded, fashioning a smile while her mind raced to fit the information into the puzzle that was Gabriel.

Lord Malinor took her hand and patted it, his fingers hot and moist as they wrapped around hers. The stench of stale wine assaulted her as he leaned close enough for his jowl to graze her cheek. "Pretty thing like you mustn't fret," he whispered in her ear. "These are dangerous times. Makes a man think of what's important. Makes a man realize he must seize the moment, for one cannot know what tomorrow will bring."

Good heavens. What was he going on about? He was smiling and squinting at her in a most unsettling fashion. "Ah, here's my mother and Aunt Julia."

She slipped her hand out of his grasp.

"We'll speak later," he said with a wink.

DAISY DIDN'T WANT to believe the latest bits of news, but it had to be true. Napoleon had escaped Elba and was on the run. Was it possible? Lord Malinor had let slip that Gabriel spoke the language fluently and knew the countryside. Was he needed to plan a defense? Why? He was known as a wastrel, not a military man.

And who was this countess?

She shook her head and sighed. Obviously an affair that ended years ago. She'd ask Graelem about it later.

As for Gabriel, she recalled the recent stories she'd heard about him, all of them possibly false. He'd been accused of drinking to excess, but he'd always been sober during their encounters. He was known as a womanizing scoundrel... well, he'd admired Lady Westhaven's enormous breasts this afternoon, but ogling was something all men did, even her sainted uncle, George, a pillar of respectability.

Gabriel was known to disappear for weeks at a time, yet his business affairs were in good order, or so Laurel had insisted during their afternoon discussion. Indeed, Laurel had been certain of it, for Graelem had confided in her about his cousin's estates, which meant those seemingly impulsive disappearances were well thought out.

Several months ago, he'd been shot by a cuckolded husband somewhere in the north of England. That was the rumor spread around town and his own grandmother had believed it. Daisy had held Eloise's hand and cried, for Gabriel had returned in such terrible shape few expected him to survive.

What if he hadn't been shot by a jealous husband, but had received those wounds secretly fighting Napoleon? His long absences could have been secret missions to France.

And his injuries coincided with Napoleon's capture and exile.

Daisy groaned inwardly.

Of course, it had to be.

The hunting lodge, the bachelor friends... his terrible reputation... all a carefully crafted sham. But not everything fit. There was the matter of that ugly little man.

What was his connection to Gabriel?

Or to the attempt on Lord Malinor's life?

Drat, she wasn't even certain there had been an attempt on his life.

"Daisy," her mother said, tapping her shoulder only moments

216 | MEARA PLATT

later. "You're talking to yourself."

She shook out of her thoughts, saw Julia and Lord Malinor drifting into the music room together, and turned to her mother with an apologetic smile. "I was thinking aloud."

"As we Farthingales are known to do from time to time." Her mother cast her a sympathetic smile in return. "But try not to do that when in company, it looks a bit... well, odd."

She wondered just how she and her mother had turned out so alike in looks and, it appeared, in temperament as well. Sophie Farthingale was still a beautiful woman, retaining much of her youthful figure and lush dark hair, though now salted with white. Her gentle blue eyes were wrinkled at the corners, but those were laugh lines, a result of a joyful household filled with mirth and affection.

Daisy had always hoped to age as gracefully as her mother. However, at times her mother was a dizzy, disorganized creature who'd forget her own head if it weren't attached. She was a scatterbrain and often talked to herself.

Oh, dear! Was she becoming as scatterbrained as her mother?

"... and keep away from Lord Dayne. I won't have the Farthingale name associated with that coward."

He isn't a coward! She wanted to scream the truth aloud, but knew it was hopeless. Neither her mother, nor anyone else, believed he had any good in him.

A small cluster of lords and ladies paused on their way to the music room, where the harp recital was about to commence. "Sophie," said Lady Beaverton, a dear friend of hers, "have you seen him yet? Lord Dayne, of course."

Her mother shuddered. "No, Miranda, and I certainly don't wish to."

Auguste Malinor was just behind them and had obviously overheard. He uttered a crude jest about Gabriel.

Daisy cast him an icy glare. What had he ever sacrificed? Or was he too insignificant for the Prince Regent's notice? She desperately wished to come to Gabriel's defense, but wasn't about to ruin the scandal that he and the Prince Regent had concocted. Had Wellington been involved in the planning as well?

She stood with her hands curled into fists at her sides, silent and unresponsive while all around her spoke of Gabriel with unmasked derision. Finally, she could take no more. "Who are we to condescend? Has the Prince Regent ever taken notice of any of you? Have you done anything worth his notice?"

Her mother's eyes rounded in horror. "Daisy!"

"My father and I," Auguste said with a disquieting sense of menace, "are well acquainted with the entire royal family and you would be wise never to forget it."

"Forgive my daughter, my lord. You see, Lord Dayne recently did us a great favor, and my daughter now believes we owe him something in return."

He arched an eyebrow. "Ah, I see. Loyalty, Miss Farthingale, is an honorable trait, but misplaced loyalty is a dangerous thing. Please excuse my earlier crude jest, but do be wary of Lord Dayne. He cannot be trusted."

"Thank you for the warning, my lord." A warning he insisted on droning into her skull each time they met. Gabriel had also expressed little fondness for Auguste. Why did the pair particularly detest each other?

"I hope we are friends again." He cast her a smile that did not reach into his cold, dark eyes.

She managed a small smile in return. "Yes, of course."

"Excellent." He let out the breath he'd been holding, a response which Daisy thought quite odd, for Auguste had never seemed to care whether or not she held a good opinion of him. "May I be so bold as to escort you to dinner after the recital?"

"Of course you may," her mother interjected before she could decline. "My daughter is honored by your notice."

He bowed to her mother and then to her. "Until later, Miss Farthingale."

She managed another smile, this time more sincere. "I look forward to it, my lord."

Her mother turned toward her once Auguste Malinor, Lady Beaverton, and their companions had walked away. "Goodness, you gave me quite a scare! Daisy, you almost ruined your chances with young Malinor. Possibly ruined Julia's chances with his father. I know we taught you girls to be honest, but sometimes it is best to keep such thoughts to yourself."

"Sorry, Mother. I don't support what Lord Dayne has done, but who are we to cast blame? Do we have the right to question his sacrifice when we've sacrificed nothing ourselves?"

"Oh, Daisy," her mother moaned, uttering a string of woes which included phrases such as "sad creature, doomed to spinsterhood" and "determined to drive me to an early grave." "No man wants a woman without the sense to keep her radical thoughts to herself."

"I'm sorry. It's just that—"

She held up her hand. "I don't wish to hear your excuses. Indeed, I blame myself for failing to train you properly. But I won't make the same mistake with your younger sisters. I'll thrash them soundly if they dare to utter an independent thought!"

"Mother! You've never raised a hand to any of us."

"And I never will," she admitted, her shoulders sagging as she let out a sigh, "but you worry me, darling. At times you make it so difficult for anyone to see just how special you are."

"I'll be an angel to the entire Malinor family if it will help set matters right."

"Ah, well. Nothing to be done about it now. Come along, child. The music has started."

"You go in, Mother. I'll follow shortly." She mumbled something about misplacing her fan, then hurried off in search of Gabriel.

Though the Baldridge home was large, she managed a quick search of the residence—the card room, dining room, and private nooks. She'd just about given up hope of finding him when she spotted him on the terrace. "There you are."

Gabriel glanced in the direction of several guests who were also on the terrace, staring at him quite coldly. "Daisy, you shouldn't be out here."

She paid the scowling guests no notice. "I know, but I must speak to you."

"You've just done so. Now, go away before tongues start wagging, this time against you."

"Are you suggesting that you care?"

He frowned. "About your reputation? I do care. Don't come any closer."

She had to meet him somewhere private, find some place far from the music room or terrace, far from prying eyes and disapproving gazes. "How's your arm?"

His lips curled in a mirthless smile. "It's fine. Nothing more than a scratch. I've been injured worse."

Her heart tightened. "The news of your row with the Prince Regent and Wellington is all anyone is talking about tonight. Do the London gossips pay you to set the town afire with scandal, or is it a natural talent of yours?"

He glanced over her shoulder as another group of gentlemen and ladies passed by and began to whisper furiously while casting him furtive glances.

"A natural talent," he replied. "Now, go away."

"Follow me." She wasn't certain whether to poke him in the nose or go after the next person who glowered at Gabriel. She was angry with everyone tonight, particularly him. He was arrogant, insufferable, and thickheaded.

"No."

She folded her arms over her chest and scowled at him. "You must."

To her surprise, his gaze turned tender. "And allow you to be tarred with the same brush as me? I don't think so."

The will to fight simply drained out of her and all she felt was a deep, abiding sorrow. "Please, Gabriel. I'm so frightened for you."

He let out a soft groan. "Don't be."

She shook her head and sighed. "I can't help it."

"I know." He cast her a mirthless grin. "You Farthingales like to meddle. But this is a dangerous business, Daisy. The only way to keep you safe is to keep you far away from me."

"Are you ordering me to forget you? Am I supposed to return to the music room and pretend to listen to that insipid harp recital?" She shot him a frown. "There's a small Grecian temple in the Baldridge's garden."

He pushed away from the balustrade. "Haven't you learned your lesson about secret meetings and gardens? You could have been killed the other night... and again today in the park." He ran a hand through his hair, obviously exasperated. "What will it take to make you go away?"

"Five minutes alone with you," she said, glancing out into the garden. "I'll go first. Don't take too long." She marched off before he had the chance to stop her.

A cool gust of wind caught Daisy's curls, loosening several as she walked toward the Grecian temple next to a torch-lit pond. She ignored the stray wisps curling about her ears and neck, her thoughts in anguish over Gabriel as she walked on, hardly noticing the scent of lilac in the air.

A row of lilac trees swayed lightly along the high stone wall at the garden's edge, and she barely heard the rush of cool water spurting from the fountain in the nearby fish pond. The tree-lined wall obscured much of the garden walk from view of the music room and would afford them the privacy she desired.

Of course, she didn't know what she would say or do when he arrived... *if* he arrived, but she wasn't worried. She'd let her heart guide her.

She ducked into the temple and waited for Gabriel, straining to hear the sound of his footsteps against the wind, but all she could make out was the lilt of the harp filling the air.

"Daisy," he said with a rasp to his voice, stepping close and tucking a stray curl behind her ear in a casually affectionate gesture. However, Gabriel was not the casual sort. His every move was well thought out. He knew exactly what he was doing and had calculated precisely how to achieve his purpose with a smile, a touch, a soft word. He was much like any other rakehell, except he seemed genuinely worried about her.

His mere touch was crumbling her defenses, not that she ever wished to defend herself against him. She didn't at all. He wasn't a rogue... well, perhaps he was, but one with well-developed protective instincts. That's what he was doing now, trying to protect her by pushing her away. "I won't keep you long, Gabriel. I promise. I just had to tell you that I believe in you. No matter what happens, no matter what anyone says about you, I know the sort of man you truly are. I won't defend you, because you've gone to great pains to make everyone loathe you and I won't ruin your plans, but in my heart—"

"Daisy, don't talk about hearts." His words sounded pained. "I need you to forget me."

That wasn't quite what she longed to hear, but telling him what was in her heart mattered, even if only to herself. Somehow, she knew it was important to him as well, even though he was determined to make her think it wasn't. "I love you."

He grabbed her by the shoulders and shook her gently. "Don't. You little fool, you can't love me."

"Why? Because it interferes with your carefully designed plans? I'm not a fool," she insisted, lowering her voice to a whisper, although they were quite alone and she doubted anyone could hear them. "I know your Scottish hunting trip has nothing to do with shooting game or debauching or running away from war. I know that Napoleon has escaped and you're needed for something dangerous."

His fingers tightened on her shoulders as she continued. "You're a hero, Gabriel. You don't run from responsibility, no matter how tortured or overburdened your soul. Everyone thinks Alexander is the Dayne family hero, but it's really you. That's what you were doing throughout the war, running headlong into battle, volunteering for the most dangerous missions. Secret missions."

She waited for the well-intentioned lie to spring from his lips, waited for the denials she knew were coming because he refused to admit he was brave or noble. He sighed and then released her, turning away to study the pond. He pretended to be fascinated by the amber torch flames reflected in the shimmering water, but she knew his thoughts were on her. "I'll be away for quite some time, Daisy."

He ran a hand raggedly through his hair. "You saw the glowers I received tonight. I'm no longer welcome in society. That's how it needs to be."

She nodded. "Will you be gone a week? A month? Years? How long do you mean to stay away?"

He turned to face her. "I don't know."

"Gabriel," she said, edging closer, but afraid to hug him for fear he'd rebuff her. "If you want me to wait for you, I will. A lifetime, if necessary. Who knows how long a war will last? Napoleon is on the march again and everyone's afraid he'll soon regain control of France. Isn't that why the Prince Regent and Wellington are so concerned?"

She paused, waiting for his response, and continued when he said nothing. "But you intend to be *hunting* by then. What I don't understand is your need for pretense. Why can't it be known that you're working with Wellington?"

He ran a knuckle gently across her cheek. "Because it isn't that simple."

"I didn't think it was." Her breath was shaky and her entire body tingled. Gabriel's mere touch was enough to turn her upside down. Her body wasn't merely tingling, it was on fire. He was doing all he could to douse that flame. It wouldn't work. She was too far gone. She hoped he was as well, for she really wanted their last moments together to be special. "But I wish you'd have some faith in me, enough to tell me the truth."

"You think I don't have faith in you?" He let out a soft, anguished laugh and drew her into his arms. "You're the only... I just wish I'd met you two years from now, hopefully when the threat from Napoleon is truly over."

"Two years? Is that how long you think this new war will take?"

He shrugged. "It could take longer."

"Very well." She tipped her chin up to meet his steady gaze. "I promise I will wait for you."

His laugh sounded mirthless. "No, you won't. You had better not. I reject your promise. I don't want you to give up your life for me. I forbid you to wait."

"Forbid? That sounded quite military and commanding, but I'm not one of your soldiers."

"No," he said softly, "and thank heaven for it. Soldiers need to obey without question, need to respond on instinct. You don't look like a soldier either. You're so beautiful, Daisy. My heart slams into my chest every time I look at you."

"Oh, Gabriel! My heart does the same whenever I look at you." She reached up and put her hands on his shoulders, hoping he'd take the hint and kiss her.

He drew away. "No, Daisy. The sooner you realize we aren't meant for each other, the better off you'll be."

Were they speaking the same language? Hadn't he just admitted that his heart soared whenever he set eyes upon her? So why was there such desperation in his voice? He wouldn't push her away unless... he knew something terrible was in the offing. Her eyes clouded with tears. "You don't expect to survive."

"Nonsense." But he set his hands against her cheeks, once again caressing them with his thumbs as more tears began to roll down. "Forget your little girl dreams. You must."

"Please," she said in anguish, her throat so constricted she could barely speak. "I can't forget you, or let you destroy yourself... your future. *Our* future together. I've grown up and my feelings for you are not just little girl dreams."

He stood still a very long moment, hardly breathing. The night had a way of heightening one's senses. Noises were sharper, scents were easier to identify. Gabriel's subtle musk scent drew her closer, made her ache to put her lips to his throat and kiss her way slowly to his mouth.

But Gabriel made no move. The only sounds she heard were of the gentle flow of water circulating in the pond and the distant, plaintive strains of a Celtic harp. Her senses were as finely tuned as the harp, her body as taut as its strings.

She understood the importance of this moment, the need inside her. An aching need that brought more tears to her eyes.

Gabriel moaned and took her securely into his arms, cradling her against his chest while she sniffled into his shirt. "Damn it, Daisy. You'll destroy me if you cry."

She held him tightly and breathed in his musk scent. She ran her hands along his broad chest and muscled shoulders, wanting to memorize every hard curve of his body. She wanted to remember his strength and stubbornness, to remember *him* because she had the horrible feeling that she would never be in his arms again. "I'm glad I met you... glad I fell in love with you."

"I won't say it back to you, Daisy." But his voice was tight and raspy, and instead of pushing her away, he drew her even more firmly into his arms, holding her so close that their bodies seemed as one. His fingers gently brushed against her hair, but he needn't have been careful, for the wind and her tearful burrowing against his chest had ruined her fashionable chignon.

She didn't care. How could she worry about the style of her hair when her life was coming undone?

He bent his head to hers and kissed her softly on the mouth, a gentle, lingering kiss that made her heart soar like a bird. When the kiss ended, he didn't pull away. She felt his lips against her cheek, mingling with her tears. "Daisy Farthingale, you complicate my life. What am I to do with you?"

"Love me," she said and instantly felt him tense. "Even if it isn't true. Just pretend for tonight. I want the memories. No matter what happens, whatever our destiny... I want to remember the kisses, your laughter and your smugness—you can be impossibly smug, you know."

He let out a light, mirthless chuckle. "I know."

"I want to remember the gentle strength of your arms around me, the heat of your body against mine. I won't ask more questions. Keep your secrets. Just kiss me, Gabriel. Make this night memorable. Please."

And he did.

He lifted her into his arms, holding her tightly, exquisitely, his large hands exploring each curve of her body, gliding up her thighs, circling her waist, and then he cupped her breast, his hand warm and gentle and knowing.

She arched into his palm, her body melting under the heat of his touch as he flicked his thumb across the hardened bud, evoking moans and passionate shudders from her. When she thought she could bear no more exquisite delight, his hand drifted lower, his fingers lightly grazing along her tingling skin on a purposeful path down her body. Somehow the silk bodice of her gown was now down about her waist, her breasts bared to the cool breeze.

Before she knew it, his mouth closed over her breast, his tongue flicking across the taut nipple, swirling and suckling, until she thought she'd shatter from the pleasure. His hand slipped under her gown and he caressed her thighs, then caressed what he'd obviously sought between her thighs. "Gabriel!" she cried in a whispered moan.

"Sweetheart, don't hold back. I want to remember you like this, so soft and beautiful in the moonlight."

He stroked her moist core, seeming to know just when and where to apply the gentle pressure. She'd never experienced anything so powerful, her entire body in flames, hot, roaring and so intense she doubted her fiery passion could ever be doused. For him. Only for him.

She nestled between his muscled legs and felt his arousal, knew he was meant to be inside her, filling her. "I love you, Gabriel."

He said nothing, just closed his mouth over hers again and began to... *oh, oh... oooh*!

CHAPTER 17

*A lady must never decline an offer of
marriage from a man of quality in the hope
that the rake will reform.*

DAISY SLIPPED BACK to the recital unnoticed and spent the rest of the evening watching helplessly as Gabriel made a drunken fool of himself. His actions were obviously planned in advance and executed with precision, though the other guests were quick to believe that he was in his cups and out of control. Lord and Lady Baldridge, finally having had enough of his offensive behavior, demanded that he leave their home.

Graelem stepped forward to take his staggering cousin in hand. "C'mon, Gabriel. You'll have a blistering headache in the morning. Sleep it off at my house."

"Your place? What fun is that?" Gabriel took an awkward swipe at Graelem and missed. "Take me to Curzon Street. I have a call to make there."

The last was said loud enough for all standing close by to hear. Daisy and Auguste Malinor, who had spent much of the evening by her side, happened to be standing beside the door. "Disgusting," Auguste remarked.

"Indeed," Daisy's mother replied, for her family was standing close by as well. She took Daisy's hand and gave it a sympathetic squeeze, for her mother knew her well enough to sense her quiet desperation. Though she disapproved of Gabriel, Sophie

Farthingale's motherly instincts were on alert now and her only concern was to comfort her daughter. The "Daisy, you're young and foolish" lecture would come later.

Graelem left with Gabriel.

The music started up again and the Baldridge guests soon returned their attention to the festivities. Daisy could only think of Gabriel, but she hid her quiet concern since Auguste Malinor was still by her side.

One thing was clear: Gabriel and his cousin had neatly arranged to put Gabriel in Graelem's home tonight. "Sleep it off at my house," Graelem had said. Was it a ruse to provide cover while Gabriel collected the supplies kept under lock and key at Graelem's without raising suspicion?

Auguste put his hand on Daisy's elbow. "The dancing has started. I believe this waltz is mine."

Daisy shook back to the present and glanced around at the other couples already on the floor. All were eager for the real fun to start now that the harp recital was over and the chairs had been cleared away. "Indeed it is, my lord."

Auguste, his expression suddenly serious, escorted her onto the floor and drew her into his arms. "Tonight I claim a waltz," he whispered smoothly in her ear, "but very soon I shall claim your heart... as you have claimed mine, my dearest."

Daisy gaped at Auguste, paying no heed to the dancers now whirling about them or her own steps as her body turned numb. "My lord, I fear you've also imbibed too much this evening."

He arched an eyebrow, his expression a mix of surprise and anger, though he quickly hid that darker, angry response. "Do you not feel the same about me?"

"Perhaps," she said, hoping to lighten the conversation, "if you did not attempt to claim the heart of every young lady you met this evening. Lord Dayne isn't the only scoundrel. You do have a reputation, you know."

He threw back his head and laughed. "You are utterly delightful. Upon my oath, these words have been spoken to no one but you."

Which wasn't quite true. She'd seen him sneak off with another young lady earlier this evening, but had no intention of confronting him about it, for she'd done the same with Gabriel. She said nothing more, allowing Auguste to twirl her about the room in time to the music.

She and Auguste didn't know each other very well. Perhaps he wished to remedy that oversight, for he had been attentive to her throughout the evening, and had taken pains to charm her family. He'd said all the right things, whispered all the pretty words that Daisy longed to hear from Gabriel and never would.

She glanced up and saw that Auguste's gaze was on yet another young lady. Was he silently arranging another tryst in the Baldridge gardens? Two seductions in one night, and the night wasn't over yet!

Nonetheless, she tried hard to like Auguste. Truly she did, for Auguste had many worthy attributes — wealth, title, good looks. But there was obviously something lacking, something about him that didn't feel right, and it was more than his wandering eye for the ladies.

Perhaps it was the fact that he'd never attempted to kiss her. She had supposedly claimed his heart, he'd just told her so. Yet, he behaved nothing like a man in love. In truth, he seemed more in love with himself than with anyone else.

He was quite agreeable and polite with her, but he certainly didn't tingle at her touch, nor did his heart thump madly whenever he glanced at her. Indeed, the smile on his face appeared forced, and his light touches seemed calculated, as though timed at precise intervals.

Daisy couldn't shake the feeling that Auguste found her tedious. Was it possible the Malinors needed an infusion of capital to maintain their business enterprises and were now waging a campaign to capture her trust fund?

Great balls of cheese! She was eager for this interminable night to end.

A month into her debut season and all she had to show for it was Gabriel, a man who didn't want her for his wife, and Auguste, a man who wanted her only for her money.

What more could a debutante ask for?

DAISY RODE HOME in Eloise's carriage hoping for the chance to confide in her, but the old dear was exhausted and began to drift off shortly after the start of their ride. "Have you finished Lady Forsythia's book?" she managed to ask with a yawn as the carriage drew away from the Baldridge home.

Daisy nodded. "Most of it. Only two chapters to go."

"Good. Make sure you finish them soon." That said, Eloise had closed her eyes and was soon lightly snoring.

Daisy's parents and the rest of the family had piled into the Farthingale carriages and departed shortly ahead of them.

After seeing Eloise to her bed, Daisy slowly walked next door to her home and was about to retire to her bedchamber when her father called to her on the stairs. "There you are, child." He had a broad smile on his lips as he summoned her into his study.

The family elders were gathered there, several of her uncles standing with fluted champagne glasses filled and raised as though in expectation of a celebration. Daisy returned their smiles, honored to be included among the elders—until her father explained the reason for everyone's good cheer.

Daisy paled and took a step back. "Auguste Malinor? Is this a jest? No! No! I won't marry him! You can't make me do it!"

A sea of surprised faces returned her horrified stare, no one saying a word until Julia let out a shriek and grabbed her by the elbow. "Impossible child! Are you attics-to-let? The son of England's finance minister has just offered for you. A *viscount* in his own right. If you refuse him, not only will you damage your reputation, but you'll ruin my chances with his father. Do you care so little for me? For Harry's future?"

Daisy tugged out of her grasp and raised her hands in exasperation. She turned to her father, silently pleading for his understanding. "There must be some mistake. I'm certain that Auguste doesn't love me."

Her father frowned as he lifted an elegant paper off his desk. "Not according to his letter."

"He wrote to you? When did he have the chance? We left the Baldridge home less than an hour ago."

Uncle Rupert regarded her in confusion, his bushy eyebrows raised. "He must have written the letter earlier, preparing to send it after the musicale. Why are you so surprised? We all noticed that he didn't leave your side all evening."

She tried to deny it, for he'd been busily arranging his trysts whenever not with her. "He'd hardly spent any time with me until today. We hadn't spoken more than two words to each other before then."

Uncle George stepped forward, his manner calm amidst the increasingly angry mumbles of the other elders. "He claims to love you, Daisy," he said kindly, for he had always had a soft spot in his heart for his nieces. "The important question is, do you love him?"

"No! And I never will! No! No! Never!"

"You've made your point," George muttered, casting her an indulgent grin to convey that she had been sufficiently emphatic in her response. Nodding, he folded his arms across his chest and turned to face her father. "That settles it, John. You'll have to refuse young Malinor. It's obvious that your daughter doesn't love him."

Daisy's mother frowned at her and then at her uncle. "George, you know I've always respected your opinion, but in this I must ask you not to meddle. She's our child and we know what's best for her. Ever since last year's unfortunate incident with Lord Kirwood's son, we've all been worried about her lack of judgment. I had hoped the Kirwood matter would teach her to be more prudent, but it hasn't. She has since gotten herself entangled with Lord Gabriel Dayne and we all know he's a wastrel." Her frown deepened as she turned to Daisy. "He's a bad influence on you and the sooner you're *properly* settled, the better. Your father will accept Lord Malinor's offer."

Daisy's heart sank into her stomach. "No!"

"Yes," was the general consensus among the family members, everyone nodding save Uncle George, whose opinion no longer seemed to matter. His objections were drowned out along with Daisy's pleas. "It isn't fair!" she insisted. "You can't make me marry someone I don't love!" Since her mother would not listen, she turned to her father. "Please, I beg you. Don't force me into this."

"The matter has been decided," her father said, looking unusually stern. "Get a good night's rest, child. You're confused and don't know your own thoughts. I'll respond to Lord Malinor's offer in the morning. Sleep on it and you'll come to know that your mother and I are right."

Tears welled in Daisy's eyes. "Father, please! Don't accept him. I'd rather remain a spinster for the rest of my days."

"My sweet child." In two strides, he was at her side, taking her into his arms and hugging her tightly. "I can't bear to see you cry. We only have your best interests at heart. Sleep on it, Daisy. Please. Come morning you'll see that you and young Malinor will make a brilliant match."

Her throat went dry and her heart felt as though it was about to rip from her chest. "We won't," she insisted, her voice strangled and raspy. "Doesn't it seem odd to you? Why would he ask me now? Something doesn't feel right."

Her mother stepped forward, hoping to ease her concerns. "You make a lovely couple. Everyone remarked on it at Lady Baldridge's this evening."

"We were polite to each other, that's all. We aren't suited. We'll make each other miserable." She shot another desperate pleading glance at her parents. "Am I to be the only Farthingale forbidden to marry for love?"

"What do you know of love?" her mother said gently, but with an undercurrent of steel in her voice that Daisy knew could not bode well. "Child, you're good-hearted and charming, but you've shown a complete lack of sense when it comes to men. We have no choice but to protect you from your own misguided choices. The matter is settled. I won't hear another word about it. Either you willingly accept Lord Malinor, or you shall be banished forever from this house. From this family!"

"Sophie!" Her father stared at his wife, obviously aghast.

"Don't soften, John. She's our daughter and I won't have her throw away her chance at happiness when Auguste is so obviously suitable."

"Suitable!" Daisy's eyes widened in anger. "Is that what I'm to be saddled with for the rest of my life? A husband who's merely adequate?" She curled her hands into fists to control her frustration. "Is that all you feel for Father? Because I'm sure that I see your eyes brighten and a smile cross your lips every time he walks through the door. And Father responds exactly the same way whenever he sets his eyes on you. Why can't I have that for myself? It's all I ask."

She closed her eyes and held her breath.

"Daisy..." Her mother cleared her throat, her voice sounding a little ragged as though she were trying to stop her own tears. "I will not bend on this. Either you accept Auguste Malinor or you shall leave this house right now."

"DAISY? GOODNESS, WHAT are you doing here? Has something happened to little Harry?" Laurel yawned as she hurriedly waddled into her parlor, having been awakened by her maid and told her sister was downstairs urgently needing to speak to her. Laurel's enormous belly peeked out from her robe, for she had casually tossed it on and not bothered to properly fasten the ties.

Daisy gave her sister a fervent hug. "No, Harry's fine. Everyone's fine."

"Except you," Laurel remarked, hugging her back. When Daisy continued to hold on to her, she gently pried herself away and sank onto one of the fat-cushioned chairs beside the unlit hearth. "What's wrong? What has happened?"

Even when swollen and uncomfortable, Laurel looked beautiful. Daisy marveled at her sister's radiance. Her cheeks were as pink as rose petals and her dark gold curls tumbled over her shoulders in reckless abandon. That was Laurel's nature, to be wild and reckless, and outspoken, yet the family had allowed her to marry for love.

For this reason, Laurel was the best person to speak to her parents on her behalf. She'd convince them to arrive at the same decision for her.

"I'm so sorry," Daisy winced at the tremor in her voice, for she was about to cry again. "I shouldn't have disturbed you so early in the morning. It isn't yet dawn."

"Not yet dawn?" Laurel rubbed the sleep from her eyes. "I wasn't sure. My schedule's been off quite badly lately, so I thought I had simply overslept. All the more reason to tell me everything. What's going on?"

Daisy began to wring the gloves she held in a death grip. "Something awful. I'm frightened and don't know where else to turn."

Laurel struggled to her feet and came to Daisy's side. "Who frightened you? Graelem will load his pistols and shoot the bounder."

"No, it isn't quite that. He needn't shoot anyone for me." She took a deep breath and began to explain. "You see, the family—"

"Them? What have the Farthingales done now?"

Daisy tipped her chin into the air. "They've banished me."

Laurel shook her head and laughed, but her laughter quickly faded at the sight of Amos carrying Daisy's trunk into the house. "Goodness! You're serious. You know you're always welcome here, even in the dead of night. I love your visits. Ah, I see it's to be a rather long visit." She turned to Amos and greeted him. "We seem to be keeping you rather busy lately. I'm sorry, Amos."

He responded with a grin. "I'm not complaining, Lady Laurel."

"You never do," Daisy chimed in. "I thank you for that."

"Amos, take my sister's things upstairs and put them in the guest bedchamber. Second door on the left. My maid will show you the way."

Amos nodded. "Oh, my mum sends her regards."

"Send her my best wishes, as well." Laurel waited until his lumbering footsteps grew faint on the stairs before returning her attention to Daisy. "Take a deep breath and tell me why the family has banished you."

Daisy glanced down at the gloves still clenched in her hands and now twisted into Gordian knots. "The most unbelievable reason you can imagine." She took another deep breath and closed her eyes. "First Gabriel and now this. Oh, Laurel! I simply can't bear it!" She tried to continue, but the words caught in her throat.

Laurel sighed. "I see this is going to take a while. Come along. We'll talk while we eat." She led Daisy into the breakfast room. "Are you hungry?"

"No." She felt ill and couldn't manage a bite.

"Well, I'm famished. Oh, I must warn you that Graelem has a

visitor."

Daisy glanced at her in surprise. "At this hour? It isn't Lord Malinor, is it?"

"The finance minister? Heavens, no. Whatever made you think of him? What's going on? You have me worried now."

"How long will Graelem be occupied?"

Laurel nudged her forward. "Not long."

Daisy realized that the only visitor who would be here at this hour was Gabriel, for hadn't that been the point of his spectacular departure from the Baldridge party? She had no desire to see him. Not now, certainly not in her present state.

She couldn't tell him what had just happened.

"What a divine aroma," Laurel said, inhaling deeply as they entered the breakfast room. "I love sausages and biscuits in the morning... and afternoon... and evening... and midnight."

Daisy stared at the dining table. "Do you mean to say Graelem has hired a cook to attend to you throughout the night?"

Laurel grinned. "Graelem indulges my every whim. Oh, Daisy, I love him so much. I can't imagine ever loving anyone else. I hope you marry as well as I have."

"Yes, well. I don't think so." She followed the scent of biscuits and saw Graelem with his back to her, serving himself from the buffet, even though it wasn't yet dawn and everyone ought to have been asleep.

Since Gabriel was nowhere in sight, Daisy hoped he'd finished his business and gone. All the better, for seeing him would only make matters worse. In any event, she wanted a private moment to spill her heart to the two people she trusted most in this world. "The family wants me to—"

Then she saw they were not alone.

Gabriel stood half in shadow by the servant's entrance, his shoulder propped against the door, seeming even larger than his already imposing height. "Daisy, what are you doing here?"

She stiffened. He was going away. He had a mission. She couldn't interfere with it, not that he'd necessarily care about her receiving a marriage proposal from Auguste Malinor... Well, perhaps he would care, but only because the two despised each other. They'd made no effort to mask their disdain for each other at Lady Baldridge's musicale.

"She's run away from home," Laurel answered for her.

Oh, crumpets. "Laurel!"

"Well, you have. Haven't you?"

Daisy turned from her sister to gaze at Gabriel. He looked handsome as ever and not at all drunk. He had on the formal clothes he'd worn earlier this evening, but his sleeves were rolled up as though he'd been working through the night. He hadn't gone to Curzon Street to visit his mistress—*thank goodness, thank goodness,* she'd burst into tears if he had—nor had he stopped at his home.

An alarming thought came into her mind. Was he preparing to leave for France today?

Gabriel pushed away from the door, a frown marring his brow. "Why have you run away from home?"

"I can't tell you." She'd sworn to wait for Gabriel forever, even though he'd ordered her not to. Indeed, he'd insisted she move on with her life and think no more of him. He couldn't have meant for her to accept Auguste within hours of vowing to remain true to him. That would make her appear quite scatterbrained and deceitful. "Please, Gabriel. Go away. This is a family matter of an extremely personal nature."

"Gabriel is family," Laurel insisted. "You can tell him anything you tell us."

True, he and Graelem were cousins, obviously very dear to each other. But that didn't make him a relation of hers. Daisy drew aside a chair from the table and sank onto it. "No, not this."

"I think it has to do with Lord Malinor," her sister said.

Daisy glanced up in alarm. "Laurel! You're not helping."

Gabriel crossed the room and knelt beside her. "What has Lord Malinor to do with your running away from home?"

"Nothing. Laurel's mistaken."

"Ah, Daisy, you're a terrible liar." He tucked a finger under her chin and forced her tearful gaze to meet his determined stare. "Tell me what's happened or I'll go straight to Malinor and beat it out of him."

Goodness, he was a bear in the wee hours of the morning. Well, so was she. Particularly this disastrous morning. "I will not. It isn't any of your business."

He retrieved the knife he kept hidden in his boot and checked to see that it was sharply honed.

"What are you doing? You won't use that thing on Lord Malinor, will you?"

He arched his eyebrow, which made him look quite menacing. "Give me a reason not to."

"I'll give you several. First, the matter is trivial," she lied. "Second, it's obvious you're about to leave on your hunt, so go. Taking the time to carve England's finance minister into little pieces will only land you in prison, and that will throw your important plans into disarray. Third, with you in prison, Graelem will be forced to take your place on this so-called hunt. I don't think it's a good idea just now."

Gabriel followed her gaze to Laurel's rounded belly and uttered a soft curse before returning the knife to its sheath in his boot. "I still want to know why you're in such a state."

"I'll tell you, but only if you promise to do nothing about it."

His jaw twitched.

"Gabriel, I need your promise."

He refused to give it.

Daisy frowned at him. "Why are you being so difficult?"

"I don't make promises I know I can't keep."

Because he was an honorable man. He'd insisted on acting honorably with her, even last night with the kisses they'd shared in Lady Baldridge's garden... She'd always treasure those kisses stolen in the moonlight... though she'd offered him far more. To be precise she'd offered her heart and her body, and she might have blurted something about binding her soul to his forever. A little excessive, she supposed. Not that it mattered. He'd touched her and aroused her, but he'd refused to take her innocence, claiming it was for her own good, though he'd been hot and hard and wanting.

She was inexperienced in matters of the heart, but she wasn't an utter ninny. She knew a noble sacrifice when she saw it, and Gabriel had nobly sacrificed to keep her chaste. Perhaps it did not amount to a declaration of love, but that look of agony on his face as he'd pulled back and eased her out of his arms had to mean something, even though he'd told her repeatedly and adamantly that it hadn't.

"Very well. I promise not to hurt him," he said, as though understanding the direction of the thoughts whirling madly in her head, and perhaps feeling some responsibility for her distress. "What has he done?"

She took a deep breath, then slowly let it out. "More precisely, it's what his son has done under the father's urging, I suspect. Auguste Malinor has asked for my hand in marriage."

Laurel inhaled sharply. "No!"

"Bastard," Graelem muttered. "I knew he was up to no good."

He and Gabriel exchanged glances.

Daisy shifted her gaze between them. "Did you know about his plans?"

The men traded looks again.

"Gabriel, please say something."

His cousin was the one who finally spoke. "Daisy, did you accept him?"

She didn't immediately answer, too intent on staring at Gabriel and wishing he would curse or threaten or fly into a jealous rage, but he just stood there as silent as a tomb. Did he not care? Had she misunderstood his motives in Lady Baldridge's garden last night?

I must have.

A man in love would fly into a jealous rage.

Daisy found his silence shattering.

Finally, he spoke. "Did you, Daisy?"

She shot to her feet, her fists clenched at her sides. "Of course not! I love *you*, not him. How could you think I'd ever consider him as a prospect?"

"I didn't." He rubbed his hand roughly across the nape of his neck and cast her a grim smile that made her want to reach out and kiss him passionately even though she was not kindly disposed toward him at the moment.

"The problem is, my father is determined to accept on my behalf. He claims it is for my own good."

Laurel gasped. "How is it possible? We Farthingales always marry for love."

"Well, that rule isn't written in stone, is it? Even if it were, the family refuses to believe I know my own mind. They consider me a fool. And since I'm considered a fool, they're going to make this decision for me."

"Because of *The Incident*?" Laurel imitated her stance, clenching her own hands into fists. "This is all my fault. You poor thing. How awful for you... and how brave of you to hold your ground against the entire family. I'll tell them the truth about Devlin Kirwood, that it was me, not you, who almost made the worst mistake of her life. It's time they were told what really happened."

Daisy's eyes rounded in alarm. "Don't!"

"You can't protect me any longer, sweetie. I was wrong to let you shoulder the blame for this long."

"But Graelem—"

"Has known I was the one meant to elope with Devlin. I told him all about it before we married." She cast her husband the softest smile. "I couldn't take sacred vows with that lie standing between us. I ought to have told the family elders as well, but I thought the matter was quickly forgotten. I'll fix my mistake right now."

She marched to the bell pull to summon a servant, but Gabriel stopped her. "It's no use. They'll never believe you." He turned to glance at Daisy. "They'll think Laurel is lying to save your hide. Don't you see? The timing is suspect."

"I'll make them believe me," Laurel insisted.

Gabriel shook his head. "Unfortunately, it doesn't work that way. They've made up their minds about Daisy and nothing you say will change what they wish to believe. The more you protest, the more entrenched they'll become, and they'll blame Daisy for putting you up to it."

Laurel let out a deflated sigh. "It isn't fair."

"Life never is," he muttered.

Laurel pursed her lips, then stared at her belly a long moment before glancing up and pinning her gaze on Gabriel. "I know how you can fix this."

"How?" he asked.

"Marry Daisy. After all, she's in this predicament partly because of you. I'd marry her if I could, but I'm her sister. I don't think

England is quite that progressive yet."

Daisy wanted to laugh and cry at the same time. "You can't ask Gabriel to marry me."

"Why not? Don't you love him? You just proclaimed it."

"Of course I do. But he doesn't love me." She swallowed hard, surprised when Gabriel took her into his arms and turned her to face him. "Nor will I accept you," she insisted, "so don't even think to make the sacrifice. I'll solve the problem myself... run away... paint warts on my nose... I'll think of something."

"Unacceptable," Laurel said, glowering at Gabriel. "How can you allow my sister to compromise her heart?"

Graelem groaned. "That's what I love about you, Laurel. Tact, you're just bubbling over with it."

"My sister's in pain because of your cousin. Am I supposed to stand by and say nothing while he breaks her heart?"

"Now, wait a moment. Gabriel never made her any promises."

"So what if he didn't? It's his fault as much as it is mine." Laurel turned to her husband with fists once again clenched.

Daisy let out a sob. "Laurel, please! I need you to remain calm and speak to Father as soon as possible, before he does the unthinkable and gives his consent."

Graelem nodded. "I'll go, Daisy. Stay here with your sister and don't despair. Your father loves you. He won't force you to marry against your will."

"Won't he?" She turned away and buried her head against Gabriel's shoulder. He felt so warm and solid, so reassuring in the tender way he held her.

"Take a deep breath," he murmured, gently stroking her hair.

Tears began to spill down her cheeks.

He stroked her hair again, his touch so soft it only made her ache more. "Daisy, I can't bear to see you cry."

"I can't help it."

He sighed. "Take my handkerchief."

She thanked him, and wished she had never met him. Perhaps then she might have accepted Auguste, not knowing any better and believing love was a companionable emotion, not a hot, desperate feeling that seized you in its grip and shook the stuffing out of you...

in a wonderful way, of course. "It isn't your fault that you've spoiled me—"

Laurel gasped. "You ruined my sister?"

Gabriel emitted a strangled oath. "I haven't been much of gentleman around Daisy, but I was most careful about *that*. Can't you see she's overset and doesn't know what she's saying?"

"I meant that his kisses have spoiled me," Daisy explained amid sniffles and tears that she seemed unable to control. "But I would have surrendered had he bothered to seek more."

"Oh." Laurel coughed.

"Well, I would have. I'm not ashamed of my feelings."

Gabriel's expression became pensive, troubled. "The Malinors are up to something. Auguste's father approached me several nights ago, curious about my intentions toward you."

"What did you tell him?"

"That I had no interest in you. That I had no intention of ever marrying, and if I did, it wouldn't be to someone like you," he said with a wince. "I didn't mean it, of course. It was foolishly said in order to maintain—"

"Your facade as a wastrel? I know." Daisy nodded, still in his arms and loving the protective way he held her.

"I thought nothing more of the conversation." He glanced over the top of her head to look Laurel in the eye. "Daisy was surrounded by admirers at the time, and I believed Malinor was just making idle chatter. I never suspected he desired her for his son. Auguste's a heartless, ambitious bastard, just like his father. If he offered for anyone, I assumed it would be for a duke's daughter, someone closely related to the royal family... not the daughter of a commoner. Had I realized his intention, I would have—"

"Called him out," Laurel said with an approving nod. "Run him through with your blade. Shot him. Beat him to a bloody pulp."

Gabriel shook his head. "Taken *responsible* measures to protect Daisy."

"That seems innocent enough," Graelem said, donning his jacket as he prepared to leave for the Farthingale residence.

Laurel rolled her eyes. "Oh, I see. Gabriel is your cousin, therefore he's absolved of all guilt?"

Daisy sighed. She knew her sister well enough to realize that when Laurel felt guilty and frustrated, she wasn't always the most reasonable person. "No one's to blame. It just happened. Now, I need it to *un*happen."

"Your predicament is clearly Gabriel's fault. He just said so himself."

Graelem frowned. "It isn't his fault at all. He didn't force young Malinor to offer for Daisy."

"Graelem, are you blind to what's really going on? If what Gabriel says is true, then why would Auguste Malinor want to marry Daisy? Is it a cruel hoax? A means to get back at Gabriel?"

Graelem shook his head. "That's ridiculous."

"Is it?" Laurel asked, still glowering. "Gabriel showed interest in Daisy."

"You're wrong. He went out of his way to keep his distance from Daisy."

"Is that so? Well, I think he did a very poor job of it. Had he properly resisted, Daisy would not have fallen in love with him. But she did, and the Malinors noticed, and now my sister will be forced to marry someone she doesn't love... or worse, marry someone who doesn't love her, but covets her because she belongs to Gabriel. You gentlemen must be quite proud of yourselves."

"Now wait a moment, love. You can't—"

"I can and I will." Laurel clapped her hands and waddled closer to Gabriel. "You're going to marry Daisy. Right now. Wake the magistrate and obtain the special license."

"Impossible," Graelem and Gabriel said at the same time.

"Nothing is impossible when love is involved." Laurel reached for a teacup on the nearby buffet and raised it as though to throw it at her husband's head, or Gabriel's. Daisy wasn't quite certain. Perhaps she meant to hit both.

"Laurel!" a voice rang out.

"Father!" She set down the teacup with a clatter. "Graelem and I were just coming to see you."

Daisy saw that her father looked haggard. His eyes were bloodshot, as though he'd been crying. Of course, it wasn't possible. He never lost his composure, though his silver hair did appear a little windblown and he'd neglected to put on his coat, another sign of his distraction. Uncle George stood beside him, his arms folded over his chest, and he was scowling at her.

Daisy realized that she was still in Gabriel's arms. She tried to step away, but Gabriel wouldn't let go of her. What was he doing?

"I hoped to find you here, but didn't expect to find *him* with you," her father said, tossing a frown at Gabriel.

The two men were of similar height though Gabriel was significantly more muscular. She knew Gabriel would never harm her father, but wasn't certain that her father would restrain his temper. He'd been through a difficult night and finding Gabriel here—and her nestled at his side—only made matters worse.

Not Gabriel's fault, of course. Except now, he was purposely goading her father by keeping his arm about her waist. Her father was responding to the goading, his face red with anger and fisted hands raised.

Daisy's heart sank.

This night could not possibly get worse.

"I know there's much to explain," Daisy began in a rush, before any of the men spoke. "I'm just not sure where to begin. Truth is, I'm not sure about anything right now."

"Be quiet, Daisy. I'm interested in what Lord Dayne has to say," her father said, his lips stretched in a tense, thin line, "as soon as he takes his hands off you."

"Yes, Gabriel. Please let go of me. My father won't hurt me. He loves me." When he finally did so, Daisy approached her father. "Please give me time to sort things out. I'm not trying to cause problems for you or Mother. Nor do I wish to disappoint Julia. I love you all."

"I know, child. We love you, too." His lips began to quiver, and Daisy knew she'd turn into an insipid, blubbering fool if her father shed a single tear. This was all her fault. All of it. She'd broken his heart. She'd broken her mother's heart. She'd disappointed her entire family and continued to disappoint, even now. She was a willful, disobedient, and unappreciative daughter.

Yet still her parents loved her despite her open defiance, which only made her feel worse. What she needed was a book on how to reform a wayward debutante, not rules on reforming a rake. She hadn't reformed Gabriel. Quite the opposite, she'd *begged* him to ruin her, to have his wicked way with her as often and as thoroughly as possible. "Papa," she said in a ragged whisper, unable to utter more for the lump in her throat.

"My Daisy. My sweet, beautiful child. *I love you so much.*"

Would she ever hear those words from Gabriel? Could she ever say those words to Auguste Malinor? He was far too political and they'd never suit. She spoke her mind and would embarrass him because, as a Farthingale, she had never mastered the art of keeping her opinions to herself.

She let out a ragged breath and then began to speak between sniffles and tears. "I wanted so much to make you proud of me. I had such hopes at the start of the season. I was going to marry the perfect man, someone honorable and heroic, rich, perhaps titled. Someone you'd approve of, because I thought that if you were proud of him, then some of that pride might just rub off on me. Oh, perhaps not right away, but in time."

"Daisy, I know we were a little hard on you." Her father's scowl began to fade. "I only want what's best for you. You're my beloved daughter and I can't bear to see you so unhappy." He paused a moment to clear the scratch in his own throat. "Your mother acted rashly in shipping you off to Laurel and will soon come to regret it. However, I think it's best you remain here for now. Laurel will need a gentle hand to guide her through the birth."

Laurel readily agreed.

"As for attending the upcoming balls, I know your mother has forbidden you to attend any social engagements until further notice, but I'll speak to her and explain why she must rescind that decision."

"Mother did me a favor, really. I'm not interested in the social whirl."

He nodded again. "Well, you let me know when you are and I'll take care of any objections from the family."

She intended to hug him, but he stopped her with a stern wave of his hand. "We're not finished yet."

"Oh." He could be stubborn at times. Wonderful and stubborn.

"I would prefer to issue this word of caution in private, but I

244 | MEARA PLATT

suppose it really doesn't matter. You'll tell all to Laurel, who'll tell all to Graelem and your sisters anyway. The point is, Lord Malinor is a very important man, one with wealth, power, and position. As his daughter-in-law, you would gain entry into the highest circles. You'd become a viscountess, one of the *ton's* leading ladies should you desire it."

"I don't."

"George didn't think you would," he muttered, glancing at his brother, who was still standing beside him with arms crossed over his chest. "I didn't either, but had to be sure. Daisy, you must realize that such men are not to be rejected lightly."

She nodded. "Believe me, I do. I sincerely wish I could marry him, but it simply won't work."

"His father drinks to excess and dresses like a peacock," Laurel chimed in, "and we all know the apple doesn't fall far from the tree."

Her father rolled his eyes. "Be quiet, Laurel."

"And I think there's something odd going on with the Malinors," Daisy said. "Did you know someone tried to—"

"You're mistaken," Gabriel said with quiet urgency.

"But I know what I saw in the park."

"No, you don't."

Her father's gaze darted from Graelem to Gabriel before resting back on her. "Am I missing something?"

"I suppose not. Never mind, Papa. It isn't important." Obviously, Gabriel didn't want her to discuss the shots fired in the park. Everyone, even Lord Malinor, seemed eager to keep the incident quiet. Perhaps it had something to do with England's preparation for war, but no one was about to confide in her. "What I tried to convey rather ineptly last night is that Auguste Malinor does not strike me as someone who would accept anything less than total obedience from his wife and you know that I'm incapable of being obedient."

Everyone nodded at that.

"You didn't all have to readily agree," she muttered, a little peeved. "So you see, to accept his offer would condemn me to a life of misery." She considered emphasizing her point by clutching her heart, perhaps bursting into wrenching sobs and swooning as her mother and Julia were known to do on occasion, but she wasn't usually one for cheap theatrics and her father knew it.

"Enough, Daisy. You've convinced me. I'll turn him down, of course."

She rushed into his arms and hugged him, understanding how serious the repercussions might be. The Malinors were a powerful family. "Thank you!"

"My family will stand behind you," Graelem said. "We can count on Julian's family to do the same."

Her father shook his head and frowned. "I will not drag Julian and Rose into this sad affair if I can avoid it."

Gabriel cleared his throat and stepped forward. "There's no need to involve anyone. I'll have a word with Lord Malinor."

"You will not!" her father ordered, surprising Daisy by the vehemence in his tone. "I've made no mention of the scandal presently surrounding you, Lord Dayne, out of deference to your cousin and your kindness toward Harry, but let me be clear. You are not to involve yourself further with my family."

"Papa!"

"Not another word, Daisy! You may not come to his defense."

"But—"

"I've accepted your decision on Lord Malinor's offer, but don't think for one moment that batting your lashes at me or tossing me one of your pretty smiles will change my mind about Lord Dayne." He turned to Gabriel. "I'm a forthright man and therefore will speak plainly. Your behavior has been reprehensible."

"No—"

"Daisy, be quiet!"

Obviously, her impulse to meddle wasn't helping. Yet, his treatment of Gabriel was unfair. Society's treatment of him had been unfair.

"Lord Dayne, you've caused enough harm to my family—"

"He hasn't! Papa, you have no right to say such a thing."

He whipped his gaze back to her. "I have every right to protect you from your own misguided affection for this man. Let me be clear. I will not force you to marry Auguste Malinor, but neither will I allow you to cavort with Lord Dayne."

"Cavort?" She let out a pained laugh, dabbing at the tears once more gathering at the corners of her eyes. "You have no worry in that regard. He's–"

"Already offered to marry her," Gabriel said, coming to her side. "Right now. As soon as I secure the special license."

Her father's mouth dropped open. "Is that so?"

In truth, all stood with their mouths agape. Daisy turned to face him, still doubting they'd all heard him right. A muscle twitched in Gabriel's jaw. "Yes, sir."

"Though you've made no secret of your disdain for the institution of marriage." Her father appeared not at all convinced.

Daisy's heart leapt into her throat, for Gabriel could only be doing this out of a misguided sense of honor. She turned to him, first pleading silently and then whispering, "You mustn't."

Gabriel shook his head and sighed. "You're wrong. This is the one thing I must do. I see that now. Wait here. Graelem and I will return shortly. Sir, I assume you'll give your permission."

"Please, Papa! You had better," Laurel said, now wringing her hands.

"I had better?" Her father turned ashen. "Blessed saints! Have you *imposed* on my daughter?"

Daisy gasped. "He hasn't. He's offering because... because... well, I don't quite know why."

"Because he loves you," Laurel blurted.

But Gabriel didn't say it and Daisy wasn't about to demand that he admit something he didn't feel. She knew what he was doing. That muscle in his jaw twitched again. He was protecting her from retribution by the Malinors. He was giving her the protection of the proud Dayne name.

Daisy stared deeply into his eyes, into those seemingly calm pools that hid so much pain. I love you, Gabriel. I know you're not a coward. I'm so sorry. I never meant to trap you into marriage.

Shortly after dawn, Gabriel and Graelem returned with a minister and special license in hand. The ceremony was brief and unsentimental. No flowers, no large family, no joyous celebration. Her father, Uncle George, Graelem, and Laurel were the only witnesses to their wedding. Her father and Uncle George left immediately afterward to break the news to the Farthingale clan.

Graelem and Laurel escorted the minister out, leaving her alone with Gabriel in the breakfast room. She hadn't even been married in a church! Gabriel stood as silent as a great stone monument for the span of two heartbeats before turning to her. "Goodbye, Daisy. Remember me kindly."

CHAPTER 18

*A lady must never reveal her innermost
feelings to a rake.*

REMEMBER ME KINDLY?

Daisy didn't want Gabriel replaced by a fond memory. She wanted to be with him, grow old with him, have dozens of children with him, some golden-haired and tawny-eyed like their father and perhaps one or two with her dark curls and vivid blue eyes.

Remember me kindly.

Would she ever see him again?

To her frustration, she couldn't tell her family of his secret mission, not that she knew much about it anyway. However, she would tell her father and Uncle George the little she knew in a couple of days, for she couldn't have them believe he'd abandoned her. She suspected that Uncle George knew quite a bit more than he was letting on. She hoped Graelem would provide more details once it was safe to do so.

Gabriel... her husband. Oh, that sounded so sweet!

She frowned, wondering what Polite Society would think once it was known that Gabriel had left his new bride alone on their wedding night to go on the *hunting* trip he and the Duke of Edgeware had supposedly planned. No doubt the marriage-minded mamas would nod their heads and agree that a forced marriage to the daughter of a wealthy merchant was a laughable affair. Gossip would abound, everyone believing that Gabriel was set in his rakehell ways and would never be a dutiful husband to her.

A shudder ran through her, for they might be right. She still had time before all eyes were on her. At least she could hide out with Laurel and Graelem for the next few days, thereby avoiding the friendly congratulations calls and those meant not to be so friendly.

By the time word leaked that Gabriel had left London, she would come up with another excuse to explain his absence. Her head hurt just thinking of the necessary deception, but her heart hurt as well, for she was worried about what would happen when he returned.

Daisy felt the ache well up inside her. She had forced him into this marriage and ruined his chance to find true happiness. "Mercy," she muttered softly. Perhaps her parents had reason to be worried about her. She was a reckless fool who'd made a complete muddle of love and marriage.

She closed her eyes and shuddered at the thought of the horrid whispers certain to spread across the fashionable London salons. *Rakehell forced into marriage at the point of a gun. Abandons new wife on their wedding night.*

Oh, Lady Withnall would run wild with that!

The sharp-eyed snoop amused herself by revealing the most intimate secrets of the Upper Crust. Daisy would not allow the little harridan to indulge at Gabriel's expense. He had come to her rescue, married her to protect her from the Malinors. Of course, he'd also married her to protect the secrecy of his mission.

He'd married her for every reason but love.

"Do you think Father has declined Auguste's offer by now?" she asked Laurel. It was early afternoon; only hours had passed since her hastily planned wedding. She wondered how the Malinors would respond to the news of her elopement. With anger? Relief? Auguste would be relieved, for he hadn't really wanted her.

"If I were in our father's position," Laurel said, giving thought to the question, "I'd delay my answer as long as possible. Why rush to face the wrath of the Malinors sooner than necessary? He'll need to gather his allies, as well. Graelem will stand with Father. So will Uncle George. Although he doesn't wish to involve Rose and Julian, I know they will insist on helping out, so we'll have the Emory family with us. We Farthingales will get through it."

Daisy shook her head and sighed. "I hope so."

Laurel cast her a grim smile. "And here I thought I was the rebellious, undisciplined daughter. You certainly outdid me, blew right past me on a gale force wind, or should I say, a *Gabriel* force wind? No mean feat. I'm proud of you. Never thought you had it in you, for you were always the one who settled arguments, kept the peace. But you've certainly rattled your saber and everyone has noticed. Napoleon wouldn't stand a chance against you."

Daisy spent the rest of the day in quiet exile at her sister's home. Each passing hour felt like an eternity, though she tried to occupy her mind by plunging into the task of organizing Laurel's household. She suspected Laurel had purposely disorganized her belongings in the hope of distracting her.

Finally, as the day wore on and evening approached, Daisy set down her book and stared across the library to her sister and Graelem, who were cozily nestled on the sofa by the fireplace. Laurel's head was resting on her husband's chest, and she was purring as contentedly as a kitten while Graelem gently caressed her hair.

Oh, the pair were so in love!

Feeling a trespasser on their privacy, Daisy turned away. What did she have to show for her love but a terse farewell from Gabriel? He would be across the Channel and in France in a day or two.

He was smart and determined. Nothing would sway him from his duty. And Graelem had finally revealed that the plan was to ride north toward the Duke of Edgeware's hunting lodge, then head east to the ship hired to sail him to France once they were certain no French spies had been following them. Apparently, Lord Malinor had been aware of the plan as well, and his confrontation in the park with Gabriel had been a well-rehearsed ruse to further throw Napoleon's spies off his scent.

However, what hadn't been rehearsed and caught all of them by surprise was the attempt on Lord Malinor's life. Or was it on Gabriel's life? No one was certain, and no one knew who'd ordered the attack, a concern that weighed heavily on Graelem's mind. She could tell by the way his brow would furrow as he attempted to puzzle it out.

Daisy was about to mention that odd-looking man she'd seen with Gabriel at the Royal Society and again in the park, but Laurel's sudden gasp brought her straight to her feet. "Another contraction, Laurel?"

Graelem put his arms around his wife, his gaze a mix of love and utter panic. "Sweetheart?"

Laurel laughed lightly. "What a pair of old women you are! No cause for alarm. I shifted onto my knitting needles by accident." She drew them out from under one of the decorative pillows thrown onto the sofa where she nestled with Graelem.

Daisy eased back in her seat with a sigh, smiling at the look of relief that washed over Graelem's face. The man was big and strong, built like a warrior. Fierce. Yet docile as a lamb when it came to his wife. He loved her with a deep, abiding conviction.

Would Gabriel ever feel half that love for her? Her father's parting words this morning resounded in her ears. Though he has done right by marrying you, I fear Lord Dayne is incapable of honest feeling. He has refused to accept commitment or responsibilities of any kind for too many years. Such a man will not change his ways now. Beware, Daisy. Your good intentions will never fix him. He's a broken man.

A broken man? Not her Gabriel, she decided for the thousandth time today. He was perfect.

She yawned and rose from her chair as the hour approached midnight.

"Where are you going? Don't leave," Laurel called out, clumsily raising herself to a sitting position.

"Why not? It's late." Daisy sighed. "Are you worried about me? I'll be fine. I'm rather enjoying the peace and quiet."

There it was again, her sister and Graelem exchanging worried glances. Did they know something she didn't?

At first, Daisy worried that there might be trouble with the baby, then realized Laurel would not be sitting contentedly in her husband's arms if something were physically wrong with mother or child. She wasn't about to upset them by suggesting there was.

"Very well, I'll sit with you a little longer." She returned to her seat, picked up her book and resumed reading where she'd left off.

Laurel eased back once more and rested her head against her husband's chest.

A short while later, Daisy tried again to leave the lovebirds alone. Again, they refused to allow her out of their sight. She adored her sister and Graelem, they'd made her feel more than welcome, but being together for the entire day was quite enough. Didn't they desire privacy? Or did they believe she was too unbalanced to be left alone? Goodness! They couldn't!

Daisy snapped her book shut.

Her sister let out a snore.

"Take her to bed, Graelem. She obviously needs her sleep."

Nodding, he nudged his wife upright and lifted her into his arms. "It's late, my love," he said when she stirred.

"Oh, I must have dozed off. Where's Daisy? I must stay with Daisy."

"I'm right here. What is going on? Will one of you please tell me?"

It happened again. The pair turned to each other, exchanged knowing glances, and then turned back to her.

"There, you've done it again. Why do you keep doing that? Do I have red spots on my face?"

Laurel laughed nervously. "Of course not. What a silly thing to say."

"You keep giving me these pitying looks. I will admit I was quite overset this morning, but I'm better now. The crisis has passed. Father has refused Lord Malinor... and I don't care about missing the Washburn's ball tonight, or missing Lady Ashton's musicale tomorrow, not that I'd be welcomed there anyway, even as Gabriel's wife. *Lady Dayne.* Goodness, that sounds so odd. A wife and a lady. Nice, but odd."

Laurel cast her an indulgent smile. "You'll reconcile with the family as soon as they've had the chance to calm down. All will return to normal within a few days... that is, what passes for normal in the Farthingale household."

Graelem chuckled as well, but his merriment quickly faded. "I know this next month will be rough on you. We'll do our best to help you through it. I think you'll be good for Gabriel. He thinks so too or he wouldn't have married you. You'll work it all out if he returns."

"You mean, *when* he returns." Daisy clenched her hands around the book she was still holding.

"Isn't that what I just said?" Graelem tried to sound casual, but Daisy saw that he'd paled a little upon realizing his mistake.

"Of course." Daisy tried to dismiss the comment, but in her heart she knew that Graelem had said what he'd meant... what he'd feared... that Gabriel's mission was dangerous, the odds heavily stacked against his survival.

If he returns.

Oh, mercy! That explained their looks of pity. Neither of them believed Gabriel would survive.

GABRIEL AND IAN spurred their horses to a gallop as they approached the White Stag Inn shortly after midnight, eager to be out of the unrelenting cold that was accompanied by a driving rain. The inn, located inland about a day's ride north of London, was on the well-traveled road between Luton and Peterborough. Gabriel had taken the detour north as a precaution, on the chance they had been followed. At daybreak, they would continue north, then swing sharply eastward and ride hard toward the seaport of Harwich, where he was to board a ship waiting to sail him to France.

Two lanterns burned brightly above the inn's entrance, a welcoming beacon in the night. The proprietor, familiar with Ian, heard their approach and rushed out to greet the riders. "Come in, Yer Grace! And yer friend be most welcome!" he said, smiling at Gabriel. "Leave yer horses in me son's capable hands. He'll take excellent care of them fine beasts. Ye must be hungry and thirsty. Will ye be wanting... er, the usual female attentions?"

"No," Gabriel said, receiving a surprised look from Ian. "That is, not for me. His Grace will speak for himself."

Ian shot him a questioning glance and nodded thoughtfully, seeming to understand this was not the time to tease him about Daisy. Their jovial banter would be saved for the next society ball, if

254 | MEARA PLATT

he lived to attend another ball. To his surprise, Ian also refused the offer of a girl to warm his bed.

"What do you think?" Ian asked later, once they had finished their meal of smoked quail and roasted potatoes, and washed it down with some excellent dark ale. "Did you notice anyone behind us?"

"No. Seems our plan is on course." He quickly scanned the common room, giving it a final look, but no one had come in after them and the travelers already present seemed harmless enough.

"Then it's off to Harwich in the morning." Ian glanced at one of the pretty serving maids and sighed. "Too bad I've decided to follow your example and become a monk. She would have given me a soft ride tonight to take the edge off the hard ride awaiting us in the morning."

Realizing the duke would not ask for her, the girl went off with another traveler, giggling as the gentleman tossed her a shiny coin and led her upstairs.

Gabriel poured himself another ale and one for Ian. The two of them sat in companionable silence watching the fire flicker in the hearth and listening to the rain fall on the thatch roof in muffled splatters. Wind howled in the distance, but the inn was well built and protected against unwanted drafts.

"Well, are you going to say something or must I?" Ian asked, finally breaking the silence. "Go ahead. We're alone now. Everyone, including the proprietor, has retired for the evening."

Gabriel glanced around. In truth, he'd been too lost in thoughts of Daisy to notice.

"Get it out of your system before you sail, Gabriel. I don't want that seething anger of yours to jeopardize the mission. Once you're in France, your only goal, your only concern, must be to destroy the French supply lines. Shall I help you along?" He shifted in his chair and leaned forward. "Old Malinor's a bastard."

Gabriel arched an eyebrow. "We've known that all along. He's always been a bastard."

"So's his son."

"He's even worse than the father." Gabriel gripped his mug of ale so tightly the handle threatened to break. "The conniving whelp, what does he want with Daisy? He doesn't love her." He slammed his fist on the table. "He can't love her."

"It doesn't matter. She refused him, married you instead. Hell, I still can't believe it. You, married. I suppose our sacred pact is shot to pieces."

"No broken hearts, no grieving widows," Gabriel said quietly. "That's the worst part of this assignment, knowing I'll soon make her a widow." He didn't bother to hide the pain in his eyes as he met Ian's gaze. "I'll need you and Graelem to look after Daisy for me. I don't trust those Malinors. Auguste wants something from her, or wants to hurt me... or her... or both of us. *Hell*. She'll be vulnerable. He'll try to use it to his advantage."

Ian shook his head. "I wouldn't worry about Daisy. The little baggage has such faith in you, such love for you. She'll cut him to ribbons if he tries anything."

It was quite something that she loved him, felt so good to have her stand by him even as false rumors of his character spread. He'd felt empty for so long, he'd forgotten that feelings such as pride, happiness, or respect still existed. "She is something special," he said with a light grin, "even if she did almost destroy our mission."

Ian shook his head and let out a genuine laugh. "Imagine, the course of the world completely undone by a pair of soft, blue eyes."

Gabriel felt the ache in his heart. "Ah, yes. Helen of Troy and Daisy Farthingale. Daisy hasn't quite changed the world yet, but she's changed me. I returned home wanting to die and the little nuisance somehow gave me reason to live."

"You might want to mention that to her upon your return," Ian said, his voice suddenly sounding tight. Perhaps it hadn't been quite the right thing to say to Ian, a man who'd gone through life without anyone to care whether he lived or died. Not even Ian seemed to care about his own survival.

Gabriel nodded. "Protect her until then."

"I will. I promise." Ian smacked his palms against his thighs and rose. "Since I don't have that special someone to make my life complete, I'll have to make up in quantity what I lack in quality. If you'll excuse me, I have an appointment with a buxom redhead called... oh, damn, I turned down the offer, didn't I?" He sighed and ran a hand through his hair. "Guess I'll retire *alone* to my quarters."

Gabriel grinned. "You could find yourself a snoopy Farthingale of your own."

Ian gave a mock shudder. "No. And don't think to do me any favors. I'm perfectly content to remain a bachelor for the rest of my days."

Gabriel stayed behind to watch the fire die in the hearth before walking upstairs and settling into his sparse but clean room. He collapsed onto the bed, too fatigued to do more than kick off his boots. Breathy female moans, masculine growls, and the sound of wooden bed slats creaking filtered in from next door, no doubt the maid Ian had passed up now with another traveler. He tried to shut out the noise, but his last thoughts before drifting off to sleep were of Daisy and how perfectly she would fit in this bed beside him.

CHAPTER 19

*A lady must never countenance a rake's
illicit paramours.*

"LAUREL, YOU LOOK ashen." Daisy set down her fork and pushed away from the breakfast table. She stared at her sister, then at Graelem. The pair were seated across from her, Graelem shoveling his breakfast into his mouth as though he hadn't eaten in weeks. No doubt it was a ruse to avoid talking to her. More to the point, to avoid answering her questions about Gabriel and his mission.

She *had* meant to ask more about it, but Laurel's condition was of greater concern at the moment. Laurel hadn't touched her food, an alarming circumstance since until this morning, she had been inhaling portions large enough to feed a regiment.

"Sweetheart?" Graelem set down his fork as well and was about to raise his teacup to his lips, but stopped to study his wife. "Aren't you hungry? Do you feel ill?"

"I'm fine," she insisted, scowling at both of them. "I wish you two would stop fussing over me. Daisy's the one who ought to be fussed over."

"No, I'm not." Quite the opposite, Daisy wished to remain quietly on her own, but not before she had more answers from Graelem. As she was about to toss him more questions, Laurel suddenly bent over and let out a soft gasp.

Daisy forgot about her own woes and quickly reached over to clasp Laurel's hand. "It's time, isn't it?"

Laurel managed a nod and suddenly gasped again. "I think my water just broke!"

Daisy and Graelem were up at once, Graelem sweeping his wife into his arms and shouting orders to his staff while Daisy hastily wrote a note and had a footman deliver it to her parents at the Farthingale townhouse. At the same time she summoned a second footman to fetch the midwife. Once both servants were on their way, she ran upstairs to help make Laurel comfortable.

It felt like an eternity, but could not have been more than half an hour, before her other sisters scrambled out of the Farthingale carriage and hurried up the steps to the front door. Daisy hurried downstairs and was waiting for them in the entry hall as Billings opened the door. She was thankful that Rose, the eldest, had come along with the twins.

"I happened to be dropping off a book for Lily when the footman arrived," Rose explained, efficiently removing her gloves, bonnet, and pelisse before turning to hug her.

"The midwife hasn't arrived yet," Daisy began to prattle at once, "and I don't know what I'm doing." Laurel going into labor wasn't her only problem. Daisy needed a capable hand to tend to Graelem, who was in a state, ranting as he paced up and down the hall outside of the bedchamber. Rose was just the one to handle him. After all, she now ran a successful pottery operation that rivaled the Wedgwood family establishment, so how hard would it be for her to manage an overset husband?

Rose also had experience with childbirth and could answer questions about it that neither she nor the twins could.

"Where's Graelem now?" Rose asked as they climbed the stairs and reached the landing only to find no one in the hallway. "I thought you said he was pacing outside the door."

"He was. Oh, dear. He must be inside with Laurel." Daisy hurriedly led them into the bedchamber that Laurel and Graelem shared. It wasn't the thing for husbands and wives to share quarters, but Farthingales were not known for their adherence to the rules of Polite Society. Laurel had insisted on sharing her husband's bed. Rose had demanded the same of her husband, Julian. Neither man had voiced complaint. In truth, each seemed remarkably content with the arrangement.

Daisy wondered whether Gabriel would consent to similar terms when he returned. *When he returned.* She repeated the words in her mind, for she wasn't about to let him die. She'd go to France herself to save him if she could.

Laurel moaned, regaining her attention. She was stretched out on the bed, Graelem seated on a stool beside the bed clutching her hand. Graelem glanced up to acknowledge their presence, utter panic and despair etched in his proud features. "Laurel's having our baby."

Dillie managed not to roll her eyes at the obvious statement. "I know," she said gently. "That's why we came as fast as we could."

Daisy tried not to cringe, but she knew Graelem was a disaster in the making. Rose, as capable as she was, would not be able to handle him on her own. The twins would have to help keep him downstairs and out of the way once the midwife arrived. "Lily, did Amos come with you, by any chance?"

Lily adjusted the spectacles on her pert nose and nodded.

"Good. Take him with you to find Uncle George and bring him here."

Daisy breathed a sigh of relief as Lily hurried off. Now to her next problem, how to get Graelem downstairs. Rose capably took the reins by stepping to his side and placing a hand on his obviously tense shoulder. "Julian was a wretched mess when my time came, but I can tell you that I wanted him out of our bedchamber for my sake. First of all, I wasn't pretty. Also, I was in a lot of pain and couldn't let it out because I knew it would break his heart if he saw me suffering. I'm sure Laurel's feeling exactly as I did."

Laurel smiled at her husband. "I love you, Graelem. Please go. You can stomp and pace to your heart's content downstairs, wear a hole in our ridiculously expensive carpets. *Please.*"

He said nothing for a long moment, then reluctantly nodded and let out a growl. "I love you, my bonny lass." He placed a tender kiss on her brow. When he rose, Daisy noticed that he was putting delicate weight on the leg he'd broken last year, or rather, that Brutus—that beast of a stallion—had crushed last year.

Daisy pursed her lips in concern, knowing by his limp that he

260 | MEARA PLATT

was in silent agony. He'd never admit it, though.

"I could almost *hear* him ache for Laurel," Dillie said in a whisper. "Love does that, I suppose. Of course, I'm too young and innocent to know about such things."

So am I, Daisy thought to herself, for she and Gabriel had not consummated their marriage, an oversight she meant to correct the moment he returned... assuming he wished to remain in the marriage and not seek an annulment.

She shook her head and sighed, refusing to think about that awful possibility.

Dillie interrupted her thoughts. "Tell me what to do, Daisy."

"I wish I knew. If only Mother were here." But the Farthingale elders had gone off to Windsor, some grand affair at the Duchess of Lowesbury's estate. Her father thought it best to continue with their plans even though her mother and Julia were still distressed about the Malinor debacle. Daisy hoped that a garden party in the countryside would calm them all down.

Laurel let out a gasp and sank back onto her pillows. "Sorry, the little imp kicked me hard. Caught me by surprise, that's all." Then she gasped again, this time letting out a grunt. "He's going to be a big oaf, just like his father."

As Laurel's gasps and groans grew more frequent, Daisy's concern increased. Where was that midwife? And where was Uncle George? "Maybe Rose had better take over up here."

"No," Laurel said, clasping her hand. "Not yet. Graelem will panic and come running back up here. Leave them downstairs a while longer."

As silence descended—except for Laurel's increasingly anguished gasps—Daisy began to fretfully nibble her lip.

Dillie was now kneeling beside Laurel, her own lips quivering as though she were about to cry. Perhaps it hadn't been a good idea to let her stay up here.

Laurel's labor continued into the early afternoon and intensified by nightfall along with the storm raging outside. The midwife, Mrs. Peebles, had arrived hours ago and remained by Laurel's side the entire time. So had Daisy, Rose, and the twins, although they had been consigned to the opposite side of the room and used as serving maids to fetch more water or blankets or other items needed for the birthing.

To Daisy, each passing hour seemed an eternity.

Graelem remained downstairs with their uncle George, still mad with worry although their uncle's quiet assurance had gone a long way toward stemming his panic. In truth, his presence calmed all of them.

Daisy and her sisters had taken turns looking in on the men and often attempted to occupy Graelem's attention, but as the hours progressed, the task grew harder. He refused to read, wouldn't play cards, and would not engage Lily in a game of chess. "You'll win," he grumbled, "as you always do."

If it hadn't been for Uncle George's solid presence, there was no telling what Graelem would have done by now. Daisy herself was tense and scared, though she would not allow herself to show it.

"Some babes are reluctant to leave the comfort of the mother's womb," the midwife said in response to Daisy's questioning glance when she returned upstairs. "These things take time."

"How much time?" Dillie asked, for Laurel had been struggling for almost twelve hours.

She shrugged her beefy shoulders. "I don't know, lass. The babe will set his or her own schedule."

"I've heard that the first is often the most difficult." Daisy clasped her hands behind her back to hide their trembling. She felt useless and incompetent, and would have been terrified were it not for Mrs. Peebles and Uncle George remaining so close at hand.

"Aye, it's true. Don't worry, lovies. Your sister is strong."

"Headstrong," Dillie muttered as though to convince herself of Laurel's ability to pull through. Everyone was worried, but afraid to admit it.

Mrs. Peebles eyed them with a surprisingly tender gaze, for she was otherwise terse and efficient. "Aye, she's a fighter and that's good."

Rose moved to the hearth to stoke the flames, anything to distract herself. "Mother managed to produce five of us."

Lily nodded. "Five girls and we were small. What if Laurel is carrying a son? He's bound to be as big as Graelem, and we know

262 | MEARA PLATT

what happened to..."

Daisy turned to her sister in alarm. "Don't say it, Lily." They all knew Graelem's mother had died in childbirth.

"I'll have none of that talk now," the midwife grumbled.

Laurel opened her eyes and glanced about her bedchamber. "Where's Daisy?"

"I'm right here. So are Rose and the twins." Daisy drew the stool back to her bedside and settled on it.

"We won't leave your side," Rose assured.

Laurel eased back against her pillows, but her relief was only momentary. "Where's Graelem?"

"Downstairs where he ought to be," the midwife said. "I don't allow men in the birthing room. They always faint and then where am I? Forced to take care of mother, babe, and big oaf of a father. No, keep the men downstairs. That's what I say."

"Uncle George is with him," Daisy assured her, forced to whisper in order to keep the quiver out of her voice. "He's in good hands."

Laurel nodded, but she seemed disappointed that her husband couldn't be beside her. "I suppose that settles it. Does he know that I'm doing well?" *Which she wasn't.* "He's so worried about me."

Daisy took her hand and gave it a light squeeze. "We're taking turns reporting to him."

As the night progressed, Daisy continued to hold her sister's hand and did the best she could to make her comfortable, but between the midwife's orders to fetch this or that, and Graelem constantly poking his head into the stuffy bedchamber and bemoaning his helplessness, she knew something or someone was about to explode.

"I believe it's our turn to keep Graelem occupied," Rose said as she and Lily started for the door. "Just shout down if you need us."

Daisy cast them a heartfelt smile.

"Good thing Lady Laurel has you girls," Mrs. Peebles said. "Will you be staying on after the birth, Miss Daisy? She's going to need your help."

Daisy had never seen Laurel so pale. Her eyes were closed and brow beaded with sweat.

Though she tried to hide it, the midwife looked worried as well.

Laurel's eyes fluttered open. She took Daisy's hand once more, and Daisy had to stifle a gasp at how cold it felt. "How is Graelem? I teased him earlier, but I'm scared. The babe won't budge. Graelem knows that I'm in trouble. He must be frantic."

"He'll be fine as soon as he hears his child squawking," Mrs. Peebles said, handing Laurel a foul-smelling concoction. "Drink this, lovey. It'll get the contractions started again and that's what we want to see."

After a few minutes, they did start up with a vengeance.

Graelem burst into the bedchamber upon hearing Laurel's scream. "What the hell are you doing to my wife?"

Mrs. Peebles held her ground, standing up to face him and matching his stance, fists curled at her sides. "Get out, m'lord."

Fear and heartache were etched on Graelem's face. "No. This is my bedchamber. That's my wife who's suffering. Who's..." *Dying.*

"And I'm the one who'll get her through it. Are ye goin' to leave or do I have to chase you out?"

Rose and Lily hurried in behind Graelem, apologizing for letting him slip by, though Daisy didn't think anyone could stop him, not even a regiment of the King's finest soldiers. None of them were handling the chore of distracting the nervous husband very well. The more insistent the midwife became, the more determined Graelem was to stay.

Daisy felt that he belonged by Laurel's side, but the midwife was experienced in such matters and she wasn't about to contradict her orders.

Graelem stood as firm as a wall of bedrock until Laurel opened her eyes and smiled at him. "Sweetheart," he said raggedly, coming to her side to kiss her brow.

"I love you," she whispered. "My sisters have been by my side all day and haven't eaten since breakfast. They could do with some food and a pot of tea."

Dillie put a hand on his shoulder. "Graelem, help me put a tray together. I'm not familiar with your kitchen."

A muscle in his jaw tightened. "We have servants for that."

"Yes," Lily agreed, "but it's late and most of them have retired for the evening. It'll be faster if we do it ourselves."

"Nonsense—"

"Please, Graelem," Laurel said. "I need you to take care of my sisters."

He protested and grumbled and finally gave in because he wasn't about to deny his wife anything. Indeed, if he could have eased Laurel's pain by taking it upon himself tenfold, Daisy knew he would have done so in a heartbeat.

"I'm glad he's gone," Laurel said, collapsing against her pillows with a groan the moment he'd closed the door behind him. "This really hurts. What did you give me?"

"Something to help along your contractions," the midwife said.

She let out a soft, writhing gasp. "It's working."

Was childbirth always this difficult, Daisy wondered? Was it possible Laurel would die? No! She put her hands together and silently prayed. *Please, don't take her from us. Protect her. Protect Gabriel.*

"The babe's stubborn, but well positioned," Mrs. Peebles said. "Your sister's built to deliver a healthy child. She's broad in the hips and strong as an ox."

"I resent being referred to as an ox," Laurel said, maintaining humor despite her obvious agony.

"Ye'll get no apology from me, since I meant it as a compliment. Be grateful that ye're not a frail, sickly thing."

Laurel voiced no further complaint, her efforts once more concentrated on birthing, but as time wore on, there didn't seem to be any progress, only pain. Daisy had just released the breath she was holding when she heard a resounding crash, then a yelp and a string of invectives that caused even the midwife to blush.

Daisy shot to her feet. "Oh, no! I think we have another problem." She and Dillie rushed downstairs, following the lingering echo of shattered glass and the clang of a silver tray striking against the marble floor in the entry hall.

"Rose and I tried to help him," Lily said, her gaze never leaving Graelem, who was flat on his back, his arms and legs sprawled, his shirt soaked with tea and covered in wet cake crumbs, butter, and marmalade. Their uncle was by his side, carefully removing Graelem's boot to examine his leg—the one Laurel's horse had landed on with its massive hooves last year.

Daisy had to take several deep, calming breaths because Graelem's leg was in a very bad position and his complexion was now green. "Uncle George, has he broken it again?"

Lily's eyes began to glisten with tears. "Rose and I offered to help him with the tray, but he insisted on taking it up himself... and he really ought to have let us help because there was too much stacked on the tray for one person to manage."

Rose nodded. "We tried to tell him so, but this is his home, and neither of us dared to contradict him after he gave us that imperious glare that cuts one to the quick... though I did continue to warn him, because he can't discharge us no matter how much we irritate him. We're family, after all."

Daisy closed her eyes and swallowed hard. "Uncle George, what can we do to help?"

"Bring down my medical bag. I have it upstairs. Dillie, go wake Billings," he said, referring to Graelem's butler, "and tell him to wake the footmen. We'll need to carry Graelem upstairs. Lily, wake Mrs. MacTavish. Her maids can clean up this unholy mess once Graelem is settled in one of the guest chambers."

"A guest chamber, my arse!" Graelem struggled to rise, but the pain proved too great so he sank back on the cold marble floor. To Daisy's relief, he seemed able to move his neck and back without difficulty. "I'll sit beside Laurel. I want to be with her if she..."

He couldn't continue, his fear of losing the woman he loved obviously outweighing the pain of an injured leg. Daisy knelt beside him. "Lie still, Graelem. Please. Laurel needs you to be strong for her. Are you dizzy? How many fingers am I holding up?"

"Seven," he responded, ending with a "damn it."

She'd held up only one hand. Five fingers. "Lie still. You need to give yourself another moment before you—"

"Fetch me a cane." Once again, he attempted to rise. "There are two by the coatrack in the back hall."

George forced him back down. "I'll kick you in that injured leg of yours if you dare to move. The midwife may call for me at any moment and I won't be able to rush up there until I've finished fixing you."

Graelem appeared ready to protest, but Mrs. MacTavish, his efficient housekeeper, rushed to his side at that moment, followed by Billings and most of the staff. "Och! I thought I heard a noise, but I never dreamed t'would be the master falling down the stairs!"

"I didn't fall down the stairs. I merely tripped on the first step," he grumbled. "My leg's not broken, perhaps the ankle's twisted at worst."

"We'll need bandages to securely bind that ankle," George said, his gaze never leaving Graelem's leg. Daisy knew what the knit of her uncle's brow meant. There could be a break, only Graelem would never admit it.

"Right away," Mrs. MacTavish said, sending off two maids to attend to the chore.

Billings and several sturdy footmen carried Graelem upstairs as soon as his leg was bound, but he fought them when they tried to settle him in the guest quarters. "Laurel's in bed, having your child," Daisy reminded him. "They can't carry you in there."

He scowled at his footmen. "Put me down right here. I'll walk into *my* chamber on my own, crawl on my hands and knees, if I must."

Daisy ground her teeth in frustration. Did she believe her time away from the Farthingale residence would be quiet? Or that missing Gabriel would be foremost on her mind? At the moment, Gabriel's mission seemed like a walk in the park compared with the problem she was about to have with Graelem.

He couldn't be allowed in the birthing room. It simply wasn't done.

There was also the problem of Laurel. One look at Graelem, and she'd climb out of bed to put her arms around him. Honestly! The pair were as stubborn as donkeys. Would she and Gabriel ever be this ridiculous? Surprisingly, she hoped so.

She met Graelem's scowling countenance and let out a sigh. "I'll try to convince Mrs. Peebles to let you in."

"Just get me in there. I'll take care of Mrs. Peebles."

Thoughts of bludgeoning and murder swirled in Daisy's head. Graelem would do anything to remain by Laurel's side. She eyed him warily. "How?"

He cast her a wincing grin, seeming to read her thoughts. "Nothing violent, I promise. Doubling her fee ought to persuade her. I'll triple it, if I must."

Within the hour—though it was a long, unsettling hour—matters were once more under control. The maids had cleaned up the mess on the stairs and hallway, and Graelem's ankle was bound.

Graelem was now seated by the hearth, but in full view of his wife's bed. "If you move from there, I'll beat the stuffing out of you," George warned, then started for the door.

Daisy followed after him. "Uncle George, where are you going?"

He patted her gently on the shoulder. "I'll be snoring in the guestroom should anyone need me. Graelem will be fine now that his leg is properly set and I've given him enough laudanum to dull his pain. As for Laurel," he said, pausing to run a hand through his hair, "wake me in a few hours if the babe isn't born yet. I'll need to relieve Mrs. Peebles and it's best I do it with a clear head."

Daisy's heart leapt into her throat. "I'm frightened."

He sighed and patted her shoulder once again. "I know it's taking a while, but there's no reason to fear. The signs still point to a healthy birth. The babe's a bit reluctant to leave the comfort of his mother's womb, that's all."

She nodded.

"Why don't you girls try to get some rest as well."

Daisy was exhausted, but she was too distressed to sleep. No doubt her sisters were just as overset. "We couldn't."

"Then have Mrs. MacTavish fix you the light repast you ought to have had hours ago. Keep up your strength, or you'll be of no use to Mrs. Peebles or to me."

"I am a little hungry," she admitted "The twins must be, too."

Since the household had quieted once more, she decided not to bother the staff. Most had returned to their beds by now and she knew her way about a kitchen well enough to manage on her own.

As she stepped into the hall and started downstairs, she saw Billings at the foot of the stairs, looking perplexed.

She cast him an assuring smile. "Why are you still awake, Billings? You mustn't worry. His lordship and her ladyship will recover."

"I have faith they will, what with you and your uncle close at hand. But begging your pardon, Miss Daisy, there's someone here to see his lordship, claims to bring news of vital importance. Waiting until morning may be too late, this person insists."

Daisy wasn't certain what to do. Graelem was in no condition to see anyone right now, but what if the vital news concerned Gabriel? "I'll see the gentleman. Show him into the library."

Billings shook his head, now appearing quite distressed. "The visitor isn't a gentleman."

"A lady?" She frowned. "At this late hour? Very well, show her in."

"Can't very well call her a lady either. She isn't the sort one would allow into one's home. I'll send her away. I shouldn't have troubled you, but she mentioned Lord Gabriel—"

Daisy gasped. "Bring her into the library at once."

"But—"

"Do as I say, Billings."

Daisy hurried to the library and lit the oil lamp perched atop Graelem's desk. She decided against ordering the servants to light the fire, for she doubted the visitor would stay long. Now anxious, she busied herself by clearing off a space on the desk and fumbling in the drawers for quill pen and ink. She wasn't certain why she'd thought to pull out paper stock and writing implements, only that they might be useful. In any event, she was on edge and needed to do something to keep her hands from trembling.

Laurel's life and that of her baby were in danger. Graelem was injured and in a laudanum-induced stupor. Uncle George was exhausted and probably snatching a desperate hour of sleep. She was exhausted, hungry, and about to face a stranger delivering bad news. Very bad news.

Daisy uttered a silent prayer that Gabriel was unharmed, but she feared it wasn't so. Was he hurt? Captured? Dead? He'd only been gone a day or so. Too soon to have engaged the French, unless Napoleon's agents had followed him and Edgeware, attacking them on a quiet stretch of road.

A gentle knock at the door interrupted her thoughts. "Come in."

Billings entered, followed by the most beautiful woman Daisy had ever beheld. She was tall and slender, and had lush red hair and smoky, cat-like eyes. Even in the harsh lamp light, she appeared to have perfect skin and a peach complexion.

"Lady Laurel?" the woman asked once Graelem's butler had closed the door behind him to lend her some privacy.

"I'm her sister, Daisy Farthingale. Er... um..." *I'm Lady Dayne now.* Oh, well. It seemed irrelevant at the moment. "And you are?"

"Ah, I see," she said with a surprisingly wistful laugh. "My name is Desiree St. Claire. I'm a friend of Lord Gabriel Dayne."

"A friend of Gabriel's?" Daisy gripped the corner of the desk tightly. She recognized the name and knew Desiree was more than a friend. She was Gabriel's mistress. *Don't cry! Don't be a ninny and cry!*

She had been told such women were brazen, tawdry. But this beauty was graceful and carried herself with regal bearing. She dressed in the latest fashion, her gown a shimmering, sapphire blue made of the finest silk, and the matching fur-lined cloak was of the finest quality. Gabriel had spared no expense on his *amour*, she realized with dismay. "You have news concerning him?"

Desiree nodded. "I do," she said in a refined French accent, "but I think it best that I speak to Lord Graelem."

"What possible interest could his lordship have... er, in any way relevant to your position with his... er, cousin?" she finished lamely, not sure why she hadn't just come out and told Desiree that she was Gabriel's wife. In truth, it hurt that this woman knew Gabriel better than she did. It quietly tore her heart to pieces that Gabriel liked this woman better than he liked her.

"Please, let me speak to him." Her accent grew thicker with dismay. "There's no time to delay. The message is confidential—"

"Gabriel keeps no secrets from me." *Liar.* "Kindly get to the point of your visit, or leave." Daisy held her chin up, retaining her composure, but inwardly, she was an utter mess. Her heart pounded through her ears, her hands trembled, and her blood ran cold with fear. She was no match for this exquisite beauty. How could she ever compete with Desiree for Gabriel's affections? Desiree was the exquisite mistress who indulged his every pleasure.

"A woman in my position must live on the generosity of men," Desiree said, regarding her curiously, no doubt because of her comment about Gabriel keeping no secrets from her. It was a lie and Desiree obviously knew it. "Some are kinder, more generous than others."

Oh, don't tell me! I don't want to know!

"Lord Gabriel is one of those men. That's why I had to come here despite the risk. I think he's in danger."

A chill ran up Daisy's spine. "What sort of danger?"

Desiree hesitated.

"Miss St. Claire, it isn't possible to see his cousin tonight. You see, he's injured his leg and is quite incapacitated."

"Oh, my!" She put a hand to her mouth, appearing sincerely distressed.

"So you'll just have to tell me what this is about."

She withdrew a parchment from her reticule. "I wrote the words exactly as he'd mumbled them. You see, I was with a certain gentleman of high position who visited me earlier this evening. Oh, he was quite drunk and unpleasantly persistent. I fear my coming here will have consequences, especially if he finds out that I was the one to warn Lord Dayne."

Daisy took it without comment.

She cast Daisy a weak smile. "I'll protect myself if the need arises," she said, a sudden cloud of sadness shrouding her gray eyes. "I've had to all of my life."

"I see." Though she didn't really. Women such as Desiree were much sought after and understood the power they wielded over men. They traded their bodies for protection, their sexual favors for lavish gifts. They lived charmed lives, or so Daisy had thought until this very moment. Desiree looked scared and lonely.

"Please go on," she said politely, no longer willing to judge the beauty for entering into one of civilization's oldest professions. "Tell me what this man said."

She took a deep breath. "He was drunk and making threats against Lord Gabriel that frightened me." She stared at the parchment Daisy held in her hand. "Lord Graelem must read it at once. But before he does, please tell him that this gentleman offered to become my benefactor."

Daisy shook her head in confusion. "I don't understand the

significance. You must receive many such offers."

"There is a strict protocol to such arrangements, a gentlemen's code of honor." Her cheeks were flaming as she spoke, for it was obviously an uncomfortable topic and Desiree couldn't have imagined she'd be explaining it to Gabriel's wife. Not that she realized she was speaking to Gabriel's wife. "Since Lord Gabriel has paid a six-month advance, I'm obligated to him until the time expires. For another gentleman to engage my services is a grave insult to Lord Gabriel."

"You make it sound rather like a contract," Daisy muttered with disgust, "and this gentleman was interfering with the terms and conditions."

"It's more serious than that. Men die over such disputes of honor."

Daisy only saw the sordidness of the arrangement, women treated as concubines and routinely abandoned as they aged, their protectors moving on to more youthful amusements.

"This gentleman would not have risked approaching me unless he thought Lord Gabriel was not coming back."

Daisy's hands began to shake, so she tightened her grasp on the parchment. "You mean, not coming back to you."

"No, I fear he believes that Lord Gabriel will not come back at all. That's why you must take what I've written to his cousin at once. He'll make better sense of the words."

"Stay here. I'll be right back."

Daisy read the note as she hurried upstairs, her mind awhirl with questions, especially since the note contained only one line:

Confirm N. will have welcome party for guest arriving at Boulogne.

The words could have been said by a friend, confirming that 'N'—didn't have to stand for Napoleon—had made arrangements for the arrival of a certain guest. But Gabriel was on his way to France and she feared the welcome party was a French regiment prepared to shoot him on sight.

Women had a sense about such things, even "'bad" women such as Desiree. And what of her? She was French and could very well be one of Napoleon's agents.

Daisy entered the bedchamber that was now serving as an infirmary. There was no help for it, she'd have to rely on Graelem's judgment. Fortunately he was as alert as one could possibly be in a laudanum-induced stupor, sitting up with tears streaming down his face as he gazed intently at Laurel.

Her uncle was back in the room, and he and Mrs. Peebles were beside Laurel, her uncle's medical bag open while he rubbed a foul-smelling liquid on a metal implement that looked like an instrument of torture. The hot, dank room reeked of foul alcohol. Rose and the twins were standing quietly in a corner, their hands clasped together. *Oh, no! Oh, no!*

Daisy knelt beside Graelem. "Take a look at this note. Please, it's important."

"Not now, Daisy."

"You must." She knew he was despondent over Laurel. "*Please.* It concerns Gabriel. He may be in danger."

"Damn, I'm so fuzzy-headed." A savage expression crossed his face as he took it from her hands and read it. "Where did you get this?"

"Desiree St. Claire." Daisy felt her cheeks heat. "She's here, in your library. Can she be trusted?"

He glanced at the parchment again. "How did she get it?"

"She wrote it down, claims she overheard... a certain gentleman visitor seeking to become her new benefactor."

His expression turned hard as stone. "Help me to my feet."

Daisy forced him back in the chair. "Are you mad? You can't walk."

"Help me," he ordered. "You don't understand."

"I do. If Gabriel's in danger, he needs to be warned." Assuming it wasn't already too late. "You're in no condition to do it."

"I must. *Blast it!* Hand me a cane." He tried to stand, but his face contorted in pain and he fell back with an anguished yelp.

"Can she be trusted?" Daisy repeated. "I'll deal with the rest." She tried to sound confident and efficient, but didn't know quite what to do. Should she report the matter to the Prince Regent? Or was Desiree part of the trap?

Graelem nodded. "She can be trusted."

"Are you certain?"

"Yes. I may have said my brain was fuzzy, but this note sobered me up fast. Tell Billings to wake the groomsman and saddle my horse. Help me up. I have to warn Gabriel before his ship sails for France."

Daisy once again forced him back in the chair, ordinarily an impossible feat, but Graelem wasn't at his best just now. "How do you propose doing it? By hopping across England like a demented frog with a busted limb? I'll go. He's my husband."

"You can't go. You're just a girl, and there are dangerous men on the road, ruffians and cutthroats who are just as dangerous as any French spy."

She glanced at her uncle, studying him as he worked with the midwife. "It has to be me. Uncle George can't be spared." She refused to say aloud what they were all fearing, that Laurel would die without him at her bedside. "Amos will accompany me."

"Fetch me paper, ink, and pen," Graelem ordered. "Wait! Bring Desiree up here, too."

Daisy's eyes rounded in horror. "Graelem! Think of your wife!"

"I'm thinking of her and the safety of every Englishman."

"I don't know what you two are bickering about," Mrs. Peebles said with a glower, "but if ye think ye're going ta bring one more person in here, yer sadly mistaken. M'lord, I'll toss ye down those stairs m'self if ye utter a word of protest."

Graelem sighed. "Who was the gentleman with Desiree this evening?"

Her heart sank into her stomach. "I didn't think to ask." In her own defense, Desiree's appearance had rattled her.

"Well, ask her now. Quick."

She hurried back to the library, hoping Desiree hadn't grown skittish and fled, but she needn't have worried. Desiree was standing in the same spot she'd left her, and now she was wringing her hands. The strain showed in her porcelain cheeks.

"His lordship wishes to know who came to see you." She ought to have been jealous of this woman and the intimacy she'd obviously shared with Gabriel, but it all seemed inconsequential at the moment.

"Auguste Malinor."

Daisy gasped. Auguste? Of course, she ought to have guessed. The blackguard meant to destroy Gabriel, first proposing to her and now trying to take Gabriel's mistress. But was he merely jealous of Gabriel and eager to see him hurt, or did he plan to betray England as well? She hurried back to Graelem, who already appeared to be instructing her sisters as he related the news to them. He set to work at once, scribbling several letters. "Rose, as Lady Emory you'll be granted an audience right away. I need you to take this letter to the Prince Regent. Use my carriage and take two of my footmen for protection."

"What about the other letter?" Daisy asked.

"That one's for Gabriel. One of Prinny's men will carry it to him." He rubbed his hands over his eyes. "Christ, everything's happening so fast. I don't know if he'll reach the ship in time."

"Rose can go to the palace, but give me that other note. I'll saddle Brutus and intercept Gabriel before he sails. As I said, Amos will escort me."

Graelem's eyes rounded in horror. "Are you mad? Yes, of course you are. You're a Farthingale. Even so, you can't go."

"He's my husband and I have no intention of becoming his widow." She wasn't going to let Graelem win this battle. "As you said, there's no time to lose. I'm the best rider and Brutus is the fastest horse. Come on, Graelem. We're wasting precious time. Where is Gabriel and what shall I tell him?" Graelem had already sealed the letters.

"I must be mad. He'll string me up by my... never mind. Oh, hell." He grabbed her hand and clasped it in his. "He must not sail to Boulogne. Napoleon's men know he's coming and have been told the name of the ship. They'll shoot him on sight. Probably blow up his ship as soon as it tucks into one of the nearby smugglers' coves. He must find himself another vessel. The one we chartered is no longer safe."

Despite his pain, Graelem smiled at her. "You never believed Gabriel was a coward, willing to abandon all to pursue his own pleasures while England stood on the precipice of war. You may as well know all of it now. You're his wife, after all. Prinny sent him on a raiding mission to France. His orders are to slow Napoleon's progress and give Wellington as much time as possible to muster our forces and coordinate with our Continental allies. It's damn dangerous, but he's been doing similar work for years and has managed to stay alive even under impossible conditions. I know my cousin well, and he won't let anything get in the way of his coming home to you."

She nodded, hoping Graelem truly did know him as well as he thought, but she couldn't dwell on their hasty marriage or any regrets Gabriel might have over it. "What do Lord Malinor and his son stand to gain by harming Gabriel?"

"We were having difficulty outsmarting the French lately, and Gabriel was beginning to suspect that someone close to the Crown was betraying our plans. Lord Malinor is in Prinny's inner circle. I have no doubt now that he and his son must have been feeding Napoleon's agents sensitive information."

Daisy's mind was whirling in confusion. "Why would they do such a thing?"

Graelem sighed. "Arrogance. Desire for power. Who knows what Napoleon promised them? Likely control of England once we were conquered by the French."

"Why did Auguste ask for my hand in marriage? How in heaven do I fit in with their diabolical plans?"

Graelem shrugged. "Perhaps he thought you knew more about Gabriel's mission than you let on, or he was simply trying to rile Gabriel into making a mistake." He grabbed Daisy's hand before she took off to save her husband. "Once you deliver the warning, get back here before your family realizes you're missing. Gabriel ought to be in Harwich by now. He's to sail on a vessel called The Golden Fleece, set to leave for France shortly after first light."

Laurel let out a scream and Graelem's thoughts were no longer on his cousin. No matter, Daisy knew what she had to do. Find Gabriel. Hand him the note and tell him to wait in Harwich for further instructions. She made a quick calculation in her head and realized it would indeed be close, but Brutus would make it if they left immediately.

She ran to the guest quarters she'd taken over during her stay and hastily changed into the rough, homespun trousers and jacket she wore when taking Brutus for his morning run, allowing her to ride astride the beast. She braided her hair and tucked it securely under her cap before running to the stable. Rose would have roused the head groom by now and ordered him to saddle Brutus and a mount for Amos.

Although riding with Amos would slow her down, she knew it was too dangerous for her to ride alone. Indeed, she would have only the moonlight and an occasional torchlight to guide her path and couldn't risk injuring Brutus over the uneven terrain. Once the first rays of sunlight peeked over the hills, she'd give Brutus free rein and let the stallion fly.

She took the snorting beast from the sleepy groomsman with a muttered thanks.

"Young Amos is saddling Defiance, a good horse, but nowhere near as fast as Brutus. I'll help the lad out, if ye'll excuse me, Miss Daisy."

"Of course." She heard Defiance kick against the wooden boards of his stall and knew that he'd be a handful for poor Amos. Perhaps he wasn't the best choice of escort, but he was a loyal and diligent retainer, and an adequate horseman.

She turned her attention back to Brutus, who was growing impatient. So was she, and scared that she might fail. There were no rules in Lady Forsythia's book about saving a rake's life. Her stomach was churning with the grinding persistence of a butter wheel. A wrong turn, the slightest mistake, or smallest obstruction would bring disaster.

Refusing to allow doubt to overcome her, she continued to speak softly to the skittish horse. "I'm relying on you. All of England is relying on you. Can you manage it?"

The beast's nostrils flared and he snorted in indignation.

"Good, for you had better run faster than you've ever done in your life." She patted his neck, still speaking softly as she reached for a knife atop a table laden with tools. "I'll take one of those." She hoped she wouldn't have to use the skills Graelem had taught her.

"What are you doing?" a voice asked from behind her.

She whirled, now clutching the weapon firmly in her hand.

"You!" The ugly man she'd seen with Gabriel at the Newton lecture and seen again in the park on the day of the shooting incident stood before her.

The blasted assassin wasn't going to stop her. She'd cut him to ribbons first. But as she started toward him, Billings lumbered into the stable, barely able to catch his breath. "Stop! Miss Daisy! He's on our side!"

"No, get back! He's dangerous."

Billings stepped between her and the man. "Lord Graelem forgot to tell you about Major Brandt. That's why he sent me after you." He clutched his chest and took several deep breaths. "Major Brandt has been following you at Lord Gabriel's urging."

"Since when?" She hadn't noticed him other than at the lecture and again at the park.

"I've been assigned to you since the Newton lecture," Major Brandt said, raising his hands to show he held no weapon, obviously still concerned about the one she held tightly in her hand.

"He's safe. He's one of us," Billings assured her, for she had yet to loosen her grip.

"That's right, Miss Daisy. Or should I call you Lady Dayne? That's why you noticed me in the park. I was watching over you."

She eased her stance and lowered the weapon which she still held in a death grip. "You did a dismal job of it."

"The Duke of Wellington said much the same thing when I reported the incident to him," the ugly man said, taking a hesitant step forward, his eye on the gleaming blade. "Lord Gabriel warned me that you were a handful. Smart as a whip and curious as a kitten, that's what he said about you. Now, would you mind telling me where you're going at this late hour?"

She quickly related what Graelem had told her.

Major Brandt ran a hand through his wispy, black hair. "Goodness! We'd better ride fast."

"We?"

"She might not look it, but my Emily's much sturdier than Defiance, and I'm a far better rider than Amos. Let the lad stay here, for he'll only delay us and every minute is precious. Indeed, we had better leave for Harwich now. I'll keep up as best as I can. You're the only one with a prayer of reaching Lord Gabriel before he sails."

He attempted to take hold of Brutus' reins, then quickly backed away as Brutus lunged forward to bite him. "We're on the same side, you devil!"

CHAPTER 20

*A lady must never play the wanton for a
rake, even in the marriage bed, for a rake
desires a traditional wife, a woman of demure
and obedient aspect, not a wanton repository
of his unbridled lust.*

DAISY URGED BRUTUS along the sodden ground, thankful the skies were clear. She had a full moon to illuminate her path and meant to take full advantage.

She pushed Brutus as fast as she dared, remembering to keep to the left of the sea breeze and follow the river into the seaside town of Harwich. Once there, she needed to find the Three Cups Inn.

A cool wind pricked at her cheeks and she felt her ears beginning to numb. Her legs were also stiff and aching. No doubt Major Brandt was feeling equal discomfort as he struggled to keep up. She patted the parchment tucked in the breast pocket of her jacket to make sure it was secure. Graelem had related its contents and she'd memorized it, but Gabriel would want to see it for himself. Major Brandt had more stunning news of his own to deliver besides the collapse of this mission. Napoleon was marching north to Paris faster than anyone thought possible, crushing Marshall Ney's troops... those who hadn't promptly deserted to Napoleon's side. The little general would soon be in full control of France, certain to rally the French citizens for another Continental war.

The road to Harwich was unfamiliar and not as well traveled as many in England, but Graelem had drawn up a rough map with excellent guide markers. Daisy picked up speed at daybreak, the beast's hooves barely touching the ground as they galloped northward then east along the river that marked the final leg of her journey. She'd lost sight of Major Brandt at least an hour ago, but knew he'd catch up to her eventually at the inn.

Gabriel would be furious that she'd braved the final leg of the journey entirely on her own, but he'd understand the necessity once he calmed. In any event, she was too cold and wet from this morning's sudden rain shower to concern herself with his response. What mattered was reaching the Three Cups Inn before his ship sailed.

Daisy was exhausted and about ready to tumble out of her saddle by the time she entered the quiet town of Harwich and guided Brutus toward the docks. It was still too early for most decent people to be about. Those who were awake at this hour were scoundrels who had been drinking all night and were up to no good.

"Now, that's a nasty-looking fellow," she murmured to Brutus, avoiding the stare of one particularly unpleasant character. She tightened her grip on the riding crop, clenching it in her fist to use as protection if the need arose.

She had never used the crop on Brutus and never would. But she had purposely brought it along for protection against unsavory characters skulking in dark alleys, men like the blackguard she had just passed.

"Blast it, I think he's following us." She quickly moved on, daring to breathe a sigh of relief as she turned the corner and spotted a ship's mast, sails unfurled in the near distance. She had to be near the inn.

"Please, let it be Gabriel's ship," she murmured and received a corresponding nod from Brutus.

"Where'd ye get that fine horse, lad?" a gap-toothed man sporting a tattoo on his arm and a sharp knife in his hand called out.

"None of yer business," she called back, lowering the cap over her eyes and hoping neither her voice nor her face would give away her disguise. He'd mistaken her for a boy, for she sat astride Brutus and not sidesaddle as a proper female ought to. Riding sidesaddle would have been a ridiculous and dangerous way to travel the extended distance.

Daisy's hands, which might have given her away, were hidden beneath a pair of worn leather gloves and her hair was still braided and securely pinned beneath the cap. Her baggy clothes, she fervently prayed, hid her tell-tale feminine curves.

"Give me that horse, ye peach-faced son of a whore."

Several men now stepped out of the shadows, each more hideous looking than the next. Too late, Daisy realized she'd made a wrong turn and unwittingly entered a most dangerous alley. She whirled Brutus about, attempting to head back to the main street, but the men quickly surrounded her and tried to block her path.

She fought them off with her riding crop, striking one across the cheek and drawing blood. He let out an oath and came at her again. Brutus kicked out with his massive hooves. Men yelped and cursed, and ultimately cleared a path for the devil of a horse. She and Brutus had just cleared the last assailant when Daisy felt a sudden sharp pain at her thigh.

She didn't stop to look, knowing there would be time to tend to the wound after she found Gabriel.

At last she saw the inn, recognizing it by its sign—three cups painted over the weathered doorway lintel—and rode behind the rough stone structure into its stable.

"Ye're bleedin'!" the stableboy cried, his eyes popping wide at the sight of blood trailing down her trousers. "Stay put and I'll get ye help."

"No! I need to see Lord Dayne. Is he still here?"

"Yes, he's—"

"Thank goodness! Take me to him right away." She slid off Brutus, then let out a yowl as she landed on her injured leg.

"Lud, that must hurt! I'll fetch clean cloths and some water."

"No! Take me to Lord Dayne at once," she insisted, though both her legs were aching from the hard ride and about to give way beneath her. Her left leg felt as if it were on fire.

"But there's no—"

"Don't argue with me!" She rested her weight on a bale of hay, leaning on it for support, and reached out to grab the stubborn boy, her intention to throttle him into obedience.

"But I can't take you to him!"

"Why ever not?" Her head began to spin and a soft but persistent ringing started in her ears. Her vision began to blur. The lad now sported two heads and both were spinning.

"Because he's right here," Gabriel said, jumping down from the hayloft and stalking to her side. "Of all the bloody... foolish... stupid... you'd better have a damn good explanation for why you're here—good Lord! Daisy, you're hurt!"

"Lud, ye called 'im Daisy."

Nausea built in her stomach. "Gabriel! Thank goodness!"

He opened his arms to her.

She took a step toward him and fainted.

"YOU CAN COME in now, Gabriel. I'm decent," Daisy called from inside her room, which had been his until she'd stormed back into his life in the most spectacular way this morning. Less than an hour had passed since he'd carried her in, set her on the bed and proceeded to remove her trousers over the complaints of the innkeeper's wife.

"Sir! Now, see here! We run a respectable establishment. Won't have such goings on under m'very nose," the woman had threatened, following him into the room with raised fist, and suddenly silenced by the gruesome sight of Daisy's thigh. "Lud! She's been stabbed!"

"I have to stop the bleeding. Help me get her out of these wretched clothes," he'd ordered, the additional coins thrown her way quickly stifling further protest.

Gabriel had thrown more coins about, to hire one of the serving girls to serve as Daisy's personal maid, to order a warm bath and scented soaps brought up for Daisy, to provide for a steady stream of food and drink brought to her room, to provide wood for the fire needed to keep the room warm and protect her from the chilling sea breeze.

As she bathed, Gabriel had walked to the High Street to purchase

Daisy a decent gown and shawl, shoes, stockings, and assorted delicate undergarments, handing the packages to the innkeeper's wife to deliver to Daisy. "Here, my wife will need these."

And now, he stood at her door, waiting for her to try on the new clothes and wondering how he would ever find the strength to part from her.

"Well, are you coming in?" Daisy called out hesitantly. "I'm decent," she repeated.

He opened the door, took one step inside, and sucked in his breath. *Oh, Lord... Lord, Lord.* She stood by the window in a stream of sunlight, ruffling fingers through her damp, dark hair to dry it, and all he could think of was how much he'd enjoy running his own fingers through that incredibly long, lush mound, as well as over the two lush mounds presently concealed by the soft, blue shawl wrapped over her shoulders.

Decent? The thoughts whirling in his head were decidedly not that.

"What do you think?" she asked, holding out her hands and slowly twirling to show off her new gown. She tossed him the most beautiful smile, one that reached her vibrant blue eyes.

"What do I think?" he repeated numbly, relieved that she seemed able to put weight on her injured leg without apparent trouble. He'd never beheld a more beautiful female, never imagined anyone could stir his heart this powerfully. "You didn't finish the plate of cheese and fruit I ordered brought up to you."

She let out an adorable laugh. "The *third* plate you ordered sent up. I'm so stuffed, I can't bear to look at another wedge of cheese or slice of apple. Gabriel, you've been far too extravagant in your care of me."

"I don't think so. You were bedraggled, quite mangy looking, really, when you first stumbled in here," he teased.

She laughed again, picked up a hairbrush and, instead of throwing it at him—thankfully—began to brush her hair. His fingers itched to take the hairbrush from her hand and perform the task of putting order to those silky strands, but he decided against it since his hands were shaking and his heart was painfully lodged in his throat.

"I suppose I did look a mess, but cool water and a chunk of lye soap would have set me to rights as capably as a warm, scented bath, fragrant oils, and delicate soaps."

"Those," he said with a chuckle, softly closing the door and walking toward her, "were for my pleasure."

She melted into his arms when he held them out to her. "Oh, Gabriel! I was so afraid I'd be too late to stop you from sailing to your death!"

He hugged her tightly, lifting her so that they were eye to eye, her delectable body nestled against his hard frame. Her feet dangled off the floor since he was much taller than she. But she smelled so sweet, he realized, burying his face against her neck, loving the silky smoothness of her skin. He planted kisses along her neck, the little upturn of her chin, and finally, with desperate longing, upon her lips.

Also sweet. So very, very sweet.

She responded as he knew she would, had hoped she would, by circling her arms around his neck and parting her lips in welcome. "Lord, I can't believe you're here. I thought I'd never see you again," he said, groaning against her mouth.

She pressed her warm lips to his, sighing softly as their mouths locked for another long, lingering embrace.

He loved the thickness of her hair, the way it fell in damp waves to her waist, the way it fell over his arms and shoulders, as if wrapping him in silk. "Gabriel, how much time do we have together?"

A lifetime, I hope. But he dared not think that far ahead. "Not much."

There was little to be done. Ian and Major Brandt were already securing another ship. Once settled, he'd be on his way, perhaps on this same early tide. But first, he'd have to toss more coins to the innkeeper and his staff, to the stable hand, probably the shopkeeper and boot maker, to keep their mouths shut about Daisy's presence here. Then he'd somehow have to return her to Graelem's home with no one the wiser that she had ever left it. Major Brandt would be the one to accomplish that task. With good weather and a few hours of hard riding, the major could deliver Daisy back to London by nightfall.

"Then we'd better not wait," Daisy insisted.

"For what?"

"Our magic moment." There was a pink blush to her cheeks as she lowered her gaze and stared into his chest. "That's how Laurel described her wedding night."

Gabriel set her down gently so that her feet once more touched the ground, but kept his hands loosely about her waist. The war was just getting underway. As the son of a nobleman he might have bought his way out, but he wasn't about to abandon Wellington at his most desperate hour. How was he to tell Daisy that his chances of returning from this mission were poor? Did he dare risk leaving her with child? Was that to be his legacy, a widow and a fatherless son left behind?

For years, he'd lived by the simple rules... no broken hearts, no grieving widows, no fatherless sons. Yet, looking at Daisy's anguish and desire, both so expressively revealed in her vivid blue eyes, he wanted to toss away all rules and just follow his heart. He desperately wanted Daisy, needed her more than he needed air to breathe.

How could he do this to her?

Her smile faded. "I'm an utter goose. You meant this to be a marriage of convenience, one easily annulled upon your return. You're not going to seduce me, are you?"

He stopped her when she tried to pull away, wanting to feel her silken skin beneath his palms. "Daisy, you don't understand. I wish it were otherwise."

"So do I," she whispered, straining the bonds of his resolve with her wide-eyed gaze.

His body was hot and about to ignite, her body serving as the spark. Lord, she was perfect. Soft and curved in all the right places. Vibrant, yielding... passionate. "I'm going to miss you desperately, you impossible little baggage. I don't want out of our marriage."

She let out the softest breath.

And burst into tears. "Then what's wrong with you?" she accused between sniffles. "Haven't you read Graelem's warning? Or Wellington's warning? The French know you're coming. They'll shoot you the moment you set foot on French soil."

"If they catch me. Thanks to you, they'll be waiting at Boulogne while I safely land elsewhere."

"And in the meantime, am I supposed to sit idly by and do nothing?"

His heart tightened. "What are you suggesting? I can't take you with me on this mission."

"I know. But there's something more you must do. For me. For us." Her hands trembled as she rested them against his chest. "I love you, Gabriel. Is this all I'm to have of you?"

She was asking him to consummate the marriage. He wanted to... she wanted to... but it was a mistake. Perhaps the most idiotic thing he'd ever done.

"It's the right thing to do," she insisted, seeming to read his mind and determined to contradict him. "You may think your way is less hurtful to me, but you're wrong. The worst thing you can do is deny me these last moments, if they're to be our last moments together. Though I fervently pray they're not. Please, Gabriel. You married me. If you're content with the bargain, then make it official. Make me your wife in more than name only."

He felt his resistance weakening.

She must have felt it, too, for she pressed her advantage. "Give me one precious memory of our life together."

He said nothing for a long moment.

Her eyes began to water and he knew she was fighting to hold back her tears. "Is this what you'll remember on those cold, French nights? Not me, soft and willing in your arms. But you and your blasted pride. You and your misguided sense of honor."

"Damn it, Daisy. Enough." He lifted her into his arms and settled her on the bed. The mattress dipped as he sat down beside her and reached out to stroke her cheek. "My friends and I made a pact... we swore to leave behind no broken hearts, no grieving widows." He thought briefly of Julia and little Harry, and knew by Daisy's expression that she was thinking of them as well.

"You had better rethink that pact, because I'm not going to live my life regretting these last moments... not that I want them to be our last moments together, but if they are, they'd better be spectacular. I'm not letting you out of this room until I have you, *all* of you, heart, body, and soul to carry with me forever. And when a Farthingale says forever, she means it. Napoleon's wrath will be nothing to mine if I don't get my way in this. Please, Gabriel. Don't walk away and leave me with nothing."

He meant to refuse. He meant to hold firm and live by the rules that had kept him safe, numb, all these years, but he made the mistake of gazing into Daisy's incredible blue eyes... eyes filled with love. For him.

To hell with pacts and to hell with rules. Had Daisy managed to get even one of Lady Forsythia's rules right? The answer was a resounding no, yet she'd captured his heart in spite of it... probably because of it. Her body felt warm and soft as he slipped the shawl off her shoulders and then did the same with her gown, loosening the laces at her bosom to bare her creamy breasts. "Sweetheart," he said in a whisper, his loins tight and on fire, his heart about to explode. "You're so beautiful, you steal my breath away."

She closed her eyes and arched into him as he cupped one soft, full mound in his palm. He teased his thumb across its pink tip and let out a groan as it hardened beneath his touch. He circled his arm around her waist to draw her closer, wanting her soft body crushed against him, needing to wrap her in his protective embrace and bury himself inside her.

He wanted to hear her breathy moans and feel the explosive heat of her passion as she reached her climax. He was lost and could no longer fight it. Giving in, he dipped his mouth to hers and took her in a long, deep kiss that roused a maelstrom of desire in both of them. Daisy was so open and passionate. She held nothing back in her response.

He slipped the gown off her luscious body, and then practically ripped off his own clothes.

Gad, you'd think this was his first time. Well, it was his first time with her. He wanted to make it right, a lifetime's worth of right. His breath caught at the sight of her bandaged leg. He'd have to be careful with that tender wound.

He settled her flat upon the bed, his gaze soaking in all of her, the cream silk of her skin, her lush breasts and their perfect pink tips, her beautiful long legs. Her hair fanned out across the crisp, white sheets, those long, silken strands as dark as coal against them. Her eyes were as bright as a May sky, a warm, gleaming azure blue.

She wanted him.

She *loved* him.

He nudged his legs between hers, settling his large body atop her slender frame, though he balanced most of his weight on his elbows. She felt so good beneath him. Too good. He was hard and ready, his skin fiery hot and his muscles tense from the strain of wanting to take it slow with Daisy.

But his wife—damn, that sounded good—was too impatient.

So was he. His finger found the nub of her passion between her thighs and he gently began to stroke her there.

Her eyes shot open and she gasped, but as he continued to stroke and tease, her surprise gave way to heat, and soon her eyes were drifting closed, her body moving against his finger as she softly moaned his name. *"Gabriel."*

Lord, she was beautiful. She wanted him. He felt her desire in the moist, liquid heat between her thighs.

An ocean breeze blew in cool, salty air through the open window. He dipped his head, kissed Daisy on the lips, and tasted the honeyed tea she had been drinking. He kissed a trail down her neck, then lower to her beautiful breasts, his tongue flicking across the budded tips, licking and tasting their silken warmth. Her breasts tasted like cinnamon and apples. She was a veritable feast for a starving man... and he'd been starved of real affection for so long. Finding it again, feeling it as sweetly as he did now, was all because of Daisy.

Only because of Daisy.

His heart thundered and blood heated as he poised himself over her and slowly entered her. Her legs wrapped around his waist as he thrust into her velvet opening with a satisfied growl.

"Magic," she whispered against his ear, her hands on his shoulders and body straining awkwardly and innocently against his, seeking a fulfillment she had never experienced before, but she would soon... any moment now, for he was pushing and thrusting... and she was arching and trembling with heat and need, her body embracing each sensation. Her legs tightened around his waist and she raised her hips to fully absorb his shaft.

Gad, he was about to explode!

Each thrust brought him closer to mindless release, to heat and fire and savage hunger, to a craving for Daisy that would never be satisfied as long as he lived. He would always want more of her.

He would always want *her.*

She was everything his heart was missing.

"Sweet heaven," she whispered, her breath soft and voice aching, "you feel so good inside me."

He thrust and tasted and ran his hands along her warm skin, his fingers skimming across her engorged, pink nipples, and then his mouth closed over one of those hard, pink tips, licking and teasing until she was once again breathless and moaning his name. His thrusts came faster, his kisses deeper, hotter, harder until he felt her shudder and heard the soft glory of her ecstasy. Her body strained, she cried out again and begged him not to stop, *not ever,* and fisted her hands in his hair. He felt the *thump, thump, thump* of her heart against his lips, then felt and heard nothing but the slow, building roar of his release, a crashing wave of pleasure that slammed and dipped and slammed within his body, lifting him in a great, heaving motion heavenward and holding him there for an exquisite eternity until all was spent—his seed spilled and his member throbbing against Daisy's thigh.

His voice was hoarse and raspy as he grunted his pleasure.

Daisy laughed. "Magic."

He grunted again, rolling her atop him so that her creamy breasts molded to his hot, damp chest. So good. So perfect. He wrapped his arms around her waist and gave her a gentle squeeze. She grinned, waiting for him to agree. "Aye, sweetheart. It was magic."

"I love you, Gabriel."

The wind blew gently through her dark hair. He kissed her again... and again... and lower because he couldn't get enough of her... and then his tongue found the sweet heat between her thighs. He stroked and swirled as she clutched the sheets and moaned his name. He caressed her until she throbbed and soared against his lips, her love for him a treasured memory for the harrowing months ahead.

SUNLIGHT STREAMED THROUGH the open window and glistened off Gabriel's gold hair. Daisy was still in his arms, floating in his arms to be precise, for she felt as light as a cloud and so happy, even though she understood this perfect moment could not last. He would leave soon. She refused to think about it. There was nothing she could do to stop him.

She absently stroked the gold hairs that glistened on his forearms, breathed in the mix of salt and musk against his hot, damp skin. They were spooned together, her back to his chest, and she savored the protective strength of his arms around her body.

"What are you thinking about?" he asked, turning her so that they faced each other, her breasts once again molding to his rock hard chest. He was big and muscled and perfect. She traced the scar across his brow, then delicately traced the welt on his shoulder where the shot fired in Hyde Park had struck him. Only a graze, he'd said. Apparently, that's all it was, though it had drawn his blood and would leave a red, puckered scar. Even his scars were perfect, not that she'd ever wanted him to suffer. But the hard years had molded him into the man he was today.

The man she desperately loved.

"I'm thinking that I'm glad Laurel and my father put a pistol to your head and made you marry me."

He let out a deep, throaty laugh. "There was no pistol. I volunteered, if you will recall. I would have offered for you eventually, perhaps not at that moment. You know that, don't you?" His mirth subsided and he turned serious. "I need you to know that no one forced me to marry you."

She nodded.

Another moment passed, the two lazily nestled in each other's arms, Gabriel running his fingers in a soft swirl against her skin. She clung to him, her hand gripping his big, muscled shoulder because she never wanted to let him go. She would have to soon. She sensed him shifting away before he spoke, and then he turned to her. "Sweetheart, I have to go."

Her eyes misted.

"I want you to smile for me. Be brave for me... a little while longer. I couldn't bear it if you cried."

She nodded again, though she doubted he was convinced.

He ran a hand raggedly through his hair. An unruly lock curled over his forehead. Another curled at the nape of his neck, just below his ear. "Promise me that you'll lead a happy life, no matter what happens or whatever you hear over the next few months."

She did, promising all he asked because it was important for him to believe she would manage life without him.

He sat up, threw his long legs over the edge of the bed, and glanced out the window again. "You had better get dressed. Major Brandt and Ian will be back soon. How do you feel?"

She cast him a tender smile. "Splendidly aglow."

He leaned forward and gently kissed her on the nose. "Yes, it was pretty damn fantastic. However, I meant how does your leg feel?"

She followed his gaze to her wound. "It's a little sore. Nothing I can't handle."

"My battle-hardened warrior," he teased. "Major Brandt is recommending you for a medal."

She laughed. "Me? That's ridiculous. Desiree is the one who saved your manly hide."

"Bloody hell," he said under his breath, his smile fading. "I'm sorry, Daisy. I never meant... she wasn't... she doesn't hold a candle to you."

She tried to hide the flicker of pain in her eyes. "She's the most beautiful woman I've ever met. You thought so, too. Otherwise, you wouldn't have taken her under your protection. Is that the proper expression? It's such a polite expression."

He glanced at her, appalled. "Appearances are deceiving. She was a necessary part of my dissolute reputation. There's nothing between us. I'm deeply grateful for what she did, for she risked her life in warning Graelem. I'll make sure the Prince Regent generously rewards her. She'll do well for herself. Such women always do."

He stood to dress, his golden body on exquisite display. She remained in bed and watched him, admiring his perfectly proportioned torso and its sinewed strength. He quickly donned his trousers and shirt, then nudged her out of bed and helped her into her gown, though he took a disproportionate amount of time smoothing it over her breasts, insisting they were woefully in need of his attention. "Tell my idiot cousin that he'd better be more careful with his injured leg."

She had been so distraught about reaching Gabriel in time to save his life that she had made no mention of Laurel's distress. *Dear heaven! Please, let Laurel survive.* She quickly told Gabriel everything.

His tawny eyes darkened and he frowned. "Sweetheart, I'm so sorry. Graelem's by her side as he should be. Your uncle is a most extraordinary man, best physician I've ever seen. He won't let her come to harm." He took her into his arms and held her gently.

She rested her cheek against his chest, wishing they had more time together, but knowing it couldn't be. At least he'd be pleased to know that the Malinors would get their due. "What will happen to Auguste and his father? Will they be placed under arrest?"

Gabriel nodded. "Hopefully tried and hanged before the month is out. I'm sorry I'll miss their disgrace. Bastards. I think they meant to shoot *you* that day in the park."

She gasped. "Me? Why?"

"It was their way of threatening me, of expressing their hatred for me. Perhaps they didn't intend to kill you, but from that range, it would have been easy to miss your shoulder and hit a vital organ."

"Is that why Lord Malinor invited me onto his phaeton? To make me an easier target?"

He gave a curt nod. "Likely."

"I hate them," she said at his nod. "I've never met two more loathsome characters."

"They'll get what they deserve. The punishment for treason is death."

She shuddered, wishing she better understood the art of political intrigue. Having been raised in a family in which everyone voiced their honest opinion and valued love over wealth, she was at a loss to understand why the Malinors, a family with more wealth than could be spent in a lifetime of profligacy, should lie and scheme to attain even more. Was it mere greed that motivated them, that left them dissatisfied and hungry for more? "Why did Auguste propose to me? First he plots to shoot me and then to marry me? It makes no sense."

Gabriel shrugged, though there was nothing casual about his anger. "I don't know. Perhaps they changed tactics and decided it was a better way to get back at me. Perhaps I'm wrong about all of it and Auguste did care for you."

"No," she said with a grim laugh. "He barely tolerated me."

His gaze softened. "The man would have to be a fool not to fall in love with you."

She caressed his cheek. "He didn't love me. I don't think he even liked me. I never cared for him either. I would never have accepted his proposal." She sighed. "Certainly not after I'd met you. I suppose it doesn't matter. None of their plans came to pass."

"But something else quite important did."

She tipped her head and gazed up at him. "What?"

"Your family will soon know they almost made a terrible mistake, one that might have cost you your life, certainly your happiness, had you not held your ground and refused to marry Auguste." Gabriel took hold of her hands. "I should have done more to protect you. In truth, I'm the one who put you in danger. Can you ever forgive me?"

"There's nothing to forgive. I just need you to get yourself back to me as soon as possible." She lifted on her tiptoes and kissed him lightly on the lips. He responded by sweeping her into his arms and stealing her breath with a not-so-gentle, devouring kiss.

"I won't cry. I promise. But I'm going to miss you," she said in a whisper.

"I'll miss you, too." He drew her against his body and held her to him as though he never wished to let her go. But he hadn't said he loved her. Why wouldn't he say it to her? He'd made love to her, exquisite, magical love, but that was merely an act of the body. Would she ever claim his heart?

She heard a light knock at the door, recognizing Major Brandt's raspy voice and the more refined tones of the Duke of Edgeware as they called to Gabriel.

"Keep me in your dreams." Gabriel kissed her one last time... and then he was gone.

CHAPTER 21

*To reform a rake, a lady must follow her
heart above all rules.*

"A PACKAGE HAS arrived for you, Lady Daisy," Pruitt said,
intercepting her as she strolled out of the dining room of the
Farthingale townhouse on a beautifully crisp afternoon in late June.
The house was unusually quiet. The children and governesses were
in the park, and most of the Farthingale horde were visiting Laurel,
who had safely given birth to a strapping Dayne male she and
Graelem had decided to name Ragnor.

Ragnor!

Well, the babe was almost four months old now and already had
the sturdy look of a Viking.

Most of the Farthingale men had disappeared hours ago, headed
for their clubs to do whatever men did at such places, though her
father and Uncle George had disappeared earlier in the day on
mysterious and urgent business from which they had yet to return.

"I'll open the package later, Pruitt. We're on our way to visit
Lady Eloise." She, her mother, and the twins were invited to tea with
Gabriel's grandmother.

Pruitt blocked the door and plunked the small, rectangular
packet in her hands. "The messenger was very keen that you open it
at once."

"Messenger?" She shrugged. "Curious."

"It looks like a book," Lily said, following her out of the dining room and now hovering at her shoulder, her eyes alight with curiosity.

"I asked to borrow one from Eloise's library," Daisy explained, "but she needn't have wrapped it for me. And why send it over when I could have picked it up myself this afternoon?"

Pruitt arched an eyebrow. "All excellent questions, m'lady. Why don't you open it and find out?"

She laughed. "What's going on? And why are you grinning at me? You never grin. What do you know that I don't?" She drew the string off the wrapper.

"Good heavens, it really is a book," her mother said, joining them in the entry hall and looking on with obvious confusion.

Daisy found herself staring at the cover of one of those mathematical books written by Isaac Newton. Of course, Lily had mastered it by the age of twelve, but she... "Newton? Newton!" Daisy's heart shot into her throat. The last letter she'd received from Gabriel was two weeks ago, assuring her that he was alive and well and would return to England sometime in July. He'd made it home earlier than expected. She couldn't bear it. She ached to see him. "Where is he?"

"Sir Isaac—"

"You know who I mean, Pruitt!" She darted into the parlor, only to find Julia entertaining Lord Lumley... him again, coming around quite often lately... and Julia was beaming. "I beg your pardon, I didn't mean to interrupt."

The pair looked as pleased to see her as a virulent attack of gout.

She backed out of the room, once more calling for the Farthingale butler. "Where have you put Lord Gabriel? The family shall find you dead at the door, this book embedded in your skull, if you don't tell me where he is right now!"

"Gabriel?" Dillie's eyes lit up. "It's about time that handsome wart-hero showed up."

"Honestly, child! This is no time to tease your sister," her mother chided. "Pruitt, spill it."

"I haven't put him anywhere. I believe he might be visiting his grandmother."

"Oh, I love you! Oh, dear! How do I look?" Daisy peered in the mirror, but saw little through the shimmer in her eyes. Her pale rose tea gown and its white lace collar were all a blur. "I'm sure I'm a mess!"

"You look beautiful," her sisters said in unison. Her mother was crying and couldn't speak.

Daisy ran out of the house, clutching the book to her bosom.

She didn't bother to stop at Eloise's front door. Watling was elderly and too slow—and having waited too many months for this moment, she simply couldn't wait any longer. She ran to the back, knowing the salon doors leading onto the terrace would be open. She burst into the room only to find Eloise sitting alone. "Pruitt said he's back! Oh, Eloise! You must be so pleased! Where is he? How does he look? Handsome as ever, I'm sure. Is he injured? Oh, dear. Why isn't he here?"

"Because he was stupid enough to wait for you by the front door," came the laughing response from the entry hall. "I ought to have known better."

Daisy whirled on her heels. "Gabriel!" His left arm was in a sling and a crutch supported his right arm. "You're hurt!"

"No, love. Never felt better." He limped toward her, a ridiculous grin on his face that faded as he drew close. "You've grown even more beautiful than I thought possible," he said in a raw whisper.

"So have you, more handsome, that is. You've lost a little weight." She wanted to rush into his arms and never let him go, but he was awfully banged up and bruised, and though he tried to hide it, she saw that he was in terrible pain. "A new scar," she said, running a finger lightly over his forehead.

"I hadn't noticed."

"Oh, Gabriel! I want to throw my arms about you, but don't dare. Look at you! You must ache all over. I fear to touch you, lest I knock you over. I've missed you so much. When did you return?"

"Only this morning. I went home first, but you were already out of the house, paying a call on your family. I meant to come sooner, but had business to settle with your father first. We met up with him and your uncle at their club."

"What for? He gave his permission to our marriage. And he's been banging his breast about the family's nearly fatal mistake ever since the Malinors were arrested. What a delicious scandal! He now thinks I'm brilliant. They all do, especially Julia. I think she and Lumley Hornby will soon have an announcement to make."

"He of the gherkins and weak nasal cavities?"

She let out a chuckle as she nodded. "He's gone up in my estimation. He worships Julia and sincerely adores Harry, who's as much of a scamp as ever. But a happy scamp, and that's what counts." She inhaled lightly. "You said 'we' met up with my father and Uncle George. Who is 'we'?"

"Wellington and I."

"Wellington!"

"He wishes to meet you, too." His grin broadened. "So does Prinny. The four of us had an audience with him a short while ago."

"You, Wellington, my father and uncle?" She stared at him in amazement. "Met with Prinny?"

He nodded. "I wanted your family to know the truth about me now that Napoleon is no longer a threat, and what better way to do it than to hear it from reliable sources? My days of intrigue are over, Daisy. My cover will now be blown and the gossips will have their day, whispering only good things about me from now on . . . well, mostly good things, I hope. It's up to some other poor sod to risk his life for king and country."

"*Thank goodness*. Where are my father and Uncle George now?"

"They'll be along soon. They wanted to give me a little time alone with you."

"My mother and sisters will be along soon as well. I tore out of the house when I saw the title of this Newton book." She held it up between them. He nudged it aside and drew her up against him.

"I'm expecting more guests," Eloise said with a gentle laugh, reminding them that they were not alone. "But I think we can all stand in the hall until you've quite finished in here." She slipped away and quietly closed the door behind her, her last glance an indulgent, tearful smile.

Daisy heard more female voices and knew her mother and sisters had arrived and would be escorted in by Watling. Eloise would keep to her word and not allow them to intrude, but all of them would be listening at the keyhole. Even now, she heard their squeals and

298 | MEARA PLATT

whispers behind the tightly shut door. They weren't in the least discreet, no Farthingale ever was. "Give me a moment, Gabriel. I'll tell them to go back home."

"Leave them be. Stop hopping about and stand still." His voice was raw and husky, and held promise of wondrous things to come. "Now, close your eyes."

She sighed. "But I want to see you."

"All well and good, but I want to kiss you first. It's been forever since I tasted your lips on mine," he said, his voice still husky and still promising wondrous things to come. "Close your eyes, sweetheart."

She did so at once.

"I missed you," he whispered, letting out a low, sensual growl as his lips descended on hers with passion and a wanting ache that left her begging for more. The book she was holding slipped to the floor and landed with a thud. She nudged it out of the way with her toe.

"Be careful with that book," Lily muttered through the door.

They both laughed. "It's good to be home," he said, his smile boyishly charming and happiness gleaming in his eyes.

"Oh, Gabriel! I prayed for your safe return every day." She carefully circled her arms about his neck and breathed in his familiar scent, the light, musky essence that never failed to throw her into raptures. She wanted to cling to his shoulders, run her fingers all over his hard, muscled body. "I don't know where to touch, where it's safe."

"Everywhere. Anywhere. Don't hold back." He tossed aside his crutch, and made use of his one good arm to draw her firmly against his chest. "You never were any good at following rules."

"I promise to reform. I'll be a most dutiful wife, a paragon of—"

"Don't you dare change a thing about yourself." His mouth closed over hers, his tongue gently sliding between her parted lips, tracing along her teeth before entering her mouth and treating her to an explosion of sensation that left her weak in the knees and trembling. He trailed ardent kisses along her neck, softer kisses along her throat... hungry kisses across her flushed lips. He splayed his hand across her back, drawing her closer still and letting out another one of those deliciously sensual growls that set her blood on fire. "Too many layers between us," he grumbled as her breasts molded to his chest.

She heartily agreed.

"I could strip you naked right here," he suggested, his eyes agleam and dancing with mirth, "but I doubt my meddlesome, matchmaking grandmother will approve." He tipped a finger under her chin and held her gaze to his. "But I have a better idea. Not sure if I can do this properly, for I'm afraid once down, I'll never get up. The servants will have to hoist me back onto my feet... too embarrassing."

"Is this one of those naughty sex games Laurel warned me about?" she whispered, for this topic was simply too scandalous for the twins to overhear.

"No." He chuckled as he cleared his throat. "Daisy, where shall I start? Eloise adores you, so does Graelem."

She laughed. "I know."

"I adore you, too." He took her hands in his. "No, that isn't quite right. I love you, Daisy. I've loved you for the longest time."

She inhaled sharply, afraid to breathe for fear of breaking the magic spell.

"You captured my heart the moment I climbed into Eloise's carriage the night of your debut ball and saw you fussing with your gown," he said, his voice a soft caress. "You thought you looked like a snowball and were dreadfully uncomfortable. I wanted to kiss you then and there, take you into my arms and tell you that you looked like an angel... my angel, for you somehow soothed my broken spirit, healed my tormented body. You gave me hope and happiness, had faith in me when all others had forsaken me. You had an unwavering faith that never faltered despite my best laid plans."

"I had no idea I was that splendid," she teased.

He kissed her softly on the lips. "You are, Daisy. All that and more."

He attempted to shift onto bended knee. "Bloody hell! That hurts."

"Gabriel!" She propped herself under his arm and hauled him up before he did permanent damage to himself. "What in heaven's name do you think you're doing?"

"Asking you to marry me. Doing it right this time. Church, flowers. Family in attendance, all seven thousand of them."

She shook her head and laughed. "There aren't nearly that many Farthingales."

"Well, feels like seven thousand," he said with a grin. "Will you, Daisy? Accept me and make me the happiest man alive."

"Yes," she said in an aching whisper. "Yes and yes and yes again. But I don't need another wedding. No ceremony, no flowers, and definitely no more Farthingale relatives! We just got rid of fifty and I'm not about to invite them back. They're too noisy and always underfoot. All I need is you. Only you. I knew it from the moment I first set eyes on you, holding naked Harry in your manly arms."

He winced. "Ah, yes. I'll never forget that pleasure. But our children will be perfectly behaved angels like their mother."

"And handsome as sin, like their father."

"I fear I'm a little worse for wear. In any event, Napoleon's defeat put an end to my dissolute reputation. No more wicked ways for me." He turned serious a moment. "I'll have a bit of work to do to make things right with my family. I can't wait for you to meet them."

"Um... you needn't concern yourself about that. Eloise and Graelem were so eager to introduce me that I've gotten to know them quite well, actually. We have lunch together once a week. Eloise has invited them here today. I'm sure they'll be along shortly."

"What do you think of my parents?" There was something in his tone that revealed the answer was deeply important to him.

"I adore them, Gabriel. Your father still can't believe you had the extraordinarily good sense to marry me, even if it was gone about poorly. He's afraid he'll wake up one morning and find it was all a hoax."

He let out a groaning laugh. "Have you met Alexander?"

"The fabulous brother that I was so keen on marrying until you upset my best-laid plans? He's perfect and proper and upright, and he's about to marry his childhood sweetheart, so it's a good thing I fell in love with you instead. He's as wary as your father is about our marriage. Not that he doesn't like me, but your dissolute ways have taken a toll on both of them. They no longer know what to believe about you."

"There's no help for it," he said, a sloppy grin on his face, "you'll have to worship me. Otherwise, they'll never believe this marriage is real. Or is it the other way around? Am I required to worship you?"

She poked him lightly on his good shoulder. "You had better, you dolt."

His gaze turned hot and smoldering. "I do. I will. Always. I promise."

Her heart skipped to a happy beat and the butterflies in her stomach were fluttering madly and cheering. "And promise to share the rest of your days with me?"

He nodded. "I believe it's part of the bargain. You're stuck with me for good."

"I wouldn't want it any other way."

"Nor would I. Daisy, I wish to fall asleep holding you in my arms each night and wake to your beautiful smile each morning. No separate quarters for us, will you promise me that?"

"I've already taken over your armoire and two chests of drawers. Oh, and your bed is quite comfortable, the only thing it's missing is you."

"I want marbles in all shapes and sizes stocked in my study, and a steady stream of little Farthingales to play with them. I want sons and daughters with dark hair and bright, blue eyes, and I want laughter to ring throughout our home. What do you say to that?"

She cast him the softest smile. "You have more rules than Lady Forsythia's *Rules for Reforming a Rake*, but I find them... quite acceptable. And speaking of Lady Forsythia's book, I read it to the very end only to find that she'd tossed out all her rules but one. Can you imagine?"

He arched an eyebrow, obviously amused by her indignation. "And what was that one rule?"

She shook her head and laughed. "To be guided by your heart."

"Good rule." He kissed her once more, his mouth warm and loving upon hers.

DEAR READER,

Thank you for reading *Rules for Reforming a Rake*. The road to happiness isn't easy for Daisy Farthingale and Gabriel Dayne. After Daisy, the middle daughter and family conciliator, takes the blame for an unfortunate incident involving a gentleman of dubious reputation to protect one of her sisters, she realizes the repercussions are far more serious than she ever expected. Her beloved Farthingale family no longer trusts her or respects her judgment. Daisy, determined to make the family proud of her again, plans to do it by marrying the most respectable man she can find. Unfortunately, her heart refuses to cooperate and she falls in love with the worst man possible—Gabriel Dayne, a dissolute rakehell she believes may be spying for the French. Only by trusting herself and standing up for her beliefs does Daisy find the happiness she deserves with Gabriel.

Book 4 in the Farthingale Series is *A Midsummer's Kiss*, the prequel to *Rules for Reforming a Rake*, *The Duke I'm Going to Marry*, and *My Fair Lily*. Yes, I'm finding that I think best backwards, especially with this Farthingale Series. The sisters have decided the order of these books and I am helpless to do anything but obey. So next is Laurel's story, and Laurel is a handful. She thinks she's in love with her childhood friend and is stubbornly determined to marry him, until she meets the handsome and equally stubborn Lord Graelem Dayne. She doesn't meet him in the usual *ton* way: Laurel's beast of a horse tramples Graelem and leaves him with a badly broken leg. That's a problem for Graelem, for he has only one month to find himself a wife or lose a vast inheritance. Since he's now forced to remain in bed for the month, he's decided that only Laurel will do—but convincing the headstrong Laurel will be no easy task. Read on for a sneak peek at Laurel's story, the fourth in the FARTHINGALE SERIES.

—Meara

CHAPTER 1

Mayfair District, London
May 1814

GRAELEM DAYNE LAY sprawled on his back in the middle of Chipping Way on this warm and sunny morning, writhing in agony and glowering at the snorting beast that had just burst through the open townhouse gate of Number 3 Chipping Way at full gallop and knocked him to the ground.

That horse, the color of devil's black, was still rearing and fighting its rider while that rider struggled to bring it under control. As Graelem tried to roll out of the way, one of its massive hooves landed with full force on his leg, cracking sturdy bone.

"Hellfire!" The excruciating jolt of pain shot straight up his body and into his temples.

He was in trouble.

Serious trouble, not only because the horse was still rearing and out of control, but Graelem's now-broken leg would make it impossible to complete the business he'd come down to London to accomplish. At the moment, he couldn't walk and his every breath was a struggle as it came in short, spurting gasps.

What was he to do now?

There would be no balls, soirees, or musicales for him for the next month, that was for certain. He'd never cut a striking figure hopping about on one leg, for he was a big oaf even when on two functioning legs.

He glanced at the angry beast.

Hellfire again! Just as Graelem thought he was about to be trampled once more, the beast suddenly lowered its massive hooves, let out a few soft neighs, and calmed. In the next moment, a blur of green velvet slid off the saddle and rushed toward him.

"Oh, dear heaven!" The sound of a sweet, feminine voice reached his ears, and a soft hand came to rest upon his much larger, rougher one to draw it off the boot he was clutching. "Sir, you mustn't touch your leg. I think it's broken."

"I *know* the damn thing is broken. Pull the boot off my leg!" He wished the rider had been a man so he could pound his fist into his face for so recklessly galloping into him and effectively destroying his critical plans along with his leg.

"Now!" he commanded, knowing the task would be much harder once his leg had swelled as it was starting to do now. Cutting through leather was no easy feat, and any attempt to do so would be far more painful than one swift tug done immediately.

"Of course. I'm so sorry!" She knelt beside him and braced her hands on the heel of the boot, letting out a sob as she apologized again.

Damn, why couldn't she have been a man?

She seemed young, hardly more than a girl.

He inhaled sharply as those soft hands began to tug at his boot.

"I have it," the young woman said in a soothing voice that flowed over him like warm honey. "Close your eyes and take another deep breath. I'm afraid this will hurt."

He let loose with a string of invectives as another dagger-sharp jolt of pain stabbed up his leg and into his temples. His heart felt as if it were about to pound a hole through his chest.

"Oh, I'm so very sorry!" She set aside the boot and turned to face him. Her lips quivered as she struggled to hold back anguished tears.

"I know, lass." He tried his best to answer gently, for she did appear sincerely remorseful. Although why he should care about her feelings when she was the cause of his misery was beyond him.

But whatever had possessed her to ride that demonic beast? Where was she going in such a hurry?

Before he had the chance to ask, he heard male voices calling out and the sound of hurried footsteps coming toward them. His blurred gaze remained on the young woman dressed in the dark green velvet riding habit. Had she really been the rider on that demonic horse?

"Amos," she said with a shaken breath, "put Brutus back in his stall before Father orders him shot." Then she turned to the other man who'd run out of the townhouse to lend assistance. "Pruitt, please fetch Uncle George at once."

"Right away, Miss Laurel."

As both men left to do her bidding, the girl called Laurel sank onto the grass beside him and took hold of his hand, cradling it in her lap. Her soft hands were shaking. As his vision cleared from the blur of pain, he caught a good look at her face and experienced another jolt. The girl was beautiful.

She was also trembling, obviously distressed by the incident. He felt the urge to squeeze her hand and assure her that all would be well. However, he dismissed the ridiculous notion at once. How could the mere touch of a chit who'd almost killed him affect him in any way but a desire for cold revenge?

Still, he couldn't deny that his anger was fading... or that his blood was heating.

He attributed that surprising effect to the pain of his broken leg.

"Sir, is there someone we can summon on your behalf? I'll send one of our footmen—"

"Lady Eloise Dayne," he said with a nod. "She resides on this street at Number 5."

"Lady Dayne? Oh, my heavens!" Laurel let out another unsteady breath. "Sir, are you by chance her grandson? The one who lives in Scotland and just arrived in town last night?"

He nodded again. "Indeed, lass. Graelem Dayne."

"You're Graelem... I mean, Lord Moray! And Eloise is your grandmother! Oh, this gets worse and worse."

He arched an eyebrow. "Those men called you Laurel."

"Yes, I'm Laurel Farthingale." She still sounded as though she were about to burst into tears. "I live here at Number 3 along with my parents and sisters, and a horde of Farthingale relations come to London for the season. We're your grandmother's neighbors. Friends, too. Though she won't be too pleased that I've almost killed her grandson. Are you in terrible pain?" She let out a quiet sob. "I wish there was something I could do to ease it."

There was, but she'd finish off the job her horse had started and kill him if he told her what he was truly thinking. *Damn.* Was he that depraved? At the very least, his senses were addled. How old was she? Old enough to be out in society, he guessed, but not much beyond her first season.

She was pretty enough to be snatched up quickly, assuming she didn't kill her beaus first.

She eased beside him and let out a mirthless laugh. "I'm in for it now. Probably punished for the entire summer," she muttered.

"Sorry, lass."

Her eyes rounded in horror. "You mustn't be! This is all my fault. Truly, it isn't much of a loss. This is only my first year out in society and I'm still quite overwhelmed by it. Everyone is so polite and mannered, I worry that I'll never fit in. My parents think I'm too spirited. That's the polite term they use, but they really think I'm a hot-tempered hellion. I suppose I am, as you've unfortunately discovered."

He tried to fashion a response, but couldn't, for he found himself staring into a pair of magnificent blue-green eyes that sparkled like sunshine on a Scottish mountain lake. His own baronial estate was on Loch Moray in the Scottish lowlands near the English border. It was a beautiful lake, almost as breathtaking as Laurel's eyes.

Damn. The girl also had a body that could bring a man to his knees. She sat too close, leaning over him in a way that got his heart pounding a hole in chest again... no, the pain was still addling his good sense.

He sank back, but couldn't turn away from the girl. She was a pretty sight indeed. It wasn't merely her shapely form, for the girl was fully clothed, the jacket of her riding habit buttoned up to her slender throat and the flowing skirt covering everything else that a man would wish to explore. He liked the scent of her as well, a hint of strawberries and warm summer breezes.

"Laurel, what's happened here?" An efficient-sounding gentleman approached them, a thoughtful frown upon his face. He carried a black satchel with him, obviously a medical bag of some sort.

"Uncle George, this is all my fault! The gentleman is Lord Graelem Dayne. He's Eloise's grandson and I almost killed him!" She repeated the details of the accident to Eloise when she came running out and paused with her hand over her heart to stare in horror at his injury.

"Good morning, Grandmama. It's not quite as bad as it looks." He got out little else, for Laurel quickly jumped in to assure his grandmother that she had been completely at fault.

Eloise glanced at him and then her gaze shifted to Laurel.

"All my fault," Laurel repeated with a tip of her chin, obviously determined to endure whatever punishment was to be meted out.

"Now, now, my dear," Eloise said. "I'm sure my grandson will find it in his heart to forgive you. Won't you, Graelem?"

He supposed he would. The girl may have been a little reckless, but she had been honest and had readily admitted her mistake. It spoke of her good character. Or was he too quick to forgive her because she was the prettiest thing he'd ever set eyes upon?

A lock of rich, honey-colored hair spilled over her brow.

He felt a sudden desire to undo the pins from Laurel's hair and run his fingers through her exquisite, dark gold mane.

Laurel's uncle said something about needing to cut through the fabric of his trousers before setting his broken leg. He nodded, not paying much attention, for his head was beginning to spin.

The last thing he recalled as he was suddenly overcome by a

wave of nausea was Laurel nudging him onto his side and wrapping her arms around him as he emptied the contents of that morning's breakfast onto the grass.

He always was one to charm the ladies.

LAUREL KEPT A hand on each of Lord Moray's shoulders to hold him up because his big body was still heaving even though he did not appear to have anything left inside him to come out. "Perfect," he finally muttered, and sank back against her, too dazed to notice he was leaning against her and not a tree or the ground.

"Do what you must, Dr. Farthingale," he said, lightly rolling his Rs in the way Scotsmen did. However, it wasn't a heavy brogue, but one mingled with English refinement, as though he'd spent time in both worlds.

He appeared the sort who moved about easily in both worlds, for there was a quiet confidence about him, even though he wasn't at his best just now. *All her fault.*

Uncle George began to quietly explain what he needed to do to mend his broken leg. "Once properly set, I'll fashion a splint around it. Then we'll help you into Lady Dayne's house."

"Graelem, it's best you stay with me until you recover," Eloise said, wringing her hands in obvious concern. "You'll need looking after for the next few weeks."

Lord Moray closed his eyes a moment and nodded. "I had planned to stay at Gabriel's townhouse, but I arrived late last night and haven't bothered to unpack yet. Will you send word to his butler to bring my belongings here?"

"At once." Eloise appeared relieved. "Gabriel's is a big, empty house anyway. What with him gone off again to who knows where on his latest misadventure—" She broke off, suddenly tense. "No matter. It's settled. You'll stay here."

Lord Moray turned toward her uncle. "Go ahead, Dr. Farthingale. Do what you must. Bloody thing hurts like blazes."

Uncle George cast her a light frown. "Hold him down, Laurel. This will only take a moment."

Since Lord Moray was still leaning against her, she merely kept her hands wrapped around his shoulders and prayed he wouldn't be too much to manage. He was far too big and muscled for her to restrain against his will. "Hold my hands, my lord. I think it will help."

He ignored the suggestion at first. However, as her uncle worked on his leg and the pain appeared to become unbearable, he finally complied. His hands felt warm on hers, and she realized she was still shivering with fear... and guilt.

She might have killed the man!

Her heart broke with each twinge of his body. He refused to cry out despite the excruciating pain he must have felt, and she suspected he was purposely trying to spare her feelings. Of course, he couldn't hide the sudden shift of his muscles at every tug and agonizing twist.

"I'm almost done, Laurel," her uncle assured, sparing a glance to smile at her. A mirthless smile, for he was disappointed in her behavior, and the tension in his expression showed it.

She was relieved of the need to say anything when her youngest sisters bolted out of the house and stopped beside her to gawk. "Crumpets! Who is he?" Lily asked, while the other twin, Dillie, edged closer to his prone body, for he'd closed his eyes again and appeared to be resting. Or passed out.

The twins shrieked and drew back when he opened one eye. "Who are you?" he shot back.

Laurel quickly introduced them and then explained to her sisters what had happened. "Eloise knows. She's preparing her guest quarters for his recovery."

Dillie cast him a wry glance. "Welcome to London, Lord Moray."

To Laurel's surprise, he laughed lightly. "Not quite the welcome I had in mind, Dillie."

"But one you'll never forget, I'll wager. I hear you're Eloise's favorite grandson."

Laurel groaned. "Yes, Dillie. He is." Which made what she did all the worse.

"Because if I were going to trample someone—"

"The point is, I shouldn't have hurt anyone," Laurel said.

"That goes without saying," Lily chimed in.

Laurel rolled her eyes. "Stop gawking at him."

However, she saw that Lord Moray was curious about the twins as well, for they were identical and impossible to tell apart. Though only fifteen, they were quite clever for their tender years... usually. Closest in age to her was Daisy. She was almost eighteen, and as the middle sister among the five of them, she was always the one to keep the peace.

Where was Daisy when she needed her?

"You're awfully big," Lily said, stating the obvious as she addressed Lord Moray once again. "You won't be easy to carry into Lady Dayne's townhouse, much less up the stairs. But perhaps if you shift your weight and —"

Dillie poked his shoulder. "I agree. You're all muscle." She cast Laurel an impish grin. "But I suppose you noticed that."

Laurel felt her face suffuse with heat. "Who's the doctor here? You two brats or Uncle George?" She truly wished Daisy were here, not only to chase the snoopy twins away. She needed to talk to Daisy in private, but it wasn't possible while everyone was about. She sighed, deciding there was nothing to be done about it now. She wasn't about to send Daisy to Hyde Park on her own to deliver a message to Devlin Kirwood. She would simply have to seek out Devlin at Lady Harrow's musicale this evening and apologize for not meeting him today.

He would understand and forgive her once she explained.

Laurel gave no further thought to Devlin, for she felt the subtle undulation of hard muscle beneath her palms and knew Lord Moray was trying to sit up. Goodness! She'd forgotten she still held him.

The twins were still beside her, inspecting him as though he were an archeological treasure. He squinted a little as the sun glinted through the leaves of the towering oak under which they were settled. "Am I mistaken or do you two really look that much alike?"

"No one can tell us apart," Dillie said with a chuckle. "Lily and I confuse everyone, even our parents."

He shook his head. "Heaven help the poor bachelors when you come out in society."

Lily smiled. "Assuming Laurel hasn't killed them all off by then."

"Don't jest about it, Lily." She tried to keep her voice from trembling, but knew she'd failed. Her eyes began to tear again. "I almost did kill him. It was a very close thing."

Lord Moray shifted slightly to gaze up at her. "Lass," he said with aching gentleness, "I'm a big oaf. It'll take more than an angry horse to put me in my grave."

Laurel's heart leapt into her throat. He had the handsomest smile and dark green eyes that could lead a girl to mischief with very little provocation. Of course, she wouldn't be that girl. She was loyal to Devlin Kirwood. "Our eldest sister, Rose, married last year," she began to prattle, for his smile was doing odd things to her. In a nice, but confusing, way. "Her husband is Lord Julian Emory."

Lord Graelem nodded. "I know him. Good man."

She liked the way the sun warmed the chestnut color of his hair.

"Done, my lord," her uncle said, regaining their attention. "Don't try to get up on your own just yet. We'll summon help."

Dillie was sent off to call for Eloise's footmen.

It took only a moment for Lord Moray to grow impatient and attempt once again to sit up.

"What are you doing?" Laurel immediately positioned her body against his back to catch him if he started to fall, for he'd been hurt enough for one day. Indeed, hurt enough for a lifetime, as far as she was concerned.

Lily rolled her eyes and began to jabber about linear planes and angles and some nonsense about gravitational thrust, which Laurel would have dismissed had she not found herself suddenly pinned between the trunk of the oak tree and Lord Moray, whose back was unwittingly pressed against her chest.

Her uncle groaned in exasperation. "Laurel, what are you trying to accomplish? You can't lift him up on your own."

"But I only meant to—" Realizing she was only making matters worse, she tried to slip out from under him. Her breasts accidentally rubbed against his shoulder.

"Lass!" Lord Moray said. "You'd better... blessed Scottish saints... er, just don't move. I'll roll out of your way."

She nibbled her lip and tried to hold back the tears threatening to well in her eyes, for he sounded so pained and his gaze was now turbulent and fiery. The blaze in his eyes could only signify anger. "I only meant to help."

"I think you've *helped* me quite enough for one day." He fell back as she moved away, knocking his head against the trunk of the oak tree with a soft *thuck*. "Quite enough."

She placed a hand on his arm to help, but received another fiery glance for her attempt. "Lass, it isn't necessary. My grandmother's footmen will help me to my chamber."

She nodded, feeling worse for causing him yet more discomfort. "Please, let me do something to make it up to you."

"No—"

"But I don't mind at all." Her tears had held off, but no longer. She let out a sniffle. "Just tell me what I can do for you—"

"Lass, it isn't necessary." His gaze was a dangerous smolder that seemed to intensify each time she tried to touch him.

The tears began to stream down her cheeks. "*Anything.* You have only to ask and I'll do it. You have my promise."

"I don't want it."

She hated feeling guilty. Why wouldn't he simply accept her apology? "You have it anyway. My *sacred* promise. What can I do to atone for the damage I've caused?"

He eyed her for a disconcertingly long moment. "Very well," he said with quiet authority. "Marry me."

A Midsummer's Kiss
is available in paperback and e-book

ACKNOWLEDGMENTS

To Neal, Brigitte (my fair Gigi), and Adam, the best husband and kids ever. I'm so lucky to have you as my family. To Bertrice Small, a friend and mentor to so many of us. To my intrepid first readers: Barbara Hassid, Lauren Cox, Megan Westfall, Rebecca Heller, and Maria Barlea. To my large and supportive extended family, who continue to show me just why I love you all so much. Sincere appreciation to longtime friends and terrific authors in their own right: Pamela Burford, Patricia Ryan, Jeannie Moon, Jennifer Gracen, and Stevi Mittman. To my wonderful web designer, Willa Cline. Heartfelt gratitude to the best support team that any author can have: Laurel Busch, Samantha Williams, Patricia D. Eddy, and Greg Simanson. I look forward to working with them on many more projects.

THE FARTHINGALE SERIES

London is never the same after the boisterous Farthingales move into their townhouse on Chipping Way, one of the loveliest streets in fashionable Mayfair. With five beautiful daughters in residence, the street soon becomes known as a deathtrap for bachelors.

If you would like to join the fun, you can subscribe to my newsletter at bit.ly/mearasnewsletter and also connect with me on Twitter at twitter.com/mearaplatt. You can find links to do all of this at my website: mearaplatt.com

If you enjoyed this book, I would really appreciate it if you could post a review on the site where you purchased it or other sites where you subscribe. You can write one for Goodreads. Even a few sentences on what you thought about the book would be most helpful! If you do leave a review, send me a message on Facebook because I would love to thank you personally.

Please also consider telling your friends about the FARTHINGALE SERIES and recommending it to your book clubs.

ABOUT THE AUTHOR

Meara Platt is happily married to her Russell Crowe look-alike husband, and they have two terrific children. She lives in one of the many great towns on Long Island, New York, and loves it, except for the traffic. She has traveled the world, occasionally lectures, and always finds time to write. Her favorite place in all the world is England's Lake District, which may not come as a surprise since many of her stories are set in that idyllic landscape, including her Romance Writers of America Golden Heart award winning story to be released as Book 3 in her paranormal romance Garden series, which is set to debut in 2016. Learn more about Meara Platt by visiting her website at mearaplatt.com.

Made in the USA
Columbia, SC
07 June 2021

39347883R00190